Jean-Pie...

The Lairds
of
Cromarty

Translated by Mike Mitchell

Dedalus

LOTTERY FUNDED

Published in the UK by Dedalus Limited,
24-26, St Judith's Lane, Sawtry, Cambs, PE28 5XE
email: info@dedalusbooks.com
www.dedalusbooks.com

ISBN 978 1 907650 74 1

Dedalus is distributed in the USA & Canada by SCB Distributors,
15608 South New Century Drive, Gardena, CA 90248
email: info@scbdistributors.com   web: www.scbdistributors.com

Dedalus is distributed in Australia by Peribo Pty Ltd.
58, Beaumont Road, Mount Kuring-gai, N.S.W. 2080
email: info@peribo.com.au

Publishing History
First published in France in 2008
First published by Dedalus in 2012

Les maîtres de Glenmarkie copyright © *Editions Gallimard, Paris 2008*
Translation copyright © *Mike Mitchell 2012*

The right of Jean-Pierre Ohl to be identified as the author & Mike Mitchell as the
translator of this work has been asserted by them in accordance with the Copyright,
Designs and Patents Act, 1988.

Printed in Finland by Bookwell
Typeset by Marie Lane

A C.I.P. listing for this book is available on request.

The Author

Jean-Pierre Ohl is a bookseller in Talence near Bordeaux.

He is the author of two novels *Mr Dick or The Tenth Book* and *The Lairds of Cromarty*, both published in England by Dedalus.

The Translator

For many years an academic with a special interest in Austrian literature and culture, Mike Mitchell has been a freelance literary translator since 1995. He is one of Dedalus's editorial directors and is responsible for the Dedalus translation programme.

He has published over seventy translations from German and French, including Gustav Meyrink's five novels and *The Dedalus Book of Austrian Fantasy*. His translation of Rosendorfer's *Letters Back to Ancient China* won the 1998 Schlegel-Tieck Translation Prize after he had been shortlisted in previous years for his translations of *Stephanie* by Herbert Rosendorfer and *The Golem* by Gustav Meyrink.

His translations have been shortlisted three times for The Oxford Weidenfeld Translation Prize: *Simplicissimus* by Johann Grimmelshausen in 1999, *The Other Side* by Alfred Kubin in 2000 and *The Bells of Bruges* by Georges Rodenbach in 2008.

His biography of Gustav Meyrink: *Vivo: The Life of Gustav Meyrink* was published by Dedalus in November 2008.

His website can be visited at homepages.phonecoop.coop/mjmitchell

Sir Thomas Urquhart of Cromarty (1611–1660) is a well-known historical figure; all the other Urquharts in this novel are entirely fictional and no reference to any person, living or dead, is intended.

PROLOGUE

Barnhill, Isle of Jura,
January 1949

It was a bright cold day in April...

The first line of his novel... All at once he hated it. Too limp, too *insipid*, too conventional. Why not just say *On a lovely April day...* while he was about it?

He'd already been through this. That other catastrophic beginning, perpetrated twelve years ago, still stuck in his throat: *The clock struck half-past two.* He'd written it, certainly, but he refused to recognise it — in the sense of recognising a child. It was like a foreign body, a splinter stuck in the flesh of his book. Heartbreaking for him with his love of the clear, uncomplicated openings of the great novels of the previous century: *Whether I shall turn out to be the hero of my own life...* Or, even better: *Call me Ishmael.* Dickens and Melville had no doubts about their art. They took you by the hand, simply, quietly, and lead you on the way. 'Today,' he thought, 'authors squirm with embarrassment on the threshold of their novel; they almost apologise for having written it.'

Right, he'd correct it when he did the proof-reading. And perhaps he could write an article about it: 'The *incipit*, a lost art?' Send it to *The New Leader* or to...

Scott Fleming's car, coming from Ardloch, was roaring down the hill. Right on time. He rushed out and set off at a lively pace but slowed down almost immediately, partly because of a coughing fit but also because he didn't want to give himself the feeling he was running away. The day was ending. He crossed the gently sloping field, stopping by the copse overlooking the sea. Down below, the boat was hardly rocking on the calm water, maintaining the fiction of a normal evening, similar to all the others. Cautiously he filled his lungs. Facing such a view it was difficult to accept the reality of the word 'sanatorium'. Across the water, the indented coast of Argyll seemed closer in the fading light; a few late sailing boats were returning to Loch Sween or to Crinan. To the south, beyond Kintyre, the peaks of Arran could still be made out; to the north Jura stretched as far as the Gulf of Corryvreckan and the whirlpool, the dull rumble of which echoed that of the generator. But then the generator cut out and for a few seconds he thought the Corryvreckan had too, out of solidarity.

'One of the most beautiful landscapes in Europe,' his friend Potts had written. A little over-stated perhaps, but that evening, at the moment of departure — and an insistent voice told him he would never return — the statement seemed obvious, giving the sea and the sky that special touch, that unified, polished look the natural world takes on once man has given it a name. He thought back to his novel: over several exhausting weeks he had typed it out himself, dragging himself from his bed to his armchair, smoking cigarette after cigarette despite the nasty cough that racked his whole body, looking out of the window at an enticing, mocking sea. *The Last Man in Europe* — that's what he was going to call it. And it had been easy, allowing his mind to roam with the red deer of Jura or watching though his binoculars a seal sprawled out on a reef, to imagine himself the last man in Europe as well. But at that same moment he decided to look for another title. He had to keep the book separate from its author. The book had to be immortal.

He heard his sister calling: 'Eric?'

And Richard's shrill voice: 'Daddy? Come on, I think we're going.'

As usual, Scott Fleming drove in silence; on the back seat Avril and Richard were playing at paper, stone, scissors. Eric watched the wind writing messages in the long grass and immediately erasing them. It was believable that this would be the last time he made this journey. Not unbelievable: unfair. Outrageous.

At Ardloch Scott's old golden retriever heard his master coming and started to run alongside the car.

'Sit, Ruby.'

'Can I say goodbye to her, Daddy?'

'Yes, but be quick about it.'

Following the dog, Richard and Avril disappeared in the Flemings' large house. Scott waited a little then grasped the steering-wheel very tightly in a characteristic posture, which gave Eric an unpleasant tingling sensation between his shoulder-blades.

'He's back,' Scott finally said.

'Who's back?'

'Urquhart of Cromarty. One of our old comrades saw him in London.'

The tingling spread, going right down his spine. He coughed.

'Perhaps it wasn't him…'

'It was him. I must do something.'

'What, exactly?'

Eric suddenly felt more tired than ever. He even thought of putting the journey off till the next day, but then Avril and Richard reappeared on the doorstep with Scott's wife. He gave her a little wave then said, with a visible effort, 'Please, Scott… I'm bad enough without having to think of all that… of all those dead people.'

'He's got to pay,' Scott growled as Mrs Fleming grasped Ruby's collar.

'Daddy! Louise gave me some cake.'

The car set off again. 'I've difficulty enough just *breathing*,' Eric added to himself.

'Stone!'

A little after Loch Tarbert, the place where the sea almost cut the island in two — it appeared on the map as a grimace of disgust — Eric dozed off and only woke up at the sound of the car doors opening outside the hotel in Craighouse where they were to spend the night before taking the ferry the next day. He realised now that it was a mistake. They could just as well have spent the night at Barnhill and got Darroch, their neighbour who drove down to Craighouse every morning, to bring them. Scott Fleming would have been put out, true, but at least that embarrassing conversation would never have taken place.

He left the others to take in the luggage and strolled past the distillery to the little harbour. Invisible in the dark, the chug-chug of a trawler was cutting the silence into concentric circles. He heard Scott's limping footsteps on the tarmac as he came back out.

'Sometimes,' Eric said without turning round, 'when I'm particularly happy with my job as a scribbler… I get this…'

Since he'd finished his book every sentence was an effort. He was soon out of breath, of course, but above all he felt there was a kind of immense space between himself and other people, an insuperable steppe. The previous night he'd had a dream of a country where speaking wasn't necessary, where one could write directly on other people's brains.

'I get this disgusting idea… The idea that my books justify my own survival… that in some way they've made me… more *worthy of living* than other people… than those who didn't come back…'

He felt Scott's eyes fixed on the back of his neck.

'I think I fought courageously, often putting my life in danger… Fortune smiled on me, there's nothing to be ashamed of in that… But when I get *that idea*, well, I feel disgusted with myself…'

When he turned round, Scott was already in the car. The two men exchanged a brief wave; the headlights swept through the sleeping village. Eric coughed. In a gesture of defiance, he lit a cigarette. The tip glowed intermittently and for the fisherman chugging along the coast he would be nothing more than a winking firefly — that thought cut the problem of the opening of his novel down to size…

He threw the dog-end into the water and watched it floating among the seaweed for a moment; then he went back to the hotel.

PART ONE

THE EDINBURGH BOOKSELLER

CHAPTER I

In which we make the acquaintance of Mary Guthrie and the good folk of Islay.

Bwaaaahh!

As it enters the Sound of Islay, the ferry always announces its approach with a blast on its siren. When I was little I used to think that was what the *Sound* was: a long lament that echoed round the shore whenever my father took me to Port Askaig. Then, when I was at school, I learnt that the same word meant a noise and the narrows. Words could wear several masks, it was disturbing, it was a bit like being bitten by the family dog. Even today every *Bwaaaahh!* from the siren reawakens the apprehensive little girl in me and I shiver at the thought of a monster lurking in the dark waters separating Islay from Jura, bellowing in pain as the ferry's hull scrapes its back.

'I'm sure he's not really a priest.'

'No, he's too skinny, too ugly.'

Port Askaig's not exactly a village, nor even a port, as it happens. Facing the slipway where the majestic ferries from the mainland, from the Big Island, as we call it, and the little shuttle to Jura tie up are just three buildings: a pretentious hotel for the tourists from Glasgow or England who have started to come in greater numbers since the end of the war, a grocer's and the *Harbourside*, Malcolm's pub. It was from there that we, Alison, Louise and myself, were watching the passengers on the ferry. Even when all the others were still no more than insects crowding the deck in front of the bridge Father Krook stood out with his tall silhouette and his tousled mop of hair.

'He looks like a monkey, doesn't he?'

'Yes, that's it, a big monkey. He came down from his tree one day and found a cassock on the ground.'

I joined in the laughter. I didn't want Louise and Alison to know what I really thought of Ebenezer Krook. I didn't even know myself.

Most of the inhabitants of Islay are Presbyterians. My father was the pass-keeper of the Catholic church in Bridgend, but in a community as small as ours his sole function was to provide board and lodging once a month to the priest from Campbeltown. My friends' reaction to my status as the 'pass-keeper's daughter' was a mixture of derision and curiosity.

'Mary, since you know him so well'— Louise had a fit of giggles —'you should watch him through the keyhole in the evening, I'm sure he must be covered in hair'— shrieks of laughter from Louise and Alison.

'Shut up,' Malcolm growled from behind the bar, 'you shouldn't make fun of priests.'

'How long is it since you went to church, Malcolm?'

'I'm a Catholic at heart.'

'And an alcoholic at liver!'

The black silhouette of Krook, facing east. He was the priest of Islay, our priest; but not for one second until the boat was tied up did he take his eyes off Jura. In the middle of the strait the shuttle and the ferry saluted each other with a blast on their unequal sirens — a poodle's yap drowned out by the powerful voice of a mastiff or an alsatian.

We sometimes used to take the ferry over to Jura when I was little. My heart would pound during the crossing, as if we were doing something forbidden, perhaps even dangerous; then we were driving along the only road on Jura, windows open when it was sunny and I was so thrilled, I breathed in so deeply my lungs hurt. The air seemed different, harsher, heavier, truer, the horizon wider, the forests denser. At the end of the road was Ardloch, a hamlet at the back of beyond permeated with a cowshed smell: an old car parked in a fallow field, a few shepherds' cottages with peeling walls and a large gabled house with a golden retriever dozing outside.

'That's where the Laird of Ardloch lives,' my mother said one day,

'A laird in this godforsaken place?'

'Never judge by appearances. In the old days the Laird of Ardloch was an important person. He sat on the council of the Lord of the Isles, at Finlaggan, with all the other lairds of the West.'

I imagined a terrifying person, all bone and beard, wearing a claymore and the clan tartan. At that time I had no idea that one day — and under what circumstances! — I would meet the real Laird of Ardloch.

For Islay, Jura is a kind of unruly big sister, savage, romantic. Wherever you are on our island, it's dominated by the Paps of Jura, 'those proud twin peaks resembling the breasts of a courtesan' as the tourist guide puts it, while all we have to show is little Ben Uraidh, the summit of which is not much higher than the chimney of Lagavulin distillery. The English tourists are charmed by our whisky, with its peaty flavour, its hints of vanilla, olives or juniper, because they find it *so very Scottish*, but some of us secretly prefer the proud simplicity of Jura whisky. Jura, a magnificent dream rising up on the other side of the Sound, fascinating and intimidating, like everything that is both very close and very different to us. Some old women used to say that, while we were asleep, our souls would go to Jura and have mysterious adventures, of which we had lost all memory in the morning.

Jura 'with its verdant valleys abounding in graceful red deer, while its dark whirlpools toss the boats about like toys in the bathtub.' I knew that off by heart. But it wasn't a reason for Father Krook to turn his back on Islay in that way! I almost took it as a personal insult. But that, of course, was something else I couldn't admit to Louise and Alison.

'How old do you think he is? Fifty?'

'No, of course not, you idiot, he's much younger. Mind you, it's very difficult to tell a monkey's age.'

Even while I was forcing myself to laugh, I was asking myself the same question. The first time I saw him I was just a little girl and he seemed very old to me. Less old, though, than his predecessor, Father Morton, whom I had dubbed 'the Saturday-night wind' because he suffered from flatulence and for the two days he was here you had to put on my brother's diving mask if you wanted to go to the lavatory. Since he couldn't hold back his farts whenever he knelt down, the altar boys had been instructed to ring the bells very loud and very long at the moment of the Elevation. His sphincter put up more resistance in a vertical position but it could still happen, in the course of a particularly vehement sermon, that 'God's anger' would resound in an unfortunate fashion and I would go red in the face trying to stop myself laughing.

Then, one Saturday evening, Father Morton was accompanied by an unknown man. 'Mr Guthrie, this is Father Krook.'

Teddy and I were doing our homework at the kitchen table. He nudged me with his elbow. 'Crook!' he whispered to me. 'That means criminal, maybe he's a thief!' and he pretended to hide his gold-plated fountain pen in his pencil case. Fortunately Daddy didn't hear. I scrutinised the new priest out of the corner of my eye, his timid, almost dull-witted look emphasised by thick eyebrows that met, a clenched jaw and prominent Adam's apple but moderated by a finely delineated mouth, a broad forehead and an intelligent look that seemed to be trapped inside dungeon-deep sockets.

I happened to be reading *Bleak House* at the time and the surname Krook immediately put me in mind of the incredible character who dies from spontaneous combustion, transformed without warning into a pile of smoking ash. It was the first time the priest made me think of a character in a novel but it wasn't to be the last.

That evening the two priests shared the same bed. 'A bloody brave chap!' Teddy declared when, the next morning, he saw Krook tuck into his breakfast with unimpaired appetite. Then Father Morton made a farewell speech, punctuated in his usual manner, before taking a one-way ticket to the land of my childhood memories, where he joined other figures such as my Uncle Toby, a pipe-smoker who couldn't pronounce *r* without producing an abundance of tobacco-coloured spittle, Mrs MacDonald, the post-mistress with black teeth and damp armpits, and Mr Campbell, the schoolteacher whose every statement began or ended with 'indubitably'.

Father Krook, for his part, settled in quarters that were scarcely less daunting: reality. For three years I hardly noticed him. Teddy could start diving again and we no longer found those disgusting spiders Father Morton created with tufts of his white hair tangled up in the plughole of the shower. But if Father Krook's hair was firmly fixed to his scalp, they had another characteristic that was even stranger and that eventually caught my attention: they could stand on end or lie flat spontaneously, without any physical assistance. They were the precise reflection of his moods; while the presence of certain people could make them rebel — Teddy, for example, and his irritating habit of walking all over the house while cleaning his teeth — that of others commanded absolute submission. At such time Krook looked like a giant poodle coming out of a grooming parlour.

I believe I came into the second category.

I had this idea one night in September 1949. In a few days' time I was going to Edinburgh, where I was to start university and stay with my Aunt Catriona. My life was about to be turned upside down. At the time I was immersed in Smollett and Fielding. ('Good Lord, Mary, why are you always reading these boy's books?' Mr Campbell would say when he ran into me in the tiny library of Bowmore. 'You'd be far better taking out Jane Austen or George Eliot. Indubitably.') I loved the interminable chapter headings such as those in *Tom Jones*, all those *In which...*, *Containing an account of...* My own life, I thought, had not yet got beyond these preambles but would soon undergo unsuspected developments. I imagined my studies would be an adventure as exciting as those of David Balfour in the company of ardent fellow searchers after truth, eyes ablaze with a passion for books, under the tutelage of masters worthy of Stevenson himself. In short, I was still unaware that university is for the love of literature what caster oil is for thirst.

This excitement combined with the unusual heat made sleep impossible. Around two in the morning I decided to go out for a breath of fresh air, wearing a too-short nightie and some old shoes my father was throwing away. The door of the priest's bedroom was open; there was no one in it.

I took the path to Caol Ila, the little distillery where my father had worked for more than thirty years. My mother and I often went to meet him half-way, on a little promontory overlooking the Sound. She would point out Rhuvaal lighthouse at the very north of our island and tell me the legend of Corryvreckan, the famous whirlpool off Jura.

'Once upon a time there was a Viking prince called Breacan who fell in love with the daughter of the Lord of the Isles and appeared before the full council one evening to ask for her hand. To prove himself worthy of the fair lady, he was required to spend three days and three nights in a boat by the whirlpool. Breacan went back to Norway and, on the advice of the Elders, had three ropes made: one of hemp, one of wool and the third woven from the hair of pure maidens. Then he returned and anchored where he had been instructed. The first night the hempen rope broke, but Breacan was saved... The second night...'

More recently Mummy had to pause often to get her breath back, but she always did so at specific points, making appropriate dramatic pauses.

'The second night the woollen rope broke, but Breacan was saved... The following night the rope of hair held until morning but then the wind got up and it broke as well...' At that point Mummy would smile, though I never knew why, and then went on, 'They say that the maidens who gave him their hair were not pure enough.' I didn't find this complicated story, with all its ropes and young maidens, particularly interesting, what I liked was the ending: 'So the whirlpool carried off the boat and Breacan died. But Breacan's dog dived in and brought his master's body back to the shore, where it was buried.' To my mind the legend passed too quickly over a remarkable episode, the dog's exploit, and I filled the gap by inventing lots of details of my own. I imagined it fighting against the current, struggling with the dead weight of Breacan, panting on the beach once it had laid its burden down and howling with grief as they buried the prince. One day, when I got back to the house, I started drawing the scene: I took great care choosing the dog's size and age, the length of its fangs, the colour of its hair. Then I did it again the next day, and the next, and the next, in different variations: a big white dog, a little black dog, sometimes even a green dog.

But my technique was so poor, I was always disappointed with the results: the dog would look like a sheep or a donkey, the sea like a crumpled plaid, but above all I was incapable of suggesting the complicated mood of the animal, its futile courage, its almost human despondency. I then had the idea of describing the scene instead of trying to draw it. It was an astounding discovery: everything became possible, everything was true. Compared with the precision, the undeniable power of words, the pathetic scrawls produced by my crayons were mere artistic flatulence. I wrote perhaps a hundred versions of the story of Breacan's dog, tirelessly putting together unusual words to create improbable sentences that were still very real, since I could read and reread them indefinitely. In one of the versions the dog was both 'monstrous' and 'minuscule', in another he 'barked like a cathedral' and 'the lice of death were galloping beneath his stomach'.

'That's very nice,' my mother said one day as she leant over my shoulder. 'Perhaps you'll be a writer. But for that you'll have to choose one version — the best.'

That prospect seemed delightfully far-off and desirable: a glorious rainbow. But I was happy not to have to decide straight away, not to have to choose the one I liked best. I couldn't bring myself to abandon all my dogs —'the jolly collie with cloth lungs', 'the singing mastiff', 'the handsome greyhound that could swim like a wave' in favour of a single one.

My mother was getting very tired. More and more often I took the path to Caol Ila by myself, taking my exercise books with me. Caol Ila: the Strait of Islay in Gaelic. But for me those words did not evoke the dark waters of the Sound or the monster lurking there; on the contrary, they designated a peaceful, reassuring place, marked out by my father's punctual comings and goings, populated by all my paper dogs. However, despite the pink and white fuchsias and rhododendrons creeping up the hillside, it eventually turned black, perhaps through its association with the English word coal. Or because of the inscription on the black mourning crepe round the spray of flowers: 'In memory of Christie Guthrie, the wife of our colleague. The staff of Caol Ila.' On that day Breacan's dog turned into a resonant statue, carved once and for all by my mother's vanished voice and I never more had the strength to invent little brothers for him. The power to make words sing had been taken from me. I started to devour those of other people.

Uncomfortable in the shoes that were too big for me, I climbed the steep path.The full moon brought out the bushes and rocks with almost glacial sharpness. Since I was leaving soon, the walk was both exhilarating and melancholy. It was the landscape of my childhood, more beautiful than anything I knew, and yet I felt a furtive joy at the thought of leaving it. At the top of the hill I turned to look back: my father's house rose up like a reproof.

I saw Krook below, leaning on a low wall. He was staring at Jura. On the other side of the Sound the Paps looked even nearer than in broad daylight. For a long time he stood there, motionless, then he suddenly started to walk up and down, like a duellist waiting for his opponent. Something, I don't know what, gave me the idea that he would have made a perfect quarrel-seeker: he had the impressive stature for it and the unpredictable character, hot-tempered, suicidal. He could perhaps have died for an adverb too many, an untimely look, a splash of wine on a handkerchief.

No, the era of Barry Lyndon was long past; Father Krook had an appointment with no one but himself. Was it the strange moonlight? Or all those vivid books I'd read? Suddenly he seemed immensely romantic to me and utterly attractive.

'If you like Jura so much, why don't you go there.'

He hadn't heard me coming. He grudgingly gave me one of those surly nods that so amused Louisa and Alison. 'There's no parish on Jura.'

'There's nothing on Jura apart from deer and a few natives who're all called Fletcher.'

That almost brought a smile from him. His hair flattened on his skull as if I'd smoothed it down with my fingers. Which was exactly what I wanted to do. I leant my elbows on the wall right next to him.

'Your father told me you're off to Edinburgh.'

'Yes, but I'll come back every weekend.' My reply slipped out so quickly it sounded like an invitation and I felt myself blush.

'So one day you'll be teaching English literature… like my mother.' Then he added, 'I take after my father more.'

He lowered his head and I could tell he'd seen something interesting close to the ground, but for the moment I didn't dare ask myself what it might be.

'My mother has two passions,' he went on, a touch of bitterness in his voice. 'The first is the Victorian novel. I suspect she married my father simply because he had the name of a character from Dickens'— Krook gave me a sidelong glance to see if I had understood the allusion. 'And as if that wasn't enough, she lumbered me with the ridiculous Christian name of Ebenezer…'

'Like Scrooge in *A Christmas Carol*.'

'She taught in Aberdeen for a long time… Now she lives near Stonehaven, on the edge of the cliffs… A little cottage, ugly, damp, uncomfortable… The locals like taking donkey rides and the beasts keep defecating on her lawn all the time. I hate the place.'

'Yes, but that must remind her of Aunt Betsy in *David Copperfield*.'

Krook shrugged. 'I really don't know why I'm telling you all this.'

He was clearly annoyed with himself, but why? Because he was talking too much or because he couldn't take his eyes off my knees?

'And I presume your mother's second passion is you?'

He gave a caustic little laugh. 'Oh, no. It's Sir Thomas Urquhart of Cromarty.'

It was the first time I'd heard the name and I was far from suspecting the importance it was to have in my life. Later on, when

21

I read that extraordinary passage in the *Ekskubalauron* in which Urquhart talks of what a word ought to be if language were to play its role properly —'*There is not a word utterable by the mouth of man, which in this language hath not a peculiar signification by itself... for the denomination of the fixed stars it offereth the most significant way imaginary: for by the single word alone which represents the star you shall know the magnitude, together with the longitude and latitude... if a General according to the rules thereof will give new names to his souldiers... he shall be able, at the first hearing of the word that represents the name of a souldier, to know of what Brigade, Regiment, Troop, Company, Squadron or Division he is*'— I recalled the moment when the name Urquhart of Cromarty first emerged from the void, already decked out in its harsh, howling consonants like a baby dressed from head to toe as it came out of its mother's womb. A linguistic symphony of its own, the drum-roll of the *r*'s, the grotesquely questioning *q*. A man contained in his own name.

But at that moment I was more interested in the lips from which it came. 'Who's that?'

'An obscure poetaster from the time of the Civil War. The author of four or five abstruse disquisitions with unpronounceable names. A Royalist, of course. Died from laughing when he heard of the restoration of the Stuarts... She claims we're related to him...'

'I've the impression you've a pretty low opinion of writers...'

He just grunted in reply.

'However,' I went on, 'you do read a book and it's not the Bible. It's a novel, I think.'

With a great effort he managed to drag his eyes away from my knees, but only to fix them on my face. His hair stood on end.

'I'm sorry,' I babbled, 'I happened to see it just now, on your bedside table... The door was open...'

'It's nothing. Only... a souvenir.'

As he said that, he stretched out his hand towards my knee but just pulled out a tuft of grass growing in the wall beside it. Then he stalked off with the long strides of a sick heron.

CHAPTER II

Krook's narrative

I doubt whether Saint Peter has a file index to help him select souls, but if he did, mine would read roughly as follows:

Ebenezer Krook, b. 3 January 1919 Aberdeen (Scotland); nickname: Mad Dog. Amateur alcoholic. Ordained 8 August 1946. Six years as the priest of the parish of Campbeltown (Diocese of Oban). Broke his vow of chastity 8 September 1953. Defrocked.

Then, under 'special notes': *Knocked his bishop flat*. The moment I grabbed Bishop O'Brien's collar I was dazzled by a sad revelation. '*Ecce homo*,' I thought, 'here is Ebenezer Krook as he really is. No other act will define you more precisely, more completely than this one. For centuries to come you will be the *Mad Dog*. That is, a grotesque character, six foot six tall, covered in freckles, with a too-prominent nose, a skeleton that sticks out everywhere and a carroty mop that responds to the brush and comb much as the barbarians of the limes did to the Roman legions: a blaze of revolt then weak submission. A long, gnarled bag of bones endowed with a good old fighting instinct bequeathed by our primitive ancestors. Six years of good conduct thrown away; six years spent patiently swaddling yourself in faith, temperance and chastity. But your bones, your muscles cast off those moral nappies; within the space of a few hours you turned back into a brute beast, a stallion and a drunkard.'

'I would like to see Bishop Moray.'

The little secretary with the impeccable cassock stank of eau de Cologne and bureaucracy. Before looking up at me he went on scribbling for a good twenty seconds with the boorishness of council officials or post-office clerks.

'Bishop Moray retired last week, as you ought to be aware, Father…'

'Krook. Take me to his successor.'

'Bishop O'Brien arrived yesterday. I very much doubt whether it's the right moment to…'

'It's extremely urgent!'

The name O'Brien had not aroused any memories, but everything came back to me the moment I saw the tall figure of the new bishop busy amongst his files and dossiers.

Our first encounter went back to 1935. At the time he was a simple parish priest at St Peter's in Aberdeen where he organised a rugby team in order to attract young people to his flock; he had played for the Scottish Universities. I like rugby, that improbable cocktail of sophisticated rules, panache from a bygone age and primitive violence. My mother's family was Presbyterian and had even counted two or three ministers among its members, though that was a long time ago. As for my father's family, as far as I knew they had managed to get along over the centuries without the least connection with any church at all — something rare in a country where the range of religions on offer is as abundant and varied as that of fish on the quayside stalls in Ullapool. 'But why *Catholic*?' my mother had exclaimed in her irritated tones. My father, sticking his pipe in his pocket, had said, 'Why not?' before setting off for the pub.

The 'pitch' was a little courtyard beside the presbytery where couch grass grew among the gravel. The field of play, indicated by lines drawn in blue chalk, included a boarded-up well and a moribund shrub sticking out of some railings like an arm from a gap in a tomb; two other shrubs, a little less stunted, served as goalposts. The other boys, mostly of Irish origin, used to go on and on about the exploits of the shamrock team but I doubt whether a single one of them persevered in that noble game after having encountered me on the pitch. At that time I was already very tall and my pugnacity made up for my lack of muscle. I threw myself into loose scrums with a kind of savage despair: I pushed, I tackled, I bit, I stamped. I was the *Mad Dog*. This was the only way I had of forgetting the torment I had no name for, the heat rising from between my thighs to set my whole body on fire and which neither Peggy Muir, nor Joanna Holmes nor even Jenny Young with her large white breasts like dough waiting to be kneaded, could extinguish. I was the roughest, toughest, fiercest of players, I couldn't care less about the gravel that scraped our knees and elbows, the coping of the well on which we bruised our backs. In a loose scrum I was always at the bottom, the place where blows are freely exchanged. And always, always O'Brien's large paw would grab me by the ears and pull me out of the maul like pulling up a weed. He would lift me off the ground and while I swung to and fro a few inches from his face, sweating, choking, foaming, kicking out, he would yell, 'The rules, Ebenezer! Fight according to the rules.' Then he would put me back down, muttering, 'Or at least be more discreet about it so that no one can see you.'

One year later he left to go to Edinburgh.

What would have happened if he had recognised me? Would I have burst out sobbing and thrown myself in his arms? Would I have continued for another ten, another twenty years to slip into this bizarre garment which emphasizes my skinniness and beanpole stature, making me look even more ridiculous? To pretend to believe a fable the magic of which had long since been diluted by the poor communion wine?

But he didn't. He looked at me, his mind elsewhere, in a hurry to get it over with, a vague, non-committal smile on his lips. He seemed tired, his former front-row forward's musculature had turned to flab. Before hearing my confession he raised himself from his seat a little and handed me a cushion for my knees.

'This… young woman, is she a Catholic?'

'Yes, my Lord. Her father's the pass-keeper of the parish.'

His expression became more severe. The fact that Mary's father was a pass-keeper seemed to make my sin worse.

'She's not to say anything to him about this. In this kind of case discretion is necessary… so that at least your sin doesn't tarnish the reputation of our Holy Mother Church. I know some people for whom it would be a godsend.'

He gestured to the left with his chin; later on I realised he was indicating the Church of Scotland building less than a hundred yards away.

'No one must know apart from her confessor.'

'I'm her confessor.

O'Brien waved my remark away impatiently. 'Might there be someone who suspects something?'

'I… I don't think so.'

O'Brien gave a sigh that was difficult to interpret, then granted me absolution.

'As a penance you will go to Benbecula twice a week in your free time to assist Father MacAuley. They say he's *non compos mentis* any more.'

Then, since I was taking my time getting up, he went on, 'Well? What else do you want? You're not the first, Father Krook, and you won't be the last. All this kind of thing is very banal, regrettable but banal. Go in peace.'

∞∞∞

I sucked in the sea air with astonishment. I had almost forgotten I was in Oban, that improbable Victorian resort where the decrepit hotels along the sea front, mimicking those of Brighton or Bath, alternated with sanctuaries of all the religions. Thus the Catholic bishop's 'palace' looked like a simple annexe to the gloomy and arrogant Alexandra Hotel, while the black tower of St Columba's Cathedral rising beside it was vaguely Stalinist and, at the other end of the Esplanade, the white — Presbyterian — Esplanade Church proclaimed out loud its plainness and Biblical rusticity.

The door of the lounge bar of the Alexandra happened to be open so I went in. It was a huge room furnished with leather armchairs of somewhat faded luxury, romantic bay windows and an impressive portrait gallery. Upon examination they turned out to be the almost complete set of the Dukes of Argyll since the High Middle Ages; looking round the walls one could follow the long march of Scottish civilisation from the ironclad semi-barbarousness of the days of Robert the Bruce all the way down to the three-piece suit via the frilly ruffs and cuffs of Renaissance lace.

'Can I help you, Father?'

The barman, unctuous and ghostly, had silently materialised behind the immense bar of varnished wood.

'Yes you can, goddammit!' The interjection slipped out, setting off a sort of earth tremor in the barman. 'I'd like a whisky. And make it a double, please.'

He glanced at the clock, visibly torn between his respect for my clerical garb and my unexpected order at that hour — it was just after half-past two. Not much more than twenty-four hours had passed since my arrival on Islay the previous day but to me it felt like a century, indeed the equivalent of a geological epoch.

After some hesitation he said, with a wink, 'But of course, Father. What whisky would you like.'

'Cheers!' I said to my reflection in the mirror. He hadn't aged a bit, the old bugger! He was giving me a sympathetic smile, just as he had ten years ago in the Aberdonian the day before I was due to enter the seminary. Finally I understood the meaning of his smile: 'I knew we'd see each other again, Ebenezer.' And now we had. But he didn't crow about it, he simply stretched out his hand towards a bottle and I did the same.

'A Lagavulin. There you are, Father.'

'And the same for me, Robert,' came a voice from the back of the room. 'And you can leave us the bottle.'

A man carrying a newspaper came in through the door leading to the hotel lobby, slowly walked across the room and sat down right next to me at the bar. He gave me a vague nod as he passed but kept a close eye on the barman as he filled his glass. He took out his wallet to pay and I immediately started to protest but then remembered I'd left my wallet on Islay and had had to spend everything I had in my pocket, right down to my last penny, on my ferry ticket. When the barman handed back his change, he waved it away saying, 'Think of it as overtime pay.'

He scrutinised me. He could have been anything between forty and sixty. His puffy eyes and drooping lids were doubtless the result of a hard night while his shuffling gait could equally well have been put down to a general lassitude, a lack of eagerness to get on with life, or the first signs of old age. However that might be, despite his numerous wrinkles — or perhaps because of them — he was handsome in his own way, like the venerable rapiers hanging from the walls of castle armouries.

That was my first sight of Robert Dennison: a forgotten cigarette in the corner of his mouth, his upper lip turned up in a grin that revealed his white teeth — so white that I still wonder whether he didn't have false teeth.

'Is it a disguise?' he asked.

'Sorry?'

'Your... dress. Is it a disguise?'

He reminded me of that American film actor, whose name I can never remember, narrow chested, a melancholy air and a drawling voice. Walking, speaking, lighting a cigarette — everything seemed to demand a slight effort. Everything except emptying his glass.

'No. I am a priest.'

'You don't say. So far I've never got pissed with a man of the cloth.'

'I'm sorry, but I'm just going to have a glass or two then I'm off.'

The man blinked rapidly several times before raising his upper lip a bit more in an odd grin.

'A glass or two that is the question. What do you think, Robert?'

'I'm not called Robert, sir!'

'No matter, Bob. Pour me another.'

He rolled his cigarette from one corner of his lips to the other and, leaning on the bar, held out his hand to me: 'Robin Dennison.'

'Ebenezer Krook.'

'Pleased to meet you. Right then, Ebenezer, how's this for a deal: I'm going to see a man about a dog which will give you plenty of time to slip away. But if you're still here when I get back, then the drinks are on me.'

Having said that, he stood up and headed straight for the toilets. Hardly had he closed the door than the barman leant towards me and rolled his eyes. 'In your place, Father, I'd beware of that fellow. He's a Red.'

'A what?'

'A Red! A Bolshevik!' he said, emphasising each word and pointing at the masthead of the newspaper Dennison had left on the bar.

I nodded absent-mindedly, wondering how I was going to manage without any money. At that moment Robin came out of the toilets. He looked neither surprised nor particularly pleased to see me still there but as he passed he patted me on the shoulder.

One hour later my 'glass or two' was a distant memory; I was even wondering how it could have occurred to me. The only alternative was to go out of the Alexandra, look right, then left and then right again, cross the Esplanade and throw myself in the sea with all the discomfort and inconvenience that would involve. Or to stay there quietly drinking, secretly hoping that a sufficiently large injection of whisky would somehow change the composition of my person, thus making Ebenezer Krook a biologically viable individual. The choice was made easier by the fact hat Robin was the ideal drinking companion. Neither too silent, nor too loquacious, he spared me both the long, lugubrious silences and the grotesque ramblings of the drunkard. Without stopping drinking, he was able to carry on a pleasant conversation and remain silent as appropriate.

Robin Dennison worked for a radical daily in Edinburgh of which I had never heard, but he had given up political journalism —'Asses! Pontificating asses! They argue about the revolution like theologians arguing about the sex of angels!'— for the sports pages. An important youth football tournament explained his presence in Oban. He also seemed, in his undemonstrative way, to appreciate my company and asked me a lot of questions about the daily life of a Catholic priest, especially about his 'salary'.

'Well I'll be damned!' he exclaimed. 'At that rate I think you can be considered a proletarian. The drinks are on me, Comrade. Beside you I could almost be seen as a *kulak*.'

But his passion for whisky seemed more genuine that his political militancy.

'Islay,' he murmured in wistful tones. 'The island of whisky. Ardbeg, Bowmore, Caol Ila, Laphroaig, Bruichladdich — the five sacraments. And Lagavulin, of course, the supreme unction. Mention my name if ever they need a journalist over there.'

'Actually my parish is in Campbeltown…'

'Longrow, Hazelburn, Springbank… that's not bad either.'

'Once a month I take the boat to Islay. As my old predecessor used to say, nowadays a priest is a starving wolf. He has to hunt farther and farther afield to fill his belly. My Episcopalian colleague and I share a church.'

'But that's Roman decadence! And I suppose you've come to ask for a rise from your boss?'

The bottles on the shelves were starting to vibrate a little, the barman's face stretched the more we drank and the Dukes of Argyll danced merrily from one age to another swapping their different costumes — doublet, dj, baldric, ruff, cuirass — across the centuries. I told him about Aberdeen: rugby, the cement courtyard, the seminary. Islay: the Guthries. And perhaps other things I've forgotten. But I didn't tell him anything about Jura, nor about the ring, of that I'm sure. I said nothing about my father, about his little rucksack buckled up on the table, nor about my mother walking up and down the kitchen, surprised, doubtless mortified but not really shattered: 'And you don't wonder what's going to become of us, your son and me?'—'It's only the fool who *becomes* anything…'

'This… Mary, was she beautiful?'

Creaking horribly, the seized-up drawers of memory released a jumbled collection of female attributes: her funny jutting-out chin, her straight hair, her little breasts that were too far apart… 'Not at all. I don't know what idiot poet it was who said it was women's beauty that led men to ruin. If she'd been really beautiful I would have been on my guard.'

I said nothing about her pale grey eyes, with their mixture of expectation, challenge and promise, no more than I alluded, for fear of being laughed at, to her extraordinary knees: round and firm, slightly bronzed, with an old scar: a fall from her bicycle had left pink marks, both an image of childhood and a reminder of its gradual disappearance. But how could I admit that I had fallen in love with the suggestive look of a pair of knees!

That was when Robin Dennison laughed for the first time.

'I'm sorry, Comrade, but you're the idiot. This famous beauty poets go on about has no more to do with desire than Cézanne's pears have with nutrition... or your Bishop O'Brien's sermons with the real teachings of Jesus Christ!'

All at once I stiffened. The bishop's words came back to mind: 'She's not to say anything to him about this... No one must know...' A hypocrite! A filthy hypocrite! I thought as I downed another glass. You couldn't give a damn about the salvation of my soul. All you care about is what other people might think and the good name of the Church. Fornicate, Father Krook, fornicate as much as you like, but be discreet about it, make sure no one sees you. And leave the pass-keeper's daughter in peace, find another woman... *Ego te absolvo*, as long as you don't cause problems.

I must have spoken out loud for the barman was looking daggers at me, as if I'd just slashed the Turin shroud. Robin filled our glasses and patted me on the shoulder.

'He's like the politicians, Comrade, the truth embarrasses him.'

'Exactly,' I said after having emptied my glass.

Then, on a sudden inspiration, I thumped the bar. 'Off we go, then!'

'Off we go *immediately!*' Dennison insisted, as he jumped down onto his feet.

I tried to do the same but the result was much less satisfying: the stool slipped from under my buttocks and I swept my arms across the bar in an attempt to find something to hold on to, which neither our two glasses nor the bottle of Lagavulin nor the huge plaster ashtray could provide; and if the first three objects fell straight to the floor, the fourth set off on a long glissade down the polished wood, knocking over as it passed — Robin told me later — a dozen crystal glasses and a similar decanter. Having reached the end of the bar it leapt into the air to finish by crashing into the ancient suit of armour of God knows which Duke of Argyll, reducing it to a pile of scrap metal.

The clatter reverberated inside my skull, temporarily depriving me of hearing. Face to face over the bar, Robin and the barman had their mouths wide open — eventually I realised they were hurling abuse at each other. Scattered across the floor, little Ebenezer Krooks looked at me sadly, imprisoned in splinters of glass floating on pools of whisky. A minute later Robin and I found ourselves out on the deserted, twilit Esplanade; my ears had sufficiently recovered for me to hear him singing an apocryphal version of the *Internationale* which celebrated Arthur Dorward, the captain of the Scottish fifteen. Afterwards a stage hand set up the empty corridors of the bishop's palace.

The little scented secretary had disappeared, in fact nothing was in its place. Someone had reversed the order of the rooms and slipped all sorts of huge objects under the carpet so that I kept tripping over them and swearing. The walls shrank away as I approached, the door knobs jumped up into my face and the doors themselves had an annoying propensity to open unasked and to turn into panels of wainscoting when I wanted to open them. I would doubtless have finished up in a broom cupboard had a huge hand, not unlike the signs glovemakers used to hang over their shops, not grabbed me and dragged me along another corridor. I heard someone address a certain Ebenezer Krook, a man of whom I had never heard. Then suddenly, at the back of a room as wide as the Forth, I saw Bishop O'Brien.

Although it didn't sober me up completely, this vision did a least trigger off a short burst of lucidity. I had something to say to this character, though what it was I couldn't remember. So, bouncing to and fro like a billiard ball among gigantic obstacles, I made several

Jean-Pierre Ohl

assertions which, as I spoke them, seemed clear as crystal but of which the bishop didn't appear to understand a blind word. On the edge of vision I saw Robin whose hand, reduced now to reasonable proportions, was taking the bishop's books off the shelves one by one.

So I squared up to O'Brien and, summoning up all my faculties to extract some morsels of intelligible sound from the gibberish filling my mouth, I positively yelled at him, 'You hypocrite! You filthy hypocrite!'

The bishop looked at me open-mouthed, then turned to Robin whom he seemed to assume was my legal representative. 'What is the meaning of this?'

'The meaning, sir,' Robin replied, without interrupting his examination of the books, 'is that Comrade Krook has come to hand in his resignation... For Christ's sake! Augustine, Aquinas, Newman, *The Imitation of Christ...* isn't there even *one* proper book in all this bumf? Oh, Shakespeare at least.'

'But *who* are you?'

'I am one, sir,' Robin declared, 'that comes to tell you, your daughter and the Moor are now making the beast with two backs.'

'What do you want?'

'Comrade Krook will not leave before he has received the compensation that is due to him.'

'You will leave this minute.'

The bishop took a step towards a bell-pull. At once I bent my knees, hunched up my shoulders and prepared to drive back the opposing scrum. 'The rules, O'Brien!' I cried. 'Fight according to the rules. Don't you recognise me? It's me, the *Mad Dog!* That's what you used to call me, isn't it?'

His eyes widened like doors opening on a memory and right at the back of it I saw the courtyard of the presbytery, the bushes, the well, the coping stones. I threw myself forward, but at that precise moment a table stuck its leg out and tripped me up so that the bishop and I fell and rolled back and forward over the floor, as I vainly looked for the ball that wasn't there, until Robin blew the whistle

33

for full time.

∞∞∞∞

'A fine tackle, Comrade.'

I sat up slowly. Around me the waiting-room of Oban station materialised little by little in concentric circles: first of all my knees, then Robin's, then the end of the bench, the tiles, another bench, the ticket office in the distance.

'No... I missed him... I just slipped and...'

'Shhh. I'm the journalist here, let the independent press have its say for once. Anyway it wasn't just the rugby tackle as such — although the man's pretty well built for his age — what counts is the symbol. To flatten your bishop, that's a bit like... spitting your father in the face, or calling your mother a whore. It's not just rugby, it's revolution.'

Happy with this turn of phrase, Robin took out his notebook and jotted it down for posterity.

'And how is it that we're...'

'...not at the police station? Just think for a moment: a drunken, fornicating priest. A bishop floored by an opponent who was giving him a stone and a half. You don't shout that kind of thing from the rooftops. Here's a shilling, go and have a cup of coffee, I'll be back in a moment.'

I obeyed him like a good boy, in fact anything else was beyond me. The coffee seemed very strong. It felt as if I were drinking it for the first time.

'Something else, Father?'

The waitress reminded me vaguely of Mary and at once the ridiculous, pitiful aspect of my situation hit me. I would have cried except that I was acutely aware that tears at that moment would have made me even more ridiculous. So I just gave the girl a smile and greeted Robin on his return with an expansive gesture. He whispered a few words to the waitress, who giggled, then he handed me a package, saying, 'First of all you need this. Then we'll see.' And he pushed me towards the lavatory.

I'll never forget the waitress's expression when I came back. First of all her look of amazement then the disapproval gradually twisting her lips as she realised, or thought she realised, the implications of my metamorphosis. In abandoning my cassock I had not just become an ordinary man in her eyes, no, I had tumbled down several rungs lower on the ladder of creation, become an animal, or even worse: a shapeless, incomplete, embryonic creature. In Lamarckian terms, stripped of my function I was a mere organ.

Robin did not share her opinion, he went into raptures about the burgundy shirt, the grey flannel trousers — too short, of course — and the dark-blue blazer with an impressive row of brass buttons that made me look like a clarinet.

'Good! Very good.'

Then he saw the ring and his expression changed. I had taken it off the little chain I wore round my neck and slipped it on my finger. The stone was as beautiful as ever, the ring as tight; after all these years I felt once more the mixture of pride and embarrassment the ring always gave me.

Robin examined the strange shape of the stone closely, then looked away for a few moments. 'A family heirloom?'

'No. I bought it in a pawnshop. For a girl, but she ditched me.'

'From a pawnshop? A stone like that?'

He shook his head, paid the bill and got up to leave. I was about to take my cassock, which I had roughly wrapped up in the torn paper, but he snatched it out of my hands and left the package on the counter. 'For Halloween,' he said with a wink to the waitress, slipping her a visiting card.

'Have you anywhere to go?'

'Not exactly.'

'You'll have to earn your living. In Scotland there are two places to find work, Glasgow and Edinburgh — Glasgow for manual labour, Edinburgh for intellectuals. I would advise Edinburgh.'

'But I'm not an intellectual.'

'Perhaps, but it's easier to pass yourself off as an English teacher than as a plumber. Then Edinburgh has one other advantage — I live there. A flat in Rose Street. It's small but it does have a spare room. Hey, where are you off to?'

'I'll be back straight away.'

'The waitress had unfolded the cassock. She was cautiously feeling the cloth as if it were the slough of some fabulous beast.

'Excuse me a moment.' I took the book out of the inside pocket and slipped it into that of my blazer. When I got back Robin had already bought the tickets.

'The train leaves soon.'

'Before we go I must ask you: why are you doing all this for me?'

Robin looked me in the eye. 'Hurry up and get on the train before I ask myself the same question.'

CHAPTER III

*In which Mary Guthrie goes her own way and fully deserves
the claim that 'she's got a crush on Urquhart'.*

Amongst the other things Herbert Geddes, a rich industrialist with a
passion for optical instruments, had left his wife — my Aunt Catriona
— were a portrait of himself as an old sea dog, a powerful nautical
telescope and a magnificent apartment in the building at the top of
Ramsay Garden. With its reds and whites, its towers and turrets, its
gables, its cut-off corners, its octagons, its balconies and slate roofs
it looked like a fairy-tale castle. But once inside you lost all sense
of its massive baroque structure and found yourself as if suspended
above Edinburgh in the gondola of a hot-air balloon. Suffering from
severe arthritis, Aunt Catriona rarely left the drawing-room. She
was a little old lady, neat and tidy, with a permanently hoarse voice
and something squirrel-like about her movements. Thanks to the
telescope, that rotated on a pivot, and the wide bow window, from
her armchair she enjoyed a remarkable panorama that went from
Leith and the Forth to the Old Town, including the terraces of the
Castle and Princes Street gardens nestling at her feet.

She was familiar with the private life of a good quarter of the
inhabitants of Edinburgh. She spent her time spying on the couples
on the park benches, the visitors to the Castle, the shopkeepers and
housewives in Princes Street, the traffic accidents at the Hanover
Street crossroads, the pedestrians going up the Mound towards the
Royal Mile. Keeping her right eye stuck to the eyepiece and blinking
with her left gave her a bizarrely asymmetrical look. She punctuated
her surveillance with stifled chuckles, disdainful sniffs and dramatic
exclamations: 'Well, that takes the biscuit!' or 'That was all we

needed!' From time to time she would turn to her husband's portrait to call him as witness to a particularly juicy scandal.

But her husband's substantial estate also included a different piece of equipment. The morning after I arrived she sent me to collect something from the nearest medical laboratory. A man in a white coat handed me a little case which was icy cold to the touch.

'I wonder what she does with them,' he said, looking me up and down. 'Are you her daughter?'

'Her niece. What's in it?'

'Today there's some platelets from a diabetic, some cells taken from a sarcoma and some tubercular tissue. Funny titbits to go with her tea. However, as long as she coughs up...'

The envelope I gave him seemed generously filled.

As soon as I entered the flat Aunt Catriona's voice assailed me. 'Come on, hurry up. It won't keep.'

On her instructions I locked the the case in a cupboard built into the wall I had taken for a safe but which turned out to be a refrigerated compartment. A little later, looking through the keyhole, I managed to observe a strange sight: the old lady had set up a huge microscope beside her armchair and was putting the samples from the case into it one by one. 'Well, well, well,' she commented in suggestive tones; then she threw herself back, gave a brief laugh and a vigorous shake of the head, took a mouthful of tea and applied her eye to the apparatus once more.

I found this discovery a little disturbing the first few days I stayed with Aunt Catriona. When, from my room, I heard her characteristic exclamations —'Oh, oh, oh!', 'Just look at that!', 'Well I'll be damned!'— I had no idea whether she was responding to the insurance agent frolicking with the little florist on the second floor of the Old Waverley Hotel or to a frisky cytoplasm.

When I went out I wasted no time getting out of her field of vision, but in the evening Aunt Catriona would greet me with a sardonic smile or a reproachful frown which made me think Uncle Herbert's telescope could go round obstacles or through walls, revealing every last detail of my doings to her. And in my dreams I saw her, using mediaeval-looking instruments, take little bits of me from my body of which the microscope immediately revealed the inherent defects: 'The little minx! It's just as I thought.'

My room, small but comfortable, looked out onto an interior courtyard of the block of flats. It was there that one evening I took volume T–Z of the *Encyclopaedia of Scottish Literature* and read what was for a long time to be the sum total of what I knew about Urquhart:

*Thomas Urquhart of Cromarty: Scottish man of letters (Cromarty 1612, Flushing, United Provinces, 1660). A brilliant mind, eclectic and disorganised, the archetype of the baroque intellectual. He first published a work on trigonometry (*Trissotetras*) then several unclassifiable books of an orotundity and pedantry which often come close to self-pastiche or a hoax:* Pantochronacanon, *a fantasy genealogy of his own family, relating it to various great figures of history and* Ekskubalauron, *containing specifications for a universal language. But the great work of his life is incontestably his translation of the books of Rabelais, whom he discovered during a journey to France. Zealous to excess (Urquhart 'completed' Rabelais' famous enumerations with neologisms of his own), his translation nonetheless marks an important date in the history of English literature: Swift, Sterne and Smollett make repeated reference to it. He was on the royalist side during the Civil War, fighting in the Battle of Worcester where, he claimed, he lost several thousand pages of his manuscripts. He was imprisoned in Windsor Castle, then exiled to Zealand. According to legend, he died of laughter on hearing of the news of the restoration of the Stuarts.*

My researches in the Main Library produced a very unusual result. The custodians of the special collection, two old spinsters called Miss Brain and Miss Douglas, were well known for their mutual affection; we called them Stein and Toklas. Miss Stein wore old-rose blouses and antiquated skirts with flounces; Miss Toklas, as tall and skinny as her friend was short and generously built, had a preference for black pullovers, which gave her the look of an interminable coal shovel. They both wore the same improbable brooch on their chests — a shipwrecked mariner on his raft — but Miss Toklas's Robinson Crusoe floated on the surface of a dreary black ocean while Miss Stein's boldly confronted two redoubtable pink tsunamis.

Miss Toklas filled out the request slips then watched with a protective eye the erratic swishing of Miss Stein's frills as she trotted from shelf to shelf, giving little cries of delight when she found the required book. But when it was a matter of getting the four available titles of Thomas Urquhart for me, no cry sounded and Miss Stein returned to Miss Toklas head bowed: 'I just don't understand it. I can't find them.'

'None of the four?'

'Not a single one.'

'Impossible!'

'Go and see for yourself,' Miss Stein retorted, cut to the quick.

Miss Toklas was no more successful. 'They're not there!'

'I told you so.'

'I just don't understand it.'

'Precisely.'

The register revealed that the last time the books — all four volumes — had all been taken out was on the same day, June 4 1949, by a certain B. Foyle.

'What a funny idea to steal *those*,' Miss Stein said, looking at me.

'We'll have to ask for a loan from another library,' Toklas added, looking me up and down. 'It will take some time.'

'It doesn't matter,' I said with my nicest smile. 'I'm not in a hurry.'

On my way back to Ramsay Garden I wondered about the mysterious B. Foyle. I was certainly a little disappointed to find that some man — or woman — had been there before me but it didn't mean my resolve weakened. At that time I hadn't yet met Professor Borel, but I can very well imagine how he would have reacted if I had confided in him. He would have leant back in his chair, with that insupportable smile on his face that made you want to tear his lips off with a pair of pincers; then, blinking in the smoke from his cigarette, he would have delivered a definitive pronouncement, something in the style of: 'My dear, I think I can perceive a kind of fairly rudimentary *transference* here. You've become besotted with this morose priest and since for you it is an inadmissible feeling, you've substituted this Urquhart fad for it simply because your... Krook mentioned the name at the very moment when your desire was taking form. All this taking place subconsciously, of course. And I'm certain that if the bugger had talked of Tolstoy instead, you'd already been on your way to Yasnaya Polyana.'

∞∞∞

Almost four years passed, marked by the slow, ineluctable decline of my enthusiasm for the academic world and embarrassed encounters with a Father Krook whose pastoral ardour was following the same slippery slope. Usually I spent the weekends working in Edinburgh. From the drawing-room I could hear the characteristic creak of the telescope on its tripod and Aunt Catriona's intermittent commentary: 'O my God, am I dreaming?', 'I can't believe my own eyes!', 'Again?', 'Lord, what a pity!' But I went home to Islay once a month, arriving late on Friday evening on the last ferry from Oban; Krook the next day by the ferry from Kennacraig. Our brief moment of intimacy on the cliff was now just a distant memory. To be more precise, he avoided me. One evening, however, I managed to squeeze a few words out of him.

Teddy had gone up to his room with his comics and my father, in slippers and dressing gown, was busy in his 'photo lab', that is the wash-house next to the garage.

'Urquhart? He was a madman from the little I know, and I've no desire to want to know any more.'

Krook finished his coffee standing up. Then, giving me a suspicious look, he asked, 'What exactly is it you want from me?'

41

'Your mother. I'd like to meet her.'

I thought his eyes were going to pop out of his head and fall into his cup, but they just gave me a piercing look. With a kind of angry snort, he left the kitchen.

The Sunday breakfasts were gloomy affairs. A little before nine the priest set off for the church with my father and Teddy; I for my part had insisted on being granted an absolute dispensation on the day of my twentieth birthday. Krook strode off towards the car with a frown, head bowed, a posture which expressed both suppressed anger and morbid resignation; there was also a vague stench of malt whisky clinging to him.

The return was even worse. 'Lucky pig!' Teddy muttered as he passed me on the stairs. Krook was close behind. Without a word he went and shut himself up in his room until it was time for the ferry. In the pub Malcolm's defence of him was becoming less and less vigorous. And even my father, despite his unfailing loyalty, finally confessed to a certain nostalgia for the picturesque and odiferous times of old Father Morton. I was soon going to have to face facts: when all was said and done my romantic duellist was nothing more that what I had first seen him as: a grumpy, miserable, boring misanthrope.

My interest in Urquhart, on the other hand, did not fade — I don't know whether that validates or invalidates the 'transference' theory. Weary of the Stein-Toklas prevarications I had eventually managed to buy the *Ekskubalauron* from Walpole's, a rather grubby bookshop in Anchor Close. To tell the truth, I couldn't get much out of it; the difficulties inherent in seventeenth-century English were compounded by innumerable references to persons and events that meant little more to me than the ups and downs of the Ming dynasty: preachers with vaguely ridiculous names, abstruse arguments between Presbyterians and Episcopalians, indecisive battles, alliances repudiated, political vendettas or rival lairds settling old scores. And as far as the style was concerned, I could not but agree with the editors of the *Encyclopaedia*: it was like a wine-skin inflated by the gas of recondite erudition, of monstrous arrogance and incurable megalomania. However, the wine-skin floated up into the air and from a distance could even be taken for a fairly imposing balloon. And when the rumblings of bombast and madness fell silent for a moment, you were surprised by the clear, sparkling sound of a fine phrase — concerning the beauty of language or his 'dear, dear Rabelais'. To put it briefly, I didn't like Urquhart in the usual sense of the word but I felt the kind of slightly apprehensive admiration for him the diplodocus and the mammoth inspire in children. In fact to me he seemed too enigmatic to be vain and too crazy to be grotesque.

Moreover the point at which I would have to finally choose a subject for my PhD was fast approaching. For most of my fellow students I 'had a crush on Urquhart' and to repudiate him at the last minute meant that in their eyes I would lose that aura of eccentricity and mute rebellion which suited me so well. Even worse, I would have gone down in my own esteem. And then Breacan's dog had started trotting round inside my head again in the form of a project, still vague, alongside my 'real' work as a student: to write the story of Mary Guthrie writing the story of Thomas Urquhart.

Also I had to find a lecturer or professor able and willing to supervise my dissertation. Foreseeing difficulties, I started my search well before the end of the fourth year. One specialist in Scottish literature could quote off by heart a letter Burns had written to a man in debt to him for the sum of twenty guineas, another knew exactly which drawer Scott kept his snuffbox in at Abbotsford. But to both of them Urquhart was nothing more than a name. For the seventeenth-century specialists he was a braggart and an obsessive writer; they invariably directed me towards Milton. The Shakespeareans advised Shakespeare — except one who oddly enough suggested Marlowe — the Dickensians Dickens. All of these academics had a vision of literature that was no broader than that of a mule with blinkers pulling the plough in some Grampian glen would have of the general geography of the United Kingdom. To find equivalents in other disciplines one would have to imagine an accountant who refused to add any numbers other than 4 and 8 or a garage mechanic who would only repair green cars.

'But you're certain this is the career you want to take up, are you?' Borel would have said, stroking the side of his nose with his forefinger, the gesture which invariably accompanies his ironic digs. 'Would you happen to be a masochist, Miss Guthrie?'

'A writer. I'd like to be a writer.'

'Oh, I see... and... don't you think you might be setting off in the wrong direction?'

I had put him at the bottom of my list though logically I should have started with him, because of Rabelais. His half-French background, his imposing exterior, his bombastic manner of speech, his fiery looks set the hearts of many of his female students aquiver, but I was wary of him.

His office was the nicely calculated combination of a bohemian student's room and a psychoanalyst's consulting-room. There was a portrait of Freud on the wall; books by Sartre and Merleau-Ponty were lying on the sofa that was covered with a grubby counterpane, and an old dressing gown hanging on the coat-peg. There was a permanent smell of coffee and cigarettes in the room. And his crumpled trousers, his too-wide pullover — very *Quartier latin* — were designed to give the impression of a stagey sloppiness of dress. Rumour had it that he had spent five years intriguing to obtain a post at the Sorbonne then had remembered that his Scottish mother knew lots of people in Edinburgh; so he had chosen exile, rather in the way a footballer who was not quite in the top flight and had been turned down by the big clubs would make do with a modest provincial team. But everything about him, from his assertive voice with its vaguely parliamentary intonation to the casual way he had of giving his lectures in slippers, proclaimed that, on the contrary, for him the position was an honour.

'Did you know, Miss Guthrie, that certain molluscs live encrusted on the backs of whales?'

Leaning over his desk, Borel gave me one of his long, piercing looks. 'Well, Rabelais is the whale and your Urquhart the mollusc. Without Rabelais there would never have been an Urquhart. The work of the latter is no more than a footnote to the work of the former. At the end of what psychological — or pathological, he added with a self-indulgent smile — process the pupil imagined he was able to equal his master, is beyond me to say, but the result is excruciating. Apart from a few neatly phrased epigrams, two or three insights in semiotics, Urquhart hasn't much to his credit. Even as a translator he's very overrated.'

'Overrated? But you're the one who said that no one since —'

'Miss Guthrie!' He cut me short in a tone of affectionate remonstrance. 'Let's not get too far away from our subject. And I believe the subject is not Urquhart — it's you!'

'How do you mean?'

'You are one of the most brilliant students of your year — no protests please, I've made enquiries. You've lost your mother, are the eldest daughter of a family of, how shall I put it, modest means in a… hmm… out-of the-way region — and despite all that you have an immaculate record. Without a doubt that indicates talent, great strength of character… but that also means you are accustomed to be first in everything and you wish to remain so.'

He sat back in his chair and neatly lit himself a cigarette. For the first time I noticed his hands: short, gnarled, slightly red. A farm labourer's hands. They performed all the expressive gestures demanded of them scrupulously, but afterwards they always returned to sit nice and flat on the table, simple, still, ready. They were more genuine than the whole of the rest of his person.

'In other words you prefer to become the leading specialist — the smoke doesn't bother you, I hope? — on a third-class writer than to be swallowed up in the mass of commentators on Shakespeare or Thackeray.'

At any other time my instinct would have been to throw the ashtray in his face, but a voice inside me told me to be patient. 'But it seems to me that Urquhart's fate, his place in his century…'

'His place! An incorrigible reactionary. A *réactionnaire*'— he gave the word the full French pronunciation —'incapable of seeing what was at stake in the politics of his time. But when you talk about

45

his life, I presume you're thinking above all about his death. That is certainly the only astonishing thing he accomplished... although... When you think about it, to die of laughter is not as original as all that. Rabelais himself gives several examples, without counting that Burmese king, whose name escapes me, who ruptured an artery on learning that Venice was a republic. A *republic*! He found that extremely funny. But then it's just a legend perhaps. After all, who can say that Urquhart didn't die of cirrhosis of the liver or cancer of the colon. No it's not to be taken seriously. However...'

He leant towards me again, giving me a beguiling smile. 'Here it comes!' the voice inside me said.

'However, let us not be too harsh on him. Our laird had a certain panache, a certain arrogance. Something could perhaps be made of that. I certainly wouldn't want to discourage a student as brilliant as yourself, Miss Guthrie, and if you were to assure me that this... crush on Urquhart is merely a trial run leading to something more substantial — a thesis on Rabelais, for example — so be it. I would allow my arm to be twisted.'

It was an open secret that Borel was desperate to find a thesis to supervise.

'Well, yes,' I lied, 'that had crossed my mind.'

'Jolly good. But let's get things clear between us. I need something new.'

'Something new?'

'Something new that justifies your work, an unpublished manuscript, some important biographical detail. Something to get your teeth into. It's exactly what I told that Miss — what was it? — Miss Foyle!'

'Miss Foyle?'

'A Vestal at the shrine of Urquhart, like yourself, though much less gifted, of course... and less obstinate, oh yes. Anyway, I only met her the once and I've never seen a line she's written. She must have tired of poor Urquhart and married a medical student.'

Very satisfied with himself, Borel lit another cigarette.

'You need to get an introduction to the Urquharts. A good old

Scottish family with their own tartan, a run-down castle, a family ghost — the whole works! I'm sure they'll have some archives, letters and I don't know what. You'll have to get someone to write a letter of recommendation.'

'Yes. I think there is perhaps a way.'

Hardly had I said this than I saw the tall silhouette of Father Krook in my mind's eye, hirsute, incensed, reproachful. But I went on nonetheless, with a touch of petty satisfaction. 'I know someone. He's called Krook, he's our parish priest. I think he's related to the Urquharts.'

'A Rabelaisian *curé*, then. Excellent. Very picturesque. Do some research, Miss Guthrie, some research. Oh yes, the casket. Unearth something about the casket.'

'What casket?'

'Don't tell me you've never heard of the Urquhart casket?'

'Never.

At the thought that he could tell me his story Borel's face lit up with an innocent joy I would not have believed him capable of. Perhaps he did, after all, possess, hidden behind his arsenal of poses and grimaces, an old store of childlike enthusiasm.

'As you know, Miss Guthrie, Urquhart fell into Cromwell's hands at Worcester. They locked him up in Windsor Castle for a few years but, God knows how, the bugger found a way of keeping in contact with the outside world. Some people say he managed to perfect his… *Ekskubalauron*, his universal language and used to send out coded messages. However that may be, he succeeded in uniting the resistance of all the royalists of the north-east of Scotland and in collecting funds to raise an army. They consisted of precious stones, it seems; money wasn't worth very much at the time and gold took up too much space. This hoard was never used and for good reason — Urquhart was exiled to Zealand then the Stuarts regained the throne. But the casket, what became of it? It is said that the Urquharts moved heaven and earth to find it, in vain as far as I know, or our Highlanders are very good at keeping their business to themselves. I took a trip to Cromarty a couple of years ago: Urquhart

House is threatening to fall down, the laird owes money to all the tradesmen in the village and even as far as Inverness. A poor fellow, a local hack told me, and certainly different from his ancestor — never a smile!'

'I'm not a private eye, Mr Borel, I'm a student of literature.'

'*Oh là là!*' Borel chuckled. 'Getting on our high horse, are we? Just think of your Sir Thomas. He had plenty of imagination, dash it, but it looks as if you have as much and more to spare. You know what they say about you in the Department?'

'Yes, I do know,' I said, getting up, 'I'm the girl with a crush on Urquhart.'

'Very well then, so go and write me a good old analytical commentary.'

Then he gave me an odd smile and a little wave with that large calm, friendly hand of his so that as I went off down the corridor I didn't quite know what to think of André Borel.

∞∞∞

Things might have turned out differently if old Gordon had died at the end of the month, as all good Islay Catholics are supposed to, instead of on 5 September 1953. He lived alone in a sort of ruinous shack that couldn't even be locked on the road to Ballygrant. Of course he hadn't left a penny to pay for his own funeral.

'I'd have him at my place,' Malcolm said, scratching his head, 'but it's too small and since John's our pass-keeper...'

To complicate matters my father, who had retired a few weeks ago, had gone with Teddy and the local football team to the Oban youth tournament. So I spent the last days of the university vacation alone with the mortal remains of Jeff Gordon, a situation that Mr Campbell, my former primary school teacher, described in a session of the local council as 'worrying, indubitably'. He telephoned the undertakers in Bowmore and the Catholic presbytery in Campbeltown without imagining I might find a living man, even a priest, much more disturbing than a corpse.

In the meanwhile Gordon was put in the wash-house. My father had forbidden us to go in because of the chemicals kept there but I managed to unearth the key at the bottom of a drawer.

'At least we won't have to tell old Jeff to keep still,' Malcolm said when he saw all the photographic equipment. It looked pretty dusty to me, the place strangely disused. The developing tanks were empty and there was no trace of the much-vaunted chemicals that were supposed to fill them. On the other hand underneath the sink I found a large number of empty gin and whisky bottles. I had always accepted my father's ability to deal with his grief without question; the pile of corpses opened my eyes. A little while later I disposed of them in our large dustbin and I think the last vestiges of my childhood disappeared with them.

The Bridgend butcher offered us several blocks of ice free of charge. 'Out of the question,' Malcolm declared. 'Jeff hated ice. He drank his whisky neat.' However he eventually accepted, out of consideration for me.

On the morning of 8 September we went down to the ferry terminal — *bwaaaah!* — to meet Krook. I hadn't seen him for three months and I was struck by his appearance. He was like a caricature of himself, an actor in overdone make-up playing the role of Father Krook. The furrows of discontent on his forehead looked as if they had been drawn in soot.

'Are you... are you well, Father?'

'Very well.'

During the drive Malcolm recounted the story of the Englishman and the ice, imitating in turn Gordon's rustic tones and his adversary's affected drawl: 'Nae, ye willna dae it!'—'But why, if you will forgive me, should I not put ice in my whisky?'—''Cause it's immoral, that's why.'

'Where are the altar boys?' Krook muttered as he put on his chasuble.

Malcolm stared at the vault with a look of embarrassment. 'At the football tournament'

The priest directed us to our places with a jerk of the chin. He stopped two or three times during the benediction trying to remember the words.

'O Lord,' said Malcolm, 'we'll never get there!'

We did get there, however, and the little band of mourners — minus the three old women who hadn't managed to make up their minds whether to join us or not — accompanied Jeffrey Gordon to the minuscule 'Catholic section' of the Bridgend cemetery. The grave seemed ridiculously small to me; the two men in black managed to lose their grip on the ropes, letting go of the coffin before it reached the ground so that Jeff's last journey finished with the sinister crack of an old boat running aground. Malcolm gulped. 'Poor old Jeff. It would have given him a real thirst, a burial like that.'

On the way back the ancient Austin Classic, of which Malcolm was so proud, broke down. As his top half disappeared under the bonnet —'It's nothing, just a bit of dust in the carburettor... What time's the ferry?'— I observed Krook in silence. I felt like giving him a good slap, grabbing him by the shoulders, shaking him and shouting at him, 'No! It's not right for a priest to look so miserable!' However the little voice I sometimes heard inside my head (for some time now it had borrowed the unctuous, pedantic tones of André Borel) persuaded me not to: *What do you actually know about him, Miss Guthrie? Being miserable demands a certain talent for it, a minimum degree of intelligence. Does he really have those requirements? What if he were just a disagreeable, sulky animal? A bear with a sore head, for example, or a monkey, eh? Yes, a monkey as your friend Alison says.*

'That's it! I've done it.'

Malcolm had dislodged the dust, but too late. And it had already penetrated a mechanism much more fragile and complicated than a carburettor, even that of an Austin Classic. From that moment on events departed from their predetermined course. It was no use Malcolm combining the smoothness of a Stirling Moss with the furious speed of a Fangio, shooting ahead on the straight stretches and taking the curves elegantly, it was ordained that we would not get to Port Askaig in time. Less than three miles from the harbour a herd of apathetic cattle blocked the road and when we reached the landing stage it was to see the last ferry disappearing to the east with a farewell bellow.

Booowah!

Father Krook showed no signs of irritation. His gaze wandered over the Jura shore which seemed almost close enough to touch. Meadows sloped gently down to the Sound as far as the cliffs that in places rose above narrow strips of sand. In the background the Paps caught the last rays of the sun, giving them a misty halo.

'You could say it's the Lord's will, eh, Father?' Malcolm said. 'How about coming to the Harbourside with us?'

Krook turned round.

'A little ecumenical ceremony — for Jeff.'

To my great surprise, after a moment's hesitation Father Krook said: 'Why not?'

At closing time it was mild and clear, a little like the night when we had talked by Caol Ila. Krook accompanied me without a word except 'Sorry' when our shoulders touched in places where the path narrowed. But he had laughed at least twice in the course of the evening.

I'd left a few old photos lying on the kitchen table and while I was making the coffee he sat down to look at them. I didn't feel drunk; on the contrary every one of my movements was unusually precise. I filled the cups to the rim without spilling a drop and placed the sugar bowl, the milk jug and the silver spoons just as my mother used to do for important guests.

'How old were you on this one?'

'Eleven,' I said sitting down beside him on the bench. 'It was my birthday. They'd given me a bicycle and I fell off at the bottom of the hill. I cried for a whole hour — I think Daddy took the photo to make me stop.'

On the photo I was sitting in the same place as now but the other way round, with my back to the table. The tips of my plimsolls just touched the ground. The hem of my skirt didn't quite hide my knee smeared with Germolene, the tin could be seen by the sink, next to the packet of cotton wool. You could also see a glass of water and the tablets my mother used to take when she felt really ill. And then on the other bench, hidden by the table, there must have been *The War of the Worlds* still in its gift-wrapping. The picture had caught my mother in a bizarre pose: her face was blurred and her hands at her throat, as if she were preparing to strangle herself. A phosphorescent, metallic monster, not unlike the one on the cover of Wells' novel, was observing the scene through the window. It took an effort to see, flooded by the flashlight, the reflection of the camera and of my father's eye.

Krook seemed fascinated by the photo: he spent a long time examining it, taking little sips of coffee. I closed my eyes and managed to feel once more the pain of the graze, the sting when I fell, then the burning sensation of the first minutes, the dull throb that followed going up to my heart: *boom, boom* — the footsteps of pain withdrawing. I could also hear Mummy's voice speaking to Daddy just before the photo: 'Just a moment, John, I'm not…' The crackle of the flash-bulb, the annoyed click of the tongue from my mother as, too late, she smoothed down her hair. I saw again Daddy's apologetic look, Mummy's grimace, his gesture, immediately repressed, towards the box of pills. I could have rerun the film of that long-gone day with great precision, I could have fallen asleep and dreamt my whole life had my knee not been visited by a large, timid hand, as dry as thirst and soft as lips. As he drew me to him, I smelt the slightly rank odour of his cassock and, through the cloth, felt against my throat the pressure of a small object he wore round his neck.

∞∞∞∞

I suppose that on waking up beside their first lover young girls have their heads full of plans: get engaged, get married have children perhaps. All that was forbidden to me. In this specific case what generally marks a beginning was just an end. Catholic priests don't get engaged, don't get married; the only children they can father are bastards. And the women who sleep with them are as out of place there as a plough on a frozen lake.

I pretended I was still asleep but opened my eyes just enough to see him sitting on the side of the bed, already wearing his cassock. Suddenly he gave a laugh; not the kind of laugh he'd had in the Harbourside, rather one that comes when you remember a grotesque episode in your own past. Your lips stay closed, an explosive sound comes from your nostrils; there is tacit agreement to call it a laugh, but it doesn't express hilarity at all. Then he muttered, 'So it never ends…'

My eyes wide open now, I pushed myself upon my elbows. 'Sorry. What did you say?'

'Nothing. It's four in the morning. You ought to go to your room.'

The logic of that escaped me, but his last words stuck in my mind. I'd have preferred it if he'd just gone ahead and slapped me. 'To my room.' I repeated.

'Yes. I'll wake you a bit before I leave for the ferry. We'll have time to… talk about all this.'

'I'll go with you.'

'Certainly not! Don't you think… don't you think we've been foolish enough already?'

Just before I slammed the door I saw him staring fixedly at the sheets.

When I woke, the guest-room bed was already made, the pillows fluffed up. Krook himself had disappeared, leaving behind as the only evidence of his passing: his wallet, the coffee cups on the table and a slight irritation between my thighs.

I sat down on the doorstep but found it impossible to order my thoughts. At times I was flooded with anger, at others I felt close to tears. To crown it all, I could hear André Borel whispering in my ear: 'And rancour, Miss Guthrie, you're forgetting rancour. That gorilla's really humiliated you, hasn't he? And you don't like that. Not in the least.' One thing alone was clear: my father was going to be back soon and the last thing I wanted was to have to deal with his questions. I packed my suitcase, left a scribbled note on the kitchen table — *Urgently need to consult a book. Off to Edinburgh. Will ring. Kisses* — telling myself that the telegram style, far from suggesting the worries of a conscientious student, recalled trashy spy films.

I made my decision on the way, Father Krook's scowl did not deter me. On the contrary, it encouraged me. It would be a nice little revenge, petty like all revenge. Perhaps he'd never know about it, but it gave me the initiative.

Discretion demanded I should avoid the Harbourside and for the first time in my life I pushed open the door of the Port Askaig Hotel. Unfortunately I'd forgotten that Alison had taken a summer job there. She gave me a strange look from behind the reception desk. On the walls were sepia engravings of bagpipers, lumberjacks tossing the caber, merry gentlemen in kilts brandishing bottles of whisky. Nothing there was authentic not even the Scotch terrier snoring on a chair with an impeccable little goatee that looked as if it had been cut by a ladies' hairdresser.

'Too late. He's gone.'

'Who d'you mean?'

'Krook. On the Oban ferry, the half-past six. He looked funny somehow. He hasn't stolen something?'

Why the Oban ferry? It was the Kennacraig ferry he should have taken to get back to Campbeltown. Alison was giving my suitcase curious looks.

'Let me have the phone book, will you?'

Only one Krook in Stonehaven: A. Krook, Raven Cottage, The Cliff. A for Amelia, Amanda, Augusta — the address and the initial seemed to fit the image I had of Mrs Krook.

'I knew it! You're going away with the monkey! He's going to abandon holy orders and the pair of you will head off for the colonies.'

'Get stuffed,' I said as I put down the phone book.

∞∞∞∞

After a brief stop in Edinburgh, where I cashed the first instalment of the bursary the University had generously awarded me on the recommendation of Borel, I took the Aberdeen train and got out at Stonehaven. Aunt Catriona, busy observing a German tourist micturating in the toilets of the public gardens, had scarcely noticed me: 'Lord preserve us! Where was he keeping *all that?*'

I wasn't particularly keen on Dickens but I had *David Copperfield* with me and I remembered a few scraps from Mr Davies' course, a mumbling, ancient specialist who probably had his information from the author himself: 'Betsy Trotwood, decent, modest and generous, represents the Victorian petty bourgeoisie. Her constant battle with the donkeys corresponds to the unproblematic affirmation of property rights; it fulfils little Davy's longing for security and rules after his long wanderings.'

At first sight it had everything: the hamlet on the heights, the little house on the edge of the cliff with its sandy yard, beaming garden gnome and stepping-stone footpath. No donkey in sight, however. The little lawn that could be seen at the back had not been mown for a long time, climbing plants were scaling the front and no one seemed in a hurry to repair the awning, bits of which were scattered over the steps while the ribs of the framework, now with no function, looked like a sort of four-person gallows. To the south, the ruins of Dunottar Castle, a long bird's skeleton perching on the mist, seemed to be waiting for some new historic tragedy to bring it back to life.

I tugged at the bell-pull twice but I could see it wasn't connected to any bell. However, after a minute somebody appeared at the door and immediately dismissed the reassuring image of good old Aunt Betsy.

'Yes?'

'Mrs Krook? I'm Mary Guthrie... a friend of your son.'

She raised one eyebrow slightly and scrutinised me, then stepped back which I took as an invitation. I crossed the hall, empty apart from a pile of broken glass, which doubtless came from the awning, while she repeated behind me: 'A friend of my son...'

'I'm sorry, I'm interrupting you in the middle of moving.'

'It's always like that, just ignore it.'

That was impossible. In the living-room no object was in a normal place so consequently they all attracted your attention. There was an empty aquarium on an ironing board, a slipper on a pedestal; the window at the back was almost completely obscured by a refrigerator, the cable of which was not plugged in anywhere; on the bookshelves there were empty bottles, tins of food, a hat, a nail file and some white pills without their container. Cardboard boxes were piled up more or less everywhere, still sealed by the red ribbon of the removal firm but covered in dust. Most were inscribed in blue or black ink: *XVIIth, XVIIIth, History — Scotland, Dickens/Thackeray* etc. Only two or three had been opened but the contents — books and bundles of documents tied up with string — were still standing beside them on the floor. It was very dark, not just because of the fridge but also because a gigantic garment bag was hanging from the curtain rail of the other window. There was a smell of mould, frying and tobacco.

'Please sit down.'

I hesitated between the settee, the dark-red cover of which was scarcely visible beneath a pile of old newspapers that had clearly been used to wrap fish and chips, and a swivel chair with a pair of knickers and a bra hung on it to dry, but finally I opted for a chair leaning against the wall. However, before I could sit down I had to remove a box, like those librarians use for index cards, containing beer mats. As I was looking round for somewhere to put it down, Mrs Krook gave a plaintive sigh: 'There. On the floor.'

It seemed impossible that such a tiny woman could have contained what was to become the interminable carcass of Ebenezer Krook. If there was any resemblance between the son and his mother it was of the same order as that between some territory and the map representing it. Mrs Krook was wearing an apron which gave her a housewifely look completely at odds with the state of the house but which she obviously wore because its big pockets were useful for keeping her packets of cigarillos and her lighter. Her teeth were yellow from the tobacco as were the index and middle fingers of her right hand, her eyes shone, her skin was dry and dull. She looked as if she was recovering from some illness, that is unless she was about to go down with one. But what really made me feel ill at ease was the way she smiled and grimaced alternatively, as if one invisible hand were stroking her neck while another was crushing her spine, or as if a defective neuron had acquired the bad habit of transmitting contradictory information to her facial muscles. She sat down in the swivel chair, between the knickers and the bra, and immediately lit a cigarillo.

'So he spoke about me, did he?'

'Yes, that is... I'm studying English literature and...'

'The last time he came to see me, he sat there, exactly where you are.'

I was twisting and turning in my chair. A scrap of wallpaper that had come unstuck was tickling my left cheek irritatingly but I couldn't move over to the right, for fear of disturbing the unstable balance of the aquarium, nor forwards since one of the legs of the chair was stuck against a tray with a dirty glass and a little pile of nutshells on it.

'It was... oh, four or five years ago. He arrived without warning and... Have you been talking about literature with him?'

'Er, well... not exactly, we...'

'Because that would have been truly extraordinary! Do you know what he said to me one day? "Mummy," he said, "whenever I happen to open a book I feel as if a crow's just come and perched on my shoulder. And the crow smells like your cigarillos." A charming lad, my son.'

As she said that, her features froze in the 'grimace' position.

'The reason I've come to see you is...'

'I've tried everything. I've given him dozens, for his birthday, for Christmas... Barrie, Du Maurier, Scott, Stevenson, Priestley. Would you like a drink?'

'No, thank you.'

She stood up and first of all went over to a toolbox, which contained a bottle of cheap beer, then to the settee where somehow or other she managed to unearth a bottle opener from beneath a cushion and finally came towards me. As she bent down to pick up the glass I noticed, beneath the sweetish smell of the cigarillo, a whiff of unwashed underwear.

'But he ignored them,' she said, sitting down again. 'I mean, he made it clear he was ignoring them! Something however tells me he wanted to...'

'But there is a book he...'

'*Martin Eden*. He never goes anywhere without it.'

She screwed up her eyes as she looked at me, then took a mouthful of beer. 'It was his father who got him to read that. Eden was his father's hero — the common man who rises above his station by virtue of his talent alone, then disappears when he's reached the summit... Except that there was nothing common about Francis — his parents ran a luxury retirement home — and he had no talent, at least as far as I'm aware, but as for disappearing, yes, that he could manage: he disappeared. Have some nuts.'

Out of politeness I looked down at the tray but I could see nothing but empty shells.

'I don't know if you can picture it: a man who had never voted in his life, who moved to another table in the pub when someone started talking politics, and then off he goes to Spain, just like that, without a by-your-leave... and there he is, rifle slung over his shoulder, crawling through the mud with those... Francoist Republicans. Can you understand that?'

Perhaps he simply wanted to be able to finish a sentence, I thought, before taking advantage of the fact that she had put the glass to her lips to point out that the Republicans weren't Francoists.'

Mrs Krook gave a little 'oh!' of apology and put her hand over her mouth, as if she'd opened the door to the men's toilets in a restaurant by mistake.

'You're right but it doesn't make any difference. The important thing is that he ran off, just like Eby when he decided to become a priest. And I warned him: "It doesn't suit you at all, Eby. It's just not you, you're too tall. And are you really *obliged* to wear that cassock?" But I expect you're a Catholic too,' she said graciously.

Involuntarily I squinted at the strip of wallpaper. 'I am but not a practising one.'

'You feel like shooting at it, don't you?'

'I'm sorry?'

'The wallpaper. You feel like shooting at it to see what will happen. You tell yourself the wall might go next, then the house, then the garden, then all the rest... as if the world were nothing but a thin layer and there was nothing behind it. You see what I'm getting at?'

Mrs Krook finished her beer, lit another cigarillo and switched on the 'smile' function. 'Don't worry, Miss Guthrie, I'm not mad. We can get down to Urquhart, if you like.'

Enjoying my amazement, she went on with a hint of irony: 'You are studying English literature, aren't you? What other interest could I have for you? Unless you've come to ask for Eby's hand in marriage... but I can't give you that, my dear, you'll have to ask that man, the one down there in Rome with his cook's hat and golf club... No, I'm sure it's Urquhart who's brought you here. All I have to do is to find the documents. Don't worry,' she went on seeing my worried look, 'I know exactly where they are.'

Her odd remark about Krook and marriage had made me feel even more uncomfortable, if that were possible, but Mrs Krook paid no attention to that. She went to the back of the room, slipped nimbly between the window and the refrigerator and opened its door. A few seconds later she was back beside me holding a shapeless satchel.

'The originals are in the bank, of course, but I've copied everything out by hand. That's *The Jewel*, a sort of *pot pourri* as the French say, by Christianus Presbyteromastix — Christian Presbyterian-eater. Unreadable, of course, apart perhaps for the section on the Admirable Crichton... a swashbuckling duellist who scoured Renaissance Italy looking for a duel with anyone with the right to carry a sword. He used to skewer his victims three times to form an equilateral triangle on their chest... And this is *The History of Urquhart House and its Pendicles* of dubious authenticity according to some but for me there's no doubt at all, it's definitely our Sir Thomas who wrote it.

You'll see that as soon as you've read the first few pages.'

'Thank you very much, I'll bring them back as soon...'

'I would very much appreciate a second visit, Miss Guthrie, but it will not be necessary. All these documents are yours. Don't tell anyone, but my passion for the Sheriff of Cromarty has cooled down somewhat recently... Age perhaps... the desire to get rid of certain things. So, as you see, you're heaven-sent. When we're young, no baggage seems too heavy, but the moment comes when we prefer to travel light, if you see what I mean? Especially as friend Urquhart is a bit of an encumbrance as a travelling companion. Have a good look at this photo: Alexander Urquhart, the great-uncle of the current Sir James... he died a bachelor at Cromarty after having spent almost the whole of his life in Florence where he went — in vain — for the sake of his lungs, his nerves and his unbridled sexual appetite. I think he must have slept with the whole of the Anglo-Saxon colony in Tuscany, men and women — except for Henry James perhaps... And the woman in the photo, that's Catherine Grant, Alexander's chambermaid, one of the fortunate recipients of his generous gifts... and the mother of his child, Saul — what a name! She put him into the care of some distant relations, the Krooks...'

'Just a moment. Do you mean to say...'

'That Francis, my husband, was the son of a bastard of Sir Alexander, that the blood of the Urquharts flows in Eby's veins. He didn't tell you that? It doesn't surprise me... like father, like son. Running away, always running away. Incapable of calling a spade a spade. *Bastards*, that's what they're called. What difference does it make? It isn't the nineteenth century any more. What does it matter who was the owner of the spermatozoon that shackled us to life, the result's just the same, isn't it?'

While speaking she was pushing me towards the door. When I was on the doorstep she turned out her pockets in search of a cigarillo, then she fixed her eyes on me: 'You know what you find in the end?'

'Er...'

'When you've finished shooting at the wall, when the whole world's unravelled and turned into a pile of sticky wallpaper, you know what you find at the other end?'

'No, Mrs Krook.'

'Your own hand, of course, your own hand.'

Dunottar castle had disappeared in the mist. Holding the satchel under my arm, I turned round again before going down the hill and I saw Mrs Krook at her window. The switch seemed to be stuck on the 'grimace' function.

CHAPTER IV

Krook's narrative.

The next day, Saturday, Robin set stage one of his plan —'making contact'— in motion: as soon as they opened we visited all the bars in Rose Street. Doubtless I could have survived the famous pubs on the street itself unscathed, but we also had to take in the strange alleys — the sadistic organiser of a fiendish treasure hunt had called them all North Lane or South Lane — going off this way and that, which meant a further half dozen torture chambers. In the mazy progress Robin's unpredictable decisions imposed on us, I was swallowed up and spewed out by more and more mysterious, cramped and murky establishments, so that by the time we'd crossed Rose Street ten times in both directions I was starting to feel like those little aquarium fish that ceaselessly explore every crevice of the décor.

I soon gave up trying to keep count of the bars I'd leant on, the glasses I'd drunk, the number of times Robin had announced 'To the next!' And if my memory of the first part of our marathon, devoted to 'warming ourselves up with Guinness,' is fairly clear, it starts to get hazy after two o'clock when Robin, having examined the whites of my eyes, decided we should drink 'with both hands': beer on the left, whisky on the right. We lunched on a pork pie opposite the Melville Monument in St Andrews Square, after which Robin wiped his lips and announced that, 'Things are going to get serious now — whisky on the left and whisky on the right.'

There's nothing much I can say about the afternoon except that we must have visited a couple of dives where Robin was well enough known to get a drink despite the licensing laws. If I had subsequently been accused of some horrible crime, my fate would have rested on Robin alone; his lucidity was unfailing despite the Rabelaisian amounts of alcohol he'd consumed, making him an ideal witness. Not once did his diction falter, not once did I see in his look the least sign of fatigue — and even less of befuddlement. I'm talking about the afternoon, of course; once the pubs opened again and we could get a legal drink, my ability to assess his capacity for alcohol became comparable to that of a legless cripple trying to assess the pace of a marathon.

When, despite everything, I endeavour, like the man with the golden brain in Daudet's story, to scratch the inside of my head with the fingernails of memory, this is all I manage to extract: haloes and the noise of flushing lavatories. All sorts of haloes: amber, black, frothy, they grew in size as my gestures grew more and more clumsy and I spilt more and more liquid; when my head dropped towards the bar they made me into a grotesque saint. All sorts of flushing noises: siphons, lock gates, cataracts, rural babblings, industrial rumblings. Robin baptised every convenience in every pub. The street noise might fade, voices merge into a distant murmur — the flushing lavatories still resounded, giving the signal to depart: 'To the next!' For me our meandering progress came to resemble a long trek beside a turbulent river towards the ocean of sheets and blankets into which Robin pushed me with a grunt.

The bed pitched and tossed at the bottom of a whirlpool much worse than the Corryvreckan itself. I had no idea where I was, the information I had about the universe could be summed up in one word: Sunday. It was Sunday, of that at least I was sure. Sunday, yes, but what time? It must be time for mass, surely. All unbuttoned, panting, sweating, I was running towards a little blue church where numerous parishioners were waiting for me, each holding a glass. The results of the the last day of the tournament were written on a blackboard by the entrance. The choirboys were wearing ridiculous caps, there was a W.C. sign over the steps up to the pulpit, which went down into the ground instead of rising up to heaven; and my parishioners, after having emptied their glasses, threw them over their shoulders at the stained-glass windows which looked like mosaics of bathroom tiles. I was frenetically leafing through my missal until I realised it was a telephone directory. 'Look under *God*,' Robin suggested but the number had no less than eighteen hundred and seventy-two figures. Then Mary Guthrie came forward out of the line to take communion. She was holding the elbow of a courtier from the period of Charles II with a moustache and powdered wig. One hand on hip, the man looked round with a conceited air as Mary said, 'Father, may I introduce Thomas Urquhart to you,' to which he added, '*Sir* Thomas Urquhart, Sheriff of Cromarty, Admiral of all the seas between Inverness and Caithness, mathematician, philosopher, man of letters, at your service.' Then he gave an extraordinary burst of laughter.

'My God, my God, why hast thou forsaken me?'

Such was the last mass of Father Krook.

Robin, impeccable, fresh as a red rose, was standing at the foot of the bed.

'What… What time is it?'

'Eight o'clock.'

'Morning or evening?'

'Morning. Monday morning. I've left something for you to eat in the kitchen. I've only got one key, which I'll leave with you. I'll be back this evening, about six.'

The strange room smelt of sweat — my own. The worn but clean floor was covered in books, newspapers, pamphlets and crumpled clothes that had obviously been swept off the bed in a hurry. There was an old Underwood typewriter on a small table.

'Where are you going?'

'Where most people go on Monday morning — to work. By the way, a friend of mine will drop by to see you later on. He might have a job for you.'

'What kind of job?'

Robin shrugged. 'In your situation I wouldn't be too choosy. See you this evening.'

After a morning spent looking at the ceiling and renewing

acquaintance with the different parts of my body, I managed to remember certain more abstract details about my person: my name first of all then the catastrophic events of the past week. I also remembered that I had eaten nothing at all the previous day. I had just finished a pot and a half of coffee and a cold omelette when the bell rang.

When I realised what type of person my visitor was I have to admit that I had some doubt as to the morality of the 'job' he had in mind for me, but my visitor was clearly used to reactions of that kind. Giving me a smile he said, before offering me his hand, 'I'm Lewis Rosewall. And, don't worry, you're not at all my type.'

I blushed in embarrassment, especially since I had just caught a glimpse of my reflection in the hall mirror: drawn, bloated, lumpy — Mr Rosewall would have had to be an 'invert' of particularly perverted tastes to harbour the least desire for my body! 'Invert' is the official term the Catholic Church uses to designate Lewis Rosewall and his friends; she would of course prefer not to have to refer to them, but since that is unavoidable, she designates them thus. I believe that the Presbyterians, with their erudition in matters of the Bible, prefer 'sodomite'; as for my school-friends, they would refer to them as 'Dundonians', doubtless the result of East-coast rivalry between Aberdeen and the capital of jute and marmalade. As for me, I have never been able to share the revulsion for homosexuals professed by Rome; I even acknowledge their distinction in having settled the problem of women once and for all and in that respect I can't help envying them, like car-drivers who have suffered a breakdown watching horse-drawn vehicles trot past.

It had taken me no more than a second to discern Mr Rosewall's preferences but that does not mean he flaunted them. He was, I later discovered, a past master in the tightrope art of allowing his true nature to appear while making that truth tolerable to the majority. Well-groomed hair and moustache, a silk cravat, a velvet jacket, features delicate without being feminine — signs anyone could interpret in their own way, depending on their perspicacity and openness of mind.

'Are you ready, Mr Krook?'

A further surprise was awaiting me at the bottom of the tenement: Mr Rosewall's wife — at least that was how he introduced her to me with a touch of formality and a hint of a smile which was probably a response to my astonishment. She was an erect, dark-complexioned, austere-looking woman, her hair still black despite her age and tightly done up in a chignon. They exchanged a few words in Spanish, then she took her leave, giving me a nod, and set off towards the West End. Lewis said nothing about his improbable Spanish wife but took me in the opposite direction, slowing down, however, outside the first pub we passed.

'Er... Perhaps you'd like a drink.'

At the very word the hard liquor that, insufficiently absorbed by the omelette and bacon, was still gnawing away at my entrails, started to rise up again.

'My God, no! Not for another week!'

'Excellent!' Mr Rosewall exclaimed. 'Robin's cure has done its job.'

Then, after a moment's hesitation, he added, 'He found you in an unfortunate situation and he thought up this... treatment to stop it turning into anything worse.'

It took me some while to relate the words 'cure' and 'treatment', which evoked the immaculate sheets of a hospital, the hushed rounds of the nurses and the faint odour of antiseptic, with the incredible pandaemonium through which Robin had dragged me from Saturday to Sunday. I had hardly noticed that we had started to go up the Mound towards the Old Town.

'What I do find rather odd,' I finally said, 'is that the "cure" has no effect whatsoever on Robin himself.'

Lewis Rosewall smiled. 'Robin has no need of a "cure". Alcohol, that for most of us is a wild beast ready to pounce, curls up at Robin's feet like a pet basset-hound. I suspect he possesses a second digestive system that is proof against stomach acids —'

'And a second pair of kidneys too!'

'Ah yes, I see what you're getting at. Alcohol goes, Robin stays.

The last time I saw him drunk was on his birthday. He'd emptied a bottle of cooking rum.'

'Which birthday was that?'

'His eleventh.'

'You've known him that long?'

'I don't know if one can say that, Mr Krook. Robin's the kind of person who at the very start makes you a gift of one part of himself so that you won't try to discover the other part. There are all sorts of labels to classify people of his type: Communist, alcoholic, confirmed bachelor, skirt-chaser etc. But none is the right one… you can believe me, I know all about labels.'

As he was talking Rosewall led me along Bank Street and the Royal Mile up into the Old Town. Some of the window displays looked as if they hadn't been changed since Mary Stuart's last shopping spree. Either side of the road the wind plunged into the closes like a mounted policeman chasing a gaggle of drunks. These steep alleys with their lop-sided steps, their rusty handrails and their scrawny cats were still haunted by the ghost of Deacon Brodie.

Everything seemed strange to me: the surroundings, my clothes, this conversation with someone I didn't know. Only one detail was familiar, unchangeable: the weight of the book in my pocket.

'We're there.'

We cautiously made our way down some slippery steps into Anchor Close and immediately found ourselves facing a worm-eaten door with a single window and a sign: *Experienced sales assistant sought*. Apart from that there was nothing to distinguish the shop from an ordinary dwelling house, but a glance through the window sent a shiver down my spine.

'No,' I said firmly, 'I can't do that.'

'Come now, young man,' he said with a laugh, 'would you have preferred it if I'd been a fisherman and suggested an apprenticeship with a fishmonger? But I'm a publisher, you know, so…'

He opened the door — the bell rang out a joyous carillon — and pushed me inside.

∞∞∞∞

'And whom did you work for previously, my boy?'

With twinkling eyes and slightly pouting lips, Arthur Walpole stroked his chin as he observed me over the top of his old horn-rimmed glasses. He was a small gentleman of around sixty wearing a grey apron and with sparse hair covering his skull in a single lock that the draught from the door had made stand on end. He squinted upwards and at this mute exhortation the lock duly dropped back into place.

Lewis Rosewall answered for me: 'God.'

'Oh, yes?' Walpole replied, showing no surprise. 'And in which branch of His enterprise?'

'The parent company — Rome.'

Walpole gave an ironic whistle. 'Are you familiar with books, Mr...'

'Krook. Not very, I have to say.'

'But you must have used them a lot in the seminary?'

'As little as possible.'

Walpole fluttered his eyelashes and glanced at Rosewall who cleared his throat: 'Arthur, might I have a private word? Excuse us for a moment, Mr Krook.'

Walpole's bookshop, hardly bigger than an average-sized room was like a shell round a central cubby-hole formed by shelves full of books. The two men disappeared into this recess, closing behind them a door on which *Private* was written in white chalk. Resisting the temptation to glue my ear to it, I started to explore the shop.

It was pretty dark despite the two bulbs that were on all the time. The books, some laid flat others standing up, seemed to have been shelved with no system whatsoever — ancient tomes bound in kid leather rubbed shoulders with paperbacks, handbooks of gardening with ancient numbers of *The Spectator*, Bibles in linen binding with the complete works of Elizabeth Gaskell. The alphabet was no more use in finding your way round this labyrinth than a shoelace would have been to Theseus in that of the Minotaur; if you happened to

find what looked like the start of a series on the higher shelves —
Addison, Austen, Brontë — it would immediately be interrupted by
intruders beginning with P or Z, only to continue on its alphabetical
way lower down, like a stagecoach after a nasty jolt. With a treatise
on agronomics as its foundation, a bold tower of Shakespearian
fascicles was attacking the *Mémorial de Sainte-Hélène: Journal
of the Private Life and Conversations of the Emperor Napoleon at
Saint Helena*. A huge black Wordsworth jammed in between two
series of the minuscule volumes of Nelson editions looked like a
Cyclops presiding over a banquet of dwarves.

Most of the titles meant nothing to the layman I was at the
time. However, I guessed that their apparent disorder concealed
a paradoxical harmony, that their places were fixed by a ranking
system as inflexible as the Tables of the Law. Whoever had arranged
this mystery must be a god or at least a kind of super-engineer
with absolute knowledge and infinite malice. One of his secrets,
however, seemed to be within arm's reach and I would doubtless
have discovered it if a fearful coughing fit had not put an end to my
reflections. Walpole, bent double, shot out of the cubby-hole with
Rosewall slapping him on the back to try and relieve his cough. It
took a good minute before the bookseller had recovered his power
of speech.

'Right then, right, Mr Krook... Although the bookshop is a little
small for playing rugby I think we will give you a "try" for a few
days.'

'But I...'

'To start with I will give you precisely the same task my dear
master and predecessor here, Doug MacDonald, gave me forty-two
years seven months and eight days ago today. Cheerio, Lewis.'

I hadn't felt so at a loss since I'd started school. I bid a reluctant
farewell to Rosewall while Walpole, laughing and giving little
coughs, was rummaging round in his cubby-hole.

'Tomorrow we will attempt to initiate you into more noble tasks,
but today it's too late. For now you can start with these.'

He handed me a brush, a dustpan and a feather duster. With a

69

gesture that took in the whole shop Walpole indicated my new field of activity, then he fetched a kind of small orange box from his desk that he started to fill with books all the while watching me out of the corner of his eye.

' "What does he take me for, the old fart." That's what you're thinking Mr Krook, aren't you?'

Perched on a stool, Mr Walpole had his back turned to me.

'Er… yes,' I admitted. 'Something like that.'

'That's what I thought of Doug MacDonald when I started.'

For a few minutes we busied ourselves with our respective tasks. Walpole carefully selected a book, placed it in the box then dragged his stool to another shelf. As for my dusting, it quickly turned out to be more awkward than I had foreseen. In the first place, the dust had a tendency to gather behind the books rather than in front; in the second, some books were covered in a veritable film, slightly greasy, against which my feather duster was powerless: if I didn't rub it, the film remained intact, if I did rub it, the greasy dust stuck to the feathers of my duster and spread over the next row.

After a quarter of an hour I sneezed explosively.

'Bless you, Mr Krook. I don't know if you've noticed, but book dust is different from all other kinds, it's almost as if it's organic… that the books secrete it… that it's their excrement, in short…'

Now he was facing me; but the malicious gleam in his eyes was never switched off, so that I couldn't tell when he was joking.

'Do you know what Doug MacDonald said to me on that first day? "The best jockeys all started out as stable-boys." I have to say that Doug was fond of equestrian metaphors. "They cleaned out the stables and shovelled up the dung for months and months before they were allowed on a horse." Well that's exactly what I intend to do with you, my lad. Familiarise yourself with the excretions of books; soon you'll be climbing on their backs and they'll carry you off to the ends of the earth. Look, tomorrow, if all goes well, I'll take you on your first training ride.'

Lowering his head a little, he looked at me from under his eyebrows while the sun, as it set, shone into the shop for the first and last time in the day.

' "Yak away, you old scarecrow. You're not going to see me tomorrow, nor any other day." Am I right or am I right, Mr Krook?'

Walpole burst out laughing then spent a good fifteen minutes coughing.

My 'training' continued for a while. I learnt how to grease the hinges of the shop door and of that into the cubby-hole; to copy out addresses on labels; to get twenty volumes into a cardboard box that seemed made for no more than ten. I also learnt how to operate the cash register.

'Doug was very proud of it. He bought it from a banker who'd gone bankrupt. Normally if you press this key the drawer will open... but the spring can be a bit recalcitrant, you have to encourage it with this screwdriver. But watch out. Occasionally the spring releases and the drawer shoots out and since you're pretty tall it would hit you more or less in the region of your... wouldn't it? Then there'd be nothing for it but to find some Turk who'd take you on for his harem, ho! ho! ho!'

Such a catastrophe seemed very unlikely, given the complete absence of customers. Since I'd arrived just one person had crossed the threshold — a tourist looking for John Knox's house.

While playing with my feather duster I discovered a small window looking out on to the Royal Mile at pavement level. 'That's right,' Walpole explained, 'we're in a coal cellar. The former owner was a friend of Doug's who rented it out to him for next to nothing and let him make a door out into Anchor Close. And that's how I can continue to pursue my not very lucrative trade for the princely sum of fifty pounds a year.'

From time to time I looked up at the strange ballet of shoes, skirts and trousers that seemed to have a life of its own.

A little before six Walpole bolted the door, sat down at the till, handed me an envelope and gestured with his chin at the orange box he'd filled with books. Then he lit a big cigar.

'If we are going to work together, Mr Krook, it is essential that you read these few books. They aren't necessarily the greatest books

71

in the world, but they're my favourites. If you don't like them, you won't like me either.'

'I don't read very much.'

'Take your time, there's no hurry. I've put a little advance in the envelope, enough to tide you over while you find somewhere to stay in Edinburgh.'

'But I'm not sure that...'

'If you decide not to come back give the money and books to Lewis. And now would you put the light out, please.'

Immediately the shop was plunged into semi-darkness. There were no street lamps in Anchor Close and the light from the Royal Mile, close though it was, gave up the ghost at the window, merely staining the darkness with a pale orange tinge. The glow at the end of Walpole's cigar was reflected in his spectacles, then went out, only to flare up again, like a lighthouse. A young couple passed in the Close, laughing. Farther down the alleyway someone whistled for their dog. Walpole, with his bizarre rig-out and manner from another age, was drifting somewhere outside time; and if it hadn't been for the distant noise of traffic on South Bridge, I could have believed I'd been transported back a couple of centuries.

'And now sit down for a minute. Have a cigar. It's the best moment of the day, don't you think? Everything's at rest. Or, rather, will *soon* be at rest. Apart from the books, they never sleep.'

Walpole closed his eyes, exhaled the smoke in a long breath, cleared his throat.

'You could almost say you don't exist any more. Our life withdraws from us. "It's the moment," Doug used to say. Have a look.'

At the back of the shop the faint light from the narrow window was spreading over the books, touching them one by one, idly, like an old hand that remembers how to caress but has forgotten desire. And each one caught an infinitesimal part of the beam and clung on to it, proudly standing erect in the sparse light.

'The moment of what? I don't know, Mr Krook... Just the moment, that's all.'

∞∞∞∞

'The Corryvreckan. It appears that Homer drew his inspiration for it when he described Charybdis…'

'Well I never! You're quoting the classics now, are you?'

My father didn't answer my mother immediately. For some minutes now we could hear, from the north-west, the tremendous rumbling that made me think of a building being demolished. However, the water was still calm and the little boat with its outboard motor, despite its fragile appearance, was performing impeccably.

'Some sailors say it's the lavatory of Europe being flushed,' he went on. 'It's less poetic but I like it better.'

I was nine. It was such a solemn moment I could hardly contain myself. For the very first time my father was taking us for a weekend away, and not on the mundane trip to Balmoral Castle my mother had been demanding in vain for months, but a real journey: the train to Oban then the ferry to Jura; a room, simple but spacious and clean, in the only hotel on the island. And then hiring a boat! Such an unlikely luxury for the man who had decided to live for as long as possible off the comfortable inheritance from his parents and whose main expenses were limited to tobacco for his pipe and a few pints in the pub. I had never dared dream I might enjoy such a piece of good fortune, though at the same time it gave me a vague sense of unease, perhaps because it was so unexpected. Or maybe because my mother, obliged for once to accept her husband's largesse, only enjoyed our jaunt grudgingly, if at all — the beds were too soft, the black pudding overcooked etc. She had made several ironic remarks about this sudden enthusiasm for the wild islands of the West and for seafaring. But the worst thing in her eyes — as I later came to understand — was the look of wonder in mine when my father, hardly listening to the advice of the man who'd hired it to us, took his place at the tiller, got the engine going first time and manoeuvred the boat perfectly out of the little port of Craighouse.

'You will be careful, won't you?'

My father, his eye already fixed on the open sea, didn't deem the question worthy of reply.

I only went to Jura twice and both times the weather was magnificent. Protected by the Paps, the east coast of the island can be like the Mediterranean. There's a dwarf palm tree growing outside the hotel, the water's blue, calm and clear. That day in particular, as we sailed up Craighouse Bay seaward of the reefs the locals call the Small Isles then northward along the wooded coastline beyond Rubh' a' Chamais, you could have imagined yourself somewhere in Greece or Italy.

But things changed farther up when we were on a level with the white house, all by itself near the top of the island, where, twenty years later I was to see the man from Jura. The Paps had been wreathed in thick cloud for some time but suddenly, like conscripts weary of standing on guard, they released their load and at once the sky darkened.

'It's three o'clock already,' my mother pointed out.

'We've hired the boat until five.'

'But the last ferry leaves at six, and we have to go back to the hotel first.'

I peered at my father's face; it had darkened too. The veins on his hand gripping the tiller made a complex web. 'It'll be all right,' he muttered, giving me a quick glance.

From the sound of the engine I could tell that we'd accelerated and I saw the little deserted beach and the white house slowly grow more and more distant. But that wasn't what was frightening me. My father was very close to me, I could touch him if I stretched out my arm, but he seemed incredibly distant, as if all of a sudden the little boat had become immense and it would have taken an interminable journey to reach him there at the other end of the bench.

'What are you doing, Francis?'

Two or three weeks previously my father had given me *Martin Eden*. He had been drinking a bit that day, I could tell that from his dignified bearing. Some men lose their dignity under the influence of drink, they gasp for breath, look pathetic, maudlin. My father, on the other hand, became particularly dignified. You got the impression that he found his dignity on the back of the chair, on the pub table, and that he lost it again bit by bit after he came out. Not that he was pathetic or maudlin when he was sober, but he lacked something, a mysterious possibility that two or three glasses — never more — could give him: *It's the story of man who wants to make his mark on the world and who, when he has achieved that, hates the way the world has become.*

'Francis? What are you *doing*?'

The rumbling was getting closer. It wasn't like other noises, nor even louder, but it devoured all other noises. It devoured them from inside, like a cancer eating away at the bones. And the words my mother spoke seemed sickly, atrophied. It was perhaps because of that, I told myself, because of their sickness, that they took so long to reach my father and that my father took so long to reply to them.

'Nothing. there's no risk this side of the point.'

It's the story of a man capable of putting up with anything to overcome a setback. Anything apart from success.

Curled up in the corner of the bench, a few million miles away from my father, I tried to imagine someone pulling a lavatory chain on a global scale. The point of Carraig Mhór was approaching — not even a point, really, just a kind of wart on the forehead of the coast with hundreds of seagulls swirling round and round endlessly, as if the spectacle of the Corryvreckan, which we couldn't see yet, were driving them mad. And our boat was no longer a boat, suddenly it was a person, very strong, very intelligent and very resolute; and its whole existence as a boat, that of the men who had sailed it, the men who had constructed it, the tree that had been used for its hull, the whole existence, not much longer on the cosmic scale, of the ground where the tree had taken root, seemed to have no other justification than to round Carraig Mhór to see what was beyond it. I was frightened but held back my tears; I was proud of my father, proud that it had been given to him to accomplish this deed.

But then something happened. What? I don't know. Perhaps my mother managed to find some slightly stronger, less sickly words.

75

My father gave a start. Reluctantly the boat made a long semi-circle and the white house reappeared in my field of vision as if it were the world itself and not us that had turned on its axis. The bench was tiny; once more I could smell the leather of my father's cap.

We never went away for another weekend.

∞∞∞

'You're going back to the old fellow?' Glancing at the clock, Robin took a big mouthful of coffee.

'No, I don't think so.'

'Robin?' came a sleepy voice from the other side of the partition. He raised his eyebrows as if he'd forgotten a woman had been sleeping in the room.

'It's up to you to decide. You could go to Leith, work on the docks. Sometimes they take people on for a week.' He gave me a quizzical look, then folded up his newspaper and handed it to me.

'Robin!'

'Have a look at the small ads. You never know.'

Once out in the street I remembered that I had nothing to do, no one to see, nowhere to go. Out in the desert it would have been depressing, in a big city it was even worse. I had never previously noticed our extraordinary propensity to go *towards* a place or to carry out some *precise* task. When you think about it, this daily miracle is truly incredible, especially as it occurs spontaneously, without prior thought. I felt myself invisible among all the people heading for work or already going about their business. There were thousands of options available to me: take a walk, go into a café, visit the Castle, sit on a bench, go back to Robin's place and spend the day in bed. But all these options were purely theoretical, like an infinite number of closed doors behind each of which there was nothing but myself.

Without noticing where I was going, I had reached the Mound. I headed for the Old Town and ended up in Walpole's shop.

'Quick, quick, Mr Krook, I'm late! My wife's waiting for me.'

He hadn't even bothered to say good morning — unless you took his lock of hair automatically standing on end as a greeting.

'I'll be back in less than an hour. And watch out for that till drawer!'

He left, laughing and coughing. And the trap in which I was to spend the rest of my life closed — I'd even oiled the mechanism myself the previous evening. Just the ping of the bell and then nothing.

They were there, all round me. In their thousands. Like the big cats in a circus assessing their new lion-tamer. Making a show of attending to their own affairs, but keeping an eye on my every move. When I went up to them, Scott and Stevenson immediately broke off their confab, only to start again once my back was turned; *The Gallic War* shrank back into the shelf in a posture that was more menacing than respectful; the little Nelson editions hauled themselves up onto the Wordsworth to have a better look at me. I took one out — *Barchester Towers* — but it only deigned to open in three places, the blank pages between each part; the other pages seemed to be stuck together, not by greasiness or humidity but out of deliberate hostility towards me. I tried to leaf through *The Vicar of Wakefield* but the paper was so fine it made me feel I had fat sausages instead of fingers. As for the first volume of the Arden Shakespeare, like a recalcitrant soldier it absolutely refused to step out of rank and remained stuck to its fellows. I started to sweat profusely and stood there, transfixed, like a monkey in a courtroom.

The ping of the bell put an end to my agony. It wasn't Walpole, alas, but a tall, thin man who seemed to have run all the way to the shop from some distant suburb.

'I was just listening to Mendelssohn on the wireless,' he said when he'd got his breath back, 'and I had this sudden desire for some Shakespeare!'

He paused for a few seconds, as if his declaration demanded some comment from me, then strode across the shop. 'Arthur's not here? Oh, yes, of course, it's Tuesday… Why is it that my lady friends always take a fancy to my library at the very moment when they're leaving me? Six months, a year living together and not a word about books, but as soon as they decide to do a bunk they stick an armful in their luggage… usually Shakespeare.'

To my great surprise he had no problem taking out the book that had put up such resistance to me only a couple of minutes ago and leafed through it with no difficulty whatsoever.

'It is remarkable, though, this obsession with Big Bill. They could swipe my first edition of Dickens with the Cruikshank illustrations or my signed Balzac, but no, it's Shakespeare they must have. Does that make any sense to you?'

The man came to the cash desk, the complete edition in his arms. 'Christopher Duff. There'll be an account for me in the ledger.'

Without hesitation I entered the amount under D, but Mr Duff didn't seem in a hurry to leave. He sat down beside me on the little stepladder (I later learnt that this was a special privilege reserved for a few regular customers) and gave me a wink.

'An odd customer, isn't he?'

'Who?'

'Walpole, for God's sake! I've known him for ages. The first time I came I opened the door and said, "Have you got the latest…" but he didn't let me finish, he simply said, "No."—"What d'you mean, no?" —"No I haven't got the latest novel by Mr Himagain, nor the fourteenth volume of the memoirs of Mrs Stillgoingstrong, any more than the latest works of Messrs Helloit'sme, Iinvariablypublishonebookayear, and Thisone'sevenworsethanthelast…" You can imagine my amazement. "But what do you sell then?"—"Only books that were published at least fifty years ago."—"Hard luck on James Joyce, Virginia Woolf and Malcolm Lowry…"—"Doubtless, but that's the rule, fifty years, not one less. It's the no-man's-land separating us from the enemy, the dyke saving us from the unsavoury flood of occasional books — superfluous books, quickly written, quickly sold, quickly forgotten." He was giving me one of his sidelong looks, you know, cajoling and indignant at the same time. Then he held out his hand and gave me a cigar! And do you know the funny thing? I buy the latest titles from MacAvoy's or Stone's, on the quiet, as if I were doing something to be ashamed of!'

When Mr Duff finally left, not before he'd warned me, with a laugh, about the danger of the cash-register drawer, I slowly looked round the shelves, two dates echoing inside my head like the tick-tock of a clock: 1953, 1903. 1953, 1903. 1953... Feeling slightly dizzy, I closed my eyes.

1903: A shovelful of coal came shooting in through the fanlight. With remarkable precision and a wealth of detail I saw myself going up onto the Royal Mile amid top-hats and crinolines. A carriage almost knocked me over. I heard a newspaper vendor shouting out the headlines: 'President Loubet and His Majesty Edward VII actively preparing the Entente Cordiale. The Wright brothers break their record for "heavier than air" flight.' And I felt almost light enough to float myself. In the air, among the stench of horse droppings and boiled cabbage, there was a sort of inexplicable gaiety with which I filled my lungs: the fragrance of my non-existent state. But the roar of a motorbike brought me crashing down to earth: 1953. My head was still spinning — I really did exist. For lack of any big decision that would give the name of Ebenezer Krook significance in a wider context, I promised myself that at least I would feed his body at certain fixed times and fortify his mind against the blandishments of old Walpole.

The noise of the motorbike had made me look up at the little window. And I stayed like that, breathing heavily as I deciphered the complex alphabet of feet and legs. Lots of 'A's, without the crosspiece; upside-down 'W's when two passers-by crossed or one overtook the other. But the flesh, insidiously, began to disturb the austere pleasures of calligraphy. A bare ankle emerged from a bootee; under the lampshade of a pleated skirt a round, firm calf was dancing a jig. And sometimes, even, a knee — a forbidden fruit at the top of a tree of nylon or silk revealing its skin: golden, sallow or white depending on the flesh tints. The books had gathered behind me, they were also watching. Men and women had written them; men and women who had lavished, or dreamt of lavishing caresses and were holding out their hands through me. And I felt carried away by this wave of exultation rising towards the heaven of the window, but it could not escape the material of my trousers and remained a prisoner, a half-formed letter, an illegible hieroglyph. The tears came to my eyes.

I needed a drink.

They were open by now. Five minutes. That was all it took me to run out, climb the steps to the Royal Mile, find a pub with two old men listening to the radio, mouths agape, as if the sound could get in more easily through that opening, and where even the whisky smelt of cat's piss. Five minutes too many. When I got back Walpole and Robin Dennison were waiting for me in the shop. From their looks I could see that something had happened.

'Nothing serious,' Walpole assured me. 'Robin got here just before me and saw some chap come running out.'

'I'm really very sorry…'

'It's partly my fault. I should have left you a key. Anyway, they didn't touch the till.' He didn't ask me where I'd been. Hands clasped behind his back, he set off on a tour of inspection of the shop.

'Aha!' he said, seeing the gap left by the Arden Shakespeare. 'Mr Duff's been ditched by his latest conquest… And that Dostoyevsky there, it's not in its place.'

'It was me who put it back there. Sorry.'

'Doesn't matter… Now that is strange…'

'What?'

Walpole slowly drew his finger across all the books on the shelf, correcting the position of this or that volume. Then, with a frown, he started again, muttering to himself as if he were reciting a catalogue from memory. Finally he took one book off the shelf.

'My friends, our man may run very quickly, but he's not a thief.'

'How do you know?'

'Not a single book is missing. On the contrary, this one is one *too many*.'

I couldn't take my eyes of the familiar little black octavo, bound by an amateur, that in general appearance looked like a huge insect that had been crushed underfoot.

Robin examined the book in turn. 'But why would this man have *brought* a book?'

'Perhaps because he'd run out of space. It's a real problem, you know. De Quincey used to move house every time his library was full. And they say that in order to avoid having to go to such extremes, Samuel Johnson fixed the number his library was to contain at one thousand seven hundred and nine, the year of his birth, so every time he acquired a new one he had to get rid of another. A cruel dilemma, it must have cost him many a tear...'

'But then why run off?'

'How should I know? He was probably afraid he'd relent at the last moment. Let's have a look. Hmm, 1909, we can't even sell it. We'll have to wait six years. Pity, it's a fine novel, and a first edition, though the paper's foxed... and then someone's gone and underlined a few sentences in red ink. What vandalism! And after that people are still surprised someone like Hitler can have existed!

'His wilful hands and feet began to beat and churn about, spasmodically and feebly. But he had fooled them and the will to live that made them beat and churn. He was too deep down. They could never bring him to the surface... There was a long rumble of sound, and it seemed to him that he was falling down a vast and interminable stairway. And somewhere at the bottom he fell into darkness. That much he knew. He had fallen into darkness. And the instant he knew, he ceased to know.'

'My God! I'd forgotten that passage. What is there more beautiful, more conclusive than the end of a great book? Death itself? Huh, we'll see when the time comes...'

He was interrupted by the growing sound of cries from the High Street. 'D'you hear that, Robin? Your demonstrators are arriving. The revolution needs you!'

Robin hung around for a few minutes talking about the non-burglar and the extra book. I concealed my inner turmoil as best I could, but once he had left my legs started to shake.

'But... you're white as a sheet!' Walpole exclaimed. 'There's really no reason for you to get in a state, young man. I was the one

81

who was remiss. Come here, I'll show you something.'

He handed me the black book and took me into the cubby-hole. Inside it seemed bigger than I had assumed. There were several hundred more books there and a desk covered in papers. Walpole pointed to a low door. 'There's everything you need in here, you see, you don't have to go out. And if you should happen to feel a different kind of urgent need…'

With a sly smile, he opened one of the desk drawers in which there was a bottle and two glasses. While he was pouring the whisky, I examined the book. Impossible and yet true. *Martin Eden* by Jack London; an older edition than mine. The last sentence of the novel had been copied out on the flyleaf in small, precise handwriting. My father's handwriting.

From that day on Walpole never left the shop without giving me a key. Every Tuesday morning, for about an hour, he went to see his wife, Mildred, in Greyfriars Churchyard, where she had taken up permanent residence — I learnt from Lewis Rosewall — on 15 December 1937.

'What does he do there? Well, what people do in graveyards. He picks up the dead leaves, he removes the moss, he cleans out the inscription. "The problem," he told me, "is the round letters, the O in Walpole, the Ds in Mildred. They get full of dust. If it wasn't for me you soon wouldn't be able to read her name. The flesh will decay, so be it, but at least we should be left with our names." '

CHAPTER V

In which the reader visits Urquhart House and makes the acquaintance of its bizarre inhabitants.

'Cromarty? You can't go wrong, Miss, it's the terminus. Go any farther and you'll end up in the water.'

I had never travelled as much as in those few days of September 1953. After Dunottar I went back to Aberdeen and took the Inverness train. During the stop at Elgin I'd rung Malcolm to ask him to let my father know that my research was keeping me in the north. And now this antediluvian motor coach was juddering through the mist on the roads of the Black Isle, clinging onto the tarmac like a drunk clutching a handrail. North Kessock. Tore. Munlochy. Hamlets with improbable names and stiff with boredom that naively believed they'd been erased from the map but which the headlights of the coach flushed out as it came round a bend. From time to time a patch of thicker mist or the chug-chug of a trawler came from the Moray Firth.

The Black Isle didn't live up to its name. It wasn't an island and it was green all over: dense, luxuriant woodland; pasture where potbellied cows seemed to be carrying out a suicide pact by eating the rich grass.

I had sat at the front in order to take advantage of the little red bulb. Avoch, Fortrose, Rosemarkie. Interminable halts, mostly outside dimly lit pubs into which the driver would plunge to reemerge a good half hour later, reeling and in jovial mood.

'Off we go, then!'

Leaning forward into the light from the bulb, I tried to make a few notes.

'But I told you, Miss, any farther and you're in the water. Mind you, I do like a dip in the sea myself... Don't you?'

The mist had just cleared, accentuating the lecherous glint in the driver's eye. The sun came out and put an end to my literary ambitions — after having reread my notes on a bench, I tore them up and dumped them in a rubbish bin — but revealed a picture-postcard village: white fishermen's cottages on a spit of land, geraniums, petunias, and public lawns going down to the bay; a bit farther inland more affluent lanes bordered by trim Victorian houses in pinkish sandstone where the rare cars looked like monsters from a futuristic novel; a sunken lane led to a tiny chapel.

I liked Cromarty right away. But how could this quiet little village have brought forth a phenomenon such as Sir Thomas? Moreover, when I enquired about Urquhart House, the broad smiles of the natives faded somewhat and their explanations became laconic. Following a map taped to an information board, I headed east, left the village and took a narrow road which soon became a dirt track.

A building rose up before me. Who better than Sir Thomas himself to describe this place where I was to spend the strangest months of my whole life? Here are his own words, copied out from *The History of Urquhart House and its Pendicles*:

If you believe as I do, dear reader, that a dwelling exactly reflects the personality of its proprietor and that the sum total of its corridors, its gardens, each of its rooms and its stables form, like members, muscles, lips and eyes, a precise image of the man who has frequented them, then read the lines that follow and you will come to know their author as intimately as you do your own mother!

Arriving from the west all you see of my house at first is the oldest part, a proud tower built in the fourteenth century by John Urquhart, faithful lieutenant of Robert the Bruce. In the family chronicle it says that Sir John died a hero's death at the Battle of Bannockburn but I owe it to the truth to record that

The Glorious Epic of Robert the Bruce *gives a quite different version of his demise: 'Now among the noble knights who came to the camp was Sir John Urquhart of Cromarty, a man of the highest courage. Messire Urquhart had brought with him twelve strong vassals and twelve casks of whisky. On the eve of the day appointed for the battle he gave a great feast in his quarters. There was drinking, singing and carousing until dawn. Then the valiant Sir John — who had emptied one cask on his own — feeling the pangs of hunger picked up what he thought was a gigot of lamb and died, impaled on his own lance from the jaw to the back of his neck. In his manly grief, the Bruce swore he would avenge his comrade-in-arms for it was clear that the English had poured a magic potion into the whisky...'*

Contrary to my father, I see nothing shameful in this version of the deeds of Sir John, since valour is not measured by the strategic efficaciousness of a feat of arms, but by the vigour and determination of him who achieves it! Moreover, Suetonius himself in his Life of the Twelve Caesars...

There followed a long digression on the military virtues. There is no need to point out that no one, not even Stein and Toklas, had ever been able to provide the slightest proof of the existence of *The Glorious Epic of Robert the Bruce.*

Five pages further on, Sir Thomas continued:

Then, at a fork in the road, the east wing of the House appears. Sir Alexander Urquhart, much valued counsellor of James IV, added it to the tower shortly before the disaster of Flodden Field. The humiliation of defeat and his grief at the death of the king had a devastating effect on his character. One October day in the year 1513 he returned home without his arms or his horse but with a horrible gash on his forehead and a gleam in his eye that had something childish about it. He immediately took up again certain eccentricities of his younger years consisting basically of wishing the bread and the pepper a good day before sitting down at table, stepping over a large box every evening (without which he found it impossible to sleep) and trying to come down the grand staircase in one single step, an idiosyncrasy which quite naturally eventually proved fatal.

His younger brother Andrew inherited the estate to which he also added certain improvements. Shortly before his death he had a pond dug out close to the crypt, where the bones of my ancestors lie and where I will take up quarters one day. In this pond he took as his second wife a tunny fish weighing a hundred and fifty pounds. A painter was summoned from Inverness to record the event but, alas, his engravings were destroyed by Andrew's son Robert, who was concerned for his reputation. As for myself, I believe that the glory and purity of the amorous sentiment do not depend at all on the anatomical merits of its object and verily, I would have no difficulty producing a number of testimonies to support that assertion. Does not Ovid write in his Ars Amatoria...

Five pages on Ovid, Dante and Petrarch. Then:

But the eccentric vigour of Sir Charles, the son of Robert (and, moreover, my revered grandfather) eclipses all these heroic deeds. You should know, dear reader, that none of the great families of the North-East is more closely connected with the history of the game of golf than the Urquharts of Cromarty. The founding of the Chanonry Club, beyond doubt one of the first in the Highlands, is attributed to my ancestor Malcolm. When, in 1457, King James II banned the game because, in his view, it 'softened the character,' and ordered the requisition of all golf courses so that they could be used for archery practice once more, Sir Malcolm openly rebelled and, ignoring the arrows, continued to practise his drive. As for my grandfather Charles, he was notorious for his infinite delays on the greens and his memorable fits of rage. He could wait up to three hours for the sea breeze to die down before putting; and once he shattered the shin-bone of an opponent with his putter for having dared to suggest that was too long.

In 1602 he was challenged to a game by his neighbour, Findrassie, one of those Presbyterian curs, who sliced his ball into the middle of the moss. Seeing this, my ancestor burst into a positively Gargantuan fit of laughter and suddenly felt a kind of explosion inside his head. This had no visible effect on his bodily functions; however, from that very moment Sir Charles considered himself well and truly dead. Back in the castle, he took to his bed immediately and did not leave it for another thirty-five years; I never saw him other than lying down. At first my father would ask his advice on the running of the estate but Sir Charles' invariable reply was: 'I'm dead, my son, can't you see that?' However, when I asked something of him as a child, he would always comply, arguing that, 'the dead, though they cannot work, are at leisure to play all sorts of games.' Thus it was that I learnt to play crappo, spittoon, come-and-go, chase-the-lady, stud-rapier, French hole...

A page and a half of the names of completely imaginary games...

verdigris, chaos, rowboat; and once a week I went, bearing written instructions, to Chanonry Gold Course to try out new techniques in his stead. His dearest wish was to construct an ideal course, where neither the wind nor the innumerable imperfections you encounter on the courses currently in use would deflect the ball from its course by even a fraction of an inch and he was starting to draw up plans to that end. Unfortunately my father refused him the necessary money. Summoned from Inverness, a sinister-looking medico declared Sir Charles insane and signed the papers putting him under his son's guardianship. Despite that I never, in my whole life, met anyone of such a sound mind as that 'lunatic'.

On the other hand I have met many individuals who, for all their whirling golf-swings, their wild gallops, their boasting and bragging, enjoyed life much less than my late lamented grandfather. He believed he was dead when he wasn't, they think they are alive when they're dead. Who can say on which side madness lies?

The 'proud keep' of Sir John must have been that large pile of stones where a pair of crows were nesting, Sir Andrew's pool had been filled in, the door to the crypt — a building in the Romaneque style of dubious taste — had been boarded up. As for Sir Malcolm's addition, a long building with a roof in a wretched state and many windows lacking glass, it evoked both an ancient ruin and a boathouse and appeared to be held up solely by the strength of the vigorous Virginia creeper in which it was abundantly swathed. I couldn't help thinking of the house of Shaws and its slow decay due to the niggardliness of David Balfour's old uncle in *Kidnapped*. As if to confirm my impression, a bat emerged from the loft and flew through a broken pane into what must have been one of the principal first-floor rooms and I almost twisted my ankle when I slipped on the worn steps leading up to the front door. I knocked on the door, convinced the bronze knocker would come away in my hand and, hearing steps approaching on a tiled floor, prepared myself to ward off the fetid breath of a rheumy-eyed hunchback who would take me to Count Dracula or Baron Frankenstein.

'Good afternoon. My name is Mary Guthrie and I would like to speak to Sir James, please.'

The butler didn't look too bad, despite his threadbare suit: broad shoulders, a good chest and bushy eyebrows which would have fitted him for the role of the family doctor or lawyer in an amateur theatre group and which seemed to have flourished at the expense of his bare skull. His haughty and disgruntled expression was presumably not a response to the sound of the door-knocker but my presence certainly did nothing to improve it.

'Sir James does not receive salesmen.'

'I'm not selling anything. It's personal.'

Fluttering his eyelids furiously, the man looked at me as if I were a speck of dust he was trying to get out of his eye.

'Wait in there.'

'There' was a large hall which had probably once been sumptuous but in the dim and distant past. A magnificent clock was silently bemoaning the loss of its pendulum. On the walls portraits of the noble ancestors of the Urquharts were starting to disappear under a uniform layer of a brown fungal growth, like corpses under spadefuls of earth. As for the vast marble staircase, swept by an icy draught, it seemed to be saying, 'I'm still here in principle but it's years since I led anywhere.' A strip of red carpet, worn down to its backing, meandered up the middle of the stairs; the brass rods and fitments that should have been keeping it in place were scattered all over. On either side of the staircase were two large symmetrical doors; the butler had disappeared through the one on the right; the one on the left was ajar and for a brief moment I thought I saw two faces in the gap. But I was even more intrigued by a third opening. It was in a kind of cubicle made of planks, too small for a room, too big for a cupboard, that had been hurriedly thrown together in one corner by a bungling handyman.

The butler reappeared in the doorway and, with a jerk of his chin, indicated that I should follow him. We went down a corridor, crossed a kind of drawing-room with sheets draped over the occasional pieces of furniture, then an equally disused dining-room smelling of mould; these two rooms also possessed a planked-off corner as badly made as the other.

And the butler definitely did have something of a servant from a gothic novel: a limp. It was only very slight and he made great efforts to conceal it, but it made me uneasy when I discovered it. One of his shoes had an extra thick sole and when he turned round and saw my gaze fixed on his left foot, he started to flutter his eyelashes frenetically.

We came to another door. He knocked three times then quickly hurried away without waiting for a reply.

'Come in, young lady, and do sit down.'

Sir James was wearing a smoking jacket, a scarf and a nightcap with a pompom. In contrast to his butler, he appeared to be exceedingly civilised, though his courtesies and kindly smile seemed as threadbare as the velvet of his waistcoat. The room was relatively comfortable: a sofa, two chairs, a big fireplace with the Urquhart coat of arms and the magnificent solid-oak desk at which he was sitting. A French window at the rear of the house gave onto a garden full of wild roses that was neglected but pleasant. The inevitable plank structure in the corner had been smeared with walnut stain.

'To what do I owe the pleasure, Miss...?'

'Guthrie. Mary Guthrie.'

We shook hands. One section was missing from the middle finger of his left hand and the skin was darker, like that of a cocktail sausage. I set off on a quick explanation for my visit, watching out of the corner of my eye the mechanical smile of the old man — sixty at least, but perhaps the nightcap gave me the wrong impression — who was absent-mindedly playing with his paper-knife and constantly teasing his shortened finger with his thumb.

'How sad,' he sighed at the end. 'How sad that the eccentrics, the dandies always attract more attention than serious-minded people and workers. Take my great-grandfather William, for example. He had all the marshes between Cromarty and Fortrose drained to build houses for his tenant farmers, but I've never seen a student keen to look at his work...'

I gave an embarrassed smile.

'Or his son, Alastair, who restored the Cromarty Courthouse, which is a museum today... And what do you see inside it? A plaque to the memory of Alastair. No, of course not! A *whole room* dedicated to that of Sir Thomas! Sir Thomas, of course, is different... A... a *genius*, isn't he? That's what people call those who pass through this life negligently scattering a few fine words, as you'd throw a bone to a dog... A witticism here, a quip there and the idlers applaud. Oh, I am tired of all that, Miss... Guthrie.'

Before he spoke my name, he raised his eyes so that he was

looking just over my head, as if there were a stage-hand behind me holding up a slate with *Guthrie* written on it.

'Very tired... But it's not your fault, is it? You're doing what you've been told to do?'

'Well no, actually. The topic is a personal interest of mine.'

Sir James gave an even longer sigh. 'You won't find anything here. This place has long since given up the meagre riches it held. It's the curse of the Urquharts. There's always been a Sir Thomas to squander the wealth amassed by a Sir William... Even the family relics have been sold off for a song. The decadence of Rome, as Cato said. It was Cato, wasn't it?'

He quickly consulted a fat encyclopaedia as the first shadows of evening started to darken the room. 'Cato, that's right. Cato the Elder, of course, not to be confused with Cato of Utica...'

I was feeling more and more uncomfortable. 'Could I perhaps still have a quick look at your archives...?'

'Oh, our archives!' he said reflectively, turning to look at the garden again. 'There's the desk, of course, but I very much doubt...'

Some way away from the house I saw two figures walking in the gloaming. Sir James must have seen them as well, for he suddenly stopped, peered at the imaginary slate, then went on in a different tone, 'Can you type, Miss Guthrie?'

'Yes,' I lied without hesitation.

Sir James nodded sagely, as if typing were a science comparable to nuclear physics. 'In that case we might be able to come to an arrangement. Good secretaries are so rare nowadays, and the rates they charge! We'll think about it... sleep on it, that's it. Come back around three tomorrow afternoon and we'll see what can be done.'

I was about to open the door of the Royal Hotel when I saw my old friend the bus driver leaning on the lounge bar. I seemed to inspire him with such an irresistible desire for a swim in the sea that I turned back to the Cromarty Arms which I had initially decided to avoid because of the strong smell of fish and chips it spread down the whole of Church Street. The next morning I just had to cross the street to go and see the Courthouse Museum Sir James had mentioned. Thomas Urquhart was waiting for me there — in the form of an automaton dressed in a blue suit with extravagant lace cuffs and collar. He was sitting on a bench at a desk covered in old parchments, a quill in his hand, waiting for inspiration, which I provided for him by slipping a shilling into the slot. A harpsichord started playing an air, overloaded with shrill arpeggios and trills and barely audible amid the crackling noises. Then the automaton came alive; smoothing down its moustache, it started to speak in a loud voice:

My Universal Language is a most exquisite jewel...

His lips moved out of synch. The porcelain was split on the right wrist, revealing an iron rod.

'Everything's from the period,' said a voice behind my back. 'That has its advantages — and its inconveniences. Look.'

The warden of the museum, woman of around fifty, was very tall and athletic looking; she was wearing khaki cotton trousers and a polo shirt with *Cromarty Cricket Club* embroidered on it. She looked more like a sports club or gymnasium attendant. To the left a little half-glassed door gave onto a cubby-hole. On the walls were photographs of cricket teams, with a sink and a gas ring below them and a glass and a half-empty bottle of whisky on the desk. Bending down, she opened a panel perforated with little holes in the desk, under the automaton.

'A wind-up Berliner gramophone, surely the first to reach this god-forsaken place! It must have cost a fortune in those days. We've just added an electric motor and if you want my opinion, even that's too much expense.'

'No one ever comes?'

'You're the first this week. There were some Americans last Friday. They thought it was very picturesque.'

Once more abandoned by the muse, Sir Thomas had frozen in his original posture, but I had the impression that something had changed, that he was looking at me with his conceited air, ready to strike up a conversation.

'Err... it's getting towards lunchtime, do you want to stay a while longer? You can if you like, you just give me a knock when you go, I live right above.'

'No thanks, that'll do.'

'Good, good, Miss... Guthrie. We really had our thinking cap on last night, you know.'

Sir James had come to the door to let me in himself.

'Precisely!' he said in answer to an imaginary question. 'We would like to propose an arrangement which should be to the satisfaction of all parties. Would you be so good as to follow me.'

The draught grew stronger as we proceeded up the stairs and I soon saw the reason: above my head a section of the roof had been blown off and the gap crudely covered over with a tarpaulin.

'The recent storm,' Sir James said apologetically, 'but don't worry, the rest of the floor is perfectly habitable.'

To judge by the state of the panelling and carpet below the gap, the storm in question had been going on for several years. To the left was a corridor with a series of doors. Urquhart opened the second and showed me into a tiny room with an iron bedstead, a chest of drawers and a porcelain washbasin covered in a network of fine cracks.

'What do you think? Miss Birdie refurbished it specially for you. A magnificent view out over the park... and this little door takes you into the library!'

I refrained from asking what these 'refurbishments' consisted of. The neighbouring room was even more sinister. The only light came from a bull's-eye window. On the floor was a crinkled, mildewed fitted carpet, on the high ceiling a large stain vaguely resembling the shape of Australia and a light bulb with no shade. One of the walls was hung with a tapestry depicting hunting scenes but because of the damp the material had stretched and the stags had come to resemble sows, the horses mules and the hunters themselves frogs and toads with hunting hats and riding crops. Against the opposite wall was a desk with an inlaid leaf: a magnificent Renaissance piece totally out of keeping with its surroundings.

'It is a bit dark but that's because of the books. As you will know, light ruins them.'

The books… The shelves were half empty, clearly having been stripped of the more valuable volumes, leaving the run-of-the-mill stuff: bestsellers from the twenties, gardening handbooks etc. Between the desk and the little window was a plank cubicle of the same style as the others. Never was there a library so little deserving of that name.

Standing in front of the desk, Sir James took out a little key and started to fiddle with it rather pointedly. 'This is my proposition, Miss Guthrie. These two rooms can be your domain for as long as you like. Every afternoon you can devote yourself to your research. All I ask in return is that you simply type out some material for my wards, in the mornings for example. You will eat with us, of course. As far as domestic matters are concerned, see Mr Par or Miss Birdie. Both their rooms are at the end of this corridor, his on the left, hers on the right.'

'What kind of material?'

'You will be told in due course. Do we have an agreement?'

My eyes went from the desk to the key, from the key to Sir James' impassible face. I agreed without enthusiasm — the key was inserted into the lock and the drop-leaf was let down with a noise like an ankle being dislocated.

'Dinner is at half-past six, please be punctual. Oh, I was forgetting, don't hesitate to use this excellent dictionary. The world would be so perfect if only people would use dictionaries! You've no idea of the number of wars and all sorts of catastrophes that could have been avoided simply by looking things up in *Harrap's*…'

As soon as Sir James had left, I dashed over to the plank cubicle. I was prepared for anything except what I found: nothing. There was absolutely nothing in it apart from a few dead flies in a spider's web. Baffled, I went back to the desk. The 40-watt bulb, much too high up, hardly managed to illuminate more than the east coast of Australia and the desk was against the light, some way away from the bull's-eye window. Still, you could not but admire its perfect workmanship, its lines that were at once imposing and delicate; what most caught the eye, however, was the surprising steel coffer it contained that had clearly been installed well after the desk had been made. It was divided into four vertical sections, each with eight drawers. The drawers, also made of steel, were about one inch high by three inches wide, had a little knob on the front and were numbered in sections one to eight, nine to sixteen, seventeen to twenty-four and twenty-five to thirty-two.

I had no problem opening the first and the second but the rest resisted my numerous attempts until I discovered by chance that the third yielded if the first one was left open. From somewhere deep inside of the desk came a *click!* of release. To open the fourth you had to close the first and third then open the second — *click!*; and for the fifth, open the first and third again, close the second and fourth. It took me several minutes to work out the combination for the sixth — first, second and fifth closed, third and fourth opened; and that of the seventh (first, second, fifth and sixth closed, third and fourth open) took me a good quarter of an hour — *click!* Once a drawer had been opened it appeared to have been permanently released and could be opened and closed at will. But it was with horror that I realised that the number of possible combinations was multiplied by two with each new drawer; there were already sixty-four for the seventh, a hundred and twenty-eight for the eighth, it was over a thousand after the eleventh and for the thirty-second and last reached the mind-boggling figure (I covered three sheets of paper with numbers to work it out) of two thousand one hundred and forty-seven million four hundred and eighty-three thousand six hundred and forty-eight!

I started to sweat.

There were signs that someone had tried to force the drawers, there were numerous scratches on the top of the eleventh and the thirty-second. But the steel had stood up to it. The drawers fitted their cavities perfectly without leaving the slightest gap. There was nothing for it but to spend your whole life — would even that be enough — working out combinations. And to find what? An unpublished epigram by Sir Thomas?

The Lairds of Cromarty

He should obtain all his desires,
Who offers more than he requires.

What treasure could there be in such small compartments?
I was going back to my room when Borel started whispering in my ear: 'Giving up, Miss Guthrie? That's not like you. Difficulties, that's what you like, isn't it? Otherwise you'd be in the Bodleian now reading the Reverend J. P. Morrow's essay *High and Low Church in the Works of Anthony Trollope*, London, 1895…'

Uncertain what to do, I went back to the desk to examine the meagre harvest from the drawers I'd opened. The first two: recent bills and letters from creditors; the third: a map of Inverness; the fourth: a diploma for the degree of Master of Arts (third class) awarded to James Urquhart, 30th June 1916; the fifth and sixth: old cuttings from newspapers. The sole interesting find, though unrelated to my research, came from the seventh: a series of sepia snapshots showing Sir James in a truly unimaginable light. He was an attractive young man in elegant dress: tails, dinner jacket, an impeccable tweed suit. Around him was Urquhart House in all its vanished splendour: chandeliers with twenty-four arms in Bohemian crystal, gleaming suits of armour, Victorian sofas and armchairs, the clock in the hall still with its pendulum. One photo, taken in the library, showed a background of handsome bindings and a collection of Chinese porcelain. The dining-room — that dusty tomb I had passed through the previous day — was set for a sumptuous banquet: poultry steaming on silver platters, champagne and cognac in profusion, waiters in striped livery.

And the guests! I could hardly believe my eyes. At some point or other all the brilliant minds and sparkling wits of the twenties had stayed at Urquhart House: from Noel Coward with his polka-dot bow tie and carnation in his buttonhole, to George Bernard Shaw with his bushy beard, centre parting and mocking raised eyebrows and Charlie Chaplin, happy to play the vagabond with a billiard queue as a cane. Here and there ravishing brunettes were in raptures at the witticisms of the illustrious company.

But the most surprising person in those gatherings was Sir James himself. Fresh-complexioned, a sensuous mouth, a large cigar always between his lips and a glass of wine or champagne in his hand, arm in arm with Noel or patting GBS on the back; fine white teeth biting into life, sparkling eyes with an almost Dionysiac fire. And his laugh, that laugh I could almost hear as he watched Charlie Chaplin do his splayed-footed walk... Where was the connection with the Sir James of today, that colourless individual, vaguely neurasthenic, dressed like a Dickens shopkeeper, who never went out and whose greatest pleasure was looking things up in dictionaries?

Two even stranger photos were held together by a paper clip. Poor quality snapshots, unlike the others, they revealed a James Urquhart who was hardly out of adolescence. In the first he had his hands round the neck of a chubby-cheeked, ginger-haired girl; with a mischievous smile he was winking at the camera. The second, dark and slightly blurred, was of the interior of a barn or stable. A woman was stretched out in the hay, her skirt pulled up. Her face couldn't be seen but her clothes and her plump, freckled arms suggested it was the same girl. Between her legs with his trousers down and hair dishevelled, Sir James had been caught in full flow. His roguish smile had disappeared, he seemed paralysed by shame and was directing a look full of hate at the photographer at the same time trying to hide behind his outstretched left hand on which one could see his shortened middle finger.

The by now familiar sound of limping steps came along the corridor. The butler entered without knocking and looked at me for several seconds before announcing, in a tone that brooked no reply, 'Dinner is in five minutes.'

'Thank you. May I ask you a question, Mr Par? What is the purpose of these sort of cupboards made of planks you see almost everywhere?'

He fluttered his eyelashes frenetically, as if his eyelids were guillotines for my use alone. 'I'm not called Mr Par!' he snapped, turned on his heel and left.

∞∞∞

On the ground floor the smell of overcooked cabbage led me to the kitchen where Sir James, the butler and a woman of about thirty were sitting round a table with no cloth. Another, much older woman, short and misshapen, was busying herself at the stove.

'Good evening, my dear. Do sit down.'

Urquhart pulled the dictionary towards himself, liberating a place at the table. 'Eagle! Serve Miss Guthrie. And... I think I asked for some beer.'

The cook put a plate down in front of me two-thirds full of a steaming, greenish sludge.

'Beer? And where do you think that is? In the shop I should imagine.'

'So why didn't you buy some when you did the shopping?'

'Not enough money.'

'What?! And the five-pound note I gave you yesterday?'

'In the first place it wasn't yesterday but the day before yesterday. And then we owed almost that much at Dawson's. You should be glad you've got cabbage and bacon.'

Eagle and Urquhart glared at each other until the laird admitted defeat with a vague gesture. 'No matter. Anyway, I've heard say that beer is injurious to one's health, that it can cause migraine and... dyspepsia. That's the word, isn't it, Miss Birdie? With a "y", I think. Oh, do forgive me, I've forgotten the introductions: Miss Guthrie, Miss Birdie, our governess...'

She was quite pretty, despite a haircut that was a disaster and a rather square chin that gave her a masculine look.

'Yes, definitely a "y",' she said, giving Sir James an exasperated look.

'But we must check. Let's have a look: dysentery... dyslexia... dyspepsia! — a "y"! I knew it!'

From then on Sir James ate with a hearty appetite, while the butler dealt with the food like an Inquisition torturer, dismembering the cabbage and slashing the bacon vindictively with his knife. As for the governess, she somehow managed to give the impression that she was eating without the amount of food on her plate diminishing at all. Eventually she put down her knife and fork and fixed a gimlet stare on me: 'Well, Miss Guthrie, has your initial research been fruitful?'

'No, not really. But,' I turned to Sir James, 'we really must talk about...'

The door opened with a great crash. I had my fork half way to my mouth with a piece of cabbage quivering on it and suddenly I could understand the terror of the poor leaf as it sees two sets of teeth closing in on it in a symmetrical trap: two young men, alike in all respects, came hurtling towards me, one from the left, the other from the right; standing over me, they immediately subjected me to a staccato burst of questions.

'How many words a minute?'

'How many pages an hour?'

'How long will it take you to do my twenty-three pages?'

'And my thirty-four?'

'Thirty-four? Hardly surprising with double-spacing.'

'And what about your margins? You could copy out *David Copperfield* in them.'

The similarity was truly amazing. To the naked eye there was nothing to distinguish between these two pale, blond young men hardly older than me. They were wearing the same white linen trousers and the same V-necked pullover with a blue border — two tennis players arguing over the net, except that in this case the net was a mirror — the same tow-coloured hair with a parting so wide it suggested incipient baldness; the same glasses with thick lenses; two pairs of hunched shoulders, two hollow chests, two pot bellies; skinny legs; child's feet in white tennis shoes; and, above all, the same unpleasant, high-pitched voices. If I closed my eyes I could imagine it was the one mouth speaking.

'When can you start?'

'Tomorrow?'

'A Remington, is that all right?'

'We used to have an Underwood, but the "k" got stuck.'

'*You* made it stick by hitting it as hard as you could.'

Sir James broke in: 'Come now! Bruce! Wallace! Not so loud. You'll frighten poor Miss Guthrie away.'

With great effort the twins managed to calm themselves and sat down at the table, one across from the other, continuing their argument about the defective 'k' in low voices. Eagle brought them two plates, saying in kindly tones, 'Eat it while it's hot.'

For a few seconds all that could be heard was was the vigorous — and perfectly synchronised — mastication of Bruce and Wallace.

'By the way, Miss Guthrie,' Urquhart said, 'Mr Par here tells me that you are intrigued by our laughter closets.'

Hearing himself referred to as Par, the butler gave a pained frown.

'*Laughter* closets?'

'I have to tell you that our family, among other curses, suffers from a congenital abnormality... an aneurysm that can rupture following an incautious exertion or a violent fit of laughter. It caused the death of several Urquharts, most notably, I suspect, that of your friend, the well-known wit, Thomas. My great-grandfather William died in the saddle trying to overcome chronic constipation... As for my cousin Silas... To cut a long story short, the aneurysm is undetectable before the accident, so that none of us can know whether we are liable to it or not, but given the uncertainty I prefer to take prophylactic... er... prophylactic...'

As Sir James was eyeing his dictionary, Miss Birdie tartly stated: 'p-h-y.'

'...measures. From a very early age I have abstained from any sporting activity, I ingest as much vegetable fibre as possible and I avoid the least risk of hilarity. As you will have noticed, I am not by nature susceptible to it but laughter is terribly contagious. I have therefore had these little closets constructed to allow those who cannot — or will not — refrain from laughing to do so in isolation.'

That was something that did not fit in very well with the photos I'd found in the desk.

'So why not warn your visitors? Advise them not to laugh or to use the closets?'

'That is what we normally do, but in your case it seemed… unnecessary.'

'Why?'

'Well…' Sir James hesitated for a moment, struggling for the right words, 'I deemed the risk to be negligible.'

This compliment warmed the cockles of my heart, especially since I could see the ironic smile playing about Miss Birdie's lips. I decided to put an end to this farce as quickly as possible: 'There is indeed no risk. I will be leaving Cromarty House tomorrow morning.'

Bruce and Wallace dropped their knives and forks and stared at me, aghast.

'I think you could have warned me about the desk. I'm not a mathematician, Sir James, and I've no taste for brain-teasers. Nor have I any intention of fiddling with drawers with no guarantee of finding any interesting documents. I thank you very much for your hospitality, but I very much regret…'

'Miss Guthrie, you're forgetting our little agreement.'

Urquhart closed his eyes for a moment, put down his knife and fork, slowly wiped his lips and said in a voice that was sweetness itself: 'We spoke of an afternoon free for research in return for a morning's typing. You've had one afternoon, so you owe me a morning.'

Even today I don't know what stopped me from upping and leaving immediately. Perhaps the sly smile of the the butler who made no secret of his desire to see me fly off the handle; or the despair of the twins bent lugubriously over their plates; or Miss Birdie's challenging look.

Back in my room, I went into the library. A Remington typewriter was on the drop-leaf of the desk, beside it a ream of paper.

∞∞∞

I stared at my watch in disbelief: six forty-five and it was still dark. My back and my shoulders were aching as if I'd spent the whole night lying on the contents of a toolbox. Someone knocked on the door again.

Bruce — or Wallace — had cut himself shaving. He was standing in the doorway, holding a breakfast tray and clutching a folder under his arm. I gave the charred bacon and translucent eggs a wary glance, but the invigorating aroma of tea set off a spurt of gratitude for the twin. Eyes lowered, a sheepish expression on his face, he looked like a lad doing room service on his first day at work in the hotel. He almost upset the tray as he put it down on the chest of drawers, then, clutching the folder to his chest, started to babble: 'We really must apologise, Wallace and I, for our bad manners... It's... it's the secluded life we lead that... We... would like to express our thanks in anticipation for everything you are going to do for us.'

So it was Bruce. I filled the mug to the brim then sat on the edge of the bed. 'What is it you want me to type?'

His eyes sparkled with excitement. He opened and closed his mouth several times, like a child who has a thrilling adventure to tell you about and doesn't know where to begin.

'Do you... like the cinema, Miss Guthrie?'

'Yes, of course... the same as everyone else.'

His face lit up even more. 'It's a book about the cinema... No, it *is* the cinema!'

'A kind of... encyclopaedia?'

'Better than that! Much better! In it we're making a list of everyone who has been involved in films... of the places where they were shot... of the characters who appear in them, including animals... It's a bit like the map of a country, but such a precise one that you could see the stones on the path and the veins of the leaves on the trees.'

'I didn't spot a cinema in Cromarty.'

'That's because there isn't one. We have our own film theatre. A 35mm Cinemeccanica IVE, better than the English or American ones... I'll show it you, if you like.'

Bruce frowned. 'First I'll have to ask Wallace what he thinks... We don't always agree, you know that's why we've shared the work out between us. He's doing the beginning of the alphabet, I'm starting from the end — thirteen letters each. When he's got to M and I've finished N we'll send it to the publishers.'

'And what's it going to be called?'

'*Cinema.*'

He puffed out his chest proudly and gave a satisfied click of the tongue but immediately his expression darkened again. 'It's such a pity… if you'd been going to stay a little longer — and if Wallace agreed — I would have shown you a film…'

After Bruce had gone, I took the mug into the library and opened the folder. It took me a few seconds before I realised what I was looking at:

Za-la-Mort Zaanstad Zab Zabulon Zacharie Zakat Zampa Zanuck Zany Zanzibar Zap Zapata Zappy Zarzuela Zavattini Zebra Zecca Zeman Zen Zenith Zetterling Zgouridi Zigomar Zigotto Zinnemann etc

A list without punctuation or paragraphs. An absurd list written down in pencil on paper torn out of school jotters, a mixture of proper names — most unknown to me — with a variety of other words. No comments, no definitions, no biographical notes. At the very best *Cinema* was nothing but a stupid pastime, at worst the outpourings of a sick mind. I had been about to laugh, but the lump in my throat turned into nauseous vomit that it took several mouthfuls of tea to clear.

Cursing Bruce and Wallace, Sir James, Sir Thomas, Mr Par — whatever his real name was — Miss Birdie, Mr Remington and Cinemeccanica, and pouring even more bitter curses on myself, I took the cover off the typewriter and set to work:

Za-la-Mort Zanstad Zab Zabu —

Three knocks on the door.

'I hope I'm not disturbing you…'

A folder under his arm, a posy in his hand: a few wild flowers crudely torn out of the ground, already wilting. Wallace looked round the room for a vase; not finding one, he simply plonked the vegetable matter on the desk and took advantage of that to steal a glance through the open door of my bedroom.

'I'm glad to see you've made yourself comfortable, Miss Guthrie.'

The voice was the same, true, but his delivery seemed more assured, as did his look, which occasionally had an almost ironic gleam.

'I hope my brother has managed to convey to you the immense importance of our work…'

More assured, perhaps, but just as mad.

'Its… metaphysical importance I would call it. It's an undertaking without equal in both its scale and originality.'

Wallace placed his hands on the back of the chair and leant over my shoulder to leaf through his brother's work. I could feel his breath on my hair, smell his aftershave, slightly more provocative than Bruce's.

'A monument, isn't that what it'll be? A monument to the glory of beauty, surpassing beauty itself… *Cinema* will be more beautiful than the cinema. I really believe you should think it over before leaving us, Miss Guthrie.'

'Give me one good reason.'

I would have liked to stand up and face him, but my knees were stuck under the drop-leaf of the desk and I couldn't push back the chair he was still holding in a firm grasp.

'Our relationship got off to a bad start, all the fault of that old skinflint… but that can always be sorted out. Do you know that lots of publishers would pay dearly to have his book in their catalogue? Which means…'

He bent down a little more until our cheeks touched, then he abruptly stepped back, walked round the armchair and leant back against the wall, facing me. Like Bruce he puffed out his chest and clicked his tongue.

'Which means that we will soon be rich and will be in a position to reward your labours at their true value.'

'But making money is not the reason why I've come to Cromarty, Mr Urquhart.'

Wallace flicked away his brother's pile of papers and placed his own in front of me. He stroked the cardboard folder while giving me a wink that even the driver of the Inverness-Cromarty bus would have considered rather bold.

'Think about it, Miss Guthrie.'

Aa Aaron Abacus Abandon Abbe Abbott & Costello Aberdeen Abnormal Abou Seif Actors' Studio…
Although written out more carefully, Wallace's *oeuvre* was of the same ilk as Bruce's. I had decided that three hours of typing would be a fair exchange for Sir James' hospitality; at the end of the first I already had calluses forming on my fingertips. I typed their contributions alternately so that one would not be jealous of the other: one page of As then one page of Zs. *Adam Adamant Addams Age & Scarpelli.* At least the unutterable stupidity of the task left my mind free to wander. *Zipper Zoom Zorro Zuiderzee.* I could still feel the unpleasant warmth of Wallace against me, his breath, his aftershave; once more I felt the pity Bruce had inspired in me. How was it that I hadn't noticed the difference the previous day? Wallace's arrogance, his smugness. Bruce's fragility. His remarkable clumsiness, as shown by the little cut he'd…

AAAAAAAAAA…

I hit the key so hard that it went through the paper and remained stuck against the cylinder. *The cut on Bruce's chin.* I thought I could remember… I could almost have sworn… no, I was sure: Wallace had cut himself *in exactly the same place!* So I hadn't had two visitors that morning but just *one!* One of the twins — Bruce or Wallace, what did it matter? — had put on an act, played at being different while the other was sound asleep or waiting for his brother to get back so that they could have a laugh at my expense. Interchangeable. Two communicating vessels, available for any liquid that would fill them: fear, vanity, desire, arrogance, contempt, affection…

Jars. Drawers. And the desk was still there, a lure, an open secret. Closed. Open. Open closed closed closed open.

Her room didn't strike me as particularly 'governessy': no cretonne curtains, no teapot kept warm in its woolly cosy, no photos of an old moustachioed uncle or a virginal niece, no Persian carpet, no china ornaments; instead a full ashtray and a heterogeneous pile of books — Wharton, James, Wilde, Marx, Nietzsche, Turgenev — pencil sketches of the park and house from various bizarre angles, an old number of *The Times* and a half-bottle of brandy. Even Miss Birdie's posture showed her contempt for the proprieties: stretched out on the unmade bed, she hardly lifted her head and continued to draw on her little sketch pad.

'Yes, Miss Guthrie?'

'I've just come to say goodbye.'

'I understand. Sir Alexander's little toy is pretty exasperating. And that's not counting the twins. But have you forgotten it's Sunday? Sunday in Scotland. No trains or buses until tomorrow.'

'Sir Alexander's?'

She looked me up and down for a moment then her glance strayed towards the window. 'Sir James' great-uncle. When he wasn't sticking his prick into some orifice or other he was messing about with mechanical devices. Complicated ones for preference. He's the one who had the automaton of Sir Thomas made that you can see at the Courthouse. And the desk. I spent quite a lot of time on it at the beginning… a whole day to open the eighth drawer…'

'Just a minute. You've already opened eight drawers? But then how is it that…'

'That they were locked again later on? There's a delayed safety catch, a kind of time switch. At one point I gave up on the desk and when I can back to it several months later all the drawers were locked again. To put it briefly, I've done my sums: if two people work alternately in twenty-four hour shifts at twenty tries an hour, they would take more than a hundred and twenty-two years to work through all the combinations for the last drawer.'

'But why?'

'Why what?'

Her funny chin was aimed straight at me, almost threateningly.

Until now I hadn't noticed how skinny she was. Her silhouette was enveloped in a loose boy's shirt and cotton trousers. Miss Birdie had a dressing-table but I could well imagine her using it to achieve the opposite effect from the one women usually aim for: thickening her eyebrows instead of plucking them, adding rings under her eyes instead of masking them and regularly wreaking havoc on her hair with a pair of nail scissors.

'Why go to so much trouble to hide trivial documents?'

'Ah, that's Sir Alexander's second brain-teaser. The brain-teaser squared, if you like. But do sit down, we've got all afternoon…'

The little chair by the dressing-table, the only seat in the room, had a cardboard box full of drawings on it.

'You can look at them if you like.'

I couldn't refrain from smiling when I saw Mr Par shaking his fist at a boy stealing apples and Eagle carving a minute roast with a huge cutlass. They were genuinely well executed comic cartoons, somewhat in the manner of the artists in *Punch*. A third, more original one, represented Sir James with his nose literally stuck in a dictionary — it came out through the binding. In the fourth you could see the twins, back to back, forming a single symmetrical creature crowned by the inscription *Me and me*. The last was a sketch of the desk.

'You're very talented.'

Miss Birdie shrugged her shoulders and went on, drawing all the while:

'There are good reasons for assuming that Sir Alexander found Thomas Urquhart's treasure. With the modest income from the estate he would never have been able to afford the luxurious carriages and fine horses he had, his seasons in London, his many visits to Italy… nor to grease the palms of the magistrates when he was mired in some nasty sex scandal. Not counting the jewels he lavished on his mistresses and lovers. Shortly before his death, he took a certain Catherine Grant into his service and made her pregnant — a catastrophe, as you can well imagine for his younger brother Stephen, James' grandfather, who would have paid dearly to get rid of the inconvenient bastard. But there was no need. Catherine Grant ran off one night without warning and was never seen again. Alexander moved heaven and earth to find her, but in vain. The only witness was the driver of a stagecoach who reported having seen a pregnant girl walking alone on the road to Munlochy. She was poorly dressed but had a remarkable ring on her finger — a ring given her by Sir Alexander and which, there is no doubt, came directly from Thomas' treasure.'

'You got all this from Sir James?'

Miss Birdie gave me an odd smile but didn't answer my question. 'It was at that point that Alexander had the idea of the desk. With no offspring he could not prevent the estate and all his goods and chattels going to his brother, whom he hated. What he could do, however, was to take the Urquhart treasure — he was the only one who knew where it was hidden — to the grave with him. Even worse, he could delude his brother into thinking he had come into possession of it and thus play one last trick on him *post mortem*. He spent the last months of his life doing this: he devised the desk and had it made by an engineer in Glasgow. Then he summoned Stephen to the library and made it clear to him that the desk contained the key to the treasure. And that brings us to the puzzle. Hypothesis number one: it's empty, it's merely an infernal machine designed to ruin his brother's life and that of his descendants. Number two: that was the impression Alexander wanted to give, but the key does in fact really exist in the form of a document concealed in one of the drawers. Number three: he counted on us making deduction number two, thus forcing us to search for years and years. Number four: he thought we would reach conclusion number three and abandon the search and the treasure. You follow me?'

'Yes. Do you know how it works?'

'At a guess it will be a system of sliding rods of different lengths, one above the other, that engage with a series of rings behind each of the drawers that retain or release them according to the combination.'

'Can it be forced?'

'With a blowlamp, yes, but then the contents would go up in

flames and with them all hope of ever finding the treasure.'

'So there's no solution.'

'Perhaps there is. In the first place we must reckon, paradoxically, on the infinite perversity of Alexander... infinite to the point of giving us a helping hand from time to time. And then there's the ring.

'Catherine Grant's ring?'

'Alexander had been ill for a long time. Tuberculosis, probably syphilis as well. His last weeks were terrible. Confined to bed, he was entirely dependant on his brother. Stephen tried everything: gentleness, threats, jokes, but the old goat held out. One night, however, in a delirious fit, he started to scream the name of Catherine. Then he laughed, laughed like a madman for several hours. And when he wasn't laughing, he was teasing Stephen, who was at his bedside, always repeating the same words: "The ring! The ring, my dear Stephen. Find the ring and you'll have the treasure. The ring contains the solution." The next morning he died laughing.'

'Like Thomas.'

'Yes, like Thomas.'

Miss Birdie took a sheet of paper out of the drawer of her bedside table. 'If you want to spend the night in the house, I don't think Sir James will dare to demand a second morning of typing, so here's something to occupy you — the combination of the eighth drawer. I've noted it down according to Alexander's own system, a nought for "open" and a cross for "closed". I hope you have a strong stomach.'

'Thank you, Miss Birdie. But I don't really understand why you're telling me all this...'

'Because I hate Sundays!' she said with a mocking smile. 'I'll do anything to have someone to talk to on a Sunday afternoon. By the way...'

I had already reached the door. When I turned round I saw that she had got up and was holding out her drawing. 'My name isn't Birdie, no more than the butler's is Par or the cook's Eagle. One of the many bizarre customs of the Urquharts was to give all the servants a pseudonym connected with golf. The estate factor, when there still was one, was called Albatross, the footman Bogey, the chambermaids Double Bogey, Triple Bogey etc. And since you like my drawings, please accept this one. You can tell me what you think of it later.'

Out in the corridor I examined the portrait. It was that of a young woman with short hair and ordinary features. Her tight lips and the slight forward inclination of the head expressed obstinacy and a touch of arrogance; her expression, on the other hand, seemed disoriented, as if it belonged to someone else.

It took a few seconds for me to recognise myself. The artist had entitled her drawing *She and she*. At the bottom her signature could be seen: B. Foyle.

I wasn't particularly surprised to find a cold lunch of roast beef and potato salad on my bedside table; under the plate was a visiting card: *With the compliments of Bruce and Wallace.*

I nibbled at it but I had no real appetite. Too many questions were going round and round in my head. Too many answers as well, probably all wrong. When I went back to the library I first of all checked the combination of the eighth drawer: OXXOXOO. It opened easily to reveal a little blank envelope. It contained the following message:

> *Dear Friend or Foe,*
>
> *Heartiest congratulations! You've succeeded in opening the eighth drawer. As a reward for your patience, here is the combination of the ninth: OXOXOOOO. There you will have the opportunity to familiarise yourself even more with the exquisite literary refinement of the author of these lines — enjoy your reading.*
>
> *Alexander Urquhart*
> *P. S. Be sure not to let this minor success go to your head.*

Click! Despite Miss… Foyle's warning, the contents of the ninth drawer hardly seemed to demand a strong stomach. It was a brochure of some forty pages, printed — but carefully printed — at the author's expense and dated 1892: *Memories of a Journey to Tuscany, Umbria and Venetia, by Sir Alexander Urquhart, knight.*

Precisely the kind of reading for a rainy autumn afternoon. I'd always been susceptible to the strange charm of the accounts the British used to bring back from their travels in Italy. The upright silhouette of the cypresses, the languorous curve of the hills, the villas, the peaceful inlets and the sound of the cicadas mingle with their memories of the mists and the cold; the beauties of the south always seem fleeting, unreal to them — both desirable and inaccessible, like the pin-up photos prisoners stick to the walls of their cells. Even as they walk across the Bridge of Sighs or along the alleys of San Gimignano, they cannot entirely free themselves of the feeling that they're dreaming and that a grumpy valet is about to burst into their bedroom, open the curtains to reveal the dreary sight of some inundated countryside, some barren moor, and bring them *The Times*, a pair of slippers and a first instalment of domestic problems.

I decided to forget everything: Urquhart House, the desk and Miss Birdie-Foyle. Just as when I was a child, I snuggled up under the covers and opened Sir Alexander's book, ready to forgive him his fiendish invention in return for a few hours dreaming in the sunshine of Italy.

Chapter One: Florence.

10th February.

Morning: Via della Fortezza. Sophia (professional). By the cunt. Hair.

Afternoon: siesta. Nothing. Bumped into the American novelist everyone in London is talking about.

Evening: a little street by the docks (got lost). Lucia, twelve, perhaps thirteen. By the cunt. Very expensive. Paid her mother.

11th February

Morning: Piazza Goldoni. Name unknown (professional?). By the arse. Huge and tight at the same time: a big animal with jowls and a tiny voracious mouth. Tell P. about her when I get back.

Afternoon: excursion to Fiesole. Garden of the Villa Medici. Nothing.

Evening: Hotel Cavour. Giancarlo (boots). By the mouth. Cheap. Too many teeth.

12th February.

Morning: Pitti Palace. Uffizi Gallery. Giotto. Paolo Uccello. Botticelli. Michelangelo. Nothing.

Afternoon: by chance found Lucia's street again. Was at school. Made do with her mother. By the cunt. Hair. Smells.

Evening: nothing.

I read through the forty pages of depravity in one go. I didn't find a glimmer of remorse in them nor even an attempt at self-glorification. There was something mesmerising about the phlegmatic meticulousness of this record of abomination. It rained the whole afternoon, large opaque drops rolled down the window, cutting me off from the world. When I closed the brochure. I felt as soiled as all those bodies of which Alexander had coldly described the workings.

Towards six someone knocked at the door. I didn't respond. After a long hesitation, Bruce or Wallace put something down outside the door and went away. Doubtless the room in the Cromarty Arms would still be free but I didn't have the strength to go. I remained prostrate on my bed, my head underneath the pillow. Several hours later, while contemplating the ceiling with its approximations of Japan and Borneo, I finally fell asleep.

'You shouldn't, young lady.'

He was there, standing up, Sir Thomas Urquhart in person. Despite the gloom I could clearly see his doublet with the slashed sleeves, his breeches and his top-boots. His moustache as well and his curly hair, much longer than those of the automaton in the Courthouse Museum.

'You mustn't tell your dreams. It was Henry James who said so:

112

every dream a novelist tells loses them ten readers.'

Not for one second did I doubt that he really was there in my bedroom, yet one detail puzzled me: how could he quote a writer who was born almost two hundred years after his death? He put his finger to his lips, telling me to remain silent.

'Whoa, my fair one. Not so fast. We'll get there soon enough. Everything will go off splendidly, I can guarantee that. Ladies much more experienced and more comely than you have deigned to allow me a certain competence in this business… Now let's see, which channel shall we choose?

He sat down at the end of the bed. I looked round for something to defend myself with, but the room was completely empty, even the wash-basin and the chest of drawers had gone. I wanted to shout, but this time it was my lips on which he placed his forefinger.

'Zounds, you are a spirited filly! Desperate to make my acquaintance, no doubt. Do not fear, I will reveal all my secrets to you — the treasure of Thomas Urquhart, you will run your fingers through his rubies, his opals. But first things first, let us spill the honey before the jewels. I certainly will not choose the mouth — too easy; the wenches always have it open in order to spout their nonsense. The cunt is too well prepared to that end… you miss the unexpected. That leaves the third route which, I have to admit, I find very tempting. But will I find the formula?'

He gave a little laugh and smoothed his moustache coquettishly. 'Let's see… nought nought cross nought cross cross. Nothing! I've lost. Oh! Oh! Oh!'

He fell on me. His hair was tickling my nostrils. He had a strong smell, that of a goat that had swum a few strokes in a lake of eau de Cologne. His hands, short, firm, calloused, slipped under my nightdress. I could have sworn I recognised them as André Borel's.

'God's truth! Is this not great sport! Let's play it again. Nought cross cross nought cross nought. It won't work any more. By my beard, my fair one's resisting! Does she require a poem to grant her favours? Come to my aid, Alcofrybas! it's a rondeau, my lady, let's hold hands.

O had but then some brave Signor
Brought her to me I waited for,
*   In shitting!*
I would have cleft her water-gap,
And join'd it close to my flip-flap,
Whilst she had with her fingers guarded
My foul nockandrow, all bemerded
*   In shitting.'*

While he was singing, he grasped my wrists and swung them from side to side to the rhythm of the rondeau.

'Nay, by my troth, the lady doesn't like poetry! What would she say to *nought cross nought nought cross nought*.'

With a horrified shiver I heard, deep within my entrails, a sharp, metallic *click!*

'Victory! The town has surrendered! The drawbridge is down. The penitent townsfolk are bringing me the keys on a velvet cushion!'

Grasping me by the waist, he abruptly turned me over. It wasn't the weight of his body pressing down on my back, on my hips, it was that of Father Krook's.

'To me, men! Lift up my litter. Carry it into the enclosure. Laugh, my friends, laugh with joy, the enemy has surrendered! Ours the glory, ours the keys of the city! Let us laugh! Aah! Aah! Aah!'

Suddenly I woke up. The tap was dripping in the wash-basin. My nightdress, soaked in sweat, was sticking to my icy skin. Someone had *really* come into my room and left the door to the library open. Barefoot, I went into the library: nobody. The laughter closet was also empty. There was a stale, nauseating smell in the room. A smell of the tomb, I told myself before shrugging my shoulders at my own stupidity. The tenth drawer was open, but all it contained was a piece of headed notepaper from the Hotel Cavour on which its own combination and nothing else was written: OXOOXXOOO.

Back in my room, I realised that I was ravenous and gobbled down the cold stew that had been put outside my bedroom door. Then I leant on the windowsill and looked out. It was still raining, the water was dripping down onto the flagstones of the main courtyard. Dawn was still a long way off but I distinctly saw, in a rare moonbeam, a man with long hair in a blue doublet and breeches; sword at his side, he was heading in the direction of the sea at a brisk pace.

CHAPTER VI

Krook's narrative.

For several weeks I refused to think about the reappearance of my father's copy of *Martin Eden.* Later, I told myself, later... The bookshop routine suited me. I was happy just to get through each day as it came, as you avoid an opponent's tackle. But the image of Francis Krook was soon to reappear and in the most unexpected way.

In general we had lunch with Robin and Lewis in a little restaurant in the Cowgate. The haggis was execrable, the haddock just about all right, but Walpole was a regular customer with his table placed a little apart from the others set with its red-black-and-gold cloth, the colours of Stewart's College FPs, Walpole's old club, a clock in the shape of a rugby ball, a photo of the great 1928 Scottish team of Dykes, Paterson, Douty, Simmers and the rest and, above all, our special bottles of Graves supplied by a Bordeaux bookseller, Pierre Cavignac.

Walpole had met him at Murrayfield in 1948 at the Scotland-France match and again in '50 and '52, their meetings enlivened by fierce arguments about Henry James — Cavignac couldn't stand 'that monomaniac homosexual'— and bets on the match result. At first the latter brought my boss a generous supply of Graves but subsequently he had to send several bottles of single malt to the Frenchman.

The lunch party always arrived in the same order: first Walpole and me, then Lewis, then Robin. Sometimes La Mujer would join us. One day she encountered Kenneth, Lewis's fair-haired little paramour, and was very sweet to him; on the other hand, the only time Robin brought someone, the Spanish woman sat there tight-

116

lipped looking daggers at Robin's girl-friend throughout the meal.

'When are you going to tell me the history of those three,' I asked Walpole afterwards.

'There's nothing to tell. Get your brain cells working.'

On Halloween there were just the four of us. For once Robin and Lewis had arrived first. Since the previous Sunday the town had been drenched in a constant icy drizzle. A strike had been going on for ever in the naval dockyards at Leith and the government was talking about sending in the police, which made Robin furious. The Edinburgh team had taken a hammering in Glasgow; Davidson had ricked his ankle badly and was doubtful for the Five Nations. Lewis's business was having problems and so was ours. In short, everything was turning sour — apart from the Graves, of course.

'I never tire of watching people drink,' said Walpole, lighting a cigar. 'It's very revealing. More even than people's politics or their sexual preferences.'

'Now you, Lewis, for example, you're nothing but an amateur... an apprentice, unmethodical and clumsy. You drink to forget, you say, but when you wake up the next day, it's even worse. Robin, on the other hand, is a professional, a strategist, a Nimzovitch of liquor; the game between him and alcohol has been going on forever. Oh, he's not stupid, he knows he's going to lose, but he puts the same care as a grandmaster into his every move. A grandmaster trying to postpone the inevitable checkmate. He castles, he forks, he takes a pawn en passant...'

With a scornful click of the tongue, Robin headed for the gents.

'As for you, Ebeneezer...' Walpole turned slowly to face me.

'You, Eby, are something different again. You're a kamikaze, alcohol is your dynamite and the target... is yourself. You need the touch of a fairy in your fingertips to disarm the bomb... or a shield to protect you from the explosion... a shield of books.'

In the middle of September I'd taken back *Tom Jones, Roderick Random, Old Mortality, Caleb Williams* and all the others without having read them. He'd said nothing then and the question of my reading had never arisen again. But on that day, when we got back from the Cowgate, he did broach it: 'I was really stupid to suggest that kind of book to you. You're no longer naive enough for their glittering surface, their arrogance, but not yet seasoned enough to see the blood beneath the ermine, the shadows beneath the brightness, the depths, the darkness of the great masters of the picaresque novel. What you need is a mirror-book, a book that will say to you: "I am like you." Here, this one for example.'

I took the book: *Notes from the Underground* by Dostoyevsky. I read the first lines with Walpole looking on attentively. *I am a sick man... I am a spiteful man. I am an unattractive man. I believe my liver is diseased...*

Back home that evening — with my first wages I had rented a little maid's room in Blackfriars Street, only a minute away from the bookshop — I went on reading to page 13, where this phrase struck me:

It is only the fool who becomes anything.

My father's terrible expression, the one he had flung at my mother as he left. The one I had repeated to myself in every possible way in my attempt to understand. I was seventeen at the time, and now I had found it again, seventeen years later: *an intelligent man cannot become anything seriously... it is only the fool who becomes anything.*

At first I was seized with a kind of rage. Rage at the Russian writer, so long dead, who had just taken away from me one of my most precious possessions. Then at my father. Had he not also robbed me? Had he not, at the last moment, hidden behind a quotation, the only message he left me being the words of another?

Then I started to think about it. Oddly enough, I'd never imagined my father reading any book other than *Martin Eden*. In my mind the man and the book were a single person: a compact unit, a door at which I'd never knocked, an infallible compass measuring the angles of life by the yardstick of some faultless doctrine. But I'd just had a rather belated insight: Francis Krook was not a novel, not even a character in a novel, be it Martin Eden or Dostoyevsky's government official. His brow was not anointed with any special unction, there was no Bible in his hand. Francis Krook was a man among other men, *a reader* among other readers, searching through all the books for the missing pieces in his own jigsaw puzzle. That was what gave me the idea and I spent the whole of November putting it into practice.

Cautiously at first. A few sentences to begin with, a page here and there while flicking the feather duster over Walpole's books. Like a mushroom gatherer who's still slightly unsure about the specimens he's picked. But they didn't kill me. The taste was quite strong but not unpleasant. *'Oblomov never wore a tie or a waistcoat at home because he liked comfort and freedom.' 'Anna Arkadyevna Karenina had friends and close ties in three different circles of this highest society.' 'On reaching the salon, Chichikov was almost forced to close his eyes for a moment, such was the glare of the lamps, candles, and ladies' dresses.'* However, nothing stirred my appetite.

Every evening, hidden from Walpole, I took a book home. As I went in, I placed it on the only table in the room and left it there while I made my dinner on a little gas ring, ate it standing up by the window and then washed the dishes. After that I sat down at the table, poured myself a glass of whisky and stayed there looking at the book until night fell. I stood up to switch on the light and only then did I open the book — at random. Mostly nothing happened, the words remained silent as they always had done. But sometimes, as I was about to close the book, a hand would shoot up from the page and grab me: *'The doctor has just left me. At last I have got something definite! For all his cunning, he had to speak out at last. Yes, I am soon, very soon, to die. The frozen rivers will break up, and with the last snow I shall, most likely, float away… whither? God knows! To the ocean too. Well, since one must die, one may as well die in the spring…'*

The Diary of a Superfluous Man by Turgenev. A voice inside me said, 'Francis Krook perhaps read this book. This book contains a little piece of Francis Krook.' And I grasped the hand instead of releasing myself from its grip. I looked on the book with a different eye, the way we look on a stranger when we hear that he used to live in our village, climbed the same trees as us, ran after the same girls. *'But isn't it absurd to begin a diary a fortnight, perhaps, before death? What does it matter? And by how much are fourteen days less that fourteen years, fourteen centuries? Beside eternity, they say, all is nothingness — yes, but in that case eternity, too, is nothing.'* Then I would read the book late into the night, unmethodically, in no particular order, skipping pages, going back to the beginning, reading the same paragraph ten times over, falling asleep with the book in my hand. When I woke, all I was left with was a headache and a vague memory, like that of a disjointed conversation with some stranger in a bar or on a station platform.

One day I happened to take home one of the books Walpole had recommended to me on the first day. It was one of the books that had pride of place in my mother's library, in a nice edition full of erudite notes. 'Oh, your mother!' my father had said one day as he passed the bookshelf, 'Your mother and her insupportable Victorians!' Those simple words ought to have disqualified it for me and so, in a kind of feeling of remorse, I left it in my jacket pocket without having read a word of it. But in the middle of the night I was woken by a nightmare. I couldn't really say what it was about, all I could remember was that the book played a part in it as well as my father's ring and a rather repugnant individual called Charybdis. I went to fetch the book from my blazer hanging on the coat-hook and sat down. No hand came out to grab me but it opened naturally at the first page:

Summary of events during this Master's wanderings.

The full truth of this odd matter is what the world has long been looking for, and public curiosity is sure to welcome.

Part of myself balked at this lapel-grabbing opening, desperately trying to catch the reader's attention, to coax him into the meshes of its net. 'Francis Krook did not read this book,' the voice said. Another voice, however, more distant but more difficult to ignore, joined in: 'But what if a little piece of Francis Krook were there as well, in this book he didn't read. *Precisely* because it's a book he didn't read?'

Now there's a *different idea*, I told myself. Absurd. Fascinating.

Without trying to understand what was going on inside me, I silenced the roars of the illiterate wild beast that I was and read a few more lines to test the meshes, then allowed myself to be caught in Stevenson's net.

The next morning, as I was surreptitiously replacing the book, I froze as I heard a voice behind me: 'Well, then, Mr Krook, did you enjoy *The Master of Ballantrae*?'

Walpole was looking at me with his mocking little smile.

'Bringing a book back is not a crime, my friend, only stealing it is wrong. And even then one can often find extenuating circumstances.'

He burst out laughing and started to cough. It was at that moment that I first understood that this persistent, dry cough was not just a mannerism, a trade mark — something very personal which belonged to him, which in a way defined him like his single lock of hair, his grey apron, his very special way of drawing on his cigar and of holding it like a blowpipe or of speaking the word 'literature' by emphasising the first syllable then just mumbling the rest — but was, on the contrary, a kind of foreign body, an enemy.

Succumbing to an indefinable sense of shame, I decided to get my supplies elsewhere. A largish bookshop on Princes Street had the advantage of staying open late. My first reaction on going in was like that of a husband coming home to find his wife sprawled out, naked, in the arms of another man, while he had left her in the morning quiet, submissive, dignified, playing Chopin on the drawing-room piano. The contrast to our little shop in Anchor Close almost made me feel sick. The harsh, cold light was shamelessly copulating with the gaudy dust-jackets of the latest bestsellers. The revolving door was constantly releasing people who seemed to have come in by chance and sucking out others who looked as if they'd just remembered an important engagement. People wandered round the shelves aimlessly, idly running their hand along a row of titles, glancing through a random book now and then, changing their mind and putting it back anywhere but in the right place; with half an ear they listened to the vapid chatter of the assistants with the other half to the *ding-ding!* of the cash register; they read for want of anything better to do, they purchased books almost without noticing.

The shop must have had four or five times as many books as Walpole's but gave the opposite impression: with no one really examining them closely, which would have distinguished each from the other, all these books were piled up to no purpose whatsoever, forming a single grotesque, shapeless, abandoned whole. In the same way, what ought to have been the main interest of the shop — the fact that it offered *all* books, even the most recent — in fact constituted an obstacle to my exploration. What was missing was Walpole's invisible hand, the hand that knew how to put every book in the appropriate place, that place where the other hand, the one that was looking for it without realising, had the best chance of happening on it.

However at the back of the shop, behind a huge cement pillar, there was a dark, quiet corner where, heaped up on a trolley presumably in anticipation of a clearance sale, were ancient, unsaleable tomes: shopsoiled or incomplete volumes, books with loose binding; but the trolley seemed to have gathered to itself everything that was authentic in the shop. I found a number of books whose more fortunate brothers sat proudly on Walpole's shelves; one of these in particular attracted my attention. When I took it to the cash desk the assistant named the derisory price with a grimace of contempt.

A few days later I was once more astonished by Walpole's perspicacity.

'Well now, how far have you got with *Great Expectations*?'

This time there was no possible doubt: the man was the devil incarnate! He could read my thoughts or, to be more precise, my books. Laughing and coughing, he explained the mystery: 'Recently you've started using the word *prodigious* all over the place. Now that's one of Dickens' favourite words, for him everything's prodigious. Kindness, nastiness, Shakespeare... even the tenderness of lamb chops. And then yesterday, when Mr Wemmick gave you his name for the book he'd ordered, you gave a sly smile; from which I deduced you were thinking of Wemmick, Mr Jaggers' clerk, and of his priceless father. From the expression on your face I can tell I've hit the mark. Did you borrow it from the library?'

Shamefaced, I confessed to the bookshop on Princes Street.

'Good Lord! From the merchants and money-changers in the Temple? If you absolutely insist on enriching a competitor, then go to MacAvoy's. He's an absolute rogue, but at least he loves his work.'

Towards the end of November something strange happened to me: I started to feel a pressing need to read the books Walpole's customers bought. I suddenly had the feeling that all these eccentrics each possessed a tiny portion of a fabulous secret, that their oddities, their absurdities, their sudden changes of mood were trifling compared with the purity, the freshness, the wholesomeness of the spring feeding them. Very soon I could have the rudiments of a conversation about the Elizabethan theatre with Mr Duff; and thanks to Mr Mitchell, I discovered Meredith.

Doliphant Mitchell was a retired teacher who had taught at a high school in Perth for forty years. The word 'customer' was not really appropriate for him as I never saw him purchase a volume; he simply dropped in at regular intervals to check that all the works of Meredith were present on the shelves. If that was the case, he would nod his head in satisfaction with approving murmurs of 'good, good.' But if just one book were missing at his inspection he would quickly show signs of irritation. He would scurry from one set of shelves to another, muttering incomprehensible words, eventually facing up to Walpole, a frown on his face, his cheeks flushed crimson, his right foot tapping the the floor uncontrollably in the furious rhythm of anger.

'And where is *The Egoist*, Mr Walpole?'

'Nowhere, Mr Mitchell, I really am sorry. It's what's known in the trade as out of stock.'

'What it is called does not concern me, sir…' Mitchell's right hand was convulsively squeezing something in his pocket.

'I can understand your indignation. Perhaps you should write to the publisher to —'

'What do I care about the publisher. You are the one I hold

personally responsible for this negligence!'

With these words he would point an uncompromising forefinger at Walpole, displaying at the same time a handkerchief stiff with mucus which he used with a resounding blast. And, since he had known the bookshop since the 1910s, when he had been a student here, he delivered a verdict worse than a sentence of death: 'You'd have never seen that in MacDonald's days.'

One day, not long after I had started to work there, he slammed the door so violently the bell was reduced to permanent silence. It was around the middle of December, well before the days when I knew *The Ordeal of Richard Feverel* and *The Tragic Comedians* like the back of my hand, that I was delighted to overhear this exchange between Walpole and him: 'Your new assistant's a pearl, Arthur... you will permit me to call you Arthur, won't you? See that you never lose him.'

'I will make a note of that... Doliphant.'

I also learnt to put up with the snuffles of Mr Briggs, even to find a certain charm in them. Briggs, out of work for several months, was endowed with a formidable chest and a wallet shrunk in inverse proportion. As soon as he came into the shop he dilated his nostrils, as if he could breathe in the books to furnish the immense warehouse of his thorax. From time to time he would buy a wretched paperback then, in the doorway, he would survey the bookshop with a last, heartbreaking look, give a profound sigh and hurry off. After he had left, I would reconstruct his route between the tables and shelves, trying to identify the book that had been the cause of his loudest sniff, and when the evening came, I took it home with me. Thus poor Mr Briggs' nasal passages and oversized pectorals led to me discovering Flaubert and Maupassant.

MacAvoy's bookshop was on the other side of Holyrood Park, quite a distance from my usual haunts but in the immediate neighbourhood of a 'prodigious' dive — prodigious in the sense that its complete lack of anything that could be described as picturesque suited me down to the ground and that no one I knew would come across me there hurriedly imbibing the quantity of alcohol I deemed necessary to make up for a whole day of abstinence. MacAvoy had prices that were worthy of Sotheby's and treated the girl who assisted him like a bondmaid before the abolition of serfdom. His little blue-green eyes didn't seem made to see with but to advertise a seafood restaurant. But when I spoke about a book, the oysters could sometimes diffract a certain light, a pale reflection of the passion I saw shining every day deep within Walpole's eyes.

'Ah! Canetti's *Auto-da-Fé*... Excellent, really, you won't regret it.'

'All the same, twenty-one shillings and twopence, it's very expensive.'

'Love doesn't count the pennies, sir.'

And he was right. I have never regretted that investment, even if, when you think about it, the twopence might seem pointless. Everything in the book fascinated me: Kien's bibliomania, Therese's starched skirt, the improbable obsequiousness of the 'remarkable young man'. The *stars of heaven.* Fischerle the dwarf. And the burning of the library at the end: *He climbs up to the sixth step, looks down on the fire and waits. When the flames reached him at last, he laughed out loud, louder than he had ever laughed in all his life.* This time I had found a book by my own means. A book that owed nothing to the memory of my father, nor to the advice, however sensible, of Walpole. It was like going hunting alone for the first time and coming home with a memorable bag. For that reason, despite his mollusc's eyes and exorbitant prices, I will always have a special affection for MacAvoy, the gamekeeper of Dalkeith Road.

Among this 'prodigious' gallery of characters, one of the minor figures made a perhaps disproportionate impression on me: Kien's janitor in Ehrlichstrasse who had made a second peephole in his door at floor level and kept guard on his knees; for him 'the world consisted of skirts and trousers.' When I was by myself in the shop I thought of him when looking through the fanlight at the women passing by on the Royal Mile.

Winter was approaching, skirts were getting longer, legs were becoming sheathed in thicker stockings, but the spectacle of women passing was no less fascinating. On the contrary, there was something imperious in the way they suggested a curve, hinted at flesh. Sometimes they passed quickly in voluptuous arabesques of dark cloth which I would then patiently go through inside my head, like a film editor; sometimes they would stand there, insisting my eye pay tribute to them — in fact a newspaper vendor had his stand there and would keep the ladies waiting for a few seconds. Soon I could recognise a good number of the women from the neighbourhood — at least those who bought newspapers — from the curve of a muscle or the contours of an ankle: *The Times* reader with the fat calves covered in varicose veins; the one who preferred the *Edinburgh Daily* with the slim ankles of a star dancer. My heart would start to beat more quickly, or I would burst out laughing at my own ridiculousness. Kien's janitor couldn't have done it better.

'You are a wise man, Mr Krook.'

How long had Walpole been observing me? I forced a smile. 'Wise?'

'I spent seven thousand nights pressed up against my wife's body. I could write a book about her face, her smell, about the softness of her skin, the warmth of her thighs... but I would be absolutely incapable of describing her ankles! It's terrifying. My memory of my wife is crippled, it stops just above her knee. If she were to come back to life for a few hours, I think I would ask her to go out to the Royal Mile and buy every one of the newspapers — even the *Daily Record* — to give me time to observe, to record the details.'

'But she was yours, entirely.'

'Perhaps, only today I would be satisfied with her ankles alone.'

In the frame of the fanlight an elegant black dress appeared; a pitiless censor, it cut off half of the white, slightly chubby calves, but a simple effort of the imagination could follow the curve up to the soft, damp fold of flesh behind the knee.

'How many nights? How many nights would it take you to know these calves off by heart? Two? Three?'

'In my opinion she doesn't deserve more than two.'

'No more than that? If you say so. And that one there?'

'Too thin. That's not a leg, it's just geometry. Five nights, no more.'

'You're not very generous, my friend. You remind me of a customer who thought *Hamlet* was "not too bad, but a bit bombastic." What are you looking for? Something worthy of Phidias? Or that one, perhaps? I'm sure she'll read the sports pages.'

The girl was bouncing the strings of a badminton racket on her knee. We could hear the melancholy *bling* of the strings, like a flamenco chord, while the wind, busy underneath her skirt, revealed a forbidden expanse and sent shivers across the flesh.

'I'd go up to ten nights.'

'That's the idea, that's being more reasonable. Are you free tomorrow?'

'Er, yes, but…'

'No questions. It'll be a surprise. There's a place I'd like to show you. A place I love above all others. We'll pick you up about seven. In the meantime go home now and get some rest, there's not a soul about and you look like death warmed up. I want you on top form tomorrow.'

I hurried off, a little surprised at his proposal but welcoming the few hours of liberty that would allow me to go to MacAvoy's. However, when I got to Dalkeith Road I realised that in my haste I'd left my wallet by the cash register so I turned back.

The shop was closed but the light was on. That didn't surprise me, Walpole often had a nap in his armchair in the cubby-hole. Without making a sound, I used my own key, picked up my wallet and was about to leave again when I heard a voice from the cubby-hole.

'I wish you'd stop taking me for an idiot!'

It was Walpole, and I'd never heard him use that tone of voice. Not knowing what to do, I froze there, my hand on the door knob.

'It's two months now that I've been waiting patiently. I thought we were friends, I thought that eventually you'd tell me what it's all about. But today I'm asking you: who is Ebenezer? What do you two want with him?'

'Nothing he would object to, I swear.' I could hardly recognise

Lewis' voice, choked with emotion.

'So why all this secrecy?'

'Good God, Arthur, can't you keep out of all this.' This time it was Robin's voice, sullen, exasperated.

'Keep out of it? How can I? Tell me that, Robin. How can one not be concerned about other people? He's part of my life now.'

'The world isn't a bookshop, Arthur,' Robin went on after a silence. 'There are problems that are a bit more complicated than those of the American editions of Dickens.'

'Complicated in what way, for instance? In the same way as that unlikely story of the man dashing off and scattering books behind him. You can start by admitting it was *you*, Robin, who brought the book. At least that would be a start.'

'And then what?'

'Then it seems to me there's rather a lot of *Martin Eden* in this business... especially for someone who doesn't read books. He was already carrying a copy around in his blazer pocket.'

'Well, well! So you check your employees' pockets, do you?'

'And all at once another appeared as if by magic and Eby almost dropped dead. I *need* him, d'you hear?'

'Calm down, Arthur.'

'He's part of the bookshop... he *is* the bookshop.'

My heartbeat only returned to normal in Holyrood Park, as I approached the 'prodigious' bar. I needed a drink. But that Saturday evening the Dalkeith Bar was infested with happy workers celebrating their pay and bawling out drinking songs. I have never really understood how alcohol encourages people to sing; for a long time I even thought the expression 'drinking song' was a cliché used by writers of cheap novels.

That left MacAvoy's. For a bookseller going to another bookshop after a day at work can be a disorienting experience. There's something comforting, restful about being a spectator at the rituals you've just been performing on your own account, but at the same time these little everyday actions suddenly seem devoid of meaning. You find yourself in the situation of an adult who's watching a child piling wooden blocks one on top of the other and wondering whether he had ever derived pleasure from that himself. The assistant, flustered, close to tears, just managed a weak smile. Perched on a set of library steps like Walpole's she was pinning writers' portraits to the wall. From time to time MacAvoy would look up from his accounts and crucify her with a 'Farther left, Miss Douglas, farther left!' or an 'Oh, come on, that's not straight, not straight at all!' making the poor girl wobble. Jammed in between two bookcases, Burns and Scott looked equally unhappy with their fate: Burns' weary, effeminate face seemed to take no pleasure in his exalted position. As for Scott, frozen in his patrician attitude and casting envious glances at the door, he was visibly waiting for a good moment to take off his frock coat and stiff collar. More at ease in a rectangle of bare wall, Stevenson was contemplating the Pacific from his balcony in Vailima. But at the barked orders of Captain MacAvoy, Miss Douglas was gradually populating the ocean of white with undesirable sailors, all unknown to me: a little man with a disdainful air and round spectacles, trilby and striped tie; another with a beard, heavily built, head on one side as if that posture had the power to straighten out a sentence he was dissatisfied with.

'But the chronology, Miss Douglas, how many times must I tell you! Henry James has to go *before* James Joyce.'

'Yes, Mr MacAvoy,' said the assistant, who had stumbled back down one step under the impact.

Miss Douglas hesitated a long time over the next photo, turning it round and round as she looked for some indication of the date which, unfortunately for her, was not to be found. When she finally made up her mind where to put it, I took a step towards it, drawn by the lean, shining face, the strong nose, the manly moustache, the big ears standing out, the bony hands caressing the typewriter and, above all, by the calm, almost amused look watching me through the smoke of a cigarette.

'Who's that?' I managed to ask and the pulse at my temple started to pound and a taste of brine came into my mouth.

The girl shot me a look of pure terror, perhaps thinking that failure to answer my question would condemn her to a long Sunday pinning up photos. But MacAvoy, swapping his torturer's mask for that of amiable shopkeeper, had already jumped down from his stool.

'George Orwell, *sir*,' he said with a touch of polite surprise. 'Everyone's talking about *1984*, but it's not his best book, far from it, believe you me.'

The name did mean something to me, of course, but nothing had prepared me for *that name* together with *that face*. 'I, er... I think I've met someone who looks very much like him. A chap called... Eric Blair.'

MacAvoy, coming back with his arms full of books, gave me a hard stare before making up his mind: 'Ha, ha, ha! Very funny. Very funny indeed. I was sure you were having me on. Everyone knows George Orwell.'

Open-mouthed, wide-eyed, Miss Douglas watched us as if we were two lions ready to devour her, only held back by the question of who was to go first.

'He was right to choose Orwell. Blair really isn't a name for a writer. Look, we've got all of them... and this is my favourite: *Homage to Catalonia*. Magnificent... and only twelve and sixpence too.'

'Yes. I'll think about it.'

By chance there was another dive on the way back; a bit less prodigious, but still welcoming and one where the drunks seemed to share my views on drinking songs.

'I'm afraid we're going to have to go home soon,' one of them said every thirty seconds, without his resolve leading to any action whatsoever.

I managed to down three whiskies and two pints of stout at a speed worthy of Jesse Owens, then adopted the more reasonable pace of a Zatopek while another drunk, the spitting image of the former, kept winking at me from the other end of the bar and giving me knowing nods.

'That really was something, wasn't it, eh?' he kept repeating, smiling at the memory of adventures together that only existed in the depths of his glass.

When I tried to pay for my last drink the banknotes transformed themselves between my fingers into sticky flaky pastry and the coins on their own initiative started a game of tiddlywinks on the tiled floor. The barman's mouth hung open in disbelief for a good thirty seconds but the only audible sound that came out was '*Chleuch!*'

'I'm afraid we're going to have to go home soon.'

I was drunk, but not so drunk that I'd forgotten the lean face, the amused look. Eric Blair or George Orwell, after all, it didn't matter. I had always had just one name for him: the man from Jura.

PART TWO

THE MAN FROM JURA

CHAPTER VII

In which Mary Guthrie learns more about the Urquhart family.

17 November
Morning:
Ealing Earl of Chicago Easter Parade Eastman Eastmancolor Eau-de-vie Ebro Echo Eclipse Edgren Edit Eisenstein...
Afternoon:
XOOXXOXXOXOXXOXOOO. Nothing.
XOOXXOXXOXOXXOXOOX. Nothing.
I met Bruce in the park just now (for convenience's sake I continue to call the timid and vaguely pitiable version of the Bruce/Wallace duo "Bruce"). I heard him running after me on the gravel avenue.

'Miss Guthrie! Wait! I want to show you something.'

He was twisting a little white rain-hat in his hands.

'Would you do me the pleasure of... of putting this on? I had great difficulty finding it, it comes straight from Edinburgh.'

'Thank you, but I don't think it's going to rain today.'

"Bruce" frowned. 'The rain has nothing to do with it. It's Laura's hat.'

'Laura who?'

'Laura Hunt, of course. Haven't you seen *Laura* — the film?'

'Yes, but...'

'I think it will suit you very well. You really do look like the actress, like Gene Tierney.'

With a childish gesture he put the hat sideways on my head then took a step back to admire his handiwork. He was exultant. 'I knew it! It's perfect. Absolutely perfect. I'll order a raincoat to match.'

I burst out laughing, which clearly baffled him. 'You... You don't like it?'

'That's not the point. I don't look at all like that woman. She has brown hair, mine's ginger, her eyes are slightly slit, whereas mine...'

'Don't you know anything?' "Bruce" broke in. 'What does hair, what do eyes matter? What counts is that your face captures the light in the same way as hers, that in front of the camera you move in exactly the same way as she does...'

'The camera? There's no camera here? This isn't a film, it's reality.'

When I tried to give the hat back to him he shook his head vigorously. 'No, no, keep it. It's a present. For your work.'

He strode off but just as he was turning the corner of Sir Alexander's wing to get to the main courtyard, he shouted at me in a voice full of conviction, 'There's always a camera.'

When I reached the corner of the building I found myself face to face with "Wallace". Either "Bruce" had run quickly enough to disappear in the house, leaving a clear field to his twin, or he had done an about-turn, straightened his shoulders a little and assumed the superior air of "Wallace". In either case it was a performance put on specially for me.

"Wallace" smiled when he saw the hat I was holding. 'My God, it's dear Laura Hunt's hat! He is a lad, my brother! You've dethroned Gene Tierney, Miss Guthrie. You're the... the lady in his thoughts.'

The look "Wallace" gave me was much less platonic. With the gallantry of an old fop he offered me his arm which I accepted with repugnance — especially when Mr Par appeared at the end of the main avenue.

'It's odd how different two twins can be, isn't it? But you must have noticed that in reading our work. Our styles are completely different. And... how far have you got with my part?'

'To the letter E.'

'Ah yes, I like that passage, one of the best I've written.'

Letting go of my arm, he threw back his head, breathed in deeply and started to declaim in Byronian tones: 'Eastmancolor Eau-de-vie

Ebro Echo Eclipse Edgren Edit Eisenstein! Beautiful, isn't it?'

'I really couldn't say. I just type it out, that's all.'

'There's no point in belittling yourself, Miss Guthrie. Whether you like it or not, you're participating in...'

'I'm not participating in anything, my dear sir. I'm carrying out my side of a bargain in order to be able to pursue my research.'

"Wallace" flickered his eyelashes several times. 'My brother's right. Even angry you're irresistible.'

He'd already reached to top of the steps when he added, 'We will reward you despite yourself, Mary. That ridiculous hat's nothing. We're preparing a very, very lovely surprise for you.'

25 November.

Morning:

Tabarin Table Taboo Tashkent Tacitus Tahiti Talmadge Talmud Tamiroff Tanaka Tantalus Tarzan Taurog Taylor Elizabeth Taylor...

Afternoon:

XOOXXOXXOXOXXOXOXO. Nothing.

XOOXXOXXOXOXXOXOXX. *Click!*

I knew, even before closing the last drawer. I've learnt to recognise the tricks of the desk: the combination of the eleventh, for example, a series of ten Os — all in all just a long burst of laughter. And in the drawer a sixteenmo copy of Rabelais' *Gargantua* with Thomas Urquhart's seal and this sentence underlined (by Thomas or Alexander?): *Ponocrates et Eudémon s'esclaffèrent de rire tant profondément que en cuidèrent l'âme à Dieu.* ('Ponocrates and Eudemon burst out into such hearty laughter that they almost split themselves and rendered their souls unto God.')

I understood its limits as well, doubtless a result of technical demands. Never four Xs or four Os in succession. Its intestines: its soft sigh, the contented fart of the mechanism when all the drawers are in place apart from the penultimate one — when only *two* alternatives are left. At such times I get up and walk round the library with a feeling of exultation that I'm ashamed of fifteen minutes later, once the drawer has been opened and its meagre secret revealed.

Not that meagre, all the same. Alexander was far too subtle not to reward from time to time the slave enchained in his galley: a crust of bread here, a morsel of fat there. A photo of the 'treasure': a marquetry jewellery casket with the Urquhart coat of arms, its size unknown for want of anything to compare it with and a visiting card pinned to the photo: 'As you can see, it does exist!' A further volume of Rabelais: *Pantagruel* in the original edition of Claude Nourry (Lyons, 1532), apparently with Thomas' own notes. Pieces of advice, most often written on the headed notepaper of the Hotel Cavour, for example the following, found in the twelfth drawer: 'Ignore the next one, it's empty. Your friend A. U.' (The thirteenth was indeed empty, I wasted four days checking that out.) Or this in the fourteenth: 'To open the fifteenth drawer yoke the seven oxen.' The combination was:

OXOXOXOXOXOXOX.

Seven oxen, true, but I only cottoned on in retrospect.

As for the seventeenth, it did reveal an extraordinary document. In a short preface Sir Alexander tells us he found it in an antique shop in a pile of archives which were dispersed after the Great Fire of 1666. The edges of the document are slightly charred but the text remains readable and the writing corresponds without any possible doubt to the few extant samples of that of Thomas Urquhart — a letter to his father, a few dedications — I'd been able to find here and there.

The Prison of Windsor Castle, 4th August 1654.
To Oliver Cromwell, Lord Protector of England

My Lord,
As you will perhaps know if you take the least interest in the fate of your prisoners, the author of this letter has now been detained in your castle of Windsor for almost three years. Thirty-five months have passed since your captain of lancers, Sir George Appleby — a most courteous and refined gentleman whom I cannot recommend too warmly to you for

future advancement — accepted my sword on the battlefield of Worcester. For one thousand and sixty-three mornings now I have woken in this cramped, though very intimate, place you have most generously put at my disposal and which, without wanting to offend you in the least, I will call, for the sake of linguistic convenience, my 'cell'. As for the number of lungfuls of healthily chill and exquisitely damp air I have taken the liberty of withdrawing from Your Grace's atmospheric stock (on loan, of course!), it comes, I believe, to six thousand million five hundred and eighty-two thousand two hundred and thirty-three, assuming a rate of forty-two inhalations per minute.

I hope, my Lord, that you will excuse my innocent mania for arithmetical precision; in our family it is passed on from father to son and is at times of great service to me. It is thanks to that, for example, that the unprecedented absurdity of my presence in this cell and the extreme urgency of putting an end to it became clear to me. Please allow me to explain this point.

There are, as it seems to me, two reasons justifying the detention of a prisoner; let us examine them one after the other.

Firstly: the prospect of future improvement.

If it should be the case that Your Grace is acting on the basis of this laudable concern, then elementary honesty demands the following clarification: your humble correspondent will not 'improve'. The nature of my hostility has nothing 'political' about it — although, on reflection, the daily harvesting of heads does seem a rather summary manner of government. Now that, like a pawn captured by Your August Hand and placed on the side of the chessboard, I can examine from the distance of a simple observer the causes of this fratricidal strife and the vestiges of the war it triggered off, the whole business seems to me scarcely less derisory than a conflict of interest between a clothier and a

139

market gardener over a stall. If, for a few years, it managed to distract me from literature, then I apologise to Homer, Virgil, Pindar and, above all, to my dear Rabelais, invoking, in my defence, the oath I swore to my father on his deathbed to fight your faction to the last. To negotiate at all on this oath would be to fall into the most abject dishonour.

Would you be so good, therefore, as to cross out the first reason.

Secondly: the desire to avoid harm.

This argument seems to be based on a more solid foundation. But then, why squander your war chest on useless expenses? Why pay for the bread to feed me, the men to guard me? I see in that a lack of logic unworthy of your reputation; a lack of logic which, happily for the coffers of your young Commonwealth, I can remedy by the following means:

There is an old saying that the Urquharts' heads are well attached to their bodies. I have therefore, in consideration of the excessive labour to which your executioners are subjected, decided to spare them futile exertions and at the same time to relieve your purse. You will find enclosed the detailed plans for an apparatus of my own invention, the 'mechanical head-lopper' (I do not dare, after putting your patience to such a test, beg your leave to have the signal honour of calling it the 'Thomasette' or the 'Urquhartine') that your best engineers, if they follow my instructions scrupulously, will be able to construct in a few hours and for the modest outlay of around thirty guineas.

Below is a description of its operation in four phases (I would particularly draw Your Grace's attention to the appurtenances indicated by capital letters):

I. The condemned man kneels on two comfortable pieces of felt (A), at the same time placing his head on a cushion (B) of velvet or some other soft material, creating the optimum sense of well-being.

II. No external aid is needed to depress the button (C). A spring unwinds and thus releases the vertical carriage (D) holding the blade.

III. The carriage, impelled by the weight (E), rapidly slides down the grooves (F), tipping over on its way the bucket of soapy water (G). Thanks to this technical refinement, Your Grace's scaffolds will always be gleaming and hygienic, even under intensive use.

IV. The condemned man's head drops into the receptacle (H) and the flap (I) immediately closes over it in a hermetic seal. If necessary, a clerk can be stationed in the room and given some appropriate task to occupy him. With a little practice, and without having to look up from the paper, he will be able to mask the unpleasant noise of the decapitation and the inevitable subsequent gurglings by clearing his throat.

It goes without saying that a two-, three- or even four-person model could be devised in the event of a large-scale revolution.

I hope that, the above being to your satisfaction, nothing will now stand in the way of a swift and economic decision being taken concerning myself. However, if Your Grace is not entirely convinced by my invention, or if, all things considered, you should deem my immediate and unconditional release as even more profitable for the public purse, I would respectfully abide by your decision and leave with you, for your information and in humble recognition of my gratitude, the letters patent for the exploitation of my invention.

Please accept, my Lord, the complete subjection and blind devotion of the undersigned,

Thomas Urquhart of Cromarty, Knight.

For more than a week I was jubilant, I neglected the desk and took page after page of notes. I'd started my thesis — at last! For the first time I had laid hands on an original document, and on one of undeniable literary and historical importance at that, even if it seemed highly unlikely that the man to whom it was addressed — Cromwell — had ever read it. The Urquhart it reveals seems far removed from the fanatical Jacobite described in the *Encyclopaedia of Scottish Literature:* his commitment to the 'cause' becomes an expression of filial piety, his passion for literature is reaffirmed and his baroque sense of humour illustrated in the most extravagant way. This also makes him much more 'modern' and also much more likeable in my eyes, without entirely killing off the hypothesis of the existence of the famous treasure, given the extent to which he seems capable of keeping several existences going, of taking several different lines at the same time.

Then, one morning, I woke with a bizarre feeling, close to hunger. I dropped my notes, the image of Sir Thomas vanished, as if swallowed up in the mist, and the desk was once more the central feature of the landscape.

29th November.
Click!

The nineteenth drawer opens. Another letter but in his handwriting this time. Whatever happens he's already won: I've forgotten Krook, Thomas, André Borel, my future academic career. All my thoughts are now concentrated on the desk. And on him, Alexander.

Dear Friend or Foe,

The complicity that ties us one to the other justifies, I believe, my henceforth calling you 'my dear'. Moreover, I know you better than you think. I know, for example, that you're not my cretin of a brother — he's not intelligent enough, nor patient enough either. The lure of profit will have curdled the little that's left of his brain. No, you are of a different calibre. A sort of artist. Yes, you practise art for art's sake. If I dared...

If I dared I would venture a guess: you are a woman! No man would have got this far. No man would have understood

142

me in this way.

The sensitivity, the determination, the… precision of a woman. You possess them and I — I possess you. You will be my thousandth woman. I have kept count since I was young and if it occasionally (often) happened that I had recourse to the services of men, it was faute de mieux, just as the Papists eat fish on a Friday. A thousand, do you hear? No possible mistake. I checked the sum last week: 998 so I had the nine hundred and ninety-ninth sent from a hovel in Cromarty; and despite the illness that is eating away at me, I fucked her as vigorously as the first. What? You don't believe me? Look, I got her to write her name at the bottom of the page:

Helen Wick

And you, my beloved, my thousandth? Will you write your name underneath hers?

PS No clues today. The love I show you is sufficient unto itself, don't you think?

PPS If, despite everything, you are a man, you should know that you bear the number 113 on your back. A pretty awful number, but a prime number at least!

I've started shivering again. Excitement? Disgust? It doesn't matter. I'm thinking of the twentieth drawer. Of the book that's being written bit by bit in side my head.

30th November

Last night I dreamt of André Borel. We were having dinner in a smart restaurant in Princes Street. The waiter looked a bit like Mr Par, though he was exquisitely polite and had no limp. Looking out of the window I saw an enormous telescope focused on us.

'Come now, Miss Guthrie, surely you're not going to inflict that hybrid and hypocritical genre, the private diary, on us? (I know what that is, I keep one myself: *The Diary of André Borel*, in five volumes, you can see that from here.) If you want to write, Mary, don't be afraid of fiction. Tell a story, for God's sake! Remember the dogs of Breacan. You had no complexes then. Be bold, for God's sake. So start by telling us what happened on 9 September, your second day at Cromarty House.'

Hardly had I woken up that I set to work. Here is the result, with no alterations and no corrections:

After I'd seen the apparition there, right in the middle of the courtyard, I couldn't get back to sleep. A little before seven, in the half-light, I went down the main staircase that the rain during the night had made dangerously slippery. Everything was quiet in the hall and in the corridor with the abandoned rooms; but there was light at the end, under the drawing-room door. Pressing my ear to the door, I could hear mutterings and the rustle of pages being turned.

As always, Sir James was wearing his smoking jacket, his scarf and his ridiculous nightcap; he seemed to have spent a good part of the night surrounded by his dictionaries, two of which lay open before him while the others formed unstable pillars on his desk. The French window was open. The smell of humus and rotting leaves mingled with the coffee of which Sir James, sliding over on his slippers with the kind of weary attentiveness that was characteristic of him, poured out a cup for me.

'Miss Guthrie! I am pleased to see you, even though I was hoping it would be Miss Birdie, that little Miss Know-all. She's been getting on my nerves with her Macabees. "There's just one c, Sir James, believe me." I knew very well it could be written with *two*. Look, there: *Maccabees*. Do you take sugar?'

'No thank you.'

He seemed delighted with my reply: 'You're right, it spoils the taste.'

He hesitated a moment, then asked, 'A little milk?'

'No milk either.'

'Excellent! It's not that I'm stingy, mind you, but…'

'Something happened, last night.'

Immediately his smile disappeared. He closed the dictionaries and stared into space for a moment. 'You've seen Sir Thomas, haven't you?'

'Everyone in the house seems to take me for an idiot, Sir James, but I can assure you that I don't believe in ghosts.'

'No, no, it's not *that* Sir Thomas I'm talking about, it's…

There was a creak of floorboards out in the corridor. Urquhart left his sentence unfinished and placed his finger to his lips.

He led me out into the garden. It was the first time I'd been at the back of the house. The feeble efforts at maintaining the park had been restricted to the immediate surroundings of the building; after thirty yards the avenue disappeared in a wasteland of random bushes, nettles and tall bracken. Despite his slippers, Sir James set a pretty good pace, his finger still on his lips. On the right I recognised a huge old oak tree with a vaguely human shape that I'd seen in one of Miss Birdie's sketches the previous day, while on the left, between two rows of silver birches which seemed to indicate a track suitable for vehicles, there appeared a dilapidated wooden structure towards which we were heading. At the door, of which the wood had half rotted away, Sir James, with much puffing and panting, raised the heavy bar and we went into the former stables of the estate. The partitions separating the stalls had collapsed but there was still a faint smell of horse dung.

I followed him up the ladder to the hayloft. 'We'll be undisturbed here.'

I recognised the place. It was where the obscene photo of Urquhart and the ginger-haired girl had been taken. The first rays of the sun were shining in through the gaps in the roof onto a pile of hay with a pitchfork stuck in it.

'We often used to come and play up here when we were children. One day he made me go up first then took the ladder away. I had to promise something or other before he put it back.'

Sir James sighed and dropped down heavily on the hay. 'I've

already mentioned our genetic peculiarities, Miss Guthrie. There's one that appears in almost every generation… Thomas is my brother. My twin brother. The father of Bruce and Wallace.'

'He… he lives in the house?'

'Good Lord, no! I wouldn't stand for that. But he comes and goes as he sees fit. Almost all the great houses in Scotland are riddled with underground rooms and secret passages going back to the days of the Civil War, the Covenanters and the great religious conflicts. He enters, he leaves, he disappears for months on end. I've never seen him from close to but I've often sensed his… presence'

'And why the disguise?'

Sir James gave a sarcastic grin. 'Perhaps he has spies here? Whether he has or not, he has certainly heard of your arrival and he's come and put on his little show. He always thought the claymore suited him and that his namesake, Thomas Urquhart, was the paragon of the family virtues, in other words arrogance, extravagance, obscenity! I presume you've read *The Master of Ballantrae*? It's his favourite book. When he was a child he always wanted us to be fighting duels, like the two Durie brothers of Durrisdeer. I was Henry, dull, boring legitimist Henry, while he, of course, was James — ironic, isn't it? James the seducer, James the rebel, flamboyant, intrepid James. He would wake me up at night, drag me off here and light candles, just as in the novel. Then we would fight with my father's old golf clubs. He always won: "There, I have you, vile traitor in the pay of the Hanoverians! Long live Bonnie Prince Charlie!" Once a candle overturned, setting the hay on fire. We only just managed to escape. Thomas got a stable lad blamed for it. My brother is not so much a man as a… fiend! Look, it's to him I owe *this* (he held out his shortened finger). A stupid game he invented: one of us had to place his hand on the table, the other to drive a knife as deeply as possible into the table between the outspread fingers. When it happened he burst out laughing. "It's your own fault, you coward. You moved!" My parents always thought I'd injured myself cutting bread. By the way, did you know that Stevenson named his characters in honour of his friend, Henry James? I read that in the *Britannica*…'

The glorious memory of this discovery wrung a smile from him. Then he rose and started to pace up and down the loft, scattering wisps of hay with his feet.

'He was my parents' favourite. Intelligent. Brilliant. He didn't need to work to succeed. Only he wasn't interested in studying. I took the exams in his name. I also took the strokes of the cane... but the worst thing, the worst, was with women. They literally fell into his arms. Attracted by anything that glitters, aren't they? And then from time to time, when he tired of this one or that he... he asked me to take his place! "We both profit from it, my dear James. I look after my reputation and you — you learn a thing or two." '

I could see James's pathetic expression in the photo; his white buttocks — two half-deflated footballs — wedged between the girl's thighs; the tendons of his neck sticking out as he turned towards the camera. Thomas had doubtless taken up position at the top of the ladder: 'Don't move!' The flash had frozen the models in a pose from a blue movie while the photographer, hidden by a curtain of light, enjoyed the joke.

'But what made you do all that?'

Sir James aimed a furious kick at the pile of hay. A mouse shot out and he jumped back to avoid it. Carefully readjusting his nightcap, he shook his head with an obtuse expression, like a baby refusing a spoonful of porridge.

'You can't know... you've no idea of the power of the man, even our parents were in thrall to him. When they died, we inherited the estate jointly: I got the paperwork, the account books, the lawsuits with our neighbours and tenant farmers, while he had the parties, the pretty women, the champagne, the hunts... in less than three years we were ruined. "Don't worry, my friend."— He always called me that and I hated it. —"Don't worry, my friend, I'll take things in hand. We just have to find good old Thomas' nest egg and that'll be that!" I was horrified, of course...'

'Why?'

'Because while we were young our mother and father kept warning us again and again against the false hopes aroused by the notorious treasure. They told us how grandfather Stephen, Alexander's brother, had shut himself away with the desk for fifteen years, how he had gradually gone mad to the point where he scratched the thirty-two drawers of the desk on his chest with a razor blade. In the Inverness clinic, where he ended his days, he would implore the doctors and nurses: "The combination! Give me the combination! *Open me! Open me, for pity's sake.*" But Thomas took no notice of that. "Stephen was a sick man, one of the poor in spirit. I will proceed *scientifically.*" Scientifically! Huh! He sold our mother's jewels, the best pieces of furniture. He had a whole library of useless books on statistics, secret codes, clockwork mechanisms sent from all over Europe. I hardly saw him for three months. He was never out of the library, he'd moved into your room "to save time" as he said. Then one night I was woken by an infernal racket — I'll never forget the moment. At the time we still had six or seven servants and I was sleeping in one of the fine bedrooms on the first floor. I went down. Everyone was there in the great hall, in their pyjamas and nightcaps. He'd taken down the portraits of Thomas and Alexander and was attacking them furiously with a penknife, stamping on them, screaming, "Bastards! Scumbags!" and a stream of even worse abuse I'll spare you. I was told that shortly before that he'd tried to blast the desk open with gunpowder, to no effect, fortunately… or perhaps unfortunately…'

Sir James gave me an odd look.

'When I came down the next morning, he was fresh as a daisy, devouring his breakfast with a hearty appetite. "Working indoors doesn't suit me," he said, his mouth full. "And this grotty estate's too small for a man of my calibre. It's… it's on your scale, my friend. So I've made a decision: I'm going to go round the world." "With what money?" I immediately retorted. "Huh! Money's no problem. I'll easily find an opportunity to employ my talents. Travel writing, for example: India, Africa, America… the wide-open spaces, my friend. Or perhaps…" His eye had just fallen on yesterday's newspaper and he abruptly stopped eating. "Or perhaps a war… yes, a jolly old war. The Urquharts have always had a special talent for warfare. Give me a coin." He wanted to copy his hero, James Durie, and let his life depend on the toss of a coin. "Oh, good old Ballantrae: *I know no better way to express my scorn of human reason.* Heads I go, tails I stay." It was heads.'

'But what war?'

'It was 1936. Everyone was talking about nothing but the events in Spain.'

I had a funny feeling, a little as if I'd found the same improbable phrase from the pen of two different writers.

'The next morning he set off for Edinburgh in great style: "Squire, prepare my armour, saddle my charger." His charger was our father's old Daimler which, moreover, broke down before he was even out of Cromarty. Since then he's never set foot in the house again... at least officially. In eighteen years he's only ever written to me twice — to ask for money, of course. The first time was in '37. He was still in Spain then, but things were going badly for him, it seemed. He wanted to come home. I managed to send him a money order for a hundred pounds. What he did with it, the devil only knows. The second time was from Stuttgart, via a vague acquaintance in Zurich...'

'Stuttgart?'

'Yes, in March 1945. Perhaps he'd tossed his coin again. But then again things were going badly. Then again he wanted to come home. I didn't reply.'

Sir James fixed his gaze on the mouse that had reappeared in a corner.

'And the mother of the twins?'

'A poor chambermaid he got rid of soon after she'd given birth. Eagle brought up Bruce and Wallace as best she could. They weren't even eight when Thomas left. I've done what I believed it was my duty to do for them...'

'Do you think they're in contact with their father?'

Seizing the fork, he made as if to harpoon the mouse that had no difficulty taking cover.

'As you can see, Miss Guthrie, I'm not master in my own house.

The twins do not take me into their confidence and other things escape me as well. I have to be on my guard against everyone here. And when you turned up, for example…'

He didn't finish the sentence and lowered his head with a guilty look.

'When I turned up…'

'You… you must understand my situation, my dear. Since the end of the war many people have been seen lurking around here. Doubtless they were looking for Thomas, they'll have wanted to get even with him. God knows what dirt… what nasty tricks he can have got up to. I thought that perhaps you were…'

Sir James raised his hand, like tennis players when they're not ready.

'Just a moment… Stuttgart: how many 't's in your opinion?'

Then there was that astounding moment: with a speed and skill I would never have believed him capable of, he threw the fork and pinned the mouse, that had just stuck its nose out, to the worm-eaten floor. Then he left me, too, rooted to the spot in that sordid loft: without a word he nimbly shot down the ladder and disappeared, muttering something about a dictionary. I could hear the *slurp slurp* of his slippers as he trudged through the mud on the track.

15th December

I'll never get there.

Of course I've always known that: the numbers remind me of it every day. But I was carried along by that blissful optimism with which only children and idiots — those who have no fear of either time or death — can start without a shudder on a jigsaw puzzle with several thousand pieces.

Yet I have worked out a rigorous system, an unvarying sequence of openings and closings which takes account of everything I have observed and which allows me to try more than one thousand five hundred combinations a day. So far luck has smiled on me: success has come at the beginning of the sequences without my needing to try more than a third of the combinations. But it's not like that for the twentieth drawer. The twentieth drawer is resisting. Thirty-five thousand attempts out of fifty-two thousand possibilities and still nothing. Will it be like this with all the drawers from now on? Am I going to end up like Stephen Urquhart? Do I have to go in search of a sharp knife already (I visualise with horror mixed with curiosity the course of the blade across my chest, the blood running down my skin patterned with rectangles) and reserve a bed in some psychiatric clinic? *Open me! Open me!*

I'm giving myself ten days for this drawer, not one more. But my determination is false from the very beginning. Even in the worst case, ten days should be enough. Then there'll be that stupid, sickening rejoicing at the component interlocking; that tiny victory over the passing of time. And I will not rest until the next component interlocks in its turn.

I don't like Miss Foyle. Miss Foyle doesn't like me. Despite that, we've got into the habit of meeting in her room once or twice a week; the reason is the same as the one that makes us doodle on a blank sheet of paper when we've nothing better to do. Sometimes our exasperation is such that the point of the pencil tears the paper but if someone were to snatch the piece of paper away from us it would be even worse.

I particularly remember our cup of tea together on Halloween. Like the first time I visited her, it was pouring down and she didn't move from her bed, just waved her chin in the general direction of the teapot.

'There's something I don't understand Miss... Foyle.'

'Barbara,' she said with ironic courtesy.

'What is your precise function here? I've never seen you working.'

'I work... at night. I try to bring a little order to this madhouse. I pay the wages and the bills... when our account's in the black. Every Wednesday I try to cajole the cleaning lady into coming back next week. The worst part is having to put up with Sir James and his lexical sparring.'

'But why give up your thesis?'

'Oh, yes, my *thesis*…'

She repeated the word in a slightly surprised tone, as if it were the name of a dance that had gone out of fashion with Beau Brummell or a species of cockroach extinct since the Pleistocene. Then, looking at me over the rim of her steaming cup: 'How's Borel?'

'I haven't heard from him for some time.'

'Did you sleep with him?'

'Did you?'

Miss Foyle shrugged her shoulders. 'Anyway, it's of no consequence,' she said, opening her sketchbook. 'Would you like to see my latest drawings?'

Another tree, even more tortured than the previous ones. Its two high, long thin branches were raised up to the sky in a parody of prayer while the lower ones were twisting round the trunk in a desperate attempt at autostrangulation. The loft of the old barn — a recent sketch since the pitchfork was still in the precise place Sir James had sent it before my very eyes. And then the portrait. As on the photos in the desk, Sir Thomas was extraordinarily like his brother but even more like his ancestral namesake as he was portrayed on the cover of his *Ekskubalauron* — minus the moustache. Hardly showing his years, while Sir James was already approaching old age, he had everything his brother lacked: strength, virility, determination. His upper lip, sightly raised, revealed powerful teeth, greedy, ready to bite while his eyes shone with a kind of calm fury.

Miss Foyle had sat up, observing my reaction. I put the sketchbook down and remarked cautiously, 'You must have seen the ghost from close to.'

'The ghost from close to! Little ninny!' And she laughed in my face.

18th December.
Click! The twentieth drawer. At last.

Flushing, the United Provinces, 8th June 1660.

My Very Dear James Braco,

It is with very great regret that I have to inform you that your friend Sir Thomas Urquhart, Sheriff of Cromarty, is no more; his soul departed yesterday evening in the most extraordinary circumstances that you will hear of below. Knowing that I am under surveillance and not wanting to compromise you through an untimely visit...

I am not a specialist in ancient manuscripts, but I think that these first lines of a letter, carefully cut out across the page, are authentic. Time has faded the black ink, the paper is yellowed, crumbling like a biscuit. The date of 8 June 1660 is shortly after the return of Charles II to England and the restoration of the monarchy, thus corresponding more or less to the date legend gives for the death of Sir Thomas. As for the addressee, James Braco, he is none other than the neighbour of Urquhart to whom his translation of Rabelais was given for safe keeping.

For perhaps the tenth time since my arrival at Urquhart House, I unpack my suitcase. Then I take out my index cards and my pencil.

I make a start on the twenty-first drawer.

23rd December.

'At least you could write to your father from time to time. He's no idea where you are.'

The crackling on the line is like a sizzling cauldron of fat and Aunt Catriona's voice a large metallic fish swimming through it; even so, she seems capable of following all my doings. All at once a multitude of metaphorical microscopes and telescopes are aimed at me. The Cromarty Arms is empty, but walking round the village just now I *really* did have the impression I was being followed.

'OK. I'll write tomorrow. Any letters?'

'A telephone call. Mr Barrel.'

'Borel.'

'You are to contact him immediately.'

My old aunt gives a little suggestive laugh and then goes on, 'Such a terribly *polite* man, isn't he?'

While the operator's putting me through to Borel, I order a beer from the scrawny barman. Across the road, in the Courthouse Museum's souvenir shop, the warden is practising her cover drive; through the other window a piece of Thomas Urquhart's wig can be seen

'Is that you, Mary? I was beginning to get worried.'

I can't remember us being on first name terms. It irritates me a bit. On the other hand he sounds genuinely pleased to hear from me and that's not so unpleasant after three months in Urquhart House.

'Doubtless you're very taken up with your research... but you mustn't forget that the University's like a train and I'm the inspector. You have to show me your ticket from time to time. I've managed to get them to agree to your absence but I'd be truly sorry if you were to lose your bursary.'

There again he sounds sincere. I try to imagine him lying back in his armchair, fountain pen in his hand, drifting voluptuously in a cloud of smoke, or sprawled out on the sofa amid piles of students' work. Perhaps with an old number of *Les Temps modernes* or the *Nouvelle revue française* under a cushion. Suddenly his bohemianism, which I had adjudged a sham, his offhand way of playing with ideas and theories as if they were children's building blocks, seem almost enviable. I don't really entirely belong to the world of André Borel, but is that a reason to live the life of a recluse in that of Bruce and Wallace?

'How far have you got?'

'Not very far. I'm making notes. Accumulating documents.'

'Good, good. But don't accumulate too many. You have to be able to stand back and have an overall view of your material. How are our lairds? Picturesque?'

'They don't wear the kilt, if that's what you mean.'

'But are they cooperative?'

'Sufficiently.'

'And the treasure?'

'Forget it. It's a legend.'

He remains silent for a moment and in my mind's eye I can see his handsome peasant's hand rummaging through the depths of the sofa in search of a packet of cigarettes.

'Pity. But I do need something, Mary. Not much. A plan. An outline of your approach. You see what I'm getting at?'

'Yes, more or less. Four or five pages full of Roman numerals and small letters — Ia, Ib, IIa etc — that no one will read and that I'll ignore completely when I come to write my thesis.'

'Exactly! You'll make a good academic. Send me that by next week and I promise you the inspector won't come round again before Easter.'

I was just about to tell him about Miss Foyle when he suddenly went on: 'By the way, I've found your Friar John of the Funnels.'

'Who?'

'Your priest. Krook. But he doesn't wear a cassock any more, he's thrown it away... or left it in some disreputable place. My colleague Mackenzie knows the Bishop of Edinburgh a bit. The business caused quite a stir among the Holy Joes. I heard talk about something *truly* Rabelaisian, a young parishioner dishonoured...'— His discreet clearing of the throat doubtless meant: I know perfectly well who the young parishioner in question is but I'm far too well-brought-up to mention her name. —'...a nocturnal visit to the Bishop of Oban, a brawl — magnificent! By now all the well-informed free-thinkers of the city swear by Walpole's bookshop. He's been working there since September.'

'Since September?' I babbled.

'Yes. The place is on the way to becoming fashionable. If Sartre were to come to Edinburgh, he'd make a detour to Anchor Close. By my troth, there's a strange fellow for you — a sort of grizzly bear in a country priest's mufti. An antediluvian mop of hair! And that unlikely ring! Perhaps he robbed his bishop's corpse to get it. It's odd, when I mentioned you to him, he pretended he didn't know you.'

'Did he? Oh, I'm sorry, I've run out of change, I'm going to have to hang up.'

It took me a good quarter of an hour to digest that conversation. The barman was listening to a speech by the Prime Minister on the radio. The warden of the Museum gathered her things together and went round the rooms, putting out the lights behind her. Then, without warning, Church Street was inundated with a downpour and soaked passers-by rushed into the pub. Just one man stayed outside, his back against the window. I felt I recognised the black overcoat, the bald head and the imposing bulk of Mr Par.

5th January

This time I was lucky. *Only* nineteen thousand combinations out of a hundred and four thousand possible ones. It's come to the point where I'm giving each drawer a face and a character of its own. The twentieth, for example, was an awful egoist with furrowed brow and thin lips, like those people who hog telephone kiosks for hours on end and refuse to give up their seats to pregnant women on the bus. But the twenty-first is cast in a different mould. Like one of Trollope's clergymen, it has bushy side whiskers, a round head, an impish, kindly look. It resisted for a moment, out of principle, but you could tell that, deep down inside, it just wanted to please. I stroked it a little to thank it.

The wind is shaking the loose slates and playing with Miss Birdies's scarf as she heads east, sketchbook in hand. A rash outing: the heavy clouds gathering over the sea seem to be just waiting for a sign to drop their load. December was even wetter than November. On Christmas Eve I went for a long walk as far as Chanonry Point, wearing Laura Hunt's hat for the first time; but the dolphins, perhaps put off by the storm, did not put in an appearance. On the library ceiling, Australia is getting a bit bigger every day, turning into a monstrous grey mass, not unlike the primitive agglomerate which, according to geologists, occupied the centre of the globe before continental drift started.

The twenty-first drawer is smiling benignly. It contains a message on plain unheaded notepaper and a fat, sealed envelope. I start with the message.

My Thousandth,

How I would love to be able to tell you that your quest is nearing its end. That, after days and days navigating the briny ocean of my madness, the port can be sighted in the telescope, a distant prospect still, but so sweet to the mariner's eye when his three-master has its sails furled like so many palimpsests, the girls are on shore to greet him in their finest attire, the rum flows in the taverns and the eyes of the fish on the market stall contemplate the void with a sceptical look.

Twenty-one drawers! Twenty-one out of thirty-two! At first sight an encouraging result, the cruise has got off to a most auspicious start; if you allow yourself to dream a little you can imagine you have rounded the Cape of Doubt, crossed the Bay of Boredom, overcome the Roaring Forties of rebellion ... Alas, if you count the number of combinations that remain you have only accomplished, my Thousandth, the thousandth part of the course. And if we compare your journey to that taken by that nitwit David Copperfield from London to Dover, which my mother inflicted on us evening after evening (perhaps thinking she might arouse in me some unlikely sympathy for human suffering), you're still wandering somewhere in the outskirts of modern Babylon.

Let us try to see things differently. Haven't you enjoyed yourself on the bridge? Inhaled the invigorating air of the open sea? Seen killer whales and dolphins? Passed the most splendid ensigns? No? Then it's your own fault. What is it other than life itself? A journey the destination of which obsesses us, a gigantic shadow between us and the beauty of the world, like that of the scaffold preventing the condemned man from seeing the flower growing between the stones of his dungeon cell and the bird soaring above the watchtower.

But enough! Let us put an end to this torture.

Let me tell you that I have just lied to you — oh, just a little

*lover's teasing. You must know that the twenty-first drawer is
not like the rest, it is a kind of fierce doorkeeper guarding
the delightful hell where I await you... for henceforward
all the others, like hounds obeying the leader of the pack,
have drawn in their fangs. You can open them however you
like with your lily-white hands. All of them, except the most
obstinate — the last one!*

I check that as fast as I can. This time Alexander is telling the truth.
As if released from a spell, the remaining drawers slide out one after
the other, down to the thirty-first. All empty. All that is left is the
thirty-second — only two million possible combinations.

'Thanks for the present,' I mutter.

*But there is more to come! No present is too good for you.
Close all the drawers except the first, the tenth, the twentieth
and the thirtieth. The door separating the living from the
dead will open before your eyes. Then, arise and walk. Come
and join me, but not before first reading the contents of the
enclosed envelope which will probably be of great assistance
to you in your journey to Hell!*

See you soon, my Thousandth.

Your devoted Alexander Urquhart.

CHAPTER VIII

Krook's narrative.

'It's extraordinary, isn't it? I mean that we're here, all four of us, in this car — exactly all four of us, you understand? All four of us among several million individuals, at this precise moment, at this precise place on the road... But on the other hand, it's not as extraordinary as all that, I mean if that's extraordinary, then *everything* is extraordinary, every moment, every second, every circumstance... It's like... in poker, for example...'

Lewis Rosewall was clutching the steering wheel rather like a little boy in a brand-new pedal car. He was concentrating so hard he forgot the accelerator for a few seconds, so that the Morris would have simply come to a halt at the side of the road if Robin hadn't stepped in. He squashed the driver's foot down, forcing the ancient machine into a wild swerve that didn't go with its venerable age.

'In poker you go into raptures when you get four aces and a king in the first deal... but you ought to go into raptures for a seven, an eight, a ten, a jack and a king. Are you with me? Mathematically every combination is equally improbable... or probable, if you prefer; we're constant witnesses to these miracles which pass unnoticed, which don't seem extraordinary to us for the simple and unsatisfactory reason that we've decided once and for all what is extraordinary and what isn't.'

Robin rummaged through the glove compartment and unearthed an old packet of cigarettes: 'Do you know what would be *really* extraordinary, Lewis? If someone could explain to me why you start spouting this homespun philosophy the moment you get your hands on a steering wheel.'

159

The discussion I'd overheard the previous evening seemed to have left no trace on Lewis and Walpole. Robin, for his part, was in a more morose mood.

'Stop arguing. Look at the countryside instead.' Walpole had pulled his head back in for a brief moment then stuck it out of the window again. The wind was whipping his face; the sun, still a little pale but already warm for an autumn morning, was gleaming on his tortoiseshell frames. After the dreary suburbs of Loanhead and Penicuik — where people in their Sunday best and on their way to church seemed to be taking part in a boredom contest which only lacked judges and numbers on their backs — the first hills of the Southern Uplands appeared, a distant mauve at first, then an intense green stippled with shadow, the meadows and woods brightening then darkening in turn as we approached. Since the little town of Peebles (there the boredom contest seemed over already; little groups were discussing the results in earnest confabulation) we had been driving along the Tweed towards Galashiels at the languid pace of the Morris; Walpole went into raptures over every stone bridge, over every successive view, over the shadows of the clouds standing out in wide stripes of dark on the horizon, over various details he pointed out to us: a fern, a fence that looked like an ornamental capital, a flock charging down a slope, white and black balls tumbling down a green baize cloth, the newly shorn sheep like bleating skeletons and others whose thick fleeces rippled like baggy clothes.

Shortly after Melrose, the car slowed down again, a sign that the driver was thinking. 'We need to take the Dryburgh road, don't we?'

Robin raised his eyes to heaven. 'For God's sake, Lewis, don't tell me you're lost again?'

'Help me instead of getting worked up.'

'Certainly not! You know that I hate cars, maps, routes and country roads. I prefer the train; then at least you know exactly where it's starting from and where it's going to.'

'So what are you doing here?'

We continued at a snail's pace for a while longer. At every crossroads Lewis frantically checked the map under Robin's sarcastic eye. Finally Walpole pulled his head back in: 'Left now, Lewis. Then right, by the big oak tree, then right again.'

'But where exactly are we going?' I finally ventured to ask.

'Ah, that's the problem,' Robin said. 'We're going to an imaginary place, a... a view you see with your mind's eye. Or, to put it another way: to a place with nothing to distinguish it from any other except for the celebrated gaze of a celebrated personage that once rested on it.'

'Scott's View,' Walpole said simply. 'A panorama Walter Scott was fond of. Whenever he passed the place on his journeys to and from Abbotsford, he would give his horse a rest there and have a cold collation himself. The story goes that on the day of his funeral the horse that was pulling the hearse stopped there out of habit.'

'We're there!' Lewis almost shouted for joy. He slammed on the brakes so abruptly the Morris nearly ended up across the middle of the road, but by some miracle or other he managed to get it onto the verge, not without flattening some splendid bracken. At our feet the Tweed, having been joined by the Yarrow and the Ettrick, had calmed down, like a mother who has found her children. To the west the Eildon Hills, three bare peaks, their slopes covered in heather, were trying in vain to catch the clouds. It was quite late in the morning by now, it had taken over three hours to go fifty miles.

Lewis took the picnic basket out of the boot. We crossed the road and headed for a little field below, but just as we were going through the gate, Walpole gestured to me and hurried off.

'You're sure it's *exactly* here?' Robin mocked, lying down on the meadow with a blade of grass between his lips. 'Might it not be down there, beyond that rock... or more to the left, in the middle of the field? Now let's see, what would a great and fabulously rich writer from the early nineteenth century eat? Chicken, perhaps, or some rabbit? If we excavate a bit we might find some of the celebrated Sir Walter Scott's leftovers.'

Ignoring his mockery, Lewis pointed down into the valley. 'Old Melrose Abbey was down there, beside the Tweed.'

'But there's not a stone left,' Robin chuckled.

'And there was a Roman encampment somewhere near the Eildon Hills.'

'Not a stone left there, either. Anyway, it would have been made of wood. Nought out of twenty as far as historical interest is concerned.'

'You need a drink, Robin. Sober you're just a wet blanket.

'Good idea,' he replied.

He searched through the basket, took out a bottle of whisky and had a good swig. Then he lay down for a little nap. Lewis looked at him for a moment without saying anything before continuing his inventory of the picnic. Shaken about by the potholes on the roads and Lewis's braking style, the cheese sandwiches looked like lumps of orange and white Plasticine.

'Dammit, the hard-boiled eggs must have fallen out into the boot.'

'I'll go and get them,' I said.

Not unhappy to be left to myself, I went back across the road without hurrying. The eggs had been squashed underneath a box of unsold books that Lewis had been lugging around for more than ten years. As I was closing the boot, I noticed Robin's jacket on the rear seat with his little black notebook sticking out of one pocket. Without thinking, I got in the car and took the notebook.

Robin's writing always made me think of tadpoles or hair swept into a corner of the barber's. On the first four or five pages all I could make out were a few names of rugby players, but farther on things changed. No more lapidary notes, no more mysterious exclamations following a match score and preceding a large empty space, doubtless intended for subsequent comments. The lines started to form a single block of text and Robin had written the letters carefully, clearly intending them to be read by someone else. After a quick glance to check that he was still lying down on the grass beside Lewis, I skimmed through a few lines. Some words were repeated: 'war', 'Fascists', 'trench', 'Huesca'. Some names as well: Urquhart, Scott, Eric. 'Eric had written some books…' 'Scott was in the war, the Great War, I mean; a piece of shrapnel had smashed his left foot…'

'Urquhart, Thomas Urquhart of Cromarty. Delighted to make your acquaintance, old chap.' I couldn't concentrate enough to read longer passages. My eyes remained fixed on the notebook, but at the same time they kept jumping from one line to another, as if contact with the page were making them smart. Then the words 'Martin Eden' appeared and a shadow blocked out the sun.

' "Time travels in divers paces with divers persons," Comrade,' Robin quoted as he opened the door.

I blushed with shame as he gently took the notebook out of my hands. 'The advantage of Shakespeare is that he has a quotation for any situation. That's why I like the chap. No need to go looking anywhere else. It's like doing your own repairs: what's the point of buying four different-sized spanners when you can get a universal one.'

He blinked as he looked at me; a dog-end between his lips moved grudgingly aside to let the words pass. 'You heard us yesterday, didn't you? Arthur had double-locked the door, you only turned the key once when you left. But what exactly did you hear?'

'Not much. Just that you were arguing.'

'All the better. I'm working for you, you know? It's not easy to remember… especially when you've spent more than fifteen years trying to forget. And writing's even more difficult, it means you're trying to make something solid out of smoke. I don't much like solid stuff, liquid's what I prefer. But I'm getting there, it'll all be down on paper in black and white. You'll only have to wait a few more days.'

He flicked the dog-end across the tarmac. 'And then, Comrade, "the bright day is done and we are for the dark." '

Walpole came back half an hour later. He seemed exhausted but happy. 'I've been right round the hill. Scott was right, this is the most beautiful view of the Borders.'

Robin propped himself up on his elbow. 'Do you mean *objectively* the most beautiful? According to the aesthetic criteria certified by the government? On a scale of one to ten? Marvellous! We must put up signs along the roads: "Great beauty on the left", "Moderate beauty on the right", "Warning! Excessive beauty — sunglasses recommended", "Optimum beauty, as seen and approved by Sir Walter Scott, Sheriff of Melrose, great writer" etc.'

'Robin! How can you be so...'

Walpole placed a hand on Lewis's arm to silence him.

'Do you know what your *beauty* is, Arthur? Several thousand tons of alluvial deposits amalgamated with quite a bit of volcanic ejecta... plus some cartloads of fossilised sheep droppings. Of course man has played his part in this work of art, has left his... mark on it too, lots more dropping and rivers of piss. And,' he went on getting up and undoing his flies, 'here is my own contribution.'

He plunged into the bracken and kept on talking, in a loud voice, while he was urinating. 'Oh, there are plenty of ridiculous buildings as well that have survived ten or twelve centuries — a blink of the eye on an archaeologist's scale. And then corpses, plenty of corpses...'

'Robin! That's enough.'

'Very fertile, they say. You want good harvests? Bury your grandfather out in the middle of the field, especially if he was big and fat. Results guaranteed. And if you have a meadow, it appears that the grass comes up a rich green that makes a splendid effect. Thanks, granddad. Oh, look, nature is imitating art: it's raining.'

The downpour arrived so suddenly we hardly had time to run back to the Morris. Soaked and silent, we watched the rivulets of rain gurgling across the road and down the slope.

'The blanket,' Walpole cried before shooting out of the car. He picked it up, but instead of coming back to shelter, he continued down the slope.

'What the hell's he up to?'

I went out and joined my boss. He was standing on a little promontory, looking at the Eildons, indifferent to the streams of water.

'It's probably the last time I'll come here, Eby,' he said when he noticed me.

'Why do you say that?'

'The little bookseller, the one who lives inside my chest. He used to be in MacDonald's. And now he wants to get out. He keeps hitting my ribs with a quarto volume. He doesn't like being left face to face with tuberculosis.'

'You should look after yourself, Arthur.'

'That's what Doctor Cameron says. He thinks he can keep me going for another year, perhaps two. "Irreversible pulmonary lesions…" He likes words like that does Doctor Cameron, they're poetry to him. But I won't go. I won't go into hospital. And above all I won't wear the mask.'

'A mask?'

'An oxygen mask. I've always been awfully afraid of masks. When I was little, a pal disguised himself as Zorro for my birthday — I fainted. Even today I can't read *The Masque of the Red Death* right through to the end.'

'Let's go and get out of the rain.'

'One minute. Just one more minute.'

He rubbed the rain out of his eyes and stared intently. I tried to see what he could see: the Eildon Hills teeming, like a Breughel picture, with weird creatures, mythical animals, Roman legionaries in shining armour, a procession of monks along the bank of the river. Rob Roy, Waverley, Lucy of Lammermuir. But there was nothing. Sullen hills, a dreary, sluggish river, dark rain like washing-up water emptied out of an upstairs window. I just managed to imagine Scott sitting on a rock, his deerhound at his feet; Scott grimacing, one hand on his heart. And then, through the rain, a horse straining as it pulled the hearse draped in black and stopping there, just there, as usual.

∞∞∞∞

'It would go better if you pulled the choke out…'

Ten times I'd tried to reproduce my father's gesture, so precise, so magnificent — *clack!* a whip-lash slapping the spine of things, giving them no choice but to obey; but instead of starting the outboard motor just cleared its throat, like a teacher interrupting a poorly learnt recitation.

'Oh, of course,' I said, pathetic, 'the choke.'

It wasn't the same man hiring out the boat but there was a family likeness. His son, perhaps, or his nephew. He screwed up his eyes as he looked at me, a half-smile on his lips, torn between amusement at my incompetence and his fear of damage to his boat.

'And where will you be heading?'

'The Small Isles.'

'Eh?'

'To the Small Isles, just there and back.'

I almost blushed at my lie. But was it even a lie? Did I know myself how I came to find myself here, on Jura, alone for the first time in a boat with a mind of its own? Perhaps after all, that's what it was: the Small Isles. Just there and back. The man turned away to wave to two workers coming out of the nearby distillery then scrutinised me again through his half-open lids. 'Are you a minister, or what?'

'Not yet. Just a seminarist.'

'Aha, a seminarist,' he said, perhaps not knowing the precise meaning of the word but finding it had a baroque and slightly grotesque resonance which went well with my lack of experience of outboard motors. 'So have a good trip, then…'

'Thanks.'

And I couldn't stop myself adding, 'I won't be gone for long.'

The man shrugged his shoulders. 'That's up to you, the boat's been hired for the whole afternoon.'

In my haste to show him that I knew how to sail a boat, I almost forgot the anchor. Then I managed to extract a stallion's whinny from the motor. Quick, quick, get away from the port, away from the man with the half-smile and from the word 'seminarist' which hovered in the air behind me, like a tourist in an odd rig-out. Towards the Small Isles. A friendly name, reassuring, slightly silly. A name from a treasure hunt, from a joke map. *Small Isles*. A Never-Never Land name.

And they soon appeared, a string of glass beads round the neck of Jura. I set course for Eilean nan Gabhar, the prettiest of them with an easy and welcome mooring. My imagination called up an alluring fantasy: Ebenezer Krook, 'seminarist', making a clumsy landing on Eilean nan Gabhar and inspecting its minuscule perimeter with all the earnestness and excitement of a boy playing at pirates; watching the seals gathered just offshore, running after the puffins on the green and white machair; dozing in the sun, tasting the salty pearls of the spindrift. My brain sent the order 'Hard a-port!' to my arm. That's what I needed: the Small Isles.

The order did not reach my arm. That happened to me sometimes, when I was drunk. But I hadn't touched a drop for years; not since I'd become a 'seminarist'. The boat went past Eilean nan Gabhar, leaving my sunny fantasy behind, then past Eilean Diomhain, finally Eilean Bhride and that was the end of the Small Isles. That just left the biggest, Jura, twenty miles of wild, almost straight coastline and, at the end, the Corryvreckan.

On the coast road I could see a group of cyclists out for a ride; a bit farther on a Ford van was labouring up a hill; and a big car was parked on the edge of a wood, the occupants watching the red deer through their binoculars. Far away to the south-east two or three yachts were tacking. It had cooled a bit, but the sun was still shining. It was like the setting for a holiday scene in a sentimental film. Then the road turned away into the hills, the yachts disappeared and I was absolutely alone with the sun and the wind. 'At the top of the island there's a big white house, Barnhill. You can't miss it. And just beyond it a little natural harbour. Don't go any farther than that.' The boat-owner had looked me straight in the eye to make sure I'd got that; then he stuck the money in his pocket.

I cut the motor — not without some hesitation as I was afraid I might not be able to get it going again. Barnhill Farm seemed less imposing than I remembered it. It was a whitewashed building, elongated, with squat sheds built on at either end that did nothing to make it more elegant; in defiance of all symmetry there was a wooden porch protecting the front door. But there were pretty little dormer windows nestling in the slate roof and the heterogeneous whole gave an impression of modesty, of quiet comfort, the result of a compromise between the practical and the pleasantly attractive. To find such a charming house at the end of the world was astounding, you immediately wanted to live in it. I couldn't resist taking up the binoculars the boat-owner had lent me and slowly scanning the façade. At first the man at the window was hidden by the glare of the sun on the glass, but then a cloud revealed him, I could even make out the black shape of the typewriter. He looked up, saw me and waved.

'It's the story of a man who wants to become a writer — a famous writer. And who, once he's achieved fame, doesn't know why he sought it.'

Martin Eden was on my bedside table, in the hotel, and suddenly it was almost unbearable to be without it. Against all reason, I had the feeling that somewhere in those pages I'd read and reread thousands of times there was a secret message, perhaps in code, a precise answer to the question: 'What must I do now?' I decided to take it stage by stage and the first was to start up the motor again. I managed it first time, without my father's nonchalant skill but with that despairing energy, which appears from nowhere and sometimes transforms the worst cowards into formidable soldiers. With a last glance at Barnhill, I saw the man come out of the house and walk unhurriedly down to a boat moored below the house.

'It's the story of a man who ends up thinking that life is an illness.'

Second stage: the little harbour to the north of Barnhill. It was a sound, neutral objective, marked out by the grave and slightly drawling manner of speech of the boat-owner in Craighouse. Once that had been gained I could take a serious look at all the possibilities: tie up in the harbour, for example, and go on foot along the coast to Barnhill and back. A nice walk through the bracken in the afternoon sunshine. A few red deer in the distance, perhaps — hadn't I got a pair of binoculars as well? Or turn back now, the boat making a long, elegant parabola. Meet the man from Barnhill fishing, go alongside, cut the motor, exchange a few words: the wind, the sun. What time is it? That's a very nice house you have. Do you live there right through the year? Then return to Craighouse, see the man with the half-smile; enjoy his hint of astonishment as I draw up along the pier impeccably. No problems? No, no problems. Everything was fine.

Or was it?

A smother of spray dashed up, wetting his face. It tasted salt on his lips, and the taste was good. He wondered if he ought to write a swan-song, but laughed the thought away. There was no time. He was too impatient to be gone.

It was a quiet little harbour. Well protected by two promontories covered in bracken and juniper, with a little stony beach and, right at the back, a tongue of grass in the shade of the bushes. An ideal stopping point. It was as if Poseidon himself had put it there to lull sailors into a false sense of security: nothing serious could happen in the vicinity of such a delightful harbour. Only then did the sound come to my ears. Why so late? Doubtless because of the wind; or because of the motor, more powerful than the one my father had twenty years ago. And I didn't recognise the rumbling that had so impressed me then. On the contrary, there was something appealing, almost joyful in that far-off din, the source of which seemed destined never to reach me. A little like the noise of a funfair in the mist when you're driving past a village and trying in vain to make out the gleam of the Chinese lanterns and the majestic orb of the big wheel.

The little harbour disappeared. This time I hadn't even tried to make my arm obey me: it was in control of the situation. Unless it was the boat asserting itself after its feigned docility. For the first time since I set off, the coast started receding to the west and the wind was blowing into my face, no longer tamed by its journey across the hills of Jura but triumphal, irresistible, like a runner galvanised by the roars of the crowd. Roars that were coming closer. The last rock of Carraig Mhòr stood aside. The Gulf of Corryvreckan was before me, bounded on the north by the inhospitable slopes of Scarba.

A roll of the steamer helped him and he was through, hanging by his hands. When his feet touched the sea, he let go. He was in a milky froth of water.

It was a kind of cosmic funfair, something to amuse the idle gods of Olympus. In my mind the Corryvreckan was a hollow, a depression, a kind of gigantic bathtub that was emptying. But what appeared before my eyes was a wall, a wall of seething water several yards wide and extending right across the gulf: the 'big wave' as the locals call it.

The motor cut out. I don't remember having ordered it to. The boat carried on under its own momentum for a bit, then started to drift straight towards the wall of waves blocking the horizon a little over a mile away. Although the boat was rolling a lot, I managed to stand up. I took off my clothes, my ring, stuffed them in the waterproof container and stood there in my vest and underpants, waiting until the swell would make it impossible for me to keep my balance. I had just one idea in mind: to do something my father hadn't managed to do twenty years ago. But I would have been hard pressed to say what that something was. A slightly stronger eddy on the port side made the boat rock; all I had to do was to let myself fall into the cold water.

Not all that cold. I'd expected an icy shock, in fact it was a more of an invigorating slap. The cold grasped me firmly, but as a friend, like being in a scrum where you can't quite distinguish your own limbs from those of the others. That was exactly what was happening to me: I was swimming without effort, carried along by a kind of collective energy, leaning on the water instead of fighting against it. I enjoyed this pleasant sensation for several minutes, then I filled my lungs and dived.

There was a moment of panic. The scrum had collapsed. I was being trampled on. The decision taken freely a moment ago had become an insupportable constraint. I pulled against the water with my arms as hard as I could, pushed up with my legs and shot to the surface, disbelieving, disoriented, too surprised by my own reaction to think of swimming. The rows of seagulls on the ledges of Caraig Mhòr watched me in silence. I sank again, almost immediately. And at the precise moment, Father Muir appeared to me.

There was a long rumble of sound, and it seemed to him that
he was falling down a vast and interminable stairway. And
somewhere at the bottom he fell into darkness. That much he
knew. He had fallen into darkness. And at the instant he knew,
he ceased to know.

The very limit of everything. The end of the book. Annihilation. Was
that what Martin Eden was looking for? What my father was looking
for? No: perhaps there was a way of approaching that limit — of
approaching death endlessly — without ever reaching it. That's what
Muir, my theology teacher, said: 'The asymptotic curve, eh? The
asymptotic curve!' An old priest stuck in his own arrogance. He never
called us by our Christian names, just used a universal, threatening
'you'. Even worse, when he was forced, in order to demonstrate a
point, to quote a philosopher, he would cast a haughty glance over
his shoulder and whistle — literally — like a hunter calling his dog.
Then Saint Thomas Aquinas, Plotinus and William of Occam would
come running, tails between their legs, and humbly lick the hand of
their master. 'The well-known paradoxes of — here, boy! — Zeno,
isn't it? The stone never hits the tree, Achilles never catches the
tortoise, the arrow is motionless. *You!* Have you understood?' Thirty
heads nodded vigorously. 'And this, whether you gentlemen like it
or not — here boy! — d'Alembert and — here boy! — Kant...' The
water was buzzing in my ears.

Wasn't it grotesque? To be thinking of Father Muir at such a
moment! While a little white fish was slipping between my thighs,
part of my brain rebelled. I looked for something to think about that
was more in keeping with the circumstances. But I could do nothing
about it. Muir was there, as tangible as the fish, as bitter as the salt
in my eyes.

'*You!* There, at the front! Do you know what there is at the end
of the asymptote?' With difficulty I managed to swallow my saliva.
Two enormous bubbles that, for a few seconds, had made the sleeves
of my vest into inflated armbands, escaped to the surface with the

noise of a lavatory flushing. 'In this space, that gets narrower and narrower but is never zero, what is it that separates the axis from the curve?' I was still looking for the answer, at the same time repulsing the advances of a huge jellyfish that was holding out its arms to me, searching for imagined ground beneath my feet, struggling against the survival instinct, choking, suffocating. *This hurt was not death… Death did not hurt. It was life, the pangs of life, this awful, suffocating feeling; it was the last blow life could deal him.*

Today I can't believe I really lived through that experience; that I struggled, that I almost drowned in the Corryvreckan. I just remember it as something I read, but with greater concentration, greater intensity than usual, like those last lines of *Martin Eden*. And when I try to go through it in my mind, it's not the sensations that come back to me, but words, *printed* words — *strangulation, pain, reeling consciousness* — in the elegant and old-fashioned fount of my 1925 edition.

'So you don't know? You still don't know what is down there? What is lurking there at the end of the asymptote? It's *God*, of course, it stands to reason! *God!*'

Despite my blocked-up ears, despite the throbbing at my temples, I thought I could hear the joyful roar of the Corryvreckan; I thought I could feel the 'great race' rising up above me, indulgent, motionless, like a gigantic mirror. 'God, of course! The one you are looking for. The one you want to serve. For you want to become a priest — yes: *you* — don't you?' And I realised that during all those years, at Father Moray's catechism classes, at Father Muir's seminars — those years that had just burst on the surface like bubbles of pure delusion — I had never, never ever, not for a minute, asked myself whether He existed. Whether God existed. And it was so funny that I opened my mouth. That I burst out laughing.

A comic gurgling. Big gulps of salty water swept into my stomach, my chest. The curve had met the asymptote. God was too big — not enough room for Ebenezer Krook. In one final effort, I looked up to gauge the distance to the surface. I didn't see that *flashing bright light… swifter and swifter*, but I saw the hand, the huge hand held out to me across an immensity of space.

'Just rest. Everything's all right.'

I was naked under a heavy eiderdown. My ribs still hurt in the place where they must have pressed down to force the water out of my lungs. Sitting on the edge of the bed, the man was speaking softly. Two deep furrows went from his nose to the corners of his mouth, suggesting gravity, suffering, which were contradicted by a quiet gleam deep within his eyes. His moustache was so thin you could take it for a shadow.

'Everything's all right. I even managed to recover your boat.'

There was a pleasant smell of coffee and cake in the room. I tried to raise my head but it began to spin and flopped back onto the pillow.

'That's quite normal, you're exhausted. What you need is sleep. You're at Barnhill Farm. My name's Eric Blair. What are you called?'

Somewhere in the house a door opened. The smoke from his cigarette drifted towards me; he waved it away, giving me a view of his hand: big, bony, with a little callus on the tip of his index finger.

'Martin Eden,' I replied, taking the sight of his jaw dropping in surprise with me into my sleep.

'Have you searched the boat?'

'No.'

'There might be some papers to identify him.'

'What for?'

'Just to know.'

The voices came through the half-open door, as did the pleasant smell that hadn't entirely disappeared. I heard the clink of a spoon against a cup. Without having to move my head I could see kitchen utensils hung on the wall and the shoulder of a man — presumably Eric Blair, I recognised his white shirt — sitting at the table. I myself was in a fairly spacious, darkened room, a living-room that also served as a spare bedroom: a few armchairs, a small fireplace, a deal corner cupboard; a chair on which my underclothes had been hung to dry. From the light filtering through the blue curtains, it must have been late afternoon. I'd been asleep for several hours.

'What does he look like?'

'About as tall as me, thin.'

'Martin was tall, too. How old would you say?'

I couldn't see the man asking the questions. He was walking up and down the kitchen, the sound of his shoes on the floor suggesting a slight limp. He had a gruff voice and spoke rapidly, brusquely.

'Twenty-five. Perhaps a bit more.'

'That fits! Martin had a son of that age, didn't he?'

'So what?'

The footsteps stopped. 'So what?!' the man standing up said. 'Bloody hell, it makes a lot of coincidences.'

Suddenly he opened the door a little wider and his face appeared. Hard, sullen features; impressive eyebrows, straight and black, meeting above his nose. The room was too dark for him to see me.

'Leave him be, Scott. He's asleep.'

The door closed. Without a sound I got up and put my ear to it.

'…owe it to his memory, don't we?'

'I don't think so, Scott. Let's leave things the way Martin wanted.'

Scott gave an irritated grunt and the voices fell silent. I tiptoed to the nearest window. Opening the curtains I saw the two boats down below; Blair had moored them to a tiny jetty. The simple fact of seeing mine again made my blood run cold: it was irrefutable proof that *it* had truly happened. I put on my still-damp underclothes and went back to the door.

'Something funny happened to me…'

Blair's voice seemed distant. I imagined his wide, downturned mouth, the faraway look in his shining eyes.

'Just now, on the boat… pulling that chap out of the water. There was something that usually only happens when I'm writing: when I'm inventing a character, giving him a body, a voice, a face… bringing him out of the void, you see what I'm getting at? Taking him out of the packaging of words to make a living being of him…

'Pshaw…'

'Well that's what happened. I grasped his hand, then his arms and he came out of the water all at once, looked me in the eye, then fainted. I'd just created him and already he didn't belong to me any more. It doesn't matter whether he's Martin's son or not, it was magnificent, Scott, magnificent.'

'That's enough of that! I'll go and wake him up.'

It only took me a few seconds to cross the room, hop out of the window and run down the slope. The motor resisted a bit, but only for form's sake. Once out at sea, I stopped to put my clothes back on. At Craighouse a young lad took the boat without comment; shivering in my damp underclothes, I felt like a slimy animal imperfectly concealed in a man's skin. I just had enough time to collect my things from the hotel and catch the old bus to Feolin, where the last ferry to Islay was preparing to depart. The waters of the Sound were brooding over old discontent. On the other side the lamps of Port Askaig gave off a pale, derisory light, like a memory that doesn't yet exist.

∞∞∞

When I arrived at the bookshop one day in late December, I found Robin Dennison perched on the step-ladder while Walpole, standing by the cash register, was going through the ceremony of the post. Already having lit his first cigar of the day, he was examining the letters without opening them, simply holding them up in front of his face, as if he had X-ray eyes.

'Bill... bill... bill... bank statement — deep in the red, it goes without saying. Oh, let's have a look at this... The distinguished publishing house of Thingummybob is pleased to announce the forthcoming publication of *Vows and Betrayals*, the second novel by Miss Whatshername. He would remind us of the phenomenal success of *Plots and Rumours*, and enjoins us to send in our order without delay to avoid disappointment as it is likely to sell out very quickly.'

Robin nodded. The invisible black notebook in his left pocket was bursting with all my conjectures. 'And that's not the end of it,' he growled. 'She's still got *Plots and Vows* to write.'

'And *Rumours and Betrayals!*'

Walpole's laugh turned into a horrible coughing fit. It wasn't something new, but for the last few weeks the little lace handkerchief embroidered by his wife had been patterned with red when he put it back in his pocket; just a few scattered spots at first, then darker, bigger patches, gradually eating away at the *A.W.* monogram, just as the illness was eating away at his lungs.

'You oughtn't to smoke so much,' I said in as expressionless a voice as possible.

He gave me a very 'Walpolian' look, three-quarters reproachful, one quarter indulgent. 'Ah! News from Cavignac. Oh, what a pity, he can't come over this year, he's having alterations done to his shop — but what about this year's bet, then. He doesn't mention it.'

'Bet against me,' Robin said with a glance at me.

'Against you? You always kept out of it. And I have to warn you, I only back Scotland.'

'Fine, I'll take France. But then I'm the one who decides the stake. All right?'

Walpole screwed up his eyes, sensing a trap. Robin was looking away. 'All right,' Walpole finally sighed. 'But I have the feeling I'm going to regret it.'

'Agreed. If Scotland win I'll give you thirty boxes of Havanas and you can continue to spit blood in peace. But if it's France...'

'If it's France?'

'You'll be in a hospital bed by tomorrow evening.'

At that moment the door opened.

'Sorry,' Walpole said without looking up, 'we're doing the inventory.'

'Oh, come now, Arthur, just for me. It's an emergency... a Shakespearean emergency.'

'Tomorrow, Christopher. Come back tomorrow.'

Gently but firmly he showed a very crestfallen Mr Duff out, locked the door and started to walk up and down. 'That's not fair play, Robin.'

'You know very well that you've really no choice.'

'Hmm. I wonder whether I had any choice even one single time in my life. What do you think, Eby?'

My only reply was a nod of the head. He looked like a deer frozen in the hunter's sight.

'Well, since everyone's against me — Come on, Scotland!'

CHAPTER IX

In which Mary Guthrie puts one foot in the grave.

'See you soon, my Thousandth.'

I put Sir Alexander's letter back in the twenty-first drawer and felt the weight of the sealed envelope. Heavy. Perhaps a large bundle. Or just very old, very thick paper. I opened it.

The first page was torn, but I had no problem putting it together with the piece in the twentieth drawer so went into my room and lay down on the bed to read comfortably:

> *My Very Dear James Braco,*
>
> *It is with very great regret that I have to inform you that your friend Sir Thomas Urquhart, Sheriff of Cromarty, is no more; his soul departed yesterday evening in the most extraordinary circumstances that you will hear of below. Knowing that I am under surveillance and not wanting to compromise you through an untimely visit... I am therefore compelled to send this news, which cannot wait, on cold parchment, when the warmth of a friendly voice might have rendered it slightly less harsh.*
>
> *As you doubtless know, I have been the factor of the Cromarty estate for over twenty years and although I have shown strict obedience to Sir Angus, I bitterly regretted, without ever concealing the fact, Sir Thomas' departure. It is clear that Sir Angus holds this attachment against me — he never loved his brother. There is nothing surprising in that, heavy draught horses, straining under the yoke, never look*

kindly on the cavalcades of thoroughbreds. When, as soon as the fall of the tyrant Crowell and the triumphant return of our sovereign lord Charles Stuart to the throne was announced, he ordered me to depart without delay for Flushing, I would have liked to believe he was eager to have his brother brought back to Scotland safe and sound; I knew full well, however, that he had a quite different intention in mind.

On the boat I made the acquaintance of Lord B. — the particular repugnance I feel for this person forbids me to write out his name in full, but you will, I am sure, guess to whom I am alluding. This conceited and cunning person had been commissioned to gather together all of Charles' subjects who had been wrongfully exiled in Zealand by the Roundheads and to bring them home without delay. When he learnt the names of my masters, he lavished the most suspicious attentions on me. I could see the desire for gold glinting in his little piggy eyes and I decided to avoid his company as much as possible.

Shortly before we landed, however, he accosted me on the bridge: 'Your masters, the Urquharts of Cromarty, are among our most gallant gentlemen,' he said, placing his hand on my shoulder.

I could do no less than bow at this compliment, then tried to continue on my way, but his hand gripped my shoulder with a strength unsuspected in one so flabby and potbellied. 'They say that Sir Thomas had collected a veritable fortune to aid the return of our great King Charles but that, alas, he did not have the opportunity to send this war chest to the sovereign...'

'I couldn't say, my lord, and the matter of the war chest seems to have been overtaken by events. We must rejoice in the restoration of the King, whether it happened with or without the assistance of Sir Thomas...'

'Of course, of course,' said Lord B. in embarrassment, suddenly letting go of my shoulder.

Although it bears but a small connection with the subject

of my letter, the particular atmosphere in Vermeulen House, where the British exiles resided, is, I believe, worth bringing to your notice. Imagine a building as big as a hospital, cold as a barracks, dirty as a hovel, with a vast internal courtyard recalling those in prisons. Imagine, above all, around a hundred men different in everything but their hatred of Cromwell; men who have often fought against each other. First the Presbyterians, dressed in black, faces as long as a day without bread, thin lips muttering prayers and curses; then the Cavaliers, the flower of Scottish nobility, ever loyal to the house of Stuart — though this loyalty has, alas, too often taken the place of political wisdom and today they greet the return of the King with little more reflection that the cock greeting the break of day. Then the English nobles, lavish with the money of the common people, niggardly with their own, pious on Sundays and frivolous on all other days of the week, brilliant when it's a matter of making a toast, ignorant when it's that of improving an estate. The only restoration they pray for is that of their privileges. And finally the rest: adventurers, courtesans, sham wealthy men and genuine scroungers, men of the cloth hiding a dagger in their boot, professional traitors caught turning their coats once too often.

Lord B. had gathered them in the courtyard. The Presbyterians were a sole splotch of black in the middle of the gaudy assembly; but the riot of colours was due more to the variety of patches than to the magnificence of the materials. It was a small world that had been cooped up together in the cramped quarters of exile and gave off a smell of stale sweat, of unwashed linen; I was very much aware of it as I pushed my way through the crowd in search of Sir Thomas. The remarkable thing was that all these men, so different from each other, had ended up looking the same. Surveying their emaciated features, their dejected expressions animated by sudden concerns, fleeting suspicions like rats scurrying across a cellar floor, I could see the same resentment at the past and the same helplessness regarding the future. Their diverse backgrounds, their membership of this or that caste or clique, only appeared in certain rituals, mannerisms, posturings devoid of meaning. There was such a heavy blanket of oblivion lying over their faith, their convictions, their desires that they reminded me of metal objects — fine gold plate, copper pans, pewter bowls — left on the bottom of the sea after a shipwreck, their distinctive features long since covered over by the same greenish slime.

Lord B. had obtained a little table, which he used as a platform, being hoisted up onto it by two strong guards. The exiles remained silent, doubtless divided between curiosity and distrust. There had been too many rumours of their imminent release which had never been corroborated by information from a reliable source. It could be a trap set by Cromwell, or even by the Dutch, the intentions of the Grand Pensionary towards them never having been very clear.

'Gentlemen,' Lord B. began, 'you all know me, at least by reputation, and you know you can trust me. No one can say, in these troubled times that have encouraged all kinds of denials, that my loyalty was ever found to be at fault...'

'Oh, listen, there's a loyal man,' came a voice not far from me. 'So loyal that, in order not to suffocate under the weight of his loyalty, he had to resign himself to dividing it into two equal parts...'

There were a few sniggers. Lord B. can't have heard the remark clearly but guessed it was a gibe; he turned crimson and his eyes scoured the the assembled throng. As for me, I felt a shiver run down my spine for I had recognised, not the voice but the inimitable style and caustic wit of your friend, Sir Thomas, my only true master. I elbowed my way round to where he stood while Lord B., signalled with his chin to one of the guards to find the troublemaker.

'Gentlemen,' he went on, 'I bring great news, news which, I do not doubt, will make you forget the humiliations of

defeat and the sufferings of exile. It is our beloved sovereign, Charles Stuart himself, who has sent me to you. He has been restored to the throne in all his majesty, the odious republic has been overthrown, the tyrants rendered harmless. In a few days you will see your wives again, your children and your estates! In a word, gentlemen, you are free! Free to return to the kingdom and to share in its glory!'

For a few seconds there was profound silence. Then, gradually, cautiously, the gathering came to life, like a limb that has been stuck in one position for too long; people shook hands, covertly at first, then openly. Soon the courtyard echoed with applause and exclamations of joy; people embraced, exchanged congratulations with those who happened to be near them. Towards the back of the courtyard I found myself beside a sickly old man, almost bald, visibly crippled with rheumatism, who bent his head in a strange manner as he looked at me; I was about to continue my search elsewhere when a horrible suspicion rooted me to the spot. The man smiled at me, raised one finger and, repressing his cough, started to speak in a voice that was hoarse but loud enough to be heard above the sound of all the hugging and kissing:

'Ah gentlemen! Your joy warms my heart! Sir Malcolm, I am delighted to see you shake young Robertson's hand even though he disembowelled your brother at the Battle of Philiphaugh. I am equally delighted to see you, Sir Patrick and Sir Charles, kissing each other full on the lips when you used to besiege, pillage and lay waste to each other regularly in the good old days of King Charles!'

Thunderstruck, the said Sir Malcolm and young Mr Robertson froze then separated; Sir Patrick and Sir Charles, after having first wiped their lips on their cuffs, looked daggers at each other. All the outbursts of friendship withered away. On his little platform, Lord B. rolled his eyes angrily and a martial clanking warned me that one of the men-at-arms was approaching. Sir Thomas (for the bent, hoary old man full of catarrh was indeed he) could have continued for a long time refreshing the memories of those around him of their former quarrels, their buried hatred, their reciprocal baseness, if I had not dragged him, against his will, through a little door into the building. This was made all the more difficult by the fact that his whole body was shaking with uncontrollable laughter.

'For pity's sake, Learmonth, let me continue! Ha ha ha! I've never enjoyed myself so much!'

'Master, I beg you, don't make things worse.'

Fortunately Vermeulen House was a real labyrinth, so that no one could give chase as Sir Thomas, coughing and laughing, led me to his apartment. The tortuous corridors, the secret staircases, all had one thing in common: they were remarkably narrow. On each landing there was a tall cupboard, like a coffin stood on end, which must have been made in situ, and each room I caught a glimpse of through half-open doors as we passed was equally bare and squalid.

Finally, on the top floor, we came to a garret with walls covered in saltpetre, barely lit by a dusty window. Books and manuscripts were lying all over the place in complete disorder. Out of breath, Sir Thomas collapsed onto a pallet.

'The imbeciles!' he muttered, still panting. 'The unmitigated imbeciles! They haven't learnt a thing! All this is just balderdash. Men come and men go. Cromwell's dead, long live the king! And that's enough for these blockheads.'

'Please, Sir Thomas, we have little time,' I begged.

He looked at me, intrigued, from behind his old man's mask. Without his abundance of auburn hair, which he had always had when I knew him, he was unrecognisable. I could not believe that this man was forty-eight, not seventy. That these rounded shoulders, this hollow chest had once filled out a courtier's dress, an officer's uniform; that dozens of women had hung on that scrawny neck, abandoned themselves to those skinny arms. On the other hand, his eye still had the glint of intelligence, and if it had lost something of its old arrogance, it had gained in sharpness and depth. I no longer sensed his old haste to get things over and done with, to exploit at once, in a sort of frantic excitement, all the numerous talents nature had given him, but instead a calm assurance directed towards a single goal. He raised his eyebrows. 'Little time? What do you mean?'

'It won't be long before Lord B.'s men turn up, Sir Thomas and they will stop at nothing to get their hands on the treasure. If you still have it, you must hide it as quickly as possible.'

'The treasure?' he repeated, horrified, one hand on his heart. 'My translation of Rabelais! Quick! We must hide it!'

In no time at all he had gathered up the scattered manuscripts and, oddly enough, was carrying them towards the window.

'No, Sir Thomas. The other treasure. Where is it?'

He looked at me as if I had just said something laughably absurd. Then he shrugged his shoulders and went back to sit down on his pallet. As he did not answer my question, I went over to the window myself. The handle almost came away in my hand — it obviously hadn't been opened in a long time. Leaning out I saw, four stories below, a dark little street from which came the sound of a carpenter's plane being used and the smell of sawdust mixed with the stench of the harbour. I inspected the walls either side of the window embrasure carefully. My master gave little bursts of laughter now and then, unconcerned about my efforts. I felt the masonry above the window and eventually discovered, wrapped round a hook, a piece of string which I untied, though not without difficulty. The creak of a pulley told me something was hanging on the other end, under the eaves; I let the string out a few inches and soon saw a marquetry box bearing the Urquhart arms coming down towards me.

'Leave it, Learmonth, they'll never find it.'

'You are wrong there, Master. They will search the house

from top to bottom if necessary'.

The key to the box was tied to the string. I opened the lock: on a bed of red felt were the most beautiful, sparkling stones it had ever been my privilege to see, their shimmer reflected on the ceiling. There were six of them, fairly small but flawless, of incomparable clarity.

'They belong to the past. To a cause that has had its day. To a man who no longer exists.'

My master's voice also seemed to come from the past, or from some strange land known only to himself. With great difficulty I tore my eyes away from the fantastic glitter. 'Sir Thomas, I know at least a hundred men who would kill their father and mother to get their hands on these diamonds. Let Lord B. and his clique get hold of them and they will use them to the worst ends imaginable. Remember the great plans you had for Cromarty, the European university, open to all without cost, set up in the park. These stones would finance the construction. There is nothing for it, we must take them back to Scotland with us.'

Despite my long experience of Sir Thomas' eccentricities, I was completely unprepared for what was to follow. At first he just opened his mouth wide, like a actor who wants to express surprise. But then he burst out into a laugh that was terrible, immense, prodigious. Head thrown back, he tried in vain to squeeze his throat to silence the racket coming from it.

'Hahaha! Learmonth. Do forgive me but... haha! it's too funny. You speak of... hahaha! of returning to Scotland... but I'm not going to go anywhere... haha! not anywhere...'

The fits gradually became less violent, the gaps between them longer, like the sound of a cart moving away along the road.

'I'm going to die, Learmonth,' he said, recovering his breath. 'Very soon. Is it not obvious?'

I had put the casket down on the table. Arms hanging down, my heart pounding, I didn't know what to say. I seemed

185

to hear in the distance, in the depth of Vermeulen House, the muffled sound of boots.

'Angus, my imbecile of a brother, will inherit the diamonds. He will buy new pairs of horses, build new stables and engage thirty men to look after them. He will commission his portrait from some ruinously expensive dauber from Edinburgh... hahaha! And if he's got a few guineas left, he'll have a pharaoh's tomb of Carrara marble made for himself!

At these words, he shuddered before going on, 'Hide the stones wherever you want, Learmonth, hide them forever. May their sparkle go out with my breath... and see that James Braco gets my translation, he will see that it is completed. If there's anything that gives the hotchpotch that has been my existence some kind of meaning, then it's in those lines, not in the diamonds...'

'You must not give up hope, Master. The doctors will treat you, you'll recover your strength and...'

I couldn't finish, Sir Thomas had burst out laughing again.

'Hahaha! Learmonth, my dear... haha! dear friend. If you utter such a ridiculous word as hope in my presence again I assure you... hahaha!... that I won't survive it. Shh! Did you not hear something?'

'They're coming.'

I immediately went to lock the door then hurried over to the window. But when I tried to tie the string round the casket again, it came off the pulley and I was left with it in my hands. After having searched the room in vain for another hiding place, I went back to my master. His face was white and unmoving, as if coated with some kind of plaster. His nose and mouth seemed to have shrunk; his eyes, fixed on the door, were contemplating something beyond words.

'Yes, it's coming,' he murmured. 'I know, I can sense it. It's strange, I've always been terrified of it... and now that I can see it coming... isn't it odd...'

A choking gurgle came from his throat. He turned towards

me, a smile of disbelief on his lips, as two blows landed on the door.

'It's truly extraordinary, Learmonth. I can see things clearly now. It's funny, death is funny... incredibly funny! A clown dressed in black! As he approaches, everything becomes laughable, that's the cutting edge of his scythe... hahaha! And everyone dies of laughter!

The plaster of his face cracked, his features fell to pieces and once more I saw his wide-open mouth. But this time the roar that emerged from it had only a distant relationship with what we call 'laughter'. It was a hideous beast trying to escape from his body — no: it was his whole body attempting to spew itself out through the siphon of his mouth.

'Hahaaa! Haaa! Learmonth! How grotesque... hahaaa! how ridiculous all this is... hahaaa! Hahaaa!'

Suddenly his eyes went glassy. No further sound came from his stiff, pale lips. He fell back onto his bed, his chest still rising and falling spasmodically: his laugh, even silent was unending. If I'd ever been a man to make that kind of gesture, I would have wrung my hands in impotence. My master was dying, the blows on the door were increasing, the angry voice of Lord B. could be heard shouting louder and louder, 'Open in the name of King Charles!'

I had picked up the diamonds and, for want of any better idea, was about to stuff them in my pockets when Sir Thomas grasped my wrist tight: was it a convulsion, a simple reflex of fear or a deliberate gesture? He had raised his head and closed his lungs as if he was desperately trying to retain one last breath; but he was still conscious and seemed to want to tell me something by the intensity of his look. He pulled my hand towards him and placed it on his mouth.

When I opened the door a few seconds later Lord B., sweating and choking with rage, burst into the room. He gave me a venomous look then, with a nod of the head, released his dogs in human clothing who started to rummage round

*everywhere. Curious faces appeared in the doorway, which
did not prevent one of Lord B.'s henchmen from unashamedly
subjecting me to a thorough search. I obeyed the curt orders:
'Take off your coat', 'Lift up your hands',without letting go
of the bundle of papers covered in spidery writing which, my
dear James Braco, are now in your hands.*

*The body search having produced nothing, the man gave
Lord B. a questioning look. At his nod of assent, the henchman
and his acolytes set about examining Sir Thomas' death-bed,
lifting up his corpse in order to pull off the shabby cover and
the old serge sheet, slitting open the mattress, even going so
far as to feel his clothes, to the scandalised exclamations of
some of the lookers-on.*

*'You will not find what you are looking for, my Lord,' I
finally said. 'I had time to talk to my master. Two years ago he
gave a packet to his usual intermediary, who was to dispatch
it to our king in France.'*

'Who was this man?'

'I don't know.'

*Lord B. subjected me to a long, hard stare. I felt as if his
greedy look were a red-hot poker turning over my most secret
thoughts like embers. After a minute of this he gave a grunt
and left the room, not without leaving one of his bloodhounds
by the door. Had he given up or was he waiting for a more
favourable opportunity to continue the search? He never had
that opportunity. I procured the help of two Presbyterians who
looked forbidding but honest and who had been disgusted
by the despicable search of the corpse. At once they went to
fetch several of their fellow Presbyterians and the macabre
little company, grouped round the head of Sir Thomas' death-
bed, immediately immersed itself in sombre meditations. In
this way the room remained occupied until the arrival of the
carpenter and his apprentice. We paid our last respects to Sir
Thomas, the nails sealed the coffin lid and that was that.*

It is here before me as I write these lines, that obscene

container made of crude planks; one of the knots in the wood fell out during transport and through the hole I can see a fragment of my master's face. From time to time the boat slopes on the swell to the point where the body slides a little in the coffin. At such times, in the half-sleep brought on by fatigue and grief, I imagine I can see the head of the corpse rolling towards me; in the creaking of the hull, I imagine I can hear muffled blows on the lid and in my mind's eye I see Sir Thomas springing up out of the sepulchre like a jovial Christ — opening his mouth to let out both his unquenchable laugh and the six fabulous diamonds I put there myself: 'Hahaha... Learmonth! How grotesque... hahaaa! how ridiculous all this is!

But nothing happens and with the next wave the head rolls the other way.

Your friend, my dear James Braco, is, alas, truly dead, my only consolation being that I was able to carry out his two last wishes. Your dedication to your friend's memory will, I am sure, see to it that his unfinished book will soon appear; and our silence will see to it that those diamonds, that he had eventually come to hate, will never arouse covetous desires. But his memory will continue to shine for you and for me alone.

Your devoted servant

Angus Learmonth

For a good half hour I walked up and down, going from my bedroom to the library, from the library to my bedroom, trying to think, weighing up the 'academic' part I could take from the letter — and immediately felt disgust at my selfish motives. The letter wasn't addressed to me, it should have been consigned to oblivion, though at least one other person had read it.

That took me back to Sir Alexander, to the desk.

Close all the drawers except the first, the tenth, the twentieth and the thirtieth. Another conjuring trick. One more hoax. Shrugging my shoulders, as if he could see me, I carried out his instructions. Nothing. The open drawers formed a staircase going down from left to right. But then something happened behind me. A grating sound at first, then another, unpleasant noise, like that of a heavy canvas sack being dragged across the floor; a draught on the back of my neck, bringing with it a fetid odour — the one I had smelt the evening Sir Thomas appeared.

The door separating the living from the dead will open before your eyes.

I turned round and saw that a section of wall had opened up opposite my bedroom. It had pivoted on a central pillar. A secret passage. Through the opening a flight of steps going round and round could be seen.

I fetched a candle and a box of matches from my room and went up to the opening. I knew very well that these stairs would have been made for some perfectly serious purpose — to hide from pillagers or Viking raids, to meet discreetly with political friends during certain troubled periods of history — and that the section of wall was controlled by a mechanism that preceded the desk by several hundred years. But as I made the revolving masonry move both ways, I couldn't help smiling like a little kid; I felt I was taking part in a brilliant treasure hunt organised by Sir Alexander.

So the setting was there: a narrow spiral staircase, the steps slippery and worn away by the years, comparable in all respects to those that were obligatory in horror films — the kind of cliché that André Borel mocked mercilessly: 'It's *absolutely* essential that the steps *gleam* in the light of the candle, it's imperative, isn't it? And a little slip that turns out to be harmless is very effective before she falls into the hands of Dracula or the hunchback servant.

'And after the steps, the passage. That's very important too, the passage. It has to be narrow — the suggestion of suffocation, you understand. Old rusty rings fixed in the wall for torches. And the air! Stuffy, very stuffy. *Stifling!* To the point where the candle flame starts to flicker... Oh, those flickering candles!'

According to my calculations, the passage disappeared to the west. This was confirmed after I'd gone about fifty steps: another set of steps opened up on the right. I climbed a few and, pushing up with my back, managed to raise the slab blocking it: I was indeed in the main courtyard. Night was falling and the house seemed immense. There was something strange about looking at it like this, from the low perspective of a little animal. I could see the light on the library ceiling. Then the storm burst and the courtyard was almost immediately transformed into the bed of a raging torrent pouring down some Highland glen. The patter of raindrops was so violent it was almost ridiculous, whipping my face, the water tumbling down the steps into the passage, while the trees, far away to the east, loomed up out of the twilight at every flash of lighting, wretched and skeletal, as if caught in the flashlight of some sadistic photographer. Hastily I left the slab down again, managed to relight the candle the wind had blown out and wiped my eyes with my handkerchief. Had I *really* seen the outline of a shadow at the window, in front of the desk?

I continued along the secret passage. Muffled by five or ten feet of soil, the sound of the rain changed: it had become a distant, mournful rumbling. After a minute or two I saw a thin rivulet of rainwater coming towards me, proof that the passage came out in the open air not far ahead, doubtless among the bracken under the trees you had to pass through to get to Cromarty on foot. And indeed, the path soon went up a gentle slope, ending abruptly in a sort of embankment. Looking up, I could see the sky through a tangle of branches.

I had a strange idea and spent a long time thinking it over as I stood there with the water trickling between my feet. Alexander had led me this far, towards the exit. Was it a sign? An invitation to give up before it was too late? Or perhaps an ultimate challenge? In less than ten minutes I could be in the village, among normal people, most of whom would never have heard of the desk, nor even of Sir Alexander, and lived in a world bounded by simple markers — work, shopping, school — and not by lines of noughts and crosses. I could take my room in the Cromarty Arms again; start on my book, if that cold animal with the changing shape, floating on the edge of my consciousness and sometimes looking up at me in the middle of my dreams really was a book. What else could it be?

For that I'd have to give up now. Perhaps close to the goal. Could that be Sir Alexander's last trick?

I stood there, unmoving, until I was almost as cold and damp as the stone. Then I made my way back, step by step, examining the sides of the passage in the light of my candle; and found something. Just before the steps going up into the courtyard there was a crevice, which before I had taken for part of some reinforcement; but when I bent down, and with the aid of the light, I could see that it widened out a little, just enough to allow a person to crawl through.

I came out in a large rectangular room. Opposite me stone steps led up to a heavy wrought-iron gate. On the long sides cavities had been made in the walls, occupied by oblong boxes. It looked like a kind of storeroom — but for storing what?

Holding the candle up high, I went to the centre of the room and I didn't need to go any closer to the cavities to see my mistake.

'The crypt! Ah, the crypt! We've made it! You can't have a good horror film without a crypt. Spiders webs, a bat, perhaps the odd rat and, if the production budget can run to it, a few fine recumbent statues.'

Each wall had four rows of four cavities, that is thirty-two in all, the same number as there were drawers in the desk. And they were all there, in chronological order from top to bottom and from left to right, like books shelved according to their date of acquisition. First of all the wall of the Ancients: heavy stone sarcophaguses with a name and an epitaph carved on them. A certain Sir Lawrence (1245–1298) led the way: 'He perished where he had sinned.' The face of the recumbent statue, with the cracks in the stone accentuating its depraved and diseased aspect, said a lot about the sin in question. Then came those I knew from *The History of Urquhart House and its Pendicles*. The voracious Sir John (1264–1314): 'His own sword alone could vanquish him.' Malcolm, the golfer (1457–1458–1460–

1461–1463) — the dates must have been those of his victories in the Chanonry tournament. From the sixteenth century onwards there were no more recumbent statues — a decline in the family fortunes or a change in funerary customs? Alexander, the melancholic (1468–1513): 'He took one step too many.' Andrew, the brute (1482–1545): no epitaph, but the stonemason had cleverly made the w into a caudal fin. Among them various unknowns: brothers, uncles, nephews, cousins. Adam, Frederick, Edward, Olipher, Quintin, pinned down for eternity by a single sibylline sentence: 'He was good', 'He loved brandy too well', 'Excelled at the hunt'. There were women as well, reduced to their first name, like pet animals: Catriona, Magdalen, Susanna, Rosalind, simple hyphens in the interminable monologue of death.

Sir Robert, Andrew's brother, (1505–1558): 'He will live on for ever in our memories.' An elegant way of suggesting that they couldn't forget him quickly enough. Sir Charles, the hypochondriac (1548–1625): 'He died twice, the second time it was fatal.' Sir Thomas the Elder (1572–1636): 'A good son, a good father, a good drinker.'

I knelt down by the last tomb at the bottom on the right. Sir Thomas the Younger (1612–1660): 'He died merrily.'

For the first time since my arrival at Urquhart House I felt a deep, powerful emotion. A sort of love mixed with regret and shame. Sir Thomas Urquhart of Cromarty, mathematician, politician, duellist, seducer, writer, linguist, had after all finally 'taken up quarters' in the crypt of his ancestors. Beneath that coffin lid lay the only Urquhart worthy of my attention, the only true treasure; my sole reason for being here which I had neglected for an illusion. A writer. Not one of the greatest, of course, but at least he'd left something behind, a nebulous, translucent aura that the tomb could not contain. *Pantochronachanon, Ekskubalauron, Trissotetras.* His words were echoing inside my head, a little like the pendulum of a clock still beating the march of time long after the death of its maker. Yes, his memory was still bright. With or without the diamonds.

Before doing what I had to do, I crossed the crypt and quickly surveyed the more recent dead in the wall opposite. There scathing, mysterious or comic epitaphs were rare. In the nineteenth century the naïve poetry, the mood of the heroic age finally yielded to stock phrases, occasional tributes. Never before had I seen so many loving sons, beloved fathers, dearest spouses or generous masters heaped up in such a small space. Then even these phrases disappeared, as if the living, smothered by the weight of the dead, had renounced their duty to remember them and left their fathers to a long, anonymous journey in the corridors of the void. Though there was one exception — Sir Alexander, of course. The wood of the excellently made coffin still looked new and a very skilful craftsman — the cabinet-maker who had made the desk? — had inlaid the lid with *trompe l'oeil* Italian landscapes and a female that looking like a gorgon cleaning her fingernails with a scythe. Then his brother Stephen and Ophelia, doubtless Stephen's wife, and finally Paul and Mary, the parents of James and Thomas, coming thirty-first and thirty-second in the championship of death. The architect of the crypt had created a kind of *numerus clausus*, compelling later fruits of the family tree to 'take up quarters' elsewhere, which probably explained the walled-up door.

I went back across to the other wall, put down my candle and knelt at Sir Thomas' tomb, asking for his forgiveness in advance. The stone lid was less heavy than I had expected and I managed to slide it back. Then I held up my candle.

It was not the remains of the writer. It was the skeleton of a man dressed in modern clothes: tweed trousers, a blazer, slip-on shoes. I turned my eyes to his hands clasped over his stomach: one joint of his little finger was missing.

As I abruptly straightened up, I bashed my head on the stone and knocked the candle over. It went out. In the absolute darkness I tried to strike a match, but the box slipped and the contents were scattered over the floor. At that precise moment another light appeared, much brighter — at first I thought it was inside my skull with the stars brought out by the pain.

'My God!'

Rubbing the huge bump on my head I turned towards the light. The beam looked like a spider's web with a thousand threads. Crouching down inside the room, Mr Par was fluttering his eyelashes frantically, a revolver in one hand, the electric torch in the other. I had only seen firearms at the pictures but his seemed pretty old-fashioned. He put it back in his pocket and, without paying me the least attention, came to kneel down on the slabs. As I stood up, still dazed, and leant against the wall, he ran the torch over the cavity in the wall. I heard another oath, then:

'Three years, eh? For three years they've been taking me for a ride!'

He leapt up. A few seconds later I was running after him along the underground passage. I would never have believed he could move that quickly; from a distance his gammy leg looked like a spring. The light very nearly disappeared, leaving me in darkness. When I came to the bottom of the stairs, he was already crossing the library. I only caught him up on the ground floor where he was opening the door to the servants' hall.

Eagle was getting ready to serve the soup. She stood there, open-mouthed, the tureen in her hand. The twins turned their heads, adopting the same expression — blank, indecipherable — they always had when they were seen together.

'Where is he?' Par said in a threatening tone.

Out of the corner of my eye I could see Miss Birdie-Foyle, head bowed over her plate, playing with a morsel of bread. Eagle put the tureen down and, looking Par straight in the eye, said, 'if you mean Sir James, he's in the village.'

'Since when?'

'He left about an hour ago. He has urgent business with Farquhar.'

The butler spat on the floor. 'Urgent, eh? A dead man can't have urgent business... for your Sir James is dead, get that into your skulls.'

There was no reaction from those at the table. Birdie-Foyle started to roll another little ball of soft bread; the twins peered at their plates. As for Eagle, she simply shrugged her shoulders: 'Dead or not, he'll have to come back — he hasn't left me a penny.'

Then, to my amazement, she fixed her eyes on me, soon followed by the twins, as if from now on I was in charge of running Urquhart House.

Sticking to Par's heels, I raced round the whole of the southern part of the house, including the laughter closets. On Sir James' desk there was a cold cup of tea and a tray with — unopened — the day's post. Par went through it once, twice, as if looking for an envelope he couldn't find. 'Confound it!' he muttered before dashing into the next room. It was a dreary little chamber with just an unmade bed, hardly more comfortable than mine, and a wardrobe without a door where Urquhart's dressing gown was hanging.

As we crossed the hall, the butler seemed finally to acknowledge my presence. 'You've been lucky, I can tell you,' he said without turning round. 'If I hadn't followed you to the crypt just now, you'd have gone for a Burton. He can't have been that far away. Seeing that we'd found out what's been going on, he must have slipped out by the secret passage.'

It was the first time I'd set foot in the northern wing. No laughter closets — doubtless because Sir James never set foot there — but the same desolation as in the other parts of the house: large abandoned rooms, dust, a few old pieces of furniture sleeping under the sheets with dubious stains and a smell composed of mould and cat's urine, although none of the animals could be seen anywhere. At the end of a long corridor we went into the twins' room: bunk beds (for a moment I pictured the struggles Bruce and Wallace would go through to obtain the upper one) and an indescribable mess on the floor. With a grimace of disgust, Par extended a foot and nudged the jumble of lead soldiers, cake crumbs, electric trains, old worn teddy bears, coloured lithographs, bits of film, marbles, cut-up cinema magazines, clothes bundled up and dropped there. In a poster pinned to the wall, Laura Hunt was about to take off her little rain-hat, surveying the chaos with a look of disbelief.

'Could you — calmly — explain all this to me, Mr...'

Twenty flutters of his eyebrows left my question in tatters. I had to follow him into another room, where pride of place was taken by an impressive projector. A sheet had been hung over the window, and a few chairs arranged in a row; there the other smells were dominated by the stench of acid recalling my father's photographic studio before his whisky period. Large reels in their metal cans stood on shelves or were piled up on the floor. Celluloid snakes wound round the projector and crackled when you trod on them, or were hanging on the wall, crucified with drawing pins. I examined a few at random: several King Kongs were playing delicately with Fay Wray's skirt; thirty sinister-looking cowboys were brandishing revolvers; frozen in terror by the shadow of a claw-like hand, young brown-haired girls were stifling cries.

He had sat down and was staring at the screen with an ill-tempered expression, like a discontened viewer.

'I'm Scott Fleming, Fleming of Ardloch.'

Immediately I could see little ruined cottages, the old car and the yellow dog. The stable smell was so strong it was as if a herd of sheep had come into the room.'

'Ardloch on Jura?'

'You know Jura?'

'I was born on Islay. Donald Fleming's a neighbour. Are you related?'

'Perhaps. We'd have to check the family tree.'

For the first time since we'd met, the butler regarded me without animosity and I no longer had the feeling a bit of me was cut off with every flutter of his eyelashes.

'It was the body of Sir James, wasn't it?'

He nodded.

'And you think it was his twin brother who killed him?'

'Obviously. Who else?' Turning to the screen, Fleming went on, 'Who told you about Thomas Urquhart? What exactly do you know about all this, Miss Guthrie?'

I replied briefly, without going into the complicated details connected with the desk and Alexander, nor mentioning the ring, but referring to Learmonth's letter. From time to time he nodded or frowned; then he started to walk up and down, causing devastation to the celluloid snakes.

'The only reason I'm here is to do him in.'

'Why? What has he done to you?'

He waved my question away as you would a fly. 'Four years ago I heard from an old soldier that Thomas had come back to Scotland and was prowling round Cromarty. So I left the farm to my sons and came here. I met... *Sir James* and got taken on as butler for wages a scullion would have rejected. And I was very proud of my trick! I was biding my time waiting until I could corner Thomas — and he was there before me all the time. Four four years I've cleaned out the latrines of this... of this... What? A Fleming of Ardloch a servant! But he's a murderer. A murderer and a traitor. I would have sunk even lower to get him. Two or three times it occurred to me that... only I just couldn't believe it.'

I would have liked to know what kind of 'old soldier' he was alluding to, but I had my own ideas about that and other, more important ones were buzzing round inside my head: 'But... if Sir James is dead, if his brother Thomas has taken his place, why the occasional disguise? Why does he play the ghost?'

'How should I know? How should I know what goes on inside a madman's head? To seduce his trollop, no doubt.'

'Birdie?'

'She arrived a few weeks after me. A student, like you. I thought she wouldn't stick it out for long in the house, she couldn't bear Sir J... she couldn't bear *him*. Then, all of a sudden, something changed. She settled in, like you. And I realised something was going on. That she had met the *other* one. How many sleepless nights have I spent, sitting in my chair, revolver in my hand, listening for sounds in the corridor. But they were careful, I never managed to catch them at it.'

'Do you mean that even she doesn't know... that there's only one Urquhart alive? Oh come on, Mr Fleming. You can't fool a person like that.'

'You don't know him. He's capable of anything. Even of cutting off part of a finger if his scheme requires it.'

When I heard this, I remembered something, an idea that had appeared somewhere at the back of my mind when I saw the hands of the skeleton in the crypt. But it had vanished when I hit my head and now it was just out of reach, carried away by Scott Fleming's flood of words.

'Perhaps she knows it deep down inside. Has known it since the very beginning, but doesn't want to face up to the reality. She's mad as well! Everyone goes mad in this house. Even me!'

'Do you think the twins know?'

'They're mad too, stark, staring mad. James, Thomas, uncle, father… it makes no difference to them. All they're interested in is their bloody cinema.'

'What are you going to do? Tell the police?'

'No, I'm not going to do anything.'

He came close to me and looked me in the eye. 'It's you who are going to do something.'

'Me?'

'You,' he said quietly. 'He's still here, I can feel it. Somewhere hidden behind these walls. I don't doubt he's there this very minute listening to us.

'What makes you say that?'

'The envelope. A big envelope with the address of an Edinburgh clinic on the back. It arrived this morning. I put it on the sideboard in his office with the rest of the post. I haven't seen Urquhart all day. This afternoon, before going down to the crypt, I went back to his office: the envelope was still there. Now it's not.'

'The cook might have moved it, or one of the twins.'

'No, it was him, I'm sure of that. He's been expecting that letter for several days now. Every morning he looked disappointed when I took him the post. He's here, I tell you. He's already killed for the treasure and he won't leave without it, especially now that it's within his reach.'

'Just a minute.'

My head was still hurting. I sat down beside him to try and review the situation: 'Before going down to the underground passage, you found Learmonth's letter, didn't you? Right then. We know that a certain quantity of diamonds was brought back to Scotland in Sir Thomas' mouth and we can assume that when Alexander found the letter he got hold of them. But there's nothing to say the treasure still exists.'

'That will make no difference to Urquhart. There's still some doubt. There is the *possibility* the treasure still exists. And we're going to use that possibility as a lure. He will lurk somewhere in the vicinity until the last drawer has revealed its secret. And you are going to open it.'

'Impossible!'

'And when you open it, I'll be there, I'll have him at my mercy.'

'Impossible, Mr Fleming. It'll take months, years, even. I can't …'

'I'm going to stay here with my gun in my pocket, following Miss Birdie like her own shadow, just in case Urquhart should do something foolish. As for you, you will go to Edinburgh.'

He suddenly seemed bored by our conversation. He went on in brusque tones: 'Look for the ring. There's an old soldier knows where it is. You're to ring him up when you get there, he'll help you if need be.'

I stared at the white sheet on which the marbling of the damp patches looked like the shadows of long-gone films. This network of 'old soldiers', had it spread its tentacles wide enough to be aware of my connection with Ebenezer Krook?

'Why would I do something like that?'

Up to that point he had shown uncompromising determination, like a dog that refuses to let go of a bone, and a sound intelligence, methodical if limited. All of a sudden, like the fleeting gleam of the first rays of the sun on a piece of pewter, his eyes lit up with more profound understanding, doubtless a legacy of his ancestors and their skill at leading men: 'For the same reason that's been keeping you here for months. If you were going to give up, you would have done it at the very beginning. You've gone mad as well.'

∞∞∞

The next morning I found a crumpled piece of paper torn out of a notebook that had been pushed under my door. It was in "Bruce's" handwriting: irregular and clumsy. The upstrokes of the 'h's and 'l's bent under an invisible burden, the downstrokes of the 'p's and 'q's scraped the letters on the line below.

> *Dear Miss Guthrie,*
> *When you wake up, could you come and meet us in the projection room? Birdie will show you the way.*
> *Your devoted admirers,*
>
> *Bruce and Wallace*

Dawn had only just broken. Doubtless happy to see me go, a sardonic sun was already shining over the horizon of the sea. I put off packing my bags and went down into the hall where the slanting rays were playing with the dust and and flushing out spiders' webs. 'You will take the ten o'clock bus,' Scott Fleming had said, 'that will give you plenty of time to make the train. You will be in Edinburgh by four.' Some people employ the future with insolent ease, other have to content themselves with the conditional. That is doubtless what authority is.

Bruce and Wallace were in such a frenzy of expectation that their impatience had almost taken tangible form: a person created in my image or, to be more precise, in the image of *their* Miss Guthrie. A ghostly self driven away by my appearance. The room smelt of sweat and unwashed children. There was now only one chair facing the screen. The twins were standing rigidly on either side of the projector in the same attitude, mouths open, their hands held out a little at either side, like a priest about to begin his prayer.

'Miss Guthrie! Did you know that there are celestial bodies that are so heavy, so dense, that a penny made from their substance would go right through a concrete wall if it fell on it?'

'And that, according to Laplace, the penny alone would weigh as

201

much as a planet?'

'Well, the planet, that is the cinematographic art as a whole: all the film that has been exposed since the Lumière brothers put end to end on a gigantic reel...'

'...and the penny is what you are going to see. A precipitate. A prodigious concentrate!'

It didn't really matter which side the voice came from: the one on the left would jump in and take over from the one on the right and vice versa, like two birds fighting over the same worm. It resulted in a kind of delivery in which words lost their meaning and just formed a kind of acoustic paste... shapeless meat coming out of the mincer.

'The enemy of art is profusion, useless abundance. You have to cut what really counts out of the mass of material with the razor of aesthetic judgment...'

'...Occam's razor, you see. Cut into the living flesh. It's paradoxical but...'

'...the material you've cut out is heavier, richer than the original magma. One single film — *the* film...'

'...takes the place of all films, and improves on them!'

'Except that there are, of course, two precipitates...'

'...two quintessences of the film, Bruce's...'

'...and Wallace's!'

'Make yourself comfortable, Miss Guthrie, it'll only take a few minutes, that's the advantage of our method, for every inch of our sacred reel...'

'...contains miles of profane reels! We tossed up. Bruce will go first, then...'

'...it will be Wallace's turn. After that you'll make your decision...'

'...in full knowledge of the facts!'

'But... what decision?' I stammered as the twins led me gently but firmly to the empty chair.

'Shhh. You will know. When you've seen the two reels you will know what to do.'

I heard them move away. One switched off the light, plunging the room into total darkness until the other set the projector going; the screen started a virginal white and was then covered in convulsive threads that reminded me both of the snakes of film on the floor and the diseased cells I'd seen through Aunt Catriona's microscope.

'Reel one: Bruce's film.'

Women bent double in a paddy-field, immediately giving way to a sinister-looking gangster crying, 'Mom! Mom!' The name *Anna* carved on a piece of wood by the sea. Two men standing face to face either side of a table; one is brandishing a revolver and shouting in French, *'Tu vas la taire, ta gueule?'* A traveller in a stagecoach. A door gives way under the weight of a man. Laura Hunt slowly takes off her rain-hat. Another door, leading into a corridor; someone's hiding behind it but you can only see their shadow. An aeroplane. Another aeroplane. The piece of wood again, but now you can hardly see the word *Anna* and it's soon covered by a wave. Another stagecoach. An oversized tennis racket. A pistol made of liquorice. A pram tumbling down some stairs. A man and a woman walking towards an altar. 'Which of the two?' a mocking old woman says. Threads. Dark. Lights.

'Reel two: Wallace's film.'

Threads. A man in a boat. A bicycle. A little boy crying and shouting: 'Papa! Papa!' A dress tearing to reveal a slip and a rounded rump. A dinosaur skeleton collapses. A man runs on a roof. Another man on another roof; he's holding a child, lets it go, cries. A man opens a drawer, fingers women's underwear. Laura Hunt dazzled by the light from a lamp. The rump of a woman kneeling under a sink. Two men chasing each other inside the Statue of Liberty. An aeroplane. A stagecoach. 'Good morning, Mr Matuschek.' Another aeroplane. A Christmas tree; some cheerful people singing Auld Lang Syne. A man and a woman walking towards an altar. 'Which of the two?' a bawdy old man asks. Threads. Dark. Lights.

'Well?'

They uttered the word together, hanging on my lips, leaning towards me like a conjurer's wand towards the invisible wave. So there must be some kind of meaning to all this; a grotesque, monstrous meaning.

'Well, Miss Guthrie? Which of us are you going to marry?'

I stared at them but did not reply; then I burst into tears.

∞∞∞

Scott Fleming's lugubrious footsteps echoed through the ground floor; since dawn he had been tapping every wall, gun in his hand, looking for secret passages. I gave my room one last look, as much to make sure I'd forgotten nothing as to imprint it on my memory. Miss Foyle wasn't in her room. It was probably best like that, I wouldn't have known what to say to her; at that point I didn't know if I was going to come back.

I waited in the hall for Fleming, alone with the time-ravaged pictures.

'I'm ready,' I said when he finally arrived, 'but I'm not leaving until you've told me everything. I'm not a golf ball, I need to know where I'm going.'

The Laird of Ardloch's stomach rumbled. He fixed his eyes on my suitcase, as if he needed to know its exact weight before picking it up. He stood there for a moment, arms dangling, head lowered. Finally, in an abrupt movement, he picked up my suitcase and I almost had to run to catch him up. The words came in short bursts, but they have all remained etched on my memory. Even today the word *Huesca* invariably evokes the bend on the road to Cromarty after which you can no longer see the house and where Scott Fleming spoke it for the first time; *POUM* brings back the backfiring engine of the old black car we passed in Church Street; and, however odd it may sound, at the word Fascist in my mind's eye I see a poster on the municipal notice board on Marine Parade: *8th January, Cromarty Arms, Grand Bridge Tournament.*

Fortunately my friend the bus driver must have been ill, or it was his day off. As I stepped onto the platform I saw the warden of the Cromarty Museum at the wheel. She tipped her cricket cap in greeting, flexed her biceps, switched on the ignition and put her foot

204

right down on the accelerator.

'The old barn!' I yelled at Scott Fleming, not quite being able to make myself heard above the noise of the engine.

'What?'

'The old barn! Go and check it out from time to time.'

Scott used his hand as an ear trumpet: 'Why?'

'I don't know… an intuition.'

'An intuition, for God's sake?'

The bus was empty apart from a small group of scouts sitting at the back. The driver gave a joyful blast on the horn as we passed the Royal Hotel, then turned to me. 'So is that your holidays over? I hope you'll come back to see us again some time.'

I thought for a few moments. I couldn't get the partial memory of the thing I'd seen in Sir Thomas' tomb out of my mind, like the face of an absent acquaintance whose features we can't remember and which remains smooth and white on the canvas of memory despite our desperate efforts to recall it. There was something wrong, but what? The last houses of Cromarty disappeared. The scouts had taken out a pack of cards.

'Yes,' I said. 'Certainly. I'll be back soon.'

CHAPTER X

Krook's narrative.

Corstorphine Road was the main road out of Edinburgh to the west and we made our way, four globules amid thousands of others — white, red, black, blue — towards the beating heart of Murrayfield, which was already athrob with clamour. There were boisterous globules already counting their chickens in loud voices; nervous ones reading the match preview in the newspaper one last time; confident, worried, cantankerous, sceptical, blasé, relaxed ones; families, groups, couples, loners. French supporters in their jerseys with the cock on them, striking up the *Marseillaise* and passing round litres of red wine while another cock, a real one, was trying to get out of a wicker basket. Some young Scots who'd come up from the Borders for the match, already pretty drunk, had turned off into an alley and were pissing against the wall and bawling *Scotland the Brave*. The urine spurted onto their jerseys in the maroon and white of Gala.

Robin joined them before catching us up at the turnstiles; he looked a bit like an executioner who's become fond of his victim and is reluctant to climb the scaffold. As for Walpole, his cheerful whistling fooled no one.

'Where shall we go? North or South stand?'

Walpole licked his finger. 'North. The wind will keep my lock of hair flat on my head. That way I won't need to hold it and can applaud with both hands.'

'If you should have anything to applaud,' Robin said sardonically.

As for myself, I was feeling a bit out of sorts. The old excitement from my Aberdeen days had come back. It wasn't unpleasant but it brought with it some memories I could have done without: Father Moray's pallid face, the smell of feet and of sweat after the match in the presbytery 'changing-room'— a boxroom where our clothes, piled up on two chairs, looked as if they too had been indulging in savage brawls; the walk home when my whole body hurt and I didn't know if I was hot or cold; dinner in the twilight between my father's silence and my mother's standard admonitions ('Eat your cauliflower, it'll get cold.'); the window of my bedroom creaking like an alarm; and the mocking look of Kate Malone lifting up her skirt on some waste ground the evening of the day I'd fractured her brother's eye socket in a scrum.

Of the four of us only Lewis seemed to be on form, in fact I'd never seem him so frisky. Sporting a pink pocket handkerchief and a matching silk scarf over his navy-blue blazer, he filled his lungs with the Murrayfield air, like a hiker on the top of Ben Nevis, and openly eyed up the young men who passed us.

'Watch out,' Robin whispered to me. 'When he's in this mood you never know how things are going to end up.'

After a *Marseillaise* played as if it were a tune from an operetta, *God Save the Queen* received almost as many jeers as cheers. The referee, a big, bald Welshman by the name of David, blew his whistle and almost immediately our men took up residence in their opponents' twenty-five.

'I have the feeling things are going to turn out well,' Lewis said with a wink at one of the young Maroons we'd seen before, a nice little blond lad with the face of a Madonna one would have rather imagined in an altar boy's surplice than in a rugby jersey.

'Yeees... I think our pack will hold out, but the backs are weak, apart from Weatherstone.'

'They're without Maurice Prat and Boniface...'

'Yes, but they've got the other Prat and Labazuy... and that young pillar of a man, Bréjassou. It appears he's very good.'

At this another of the Maroons intervened. I don't think alcohol sharpens the faculties of those who have some but I'm sure that, like a magnifying glass, it increases stupidity that's already there by a factor of ten. Our man smelt more strongly of hops than a whole barrel of Tennent's. He had an ape's receding forehead and a slack lower jaw going up and down like an out-of-control lift with a big, black, furred tongue acting as lift-boy.

'Don't you worry, granddads, we're going to murder them. These French, they're just a load of… pansies.'

He said this looking Lewis straight in the eye and all the rest, apart from the little blond lad, burst out laughing.

I couldn't see the expression on Lewis's face — Weatherstone had started to jink his way down the left wing. It wasn't the wind that was making the hairs on my arms stand on end and my spine tingle, it was the rugby feeling coming back to me: the intoxication, the strength and the skill. Shoving, pulling down, ripping out. Your limbs full of painful life. Running, tackling, picking up. Even the ring on my finger was alive. I was surprised to find myself with my arms in the air, shouting with the others. But Vannier, the French full back, got the ball and found touch. Furious, I ripped off my blazer and flung it to the ground.

After this, Robin handed out the first round of whisky, Walpole lit a cigar and the whole of Murrayfield relaxed, like a cat that's just seen a mouse escape and settles down to wait for another chance to pounce.

It came, only a few minutes later, from an extraordinary up-and-under launched by Marshall.

'Things are going to be hot where that comes down,' Lewis said.

The Scots rushed forward. Vannier failed to make the mark, leading to a savage loose scrum. The forwards locked in a compact mass, a kind of undulating anthill. The three-quarters, facing each other not knowing which side the ball would come out were like figurines waiting for the magician to wave his wand before coming to life. With the rest of the stadium I was holding my breath. For a few seconds nothing else mattered, neither the petty concerns of the tens of thousands of spectators nor the great concerns still shaking the world outside; neither what had happened yesterday nor what would happen tomorrow; neither Robin's little black notebook, nor even death. Nothing apart from whether the referee would hand the ball to Dufau or Fulton.

There was a blast on the whistle.

'Bloody Taffy!' the tall Maroon yelled. 'He's on the frogs' side!'

Robin shrugged his shoulders. 'We killed the ball, the others get the put-in, that's quite normal.'

'And now, look. They're turning the scrum. Is that normal?'

'Done like a Frenchman, turn and turn again,' Walpole declaimed.

'*Henry VI,*' Robin said.

The man from Galashiels looked at them, shaking his head, and spat on the ground.

'Good Lord, what did you have to eat this morning, Lewis?'

Lewis spent the whole of half time wooing his altar boy, offering him a sandwich, Robin's flask and a ticket for *Dido and Aeneas* at the Queen's Hall, all this to the horrified looks of the other Maroons who were visibly waiting for the opportunity to administer a regular thrashing — perhaps in some alley after the match — while the one most intimately concerned was trying to keep Lewis at bay and calm the others down at the same time.

'Robin, my friend,' Lewis said as the players lined up for the second half, 'you have to let yourself go from time to time, you know something about that…'

'In your case I have the impression that letting yourself go means getting your face smashed in.'

Doubtless given a good tongue-lashing by their coach during the interval, the Scottish team lined up for the kick-off with aggressive intent. The play became rougher. At first the French pack retreated beneath the Scottish battering ram and young Bréjassou had to call on the trainer for an injury to his shoulder.

Cries of 'He's shamming!' could be heard here and there in the stadium.

'There! You see?' the Borderer exulted. 'They can't take it. Pansies, I tell you!'

'This time he's gone too far.' Before we could hold him back

Lewis had gone over and faced up to the beer-barrel.

'You're watching, but you don't see. You claim the ref's biased, you insult our opponents, but you don't know a thing about the game. You're no better qualified to talk about rugby than a slug crawling over a page of *Endymion* is to comment on Keats. Do you know what rugby is, sir?'

Totally flabbergasted, the other man stared at him, wide-eyed, mouth open, lower jaw stuck on the ground floor.

'This is rugby, listen: *Now he sits, angrily awaiting his mate./ Here she comes, like a left wing-threequarter cutting through toward the goal/ in sun-lamped fog at Rosslyn Park at half-past three in halcyon days.*'

Like driving in a nail, Lewis repeated the last line and finished: 'Malcolm Lowry. *Kingfishers in British Columbia.*'

Before the man could recover from his surprise, Robin handed me my blazer: 'Let's get out of here, it's going to turn nasty.' But as we were dragging Lewis up the gangway, the heart of Murrayfield was gripped by a kind of coronary: Bréjassou, revived by the magic sponge, was galloping along like a three-quarter. He took the ball from Pomathios and touched down in the corner. 3-0.

'Greetings from the pansies,' Lewis bawled, waving his silk scarf.

We made it to the top of the steps where a few middle-aged Frenchmen of the less belligerent type had infiltrated the Scottish crowd. The atmosphere was serious but polite. To understand each other the two camps had developed a kind of pidgin worthy of Tarzan or Gunga Din, accompanied by grimaces and much cryptic waving of hands: 'Your men strong… Your scrum… boom boom!'

His lock of hair exposed to the wind, Walpole seemed more frail but he still had hope, as did the rest of us. For we were attacking, attacking without respite. Weatherstone, then Marshall, then Cameron, then Weatherstone again. It was odd: our hope, instead of weakening with every second that passed, as would have been logical, grew stronger. A rugby match is a living being endowed with consciousness, I told myself. It is born and dies at a blast on the whistle; it swells, growls, goes this way and that for a little over an hour, ignoring the rest of the world, full of its own importance, of its unique character; but, just as absurd and blind as man, it doesn't believe in its own end. In the eightieth minute players and spectators are still looking to the future. The final whistle is like death: certain and yet unimaginable.

'And… what happens if it's a draw, Robin?' Walpole said.

Fulton had just ripped the ball off Dufau and passed it to Cameron. The whole stadium was on its toes as Weatherstone slalomed along the touch-line between Vannier and Domec, a few yards from the corner flag. He was about to dive over the line when Mias came across and pushed him into touch. The 'Aaah!' of disappointment from thousands of throats would have been enough to inflate an airship. Walpole was coughing his guts out. The referee blew for time and in a deathly hush Weatherstone quietly handed him the ball, just as I had given it back to Father Moray hundreds of times. Time, real time had taken over again. The world once more shook with our concerns, both great and petty.

'Sorry, Arthur,' Robin muttered.

Half an hour later, when I checked the state of my finances as I entered the 'prodigious' dive, I found the black notebook in my blazer pocket. As an epigraph, Robin had written:

'What's past is prologue.' *The Tempest.*

∞∞∞

The first time I saw Thomas Urquhart was on the Paris-Barcelona train.

The pub clock struck six. I closed the notebook and took another sip of beer. My hands were trembling. It was perhaps the tenth time I had read that sentence without managing to get any farther. I had the feeling that to get through Robin's narrative I would have to learn to read again. The stove was purring quietly, the mugs clinked on the bar; two old men in caps were tirelessly discussing Weatherstone's

211

failed run for the line. I decided to get back to the notebook, to decipher the words one by one, like a primary schoolboy: 'I... hate... trains...'

I hate trains, they're even worse than cars. Whenever I close my eyes and imagine that ridiculous mass of scrap iron going full speed ahead, it makes me feel sick. And then the lavatory's always occupied. And when it isn't I feel like spewing up when I see the rails going past at the bottom of the bowl, but I can't stop myself watching them...

The lads in the carriage — almost all of them volunteers for Spain, including quite a few from Britain — were crammed together on the seats or standing in the gangway talking politics and passing round bottles of drink. All these people. All these people who're so sure they know where they're going. In a car you can always change your mind, turn off, but on a train! You have to be terribly sure of yourself to get on a train.

'What was he called, that bloody frog?'

'Mias! For God's sake, that's the hundredth time I've told you.'

I went to get another beer.

Robin: an odd mixture of brusqueness and casualness. He had managed to restrain his handwriting but not his style. Robin the Peremptory, Robin the Versatile whom I had heard express the opposite view about cars and trains while we were driving out to Scott's View. He was there in the tightly packed pages of his black notebook, just as he was in himself. But I sensed something else between the lines, something firm, irrevocable; something you can't escape from, even if you are called Robin Dennison and yawn as you watch life's certainties floating past like mist on the Forth.

I had relearnt how to read. The stove, the clock, the table ceased to exist and all the noises of the pub merged into a hypnotic hum, a murmur from a dream.

Urquhart had taken a whole seat to himself; on it he had placed a huge leather suitcase and a sports bag with three golf clubs sticking out. He was observing the tumult around him and noting something down in a little jotter from time to time. No one had come to ask him to give up the places his luggage was occupying; everyone had decided to ignore him. Why didn't you do the same, eh? Why is it that Robin Dennison has to get involved in things that are nothing to do with him?

He raised an eyebrow and looked daggers at me. Then suddenly his face lit up. Afterwards I told myself it was perhaps because he'd noticed the press card sticking out of my breast pocket. Like a fool I always kept it handy; I had the feeling that it somehow justified my existence. 'Of course! Please, do sit down.' But I was still the one who had to lift his bags and put them on the luggage rack. 'You're Scottish, my friend, I'd swear it.' His cheeks were freshly shaven, he had large, very white teeth and a skull that was slightly domed, like a gorilla's. He leant over to me: 'Has anyone ever told you that you have the face of a movie actor?'

I thought about that remark later, after the war. One day I'd been to the pictures with that Minnie — Minnie or Grace or Janet, the devil only knows what the woman was called — and suddenly she exclaimed, 'Look! It could be you.'

There's nothing I find more boring than the cinema, apart from the theatre, perhaps — except for Shakespeare, of course — or opera; or museums, especially modern art. There have been times when I've gone into a museum as fit as an Olympic athlete and left completely washed out to the point where I was looking for a lawyer to make my will. And once I dumped a girl because she wanted to take me to the pictures.I said goodbye to her in the queue and went off to get plastered.

'But Robin, it really is the spitting image of you.'

OK, so I looked at the screen. And I saw that Yankee actor with his too-big head — in relation to the rest of his body,

I mean — his ridiculous chest, the bags under his eyes and wrinkles on his forehead; the corners of his mouth hung down as if he'd attached his braces to them; with his hangdog look and sad little smile that seemed to be saying, 'Come on, hit me harder, it doesn't hurt enough yet.'

Oh yes, that Maggie was an absolute idiot.

And then the actress appeared. She was half his age and a real beauty. The kind of girl you could even go and see La Traviata *with, or a Kandinsky exhibition. And then she starts hovering round the old spaniel. Seems to fancy him. But he hardly moves a muscle. At most he tries to hitch up the braces on his mouth, revealing a bit of his teeth, which makes him look even sadder. And when the girl says to him, 'If you need me, just whistle,' he rolls his pygmy shoulders a little and gives the cameraman a look of consternation.*

She was right, dammit! It could be me.

But I digress. It's because I haven't talked about that for ages. Because it's ages since I talked about anything. People who never talk about themselves end up going a bit mad. They can't help thinking that all those things they haven't said are stored up somewhere deep inside themselves and increase in value, like a fine wine. And then one day, when the opportunity arises, they go down into the cellar and uncork the bottle but the wine has turned to dust, at best to vinegar. Sorry, gentlemen, you end up with nothing to drink...

'Of a movie actor? No, no, I can't see that.'

'But you have, you have, I assure you, Mr...'

'Dennison.'

'Urquhart, Thomas Urquhart of Cromarty. Delighted to make your acquaintance, my friend.'

I shook the fellow's hand while looking him straight in the eye. And I felt something wrapping itself round me, something very dangerous, like that poisoned shirt — I can't remember what it's called, some Latin name. I looked all round and I saw a young chap, he seemed nice and, moreover, was opening a bottle of rough red wine. And I told myself, 'Robin, you're going to get up and go to the chap with the bottle. He's a good chap, a chap who won't cause any bother.'

But no. The other fellow, this young laird, this Cromarty, was more interesting. Perhaps because, unlike the rest, he seemed to be out of place on this train. I couldn't imagine why he was there, with his jotter, his big suitcase and his golf clubs.

'And what is it you do, Mr Dennison?'

'I'm a journalist.'

'How interesting! I've always dreamt of being a journalist.'

He made a note in his jotter and gave me a cocky glance. 'Well, this is it, isn't it?'

'Sorry?'

'War. We're heading straight for it, aren't we? What newspaper are you working for?'

'I'm not going for the newspaper, I'm going to fight.'

It may seem odd, but that was the first time I had formulated the idea clearly. To my colleagues, to my fellow boozers in the pub, I'd just said, 'I'm off to Spain.'

'So am I,' Urquhart said, nodding his head vigorously. Seeing me squinting at his golf clubs, he smiled: 'Just on the off chance, you never know...'

At that I told myself that the fellow really was mad and that it would be better to get up and skedaddle before the Shirt of Whatsit got too tight. The problem was that there weren't just golf clubs in his sports bag; he rummaged round in it with his hand — a sort of large, slightly weary claw — and took out something against which all the nice young chaps in the world with their bottles of rough red wine are powerless...

'Personally I don't much care for whisky, but I always carry a bottle with me, just in case. It seems that it's not that bad.'

Not that bad! The bugger was having me on! It was a twenty-year-old single cask Lagavulin; two weeks' pay for a grubby little journalist, perhaps even a little more. Two or three blokes around us had a quick glance at the bottle then looked away. Urquhart even had a little crystal glass, which he filled. I took a sip and I had to admit that the poison of Whatsit's shirt did indeed taste good.

'Perhaps you can help me my friend. How do we go about it?'

'Go about what?'

'Fighting, of course. That's why we're all here, isn't it?'

He had raised his voice a little but the men around us didn't look this time, they just continued talking among themselves. The Lagavulin did everything you can ask of a whisky: it warmed, lubricated, simplified. The words come out more easily. You don't need to rack your brains to decide whether you should say them or not, nor what they mean; they're there, that's all. But I still didn't answer straight away. There was still a long way to go, both for the train and the bottle. (That's another irritating thing about railways: time. Or, rather, the ridiculous fiction that you can master it by keeping to a timetable — the express at eight forty-two, the fast train at three forty pm — while in fact time's just a huge intestine that digests you at its own pace and excretes you whenever the fancy takes it. At least the Spaniards don't delude themselves like that: their trains depart and arrive when they can.) Of course I did have a contact in Barcelona, but... 'A contact? Excellent!'— A glass of whisky. But the information was — how should I put it? — of a confidential nature... I couldn't give it to just anyone. 'Of course. I understand perfectly.' We would have to get to know each other better. 'An excellent idea! Let's get to know each other.'— Another glass.

And he talked. About his ancestor, Thomas, the writer —'A rare fellow!' About The Master of Ballantrae. *About a certain putt he made at St Andrews. Not a word about himself. But then I hadn't said anything myself either. We weren't in Spain to bare our souls, we were there to go to war. What right did I have to stop him fighting? His rifle was as good as mine — doubtless better than mine.*

'John McNair,' I said as the train entered the station. 'He's the ILP representative in Barcelona. I'm sure he'll be able to tell you what to do.'

'John McNair, eh? From the ILP...' He noted the name down in his jotter. 'Thank you very much, Mr Dennison. But first of all I must consult my friend, the coin.'

Dumbfounded, I watched him take out a shilling coin.

'Heads, the Republicans, tails the Fascists.'

This time almost all the occupants of the carriage turned towards us. And I felt their looks weighing me, judging me, tying me to Thomas Urquhart, stifling me worse than the Shirt of... ah, now I remember: Nessus. Who knows, if Robin Dennison had had a better memory and a more accommodating bladder he might have been the Mark Twain of modern times.

In a deathly hush, scarcely disturbed by the squeal of the brakes, the coin flew up into the air.

'Heads! Long live the Republic!' He looked us in the eye, all of us, one by one. Then he burst out laughing. 'Oh, come now, Mr Dennison. I was joking, of course.'

And he was still laughing a little later as he disappeared into a taxi — for good. At least that's what I hoped.

Eric is absolutely right, one of the most important words in Spanish is mañana. You'll have the cartridges for your rifles mañana. You'll go to the front mañana. Goodness knows how many mañanas I spent champing at the bit doing stupid exercises in this flea-ridden barracks the POUM have taken over in Barcelona. Sometimes we paraded down the Ramblas with our red-and-black scarves and our unloaded rifles or even without rifles at all. And people cheered us as if we were real soldiers. Our 'company': a group of young Spaniards with nothing but down on their faces — the others had been at the front for several months — a handful of foreigners, including a Belgian, who was our captain, and two other Britons.

From a distance the two Britons looked rather similar: two tall chaps, all skin and bone, taciturn, rather severe-looking. But when you got to know them your impression was that they would never have become friends if it hadn't been for the war. Eric had written books — I learnt that from a young German militiaman called Willy Brandt in the Hôtel Continental — one of which described his life as a colonial policeman in Burma. But he never talked about it, neither about his books, nor about Burma. Scott had been in the war, the Great War, I mean: a piece of shrapnel had smashed his left foot. He would cross the barrack square dragging his foot a bit and shooting furious looks to the right and left in case anyone should be laughing at him. Together with Georges Kopp, the Belgian, they were the only ones among us who knew how a firearm worked.

But apart from that they were different in everything. You only had to exchange a few words with Eric to realise that his gruff manner was merely a façade. He would talk with fervour and intelligence about anything except himself. He had political jargon at his fingertips without hiding behind it, but he also knew how to find the right words to instil a minimum of efficiency and discipline in the young recruits, so that he became what you might call our drill sergeant.

When he saw that, Scott wanted to do the same. But he had to bawl out the orders, while it was enough for Eric to use gentle persuasion, and the Spaniards soon nicknamed Scott 'Hopalong'. He was rough and brusque, a caricature Highlander straight out of the times of Bonnie Prince Charlie. I'm sure he would have got on well with some of the Fascists on the subject of religion and the divine right of the monarchy. How could a fellow like that end up in the militia of the POUM, a fiercely revolutionary and anticlerical party?

It was doubtless the result of a linguistic misunderstanding. 'I'm against rebellion,' he told me one evening after we'd had a bit to drink. That was the be-all and end-all of his political doctrine. 'And the rebels are the Francoists.'

Eric attracted him like a magnet. Eric's calm; his modesty; his easy way with words, while Scott would spew them out, rolling his eyes and scowling as if they were bits of gravel or pieces of nutshell.

I remember our first night at the front, outside Saragossa, surrounded by a horseshoe of high mountains. There was nothing specific to conquer, no village, no real fortress, just 'positions' facing each other either side of the gorge. And it was freezing cold. I remember dreaming of Thomas Urquhart's whisky: I was taking great gulps but waiting in vain for the heat to spread through my veins. Instead the cold just got worse, the alcohol turning my intestines into long tubes of ice and Thomas Urquhart started to laugh: 'What do you think of this poison, my friend?' And as I lay on the ground, dying in pain: 'Oh, come now, Mr Dennison. I was joking, of course.'

We were six or seven hundred yards away from the enemy. To hit a man at that distance (the Fascists guns were hardly any better) was something of a miracle. But still, from time to time a bullet would pierce the flesh of a thigh or even go right into a skull. That would have pleased our pseudo-metaphysician, Lewis Rosewall. There was a risk but not a more likely one than a car accident or a heart attack, but it was still there, lodged in our minds, feeding on the brief vision of this or that soldier who had been maimed or killed by a bullet without warning. And that was our sole ally against boredom. For that is one thing you should know about war: our enthusiasm for the idea behind it, the passion it arouses, only last for a few weeks when you're hungry and cold and get a mere three hours' sleep at night. Then the sole power capable of making men get up is boredom

The Lairds of Cromarty

I'm on pretty good terms with boredom as long as there's something to drink, but we soon fall out when that's not the case. Having said that, I have never seen a man more tormented by boredom than Eric Blair. Every time Kopp asked for two volunteers to go and 'inspect the enemy positions,' he would jump up, with Scott Fleming following in his wake like his shadow. Or, when food was getting low, he would merrily announce, 'I'm out for potatoes.' That meant crawling on his stomach to the east without cover to an abandoned field where a few miserable tubers were still growing. And there were our two comrades advancing through the mud, snow and scree with the Fascist bullets whistling over their heads like a statistical formula. Scott was in his element there, perhaps because beneath the air of a Highland laird, he was a simple farmer at heart. Or perhaps because no one asks a man crawling along on his elbows whether he's lame or not.

Towards the end of January Eric, Scott and I were sent to the Monte Oscuro section to join the majority of the British contingent formed by the ILP.

Throughout the journey — three hours in the back of an old mail van, in total darkness, without even being able to take a drink out of our bottles it was so juddery — I played with the idea of seeing 'my friend' Thomas Urquhart again at Monte Oscuro. It was like when I was having a fag in the school lavatories and imagined the deputy head hammering on the door — just to make myself feel afraid. I couldn't forgive myself for having let him have the contact in Barcelona. I'd even had a couple of words about him with McNair, who didn't seem the kind of man to accept any Tom, Dick or Harry in a political unit, especially not a maverick with a bizarre turn of mind and a set of golf clubs.

It was almost dark when we arrived but when we got down I still blinked and looked all round. Some men, with nothing better to do, had come to see the new arrivals; no trace of Urquhart.

'But where are the shelters?' Scott asked. He was in a bad mood.

'Over there,' a chap with an Irish accent said nonchalantly. He was pointing to some sort of caves dug into the hillside. I was all in. While Eric got to know the others and Scott went off in search of some tobacco, I plunged into the first cave. I later learnt that it was called the 'Palace' because it was by far the most comfortable. You could almost stand up in it and a little natural chimney allowed the smoke from the camp-fire to escape. There were half a dozen sleeping berths, but none was free — clothes and personal items had been left beside the straw mattresses; a man was dozing on one of them. I was about to leave when I heard a characteristic 'plop' from the back of the cave.

Recognising it at once, I went towards the noise. A few yards further on the cave bent round and widened, but a little subterranean stream made it too damp for the straw mattresses. There, quivering in the faint light of a tallow candle, a man was standing up, a golf club in his hand. The ball rolled across a flat rock and dropped into a crevice.

'Par!' Urquhart exclaimed before he saw me. 'Mr Dennison! I am truly delighted to see you. I bring you greetings from our mutual friend Mr McNair.'

I gave him a nod and turned on my heels. As I went past the man lying down, I saw him raise himself up on his elbow. It was one of the Spanish machine gunners attached to the company.

'Lo conoces?' *he asked.*

'Un poquito. Es escocès como yo.'

'No me gusta este hombre… No me gusta ni un pico!'

'Porque?'

Without replying, the Spaniard rolled up in his blanket and turned to face the wall.

I was given a billet in another cave, one with a much

lower ceiling and narrower in which the smoke stung our eyes and made us cough. But I never really regretted not having a mattress in the 'Palace' nor hearing the odd plops of Urquhart's golf balls.

If my memory is correct, your father arrived the next day.

'Mias! I remember now.'

'You took your time.'

The pub had emptied without my noticing, there were only the two old men left and another distressed-looking chap standing by the stove, that had gone out, holding out his hands over the vague memory of heat. Seeing me look up, the landlord said, 'Do you want another drink? It's so quiet I might as well close the place.'

Deciding I'd had enough, I headed for Blackfriars Street, but when I reached the building where my flat was situated, I was seized with panic at the idea of continuing to read the notebook at home — in that little room shaped like a coffin in which the reek of the previous days' food stuck to the walls like out-of-date calendars. I went back to High Street and into Anchor Close. There, too, smells persisted — the smells of books, of dust, of Walpole's nauseous cigars and even that of the empty cardboard boxes that still smelt of the warehouse and the sweat of the workers there — but they were all part of a whole, they were alive. I pulled the chair underneath the bulb at the back. It was cold. I went into the cubby-hole and fetched Walpole's nightcap, slippers and blanket. As I sat down, I imagined the picture the rare passers-by would see: *a bookseller reading in his shop*, an illustration straight out of *Punch*. I settled into my own image as if into an old, worn but comfortable armchair. I was ready.

The lorry bringing him had broken down on one of the first hairpin bends up the mountain.. Whilst all the others had gone back to the nearby village to wait for it to be repaired, your father had set off alone — a four-hour walk, pure purgatory given the state of his boots, which were in an even more pitiful state than mine. We saw him coming when he was still quite some way away. For a whole hour he was no more than a black speck on the stony road; he looked as if he wasn't making any progress.

'A packet of cigarettes that he'll get here before dark,' Urquhart said.

'You're on,' said Scott.

But three-quarters of an hour later the black speck had turned into a man of about forty his face showing the effects of sunburn, which was horribly painful at that altitude and redheads with pale skin suffered worse than others. The packet of cigarettes changed hands.

When Benjamin, our captain, asked him his name, he said, 'Martin Eden.' It rang a bell, of course, but why is there always such a clutter inside my head? Educated people only have to stretch out their hand, all the information they need is neatly stacked on their mental shelves. I have to get it out of a huge, shapeless sack.

Eric looked surprised and that was very rare for him: 'Martin Eden? Is that really your name?'

Your father turned towards us. I tend to forget what he looked like, especially since I've known you. You're both very similar and very different. In my memory I see him with bushy eyebrows, like yours, while Scott says his were thin. And conversely, when you pick up a book, I expect you to take your glasses out of your pocket — but you don't wear glasses — and to make that odd little gesture he always did, the little flick he gave the cover, as if to wake up the characters sleeping inside the book. But your voices are the same, I'm sure of that. And your way of counting silently up to three or four before replying to even the simplest of questions.

And now your father counted up to ten: 'Why? Does it make any difference?'

Eric didn't reply but you could tell from his obstinate expression that he wouldn't give up until he'd sorted the matter out.

223

Nothing much was happening on Monte Oscuro, but the enemy was only about three hundred yards away and a Fascist machine gun would start spitting out bullets the moment a head appeared above the trench. It was a real rather than a statistical danger and, given that there were no potatoes to be got, there was no need for Eric and Scott to undertake their little excursions. But what irritated Scott most of all was the long conversations between Eric and Martin. At the beginning he had tried to join in; he sat down by them to have a smoke, listened to them, grunted now and then. But the two others were talking of things that were beyond him: books he hadn't read, philosophers whose names he couldn't even pronounce. Eventually he would wander off, puffing away furiously at his pipe.

It wasn't that Eric and Martin had become friends; more than once after one of their conversations I had the impression that Eric seemed relieved when he came to join us — Scott, the Irishman and myself — for a game of cards. But first he would often take out his little notebook to write something down. He found Martin intriguing. I wonder if at one point he didn't have the idea of using him as a character in one of his novels.

'Well, what's he really called?' I asked him from time to time.

I had eventually remembered that Martin Eden was the title of a book, but by whom? Eric didn't seem to have his mind on the game and misdealt: 'The devil only knows! Devil take me if I understand anything about the fellow.'

'Oh, bloody hell!' Scott exclaimed. As usual he had a hand full of twos and threes.

As far as being incomprehensible is concerned, Thomas Urquhart of Cromarty was not to be outdone. Some of the militiamen did the same as the chaps in the railway carriage:

they ignored him. Others spat on the ground when they saw him; they didn't like his condescending manner, nor his way of addressing us as 'my dear sir' or 'my friend' when we all addressed each other as 'Comrade'. There were all sorts of rumours about him: for some he was a Fascist spy, for others a madman who'd escaped from the asylum. But you couldn't ignore him between the rare skirmishes: no one could match him at unearthing tobacco, candles, sometimes even hard liquor he obtained through barter with the few peasants who had not yet fled the conflict. He livened things up with his unbelievable bets and had even managed to organise a golf tournament in the 'Palace'.

'Everyone has their weak point,' he often told me. 'Find it and you'll have them eating out of your hand.'

And that's exactly what happened; most of us ended up regarding him as a necessary evil, a kind of bizarre mascot, feared, hated and tolerated in equal measure. I couldn't forget that a strict militant of the calibre of John McNair had been caught in his web.

'Now you, Mr Dennison, haven't just one weak point, but two: alcohol and women. Am I right?'

That day he was wearing a kilt, a tartan plaid in the clan colours and an improbable kind of beret with a feather in it. A Scotsman out of an operetta. But I wanted to play along, I wanted to know what he was after.

'I'm not interested in women, Urquhart, it's women who're interested in me. As you said yourself: I look like a film actor. Short, ugly, but a star all the same. I just have to turn up somewhere and the most beautiful women are hanging round my neck.'

'That's marvellous! You must be spoilt for choice.'

'Yes, I know, free will as the bigwigs in the Party say. But I find choosing very tedious, a real chore. You could spend your whole life at it, examining, weighing up, deliberating. No, it's better, more comfortable, to decide on a principle: a

definitive no or a universal yes. And since a definitive no is physiologically untenable, I've opted for the universal yes.'

'Fascinating! And it's the same with alcohol?'

'Indeed.'

'Well, my friend, I know a place not far from here where you can drink beer and Asturian cider. And I'm willing to bet anything you like that you'll be interested in the woman who serves them.'

Like all my comrades, I'd heard of this other POUM position. It was on our right, five hundred yards as the bird flies, and it was right next to one of the richest farms in the area and therefore better provided with all kinds of things than ours. Three young Spanish women cooked there, it seems, and fought alongside the men at times. But to get there under cover you had to go down the north side into the valley then climb back up by a goat track; a good half day's walk in all.

'Not true, Mr Dennison. I know another route. We'll be there in less than an hour. If you don't fancy the woman who serves you, at least you can drink your fill — it's my treat.'

'And if I do fancy her, what's in it for you?'

'Let's say... a little favour you will do me when the time comes... and of course you'll be free to refuse if that seems preferable.'

A funny bet.'

'One has to change the rules from time to time, otherwise life would be deadly boring.'

Seeing us about to leave, Benjamin seemed put out. *'Where are you off to?'*

'Gathering wood,' Urquhart lied with his customary aplomb.

'See you're not late. Things are going to liven up, perhaps even before tomorrow.'

'Oh yes, mañana,' I mocked.

At first it seemed to be easy, an embankment protected

*the ridge path from Fascist bullets. But half way along there
was a steep drop and you had to cross a scree slope above the
road to Alcubierre to get back on the track on the other side of
the ravine. In this sector possession of the road was not clear,
any convoys could be exposed to fire from either camp so no
one ventured out there.*

'We won't get through,' I insisted.

'They don't keep this bit under surveillance.'

'All it takes is one sniper. It's too risky.'

'Would you be afraid, Mr Dennison?'

*So there I was, stumbling over the loose stones in the
wake of the feathered hat. And cursing that absolute cretin
that went by the name of Robin Dennison. But Urquhart was
right, the Fascists didn't waste a single bullet. I should have
thought it odd, but then everything about Urquhart was odd.
And I was thirsty. Your thought processes don't work properly
when you're thirsty.*

*There were three women at la Granja but she was
simply called la Mujer, with a capital 'm'. When I saw her I
immediately understood why.*

*She served us cider in earthenware bowls — I would never
had believed that an alcoholic drink from apples could be so
strong. La Granja was a typical farm of the region, large and
solid, with regular supplies from the people in the valley, its
own well, wine cellar and larder full of provisions left by the
owner, a local bigwig with Fascist sympathies. It even had
latrines that were almost worthy of the name and for the first
time for two months the air I breathed didn't reek of the smell
of shit. But my decision to return to la Granja at all costs,
despite the scree slope, the risk of Fascist bullets, with or
without Urquhart — preferably without him — had nothing to
do with this unexpected comfort. While the laird droned on, I
didn't take my eyes off la Mujer; after a quarter of an hour I
felt as if I'd known her for ever.*

'Have you noticed the ring?'

I looked at la Mujer's hands as she cleaned a rifle with a gun-sponge — on our sector of the front the mere ownership of such an implement was a visible sign of wealth. Her fingers were long, fine, deft, but had no rings at all. Not even a wedding ring.

'I'm not talking about that woman, Mr Dennison, I'm talking about our friend Martin Eden.'

'What ring do you mean?'

The one he carries attached to a little chain round his neck. I saw it yesterday while he was shaving.'

'No, I've never noticed.'

'That's impossible, Mr Dennison,' Urquhart said in the tone of a friendly reproach. 'You sleep in the same dugout, your palliasses are side by side. You must have noticed it.'

'So what?'

'Ah, señorita, allow me to introduce my friend Mr Dennison who is already, I believe, one of your most fervent admirers.'

As she filled our bowls with cider, la Mujer gave me a long, impenetrable stare. I couldn't tell if she understood English beyond a few rudimentary expressions. The burning sensation of the cider went all the way down to my groin.

Urquhart clinked glasses and gave me a wink. 'I have the impression she fancies you.'

'It's what I was saying. They all just fall into my arms. But you haven't won your bet yet, Urquhart. It's she who has to appeal to me, not vice versa.'

'Of course, of course! Now to get back to that ring: it's truly remarkable, an uncut diamond set in a gilt band. Now I have every reason to believe that this jewel belongs to my family, that Mr... Eden has acquired it by... let's say questionable means. Of course, there's no question of my accusing him without proof.'

'So what?' I repeated, as a lump of fear and hatred took the opposite route to the cider.

'Well, if an impartial observer could subject the aforesaid ring to a close inspection, say when Mr Eden was asleep, I have to say that I would be eternally grateful.'

I pushed back my chair sharply and was on my feet at once. For the first time for ages I felt a bit dizzy and I couldn't say what was the cause, the cider, the woman, Urquhart or a combination of all three. I looked at la Mujer, our eyes met. The rifle, spotless, was gleaming in her hands and I told myself that this time I was going to have to make a choice. As I left, I heard Urquhart holding forth on the fermentation of cider. Not long afterwards, on the scree, I set off a heavy volley of fire from the Fascists; I owe my life to good luck and thick mist.

Informing has always seemed as despicable to me as treachery. Poor Robin Dennison who believes in nothing but always pretends to believe in something. Idiot! Idiot! When I got back to our position I didn't go to see Benjamin, but Eric. On sentry duty in the most advanced trench, he was vaguely keeping an eye on the enemy trenches while glancing at his notebook from time to time. He was wearing, over four or five layers, the roomy corduroy jacket Henry Miller had given him when they met in Paris. He seemed nervous and tired.

'I can't understand why Scott detests Martin so,' he said.
'Jealousy.'

Eric considered the idea for a moment, then shook his head. 'How can one be jealous of a ghost?'

'When you're unhappy you can be jealous of anything.'

A bullet whistled through the mist above our heads. Instinctively we ducked.

'The fellow has no past. Or a future, just a present. And he stole his name from Jack London.'

Jack London, of course! It came back to me now. On a sledge pulled by a team of white dogs. With two or three gold prospectors with hollow cheeks and feverish looks. He was a hard drinker, I believe, somewhat in my own style, never really drunk. Endurance, the worst gift nature can give you.

'What about a ring? Could he have stolen a ring as well?'

I told him everything: my conversation with Urquhart and the business with the scree slope. Why had the Fascists, in broad daylight and with a great befeathered beanpole in their sights, not let off a single shot while two hours later they wasted ten cartridges on a dwarf crawling through a pea-souper?

Eric jumped up — a bullet almost tore off his left ear. The one disadvantage tall people have compared with us runts is that they often forget they are tall.

'I'm going to talk to Martin.'

That evening in the dugout Eric Blair was leafing through a book I had never seen in his hands before. And your father, very calm, even more calm than usual — so calm you almost had the impression he wasn't there at all — came up to me so quietly he made me start: 'Would you have a box of matches and some paper.

Then, going back to his mattress: 'Thanks.'

The next day for the first time he waited for the chap who brought supplies and took the post. He gave him a little package the size of a box of matches.

The dog from next door was barking in Anchor Close. It was getting colder and colder. I stood up and walked round Walpole's cubby-hole thinking about that spring day in '36 when the ring had arrived.

When I got back from school my mother was sitting at the kitchen table leaning on her elbows, frowning, her fingers at her temples, her eyes fixed on the package. She could have been a clairvoyant over her crystal ball.

I went round the table and looked over her shoulder. My heart started to pound as I read: *Ebenezer Krook, Flourmill Rd., Aberdeen.* The ink on the stamp was smudged, you could just make out: *Barcelona.*

'Does that mean Daddy's dead?'

She started, but hardly looked up. 'It's his handwriting. I don't think the dead can write.'

On the stamp were two intertwined flags, one black-and-red, the other red. Two unknown sets of initials: *CNT, UGT, todo por la alianza.*

'Come on, it's for you, open it.'

I cut the string that was much too thick for the tiny parcel. The matchbox emerged; on one side of the cover there was a dancer taking a monkey for a walk, on the other the monkey was alone, holding up a bottle: *Anis del mono.*

Once the science teacher had asked us to bring a butterfly to the lesson. After numerous failures, I had gone to find my father. And now I saw him again, stiff and silent, holding a net specially bought for the purpose. He obviously had no idea what to do. He was just as clumsy as me, but he put a lot of effort into it. I felt uncomfortable, it was really very odd to see my father waving a butterfly net. But I also found it moving, for it was also a gesture of hope. We eventually managed to trap a tiny yellowish specimen and put it, half-dead in a matchbox, together with a lettuce leaf.

The first thought I had — and it was so stupid, I blushed with shame — was that my father was sending me a butterfly.

'The ring,' my mother simply said, as if she were reading a signpost.

The imaginary butterfly had flown off. All that was left in the palm of my hand was a cold object with a dull gleam. At once sympathetic and enticing, the monkey on the box held out his bottle of absinthe to me.

And then, one day, mañana finally arrived. For some time things had been going on as usual; I went to see la Mujer every day, and I felt very odd. My heart would be pounding as I walked much faster than usual. In a whole week, she didn't say the least idiotic thing, as Marge, Ginny, Pat or the others would have done, she just looked at me with her big black eyes. Or she would talk of ordinary things, things to do with life at la Granja. Her Spanish accent seemed to caress the English words, like a soft brush, giving them a new gloss. After we had made love in the barn, she ran her fingers through my hair to take out bits of straw. For there was no cinema around, no opera, no Kandinsky exhibitions, just the straw, the cider, la Mujer and me. By deduction and cross-checking I've come to the conclusion that that is what is called 'happiness' in novels. Except that, when you haven't been forewarned, you feel something disturbing's happening to you. You're on your guard. You're watching out for the moment when it will end.

Eric and I had decided to say nothing to Benjamin, nor to anyone else. Urquhart was lying low and hadn't tried anything against your father. Moreover there was nothing to back up the idea that he was a spy. The Francoists would generally take potshots at me when I crossed the scree, but not always. They had to take a nap now and then and that's what could have happened the first time with Urquhart. As he said himself, you don't accuse a man without proof.

Then one day a Fascist aeroplane flew over our trenches. It didn't drop any bombs — our 'position' wasn't worth the bother — but copies of their rag, the Heraldo de Aragón, *announcing the taking of Málaga. That same evening, as if the news had given them wings, the Fascists brought up several machine guns and started to spray us with bullets — to no great effect, except that it kept us stuck in our trenches; it would have taken heavy artillery to do any real damage, but they were as short of munitions as we were ourselves. However, the report of the loss of Málaga had spread all along the front, morale was low and that was presumably why our strategists decided to respond with a coup of their own: to take Huesca. 'Mañana we'll be in Huesca.'*

We were transferred thirty miles away from Monte Oscuro to supplement the forces besieging the town. Since the

Fascist line was well over half a mile away, the little game of night patrols started again, much to the delight of Scott and Eric. Their purpose was to keep an eye on the enemy and reconnoitre the terrain in preparation for the coming attack. Then, one night while I was dreaming of la Mujer in our quarters at la Torre Fabian, our sappers really got to work and in a few hours threw up a new breastwork under the very noses of the Fascists. 'Mañana. It's tomorrow.'

This time it was true.

Towards three in the morning, Smillie, our new captain, woke us and told us to stand to. In the distance we could hear the sound of the sappers' picks and a few isolated shots. The attack was to be launched from a little abandoned hamlet a few hundred yards to the west. Once there, the rumour started to circulate that they were going to give us hot coffee with brandy and your father went off to see what news there was. It's odd how such little things can become important at certain moments, even for those who like neither coffee nor brandy. Eric, Scott and I met up again in a barn that had been half destroyed by the bombardment. The remains of the floor had been prised up with a spade to make a fire. As was his habit, Scott took out his pack of cards. From time to time one of us looked out of the door and asked what was happening about the coffee. 'The coffee? Mañana,' a mocking voice replied. We hardly looked at the cards we were holding; two or three times I opened my mouth, but I didn't even feel like finishing what I was saying and the words died away amid the crackling of the planks. Fear, real fear, isn't like happiness, you recognise it immediately, even if it's the first time. Beyond a certain percentage, a statistical possibility becomes a certainty and the twinges of anxiety turn into a good old panic that ties your stomach in knots and makes your heart sink into your boots.

'It would be better if we had a fourth,' Eric eventually said as he played a card. At that moment Urquhart appeared at the

door of the barn.

My first reaction was that he really did have a sense of the dramatic. My second was that I had perhaps got things seriously wrong with my scruples and if something should happen because of this individual it would be to a large part my fault. He took off his feathered bonnet came over to the fire and lifted up his kilt to warm his thighs.

'In my opinion that's not the ideal outfit for crawling through the mud... Comrade Urquhart.' Eric had emphasised the word 'Comrade'.

'My dear Mr Blair, for want of warmer clothes my ancestor Francis Urquhart took part in the Battle of Culloden in this outfit and, according to all reports, covered himself in... glory.'

Scott sniffed contemptuously. 'One of my ancestors was at Culloden too.'

'That's very interesting, Mr Fleming. And which side was he fighting on?'

For a dyed-in-the-wool Highlander such as Scott to suggest that one of his ancestors could have betrayed the Stuarts and supported the English was the ultimate insult. For a moment I thought things were going to turn nasty, but Eric put his hand on Scott's shoulder and Urquhart went on with a laugh, 'I was joking, of course, Mr Fleming. I have no doubts as to the loyalty of your family. What are you playing? Bridge?'

A further sniff from Scott.

'Oh Hell,' Eric said as he shuffled the cards.

'Hmm. What if we were to play something more appropriate to the circumstances? The truth game, for example.'

Scott looked flabbergasted. I was about to make one of my jokes, but Eric got in before me: 'Very well. You to start.'

'Thanks.'

Deciding that he had warmed himself enough, Urquhart came and sat with us on an upturned crate, after first having dusted it with the back of his hand. 'First question, gentlemen, in fact the only one that it's worth asking since we are perhaps going to die in an hour or two: why are we here?'

Silence. We all stared at the fire. Eric the intellectual. Scott the rough diamond. Robin the clown. It was a question I'd asked myself a thousand times, especially since I'd met la Mujer. There's really no answer to it once you've eliminated all those from the various professions of faith and breviaries. Why risk dying when you don't have to? When you don't believe in anything apart from your own life. And when, deep down inside, you are convinced there is no tune more stirring than the one whisky plays on your taste buds, no political programme more satisfying than a cigarette between your lips, nor future more glorious than a woman's hand taking a wisp of straw out of your hair? Do certain words have to be blown up with the bicycle pump of rhetoric until they become lifebelts, marker buoys for the blind among us: justice, courage, liberty, revolution? Or do these words truly designate something that has meaning beyond the letters that spell them? Plato, the ideas, Occam's razor and all that stuff. Grist for your mill, Lewis...

'Well, Mr Dennison?'

'Because I had to get out of Edinburgh. The rent had become too expensive.'

Eric gave a sad smile. Urquhart guffawed: 'Isn't that just our journalist friend! Full of humour and... as slippery as an eel. Do you know what my namesake, the literary genius Thomas Urquhart said? "Irony is the sword of the strong, humour the shield of the weak." But perhaps that doesn't really mean anything... Thomas loved witty turns of phrase, even empty ones. Mr Blair?'

Eric, as was his way, did not try to evade the question. He lit a cigarette and took his time, as if the question had been put by Socrates himself and not by someone like Urquhart who was just trying to stir things up. 'When I was on the train,

235

at the border,' he finally said, wreathed in smoke, 'I didn't yet know whether I was going to fight or not. But I suppose there are certain moments when men have to do certain things at least so as to find out if they are capable of doing them.'

'Excellent! Beautifully put! Sir Thomas would have adored it! And of course your decision has nothing to do with a possible... literary project?'

'It seems to me that I could have written a book on the war while quietly holed up in the Hotel Continental, or even in London. That is what many of my colleagues are doing.'

'Nor anything to do with Burma, either? A kind of... expiation? For having been a colonial policeman, "a cog in the wheels of despotism"— your own words, I believe. Bitter memories for a socialist, I would imagine... though for my part I have the greatest respect for those charged with the maintenance of order.'

Now I really admired Eric Blair. It was a trap that was difficult to get out of without losing your calm and thus justifying the one who had set it. But he didn't get hot under the collar, he looked Urquhart steadily in the eye. 'If you know my book, you already have the answer to that question.'

'Of course, of course. I'll reread it when I get time. That leaves Mr Fleming.'

'Pah! This is a stupid game,' Scott muttered.

'You should have said so before.'

'And what about you? Why don't you answer the question?'

'No problem. Here is my reply.' Urquhart rummaged round in his pocket and showed us a coin. 'My only treatise on morality; my spiritual adviser; my vade-mecum. If you start out from the principle that all decisions are equally valid — that opinions, enthusiasms, moral aspirations are for man what horseflies are for ruminants and send you running all over the field, make you swish your tail, stamp your feet and roar with no regard for the most elementary concern for elegance — then, gentlemen, a coin is the only solution. Our

*sole freedom resides in tossing it up and accepting its verdict.
At this very moment while I'm talking to you here, I could be
a doctor in a charming spa, a prospector in the Klondyke... I
could be chopping down the Amazonian forest, sowing seeds
in the Sahara, making the Antarctic ice-cap melt if the coin
had so decided. And as a result I sleep the sleep of the just
and am the happiest of men.'*

Scott grimaced and spat on the ground.

*'It hurts, doesn't it? The wound in your foot. It was at the
Somme, I believe?'*

Eric's eye met mine.

'It's very odd,' Urquhart went on, *'the way people have of
seeing shame where there's just a slight physical deformity. A
limp, what is that in the light of infinity? But I can see that one
might deem it desirable to compensate for this... distortion
with a stance of extreme moral rectitude. All the more so
when the said wound was inflicted on you... by your own
comrades-in-arms...'*

Scott suddenly straightened up and stiffened.

*'Oh, it's not an isolated case... exhausted, disheartened
troops from whom some obscure colonel eager for promotion
demands an impossible effort; a despairing advance, a ...
pragmatic retreat. And the obscure colonel orders the artillery
to fire on their own men.'*

I never found out how Urquhart had heard of the affair
but Scott's reaction spoke for itself. All at once he went white
as a sheet and had great difficulty breathing.

'Who... told you that?'

*'Oh, I can't remember, but these things always come out
eventually. Our Welsh friend, no doubt; he wasn't far from
you on the front... or... well now, perhaps it was Mr Eden.
Didn't we talk about that terrible battle of the Somme, Mr
Eden? You had a cousin, didn't you?'*

Your father, holding a pot of coffee, was standing in the
doorway. He looked at us one by one, trying to understand

what had happened. But he never knew for at that very moment we heard Smillie's voice shouting, 'Fall in! Everyone fall in! This time it's for real!'

You must know how it is: being unable to concentrate on something because of a urgent desire to pee. Your bladder blows up, just like a balloon; the balloon gets in the way of the book you're reading, the meal you're eating, the discussion you're having with someone. The world, reality is reduced to one thing alone: to have a pee. To have a pee at all costs. Well, that's what happens when I try to recall that famous 'attack', the only real fight I took part in while I was in Spain. I'm not saying that when it came to it the need to have a pee stopped me doing what had to be done. (What was it, anyway that had to be done? To show 'heroism'? Just 'courage'? To reach the 'objective'? Kill as many Fascists as possible? Or simply to obey orders and stay alive without appearing too cowardly?) But I did it in a kind of trance with just one thought in my mind: that it should all be over as quickly as possible so that I could go and have a pee. And today the memory of that very personal pain — in general pain is caused by something beyond your control, a sharp edge, a punch, an illness, while that pain is brought on by you yourself — veils everything else. The pain was intense. Revived by the cold, fear, my pelvis rubbing against the ground, we crawled along the trench dug by the sappers making as little sound as possible so as to surprise the Fascists. All the same, the mud went plop, plop as we moved along and the noise hurt as well. I was almost thinking of peeing in my trousers, I almost envied Urquhart his kilt, which would have made the operation much easier.

But I held on. I suffered in silence. Man is not an animal, he doesn't descend to things that are beneath him, that is unless he's very afraid... Bullshit! If I had to do it again...

However, I had taken precautions. Just before the assault began, Eric and I slipped away for a moment. It was majestic

*as our two jets soared up into the sky and fell back down onto
the ground with a soft hiss and a little wisp of steam.*

'We're in great form today,' Eric said.

'It must be the coffee...'

'Or the fear!'

And we laughed like two little kids.

*'Do you really think Martin might have been spreading
that story about Scott?'*

*'Certainly not!' Eric said as he buttoned up his flies.
'Even if he did know about it, he wouldn't have said anything.
Since we've known him he hasn't said more than a few words,
except to me. And even then we just talk about books.'*

*A little later, while we were hiding at the bottom of a
gully waiting for the signal, he added, 'I've no idea whether
Urquhart was serious just now, with all that stuff about his
coin. I don't know if it's possible to stake your life on heads or
tails. But what I do know is that Martin wouldn't even bother
to toss the coin. Have you read* Bartleby?*'*

*I felt like telling him that this muddy hole wasn't the best
place for a lecture on literature, nor me the best audience. Yes,*
Bartleby *did ring a bell, but I'd have to rummage through a
dozen dusty trunks inside my head to find it. Fortunately, Eric
didn't expect an answer.*

*'I'd prefer no to...' That's what Martin would say as he
was about to toss the coin.'*

'Which means?'

*Smillie put a finger to his lips and set off down the trench.
Martin followed him, then Urquhart, then all the rest. Scott
was looking for Eric.*

*'Nothing... or perhaps just this: the most secret people
are those who don't have any.'*

'Any what?'

'Any secrets. Off we go, then.'

*I wondered whether old Walpole would have enjoyed
pissing by moonlight in the company of his 'dear Walter*

Scott'? Whether the realisation that the master dressed like everyone else and was subject to the same calls of nature might not have — how shall I put it? —'dampened' his admiration. It didn't bother me at all when, later on, I read George Orwell's books. On the contrary, I liked to remember that moment. I enjoyed the knowledge that those words had been written by a man who had pissed by moonlight with me. It added to their truth, their force, in which I recognised something of the great beanpole who went along the trench in front of me and who gave me confidence, not because he was stronger, bolder than the others, but because he seemed to be crawling with a very precise aim in mind — and not simply that of disembowelling Fascists or saving his own skin. The same aim as he was pursuing in his writing. I'm not clever enough to say what that aim was, it sufficed that I knew he had one. That he hadn't just tossed a coin.

The Fascists. We started to smell them two hundred yards from the redoubt we were supposed to take. The smell of their cooking. Of their shit. So similar to ours. We had reached the last parapet, from now on there was no more protection, the trench stopped. We had to crawl across the no-man's-land without making a sound and as quickly as possible, then cut through their two lines of barbed wire and fall on them, hoping that the surprise would make up for our weakness — there were only fifteen of us; the bulk of the brigade, including forty Germans, was concentrated on another, more important redoubt two hundred yards to our right. Later on, if the plan worked, they would come to back us up.

A Spaniard by the name of Jorge took out his wire-cutters, the only pair we had. I would never have believed a wire could make so much noise when it snapped. Fortunately it had started to rain heavily. We spread out and, like huge insects bogged down in the mud, advanced a few more yards, so slowly that I could have described every clod, every drop of water in minute detail. Then the parapet was there, rising up in front of us, and on the scale of clods of earth and drops of water it looked like an impassable mountain ridge. As had been arranged beforehand, Smillie threw the first grenade. They were crap and one in every five would go off in your hand — that's if they went off at all. But this one did explode, only not far enough away, before the parapet. And that was when the shooting started, it was the only time I managed to forget my bladder. It seemed impossible to get through such a hail of bullets. But you have to tell yourself that the enemy were afraid as well; that they were shooting badly, or at random, just to make yourself feel less nervous. Taffy got a graze, that was all.

Then Eric threw a grenade in his turn and far enough this time. Scott did the same. We heard the cries, the shooting subsided a little and Smillie shouted, 'Forward! Charge!' As in the war films Bonnie used to take me to see.

It all went very quickly, as quickly as the mud, the slope of the parapet and the weight of our ancient rifles and bayonets allowed. Our grenades had destroyed their huts. One poor devil was groaning underneath the wreckage, one blood-soaked arm clasping his stomach. Just a lad wrapped up in half a dozen layers of clothes, just like us. It was much more difficult now to call him a 'Fascist', it even seemed slightly ridiculous. Two others appeared from behind a partition wall that was still standing and hurried off along the trench, one to the left, one to the right. Eric hesitated for a second then set off after the one on the left, trying to bayonet him between the shoulder blades. Scott did the same with the other. We could see them running with great awkward strides, boots flying through the air, with their bayonets, while the others hopped from side to side and arched their backs as they tried to avoid them; it all looked grotesque. By the time Eric and Scott returned we had already examined the redoubt: no 'spoils' worthy of the name, neither a rifle nor a machine gun. Just two boxes of ammunition, but that, alas, was not what we

241

were most in need of. The first part of our mission had drawn a blank.

The second was to hold the position for as long as possible, at least until the Germans had taken the other redoubt. I was just about to undo my flies when someone shouted, 'The Fascists! They're coming back!' In actual fact it was three of our Germans in shock-troop uniforms who emerged from the trench on the left and told us that the attack had failed. They'd run into two machine guns and a mortar, most had been killed and the Fascists were hunting down the survivors. No question of having a pee now, we had to block the trench with sacks of soil, hoping we would be able to repel them. While we were getting on with that, however, Paddy Donovan, whom Smillie had sent to get news, returned with the order to fall back. I remember that Eric and I burst out laughing. This time it really was too ridiculous. What, all that for nothing? And as we clambered back over the parapet carrying two boxes of ammunition, each weighing a hundred pounds, we were still laughing, but not for long: a machine gun less that two hundred yards away on the right started to spray us with bullets while sustained gunfire from at least ten rifles came from the left. On top of that were the shots from behind, our men having briefly taken us for Fascists. At the foot of the parapet I heard someone shouting and I thought I recognised your father's voice, but we couldn't see anything and the hail of bullets drove us on like the shepherd's crook does a herd of sheep.

It really was pandaemonium. We zigzagged across no-man's-land, getting stuck on the barbed wire, retiring, going forward again, seeing two parapets with no idea which was ours and which the Fascists' since they followed the topography of the terrain, winding along like the meanders of a river. Soon a mortar joined in. Jorge fell beside me, dead. I still can't say how I managed to reach the right parapet, at almost exactly the same point where we had launched the *attack. Several had made it before me, including a few who were seriously injured, one of whom was Donovan. Eric had a nasty cut on the thigh from falling on something; Scott had bandaged it with a piece torn off his own shirt but it was still bleeding.*

'Where's Jorge?' Smillie asked.

'Dead,' I replied, as in the film, that blasted film that I couldn't get away from.

'Eden? Urquhart?'

No one replied.

'It seems to be calming down,' Smillie said after a while. 'We'll have to go and see if we can find them.'

It was true. The shooting seemed to have moved away by several hundred yards. Not realising that the attack had failed, the machine guns of another POUM position, on the other side of us from the Germans, were still firing and the Fascists were transferring their troops to that sector.

'They can go to the devil!' Scott muttered, but no one apart from Eric and I heard him.

'I'll go, if you'll give me the time to have a pee.' Unbelievable! It was indeed the voice of Robin Dennison. My voice. And while I was relieving myself, filling myself with that delightful emptiness, that marvellous disappearance of pain, another voice — also mine — was screaming in my ear, 'You stupid idiot! This isn't a film, a sodding bloody film!'

So there we were, together in no-man's-land: Taffy Davies, El Diablo, as they called him because of his little pointy ears, though I think his real name was Ezekiel, and me. Me, Robin Dennison, plagued by the thought that I'd forgotten something important. The terrain, laid waste by the shells, was unrecognisable. We didn't even know whether it was best to crawl or run. We started by running, but when a Fascist machine gunner spotted us, we went back to crawling. Ezekiel and me, that is, for Davies was killed in the first burst of fire. There was still a lot of firing on the right and just as I was thinking that it was possible, that there were no Fascists in front of us and that the machine gunner had forgotten us, the sky was split by a whistling noise and Ezekiel was blown away. Lifted off the ground like a puppet by the shell. I dug myself into the mud, my hands clasped on the back of my neck. When I looked up again, the Fascist parapet was in front of me, quite close; there, on the other side of the barbed wire, your father was stretched out, groaning. And bent over him, a torch in one hand, a dagger in the other, was Urquhart.

I frantically looked for the gap Jorge had cut in the barbed wire. It was probably twenty yards to the left or thirty to the right; as good as twenty or thirty miles away, given that I couldn't get up to run. The wire-cutters, that's what I'd forgotten, those blasted wire-cutters. The intervals between the shots became longer and longer and soon there was an eerie silence. I saw Urquhart move his hand towards your father's neck and grasp the chain. I heard his enraged cry when he saw that the ring wasn't there. Then your father's head slumped down on the side facing me; Urquhart turned to face me as well. I could see them clearly in the light of his torch and assumed they had recognised me. They looked at me for a few seconds, like actors waiting for the director's instructions, as if saying, 'What do we do now?' Urquhart especially seemed disoriented. He rubbed his face with his hand, then slowly stood up and climbed over the parapet.

Snap, snap. Scott had materialised at my side, the wire-cutters in his hand. I'm sure Peggy would have clapped, but the scriptwriter must have made a little mistake: it was too late; too late to catch the miscreant. While I bent over your father, Scott climbed up after Urquhart and peered up and down the trench on the other side. Urquhart had disappeared to the left, towards the Fascists. There was an exchange of Spanish exclamations, but no shots. None of us were to see him again, at least not in Spain.

Too late to save your father as well, he was losing too

much blood and was dead before we got back to our lines. Going through his clothes we found nothing personal at all, no papers, no letters, not even a watch or lighter with his initials. Only the book, Martin Eden, *that for some reason or other I stuck in my pocket.*

A few weeks later, Eric Blair once more forgot how tall he was; early one morning a Fascist bullet went through his neck because his head was sticking up out of the trench. Seeing him spit blood on the stretcher I was fairly sure he'd be dead in a quarter of an hour. 'He's fucked,' someone said. You can't imagine a bullet could go through a man's neck without cutting the carotid artery, but that's what happened. Ebenezer Krook, you owe your life to a statistical blip, otherwise you'd be at the bottom of the Corryvreckan. But you mustn't think that statistics nods off between two striking events, no, it's at work all the time. Just imagine, for example, that my bladder had been a bit bigger; or that I hadn't forgotten the wire-cutters; or that that blockhead Scott had set off with me into no-man's-land instead of appearing like the Masked Avenger a quarter of an hour too late. Who knows? Perhaps your father could have been saved. I've seen other similar wounds, sometimes all you need is five minutes: you can lose plenty of blood in five minutes.

A philosopher — just don't ask me his name! — once said, 'Why is there something rather than nothing?' That, it appears, prevented him from sleeping throughout his life. But it's another question that makes me turn over and over in my bed: 'Why is there something rather than something else?' And I believe I'll never find the answer to that, not even at the bottom of a bottle of twenty-year-old Lagavulin.

'That… what was he called?… that Weatherstone, he failed. He didn't find the asymptote.' Professor Muir is holding the tiller.

My father, sitting beside me, is looking into the distance. He's wearing a black-and-red jersey.

'You have to slip through, do you hear? Yes, *you*. Slip through.'

The boat is gliding along an infinitely gentle curve, the sky is a brilliant white, the water is no more than five feet deep, and I can see strange things among the seaweed: a ball, a monkey.

'What do you feel like when you're dead?'

My father seems amazed that I am endowed with speech. He bends his head down as he looks at me, as if I were just a photo of myself, an old blurred snapshot taken at the seminary. He picks me up by one of the corners and turns me over to read the date.

Muir lets go of the tiller and starts to bustle about. 'The asymptote! We're almost there.'

The monkey walking along beside us under the water is looking more and more like Robin Dennison. If I put my hand in the water, I could stroke his fur, grasp the bottle he was clutching to his side. He laughs, then disappears. The boat goes between two high glass walls.

'Complete,' my father says watching a butterfly take off, 'you feel complete.'

∞∞∞

Knock, knock.

Not knowing where you are when you wake up is something that can happen to anyone. But this was different. Even after having recognised Walpole's bookshop there was a part of me that refused to return to the fold. The light bulb was me; the hand knocking on the window was me too. There were shapes dancing on the ceiling — me — sounds hiding behind the books — me again. Fanlight-me; shelf-me; Shakespeare-me.

Knock-knock-me.

But when I stood up all these bits came back, as if they were iron filings and my body a large, bizarrely shaped magnet. I suddenly felt heavier, more compact. The dream was still present, like a visitor who has just turned round having forgotten his umbrella.

'Is the bookshop open?' Robin said, a bottle of Lagavulin in his hand. It had been raining. His macintosh smelt of a Sunday by the sea.

'The bookshop, no; but the bar, yes.'

'Perfect. You weren't at home, so I thought…'

As I closed the door behind him, the wind slipped into the room and leafed through the account book beside the cash register.

'Where's Walpole?' I asked as I went into the cubby-hole.

'At Greyfriars, I think. We gave him time to go home, until Monday morning. But the hospital has already been arranged. He's going to give them a hard time.'

When I came back with the glasses, he had placed the little stepladder beside the chair, underneath the fanlight. Saturday evening, eight o'clock. Out in the Royal Mile the news-vendor was shouting out the headlines of the evening edition: 'Scotland lose.' A few disgruntled supporters were taking out their disappointment on a few tin cans while young people were meeting up to go out for a drink and to the dance hall. It was a mild January, but anyway the girls would have put up with the chilliest of winds to show off their new nylon stockings. Several pairs of bootees were pacing up and down the pavement; an ideal moment for the 'nights' game.

'Three nights,' Robin declared, emptying his glass.

'And la Mujer? How many nights?'

He gave me a glance as he lit a cigarette. 'With la Mujer it was the afternoon.'

'But what happened? And what's Lewis got to do with all this?'

'Lewis? Nothing. When the Republican government, manipulated by the Communists, dissolved the POUM militias lots of the soldiers had problems. I advised her to come back to Edinburgh with me. She said yes, but it wasn't the same any more. There's cinemas in Edinburgh, museums, other women. Lots of other women. And not a single wisp of straw. Nor Asturian cider. I felt as if she'd lost her capital letter. She was an undesirable in Spain and no longer desired in Scotland. So we thought up this idea of an unconsummated marriage — a marriage of convenience if you like — with Lewis. That's all.'

'To put it in a nutshell: you didn't love her any more.'

He refilled our glasses, gave his own a close inspection, then chuckled. 'How did that frog put it? *Love is the infinite placed within the reach of poodles*. My God! That nylon's a magnificent invention, don't you think? They look as if they've got bare legs. Jesus, just look at those calves! Five nights! Getting back to Spain, is that all you want to ask me?'

I nodded.

'As you wish... Hey, look, those aren't bad either — and she really *does* have bare legs. She must be hotblooded and that's always a good point...'

The whisky was going straight to my head, transforming my brain into one of those repulsive organs awaiting the resurrection steeped in formaldehyde in laboratory cupboards. Fascinated, I stared at the motionless legs. A gust of wind ruffled her skirt.

'Pity about that nasty scar on her knee... It's odd, she's not moving, she seems to be looking for something. Hmm... let's say two nights.'

The legs disappeared. A few seconds later steps could be heard in Anchor Close, then a face appeared at the display window.

Robin looked at me. 'I think we have a visitor.'

CHAPTER XI

*Which concerns a music box, a cricket bat and the sad end
of Laura Hunt.*

Aunt Catriona was everywhere. Hung over the back of a chair, her
cape mounted guard. There was a little note on the telescope stand:
Don't touch. Another on the Frigidaire: *Make sure you close the
door properly after use*. On the pantry door: *Put everything back in
exactly the same place*. On the pillow in my bedroom: Make the bed
every morning. In every room I could smell that characteristic blend
of heady perfume, bad breath and musty slippers that followed her
everywhere like an old dog. Even though I knew very well that the
International Conference on Optics in London would go on for three
days, I felt I could hear her footsteps in the corridor of the flat. It was
like living in a heart stuck between two beats.

She hadn't really left Edinburgh. She cleared her throat when we
kissed in the hall, when we opened the door to her bedroom — my
bed was too small — despite the *No Entry* note on the door. I could
see her out of the corner of my eye while we were making love:
standing in the doorway, wrapped in the gloom of the corridor, she
nodded her head with a knowing look. And now, on the bedside table
she had her gaze fixed on me through the eyes of a large china cat.

Krook grunted in his sleep. Taking infinite precaution, I lifted up
the blankets and slipped out of bed and walked round it. The ring
was there on the mat covering the other bedside table, by the base of
the brass lamp and Herbert Geddes' compass.

Why don't you ask him, Mary, just ask him.
He'd refuse.
Why? Why would he refuse to help his father's old comrades?
I don't know. He'd refuse, that's all.

My God, Mary, you really do have the makings of a professor of literature. You think you know everything.

In a quick swoop, as if to catch myself unawares in a game of scissors paper stone, I grabbed the ring. Followed by my aunt, who successively took on the form of the coat rack, the shadow of the telescope and the tall standard lamp, I went into the sitting-room, to the glazed bookcase — *Not to be touched on any account* — picked up the microscope and put it on a table.

I have never worn jewellery, perhaps simply because no man, not even my father, had ever expressed the intention of giving me any. 'All that glitters is not gold,' he would say when I talked about Alison and her big gold-plated earrings. The jewellers' vocabulary fills me with a complex mixture of disdain, irritation at my own ignorance — I'd be incapable of distinguishing between a ruby and a sapphire — and a faint tinge of jealousy. All I could say of Krook's ring was that it seemed to correspond to what is called an uncut diamond in the books of Wilkie Collins, that it had no facets (I had stupidly hoped the number of facets would bear some significant relationship to Sir Alexander's desk), that is was very ugly and also — probably — very valuable. After a brief hesitation I tried to slip it on my ring finger — it stuck at the knuckle. 'Hmm, Hmm,' said Aunt Catriona's cape. Krook must have very slim fingers for a man of his size, odd that I hadn't noticed. I was naked in this freezing room with its big uncurtained windows and I felt like going back to bed and snuggling up to him so that I could check his fingers.

But I didn't. I placed the ring on the stage of the microscope and focused the lens. Either side of the bezel was a date, 1855, and some initials: A. U. There was nothing on the outer surface of the ring, but on the inside — my heart missed a beat and the standard-lamp-Catriona nodded its shade — was a series of engraved letters, O and X, going right round. Thirty-two letters, of course.

XOXOXOXOXOXOXOXOXOXOXOXOXOXOXOXO

The very simplicity of the combination was an insult. A young child would probably have tried it before any others. It suggested to me that that was what Sir Alexander had in mind, to treat me like a child. To show me how stupid I was. Well I wasn't his 'thousandth', his hand-picked disciple, the only one worthy of pitting her wits against the master. When it came down to it, I was nothing but an idiot.

I put the microscope away, switched off the light and stood by the bow window for a while. A couple were kissing underneath a lamp in Princes Street. 'Well done! That's a nice mess you've got yourself into,' said telescope-Catriona. 'You've got what you wanted, eh? Are you pleased with yourself?' It made my flesh creep.

XOXOXOXOXOXOXOXOXOXOXOXOXOXOXOXOXOXO

'Is that what all this is about?'

I shuddered as I thought of Krook asleep on the other side of the wall. Idiot! Idiot! But perhaps it wasn't too late to repair the damage. I'd replace the ring and get back into bed without Krook noticing. I wouldn't even go back to Cromarty — let Scott Fleming sort things out himself. You've won, Sir Alexander, goodbye. Goodbye to the Urquharts. To hell with André Borel. I'd do a thesis on Shakespeare or Thackeray or Lord Byron... Or why not on Dickens with that old fogey Davies? It didn't matter as long as I stayed in Edinburgh. With Krook. And, above all, didn't write that stupid novel. Leave Breacan's dog where it was best off, in other writers' books. The couple were still locked in their embrace; I felt like opening the window, shouting encouragement, applauding them. I was feeling much better already.

I crept out of the sitting-room but as I was about to go back into the bedroom, something stopped me. That wasn't enough. Wake him up, that's what I had to do. Explain everything to him. It would be much more dignified. A new beginning. With my hand on the door knob, I ran through possible openings: *You mustn't think...* No. *The ring has nothing to do with...* Not that either, no denials. *I'm sorry, Mr Krook...* or, better: *I'm sorry, Ebenezer...* Eby. *I'm sorry, Eby, I've been a fool.*

He was waiting for me in the bed, sitting up, arms folded, eyes wide open. I could see their angry gleam in the half-light. I had my sentence ready but even before I opened my mouth I knew it was no longer relevant.

'I'm sorry, Eby —'

'This has got to stop!'

He breathed audibly, as if a doctor were sounding his lungs.

'What… has to stop?'

'*This!*' he said with a sweeping gesture that took in the unmade bed, our clothes on the floor and, doubtless, me as well. 'I have decided that from now on I will not touch a woman again. That's why I wanted to be a priest. To have done with lust.'

Trying to remain calm, I went to sit down beside him. He didn't move but his every muscle was taut to breaking point.

'That's absurd. Fasting doesn't get rid of hunger. On the contrary, it arouses it.'

'Not if you can reach a certain stage… if you fast for long enough.'

'You die.'

I waited a few moments, then said, 'If it's because of the ring…'

'I don't want to hear any more about that blasted ring! It's caused enough harm as it is.'

As he spoke, he got up and started gathering his clothes one by one. 'Don't you understand? It's like a wave that keeps coming back. It has to stop, otherwise I'll be…'

'It will never stop, Mr Krook,' I said, handing him the ring, which he slipped into his pocket.

He seemed amused by my tone of voice. His breathing calmed down. He gave me a long look, from head to toe, then bent down to pick up my pullover and placed it delicately on my shoulders, as my father used to do with the towel when I got out of the tub. Finally he mumbled a goodbye and two other words I didn't immediately understand.

'What… what did you call me?'

In his blazer that was too small for him and too thin for the time of year, unshaven, his hair sticking out on all sides, he looked like a tramp I'd seen on a bench in Charlotte Square the previous day.

'Two-nights. Goodbye, Two-nights.'

∞∞∞

'You and your intuition! I almost got my death of cold mounting guard outside that bloody barn!'

'Perhaps he spotted you?'

The Laird of Ardloch swore horribly and set off up the main staircase. There had been a lot of rain while I was away. On the landing the moon was reflected in a large black puddle and the twinge of sorrow the gloaming brings was accompanied by the relief you feel at getting home just before night falls.

'Where's Birdie?'

'No idea. She's not been seen since — shhh! Listen.'

Fleming froze in a grotesque posture, neck stretched out, one finger raised. Then he tapped the wall in various places with his ear against the wood panelling.

'He's here, I can feel it.'

'But how are you going to flush him out?'

'It's enough to be one length ahead. I've made my preparations, as you'll see.'

The inlay of the desk and its brass handles were shining in the darkness, but when Fleming lit the ceiling light, it suddenly seemed smaller to me. Still as beautiful, true, but less intimidating, doubtless because I now possessed the key to it. Fleming had fixed a bolt to the door into the corridor, as he had to the one to my bedroom, and a heavy iron bar blocked the revolving section of wall.

I stroked the lid before opening it, then silently contemplated the drawers, every detail of which I was familiar with — a slightly twisted handle here, a scratch there. There was something moving, a kind of pathos, about this proud mechanism that was about to succumb.

'And what if the opposite of what we expect should happen?'

'Not so loud!' Fleming commanded. 'What do you mean?'

'Suppose he's laid a trap for us, that he's quietly waiting for us to find what's to be found, then he eliminates us?'

'That's a risk we have to take. Get on with it.'

XOXOXO

Perhaps life itself has little more mystery, little more charm than a completed crossword puzzle left in a waiting-room. Or a cheap detective novel once you've worked out who the murderer is. With each drawer that opened I felt as if part of myself were being torn off. *Click!* The past first of all. The hunger of childhood, gluttonous, systematic. The slices of bread and jam gobbled up, the pages devoured, as if there had never been bread or books before us and as if some evil spirit might make them disappear at any moment. Running along in front of my father at Caol Ila, an unfailing delight, day after day. *Click!* Then adolescence. Daydreaming beside footpaths. The voluptuous, agonising state of uncertainty. Swinging on the trapeze of life while you're waiting, before leaping into the void, for the reassuring net of love, marriage, work and its responsibilities to be woven. The giggling fits, the walks along the landing stage with Louise and Alison. *Bwaaah!* The ferry has left; we'll definitely get the next one. *Click!*

'What are you waiting for?'

XOXOXOXOXOXO

Then the future. *My* future. The drawers were stealing all my possible futures, one by one. My thesis accepted. André Borel in his best bib and tucker, slippers on his feet; the candlelight supper in the best restaurant in Edinburgh. 'Now you're *truly* one of us, Mary.' His mannered voice lisping the song of love, his peasant's hand on mine, tapping out the rhythm of desire. *Click!* A publisher's ante-room. An immense office cluttered up with books, a daunting figure whose face suddenly lights up with a smile, 'I think we may be able to do something with your manuscript, Miss Guthrie…' *Click!* The Royal Mile on a sunny summer's day. The crowds, cries, laughter. I accidentally jostle someone. 'Sorry.' It's Krook. There's something different about his look. His hair is well groomed, his clothes well cut. 'Hello, Mary.'

XOXOXOXOXOXOXOXOXOXOXOXOXOXOXO

Click! I open the thirtieth drawer. I had nothing left, neither past nor future. I was entirely contained in the action of my hand that slowly, more and more slowly, was approaching the thirty-second drawer; that was going to grasp the handle, to become part of a dead image of myself in one of Daddy's photos: 'Don't move now.' *Click!*

'For God's sake, are you going to open that drawer?'

I held my breath, grasped the handle. The thirty-second drawer wouldn't open.

'Let me try.'

Fleming pulled and pulled, bracing himself on his good leg. To no effect. He peered round the room, as if a joker must have hidden the outcome of his plan somewhere. In the rafters above our heads a mocking owl hooted. Then it fell silent drawing a long blanket of silence behind it.

'You... you must have made a mistake.'

'There's no possible mistake.'

'There must be! You should have brought the ring with you.'

I looked at the desk. It couldn't end like this. I reached out to the thirtieth drawer, but just as I was about to grasp it, it slipped out of my fingers, like a lively, mischievous little animal. It slid back into its housing. *Click!* The twenty-eighth did the same, then the twenty-sixth, *click! click!* and so on *click! click! click!* until all the drawers were closed and the desk was once more a massive, inviolable, arrogant sanctuary. As on the first day. As if none of the drawers had ever moved.

Then, finally, the thirty-second opened: empty.

'Bloody hell!'

Fleming swallowed, opened and closed his mouth several times, but said nothing. Then a note sounded, hesitant, fragile, crumbling; it could only exist in absolute silence and it had waited for that before taking flight, like a butterfly venturing into the still air after a gust of wind. The note remained, hovering in the room until another came to join it; for a moment the two notes played hide and seek, spinning round Fleming's flabbergasted face, then flew away, whispering, from a third note that, after a brief display, shot up to hide in the depths of Australia on the ceiling. The fourth, fifth and sixth poured

255

out and disappeared almost in concert, metallic small fry immediately swallowed up by the eighth with its broad carp's back while the ninth was already rippling in our ears in eel-like undulations before slipping off between two books. The eleventh and twelfth gathered up the scattered fragments of their predecessors and the thirteenth drew the curtain with a shrill arpeggio.

'A music box!' was all Fleming could say.

I would never have thought him capable of marvelling at a few notes. There must be, hidden inside the desk, the soul of a nightingale or of a castrato from the time of Monteverdi.

'A music box,' I repeated, as if henceforth our tongues could form no other words than those three.

Then I felt a very faint sense of unease rising inside me, the same as I used to feel as a child, when I woke on a day for which something unpleasant was planned, even before I knew what it was — a test at school, a visit to grandfather or an injection at the doctor's. 'I've already heard that tune…'

Immediately the spell was broken. His usual self once more, Fleming grabbed me, shook me and, forgetting his own instructions, shouted, 'Where? Where have you heard it?'

'I don't know. I can't remember.'

Something moved behind the wall. Someone went tearing down the secret steps. Fleming rushed over to lift the bar but the opening mechanism didn't work.

'The shit! He's jammed it from inside.'

Holding his torch, Fleming dashed out of the room and I set off after him, following, on a parallel course, the ghost of a tune that still escaped me. By the time we'd got down the main staircase and across the interminable hall, Urquhart must have been at the end of the underground passage. When we reached it he had disappeared. But in which direction? Down towards the Moray Firth and MacFarquhar's Cave, an ideal place for a hidey-hole? Or to the main road, where perhaps Birdie was waiting for him in a car? Had he heard the music box, recognised the tune and guessed what its message was? Fleming was turning round and round, looking in all directions, like a marionette three showmen were each trying to control. And I was dressing up my musical doll in horrible clothes: crackling, creaking, white noise, static interference.

'The automaton.'

'Eh?'

'The automaton, it's the music that goes with the automaton.'

'Ridiculous,' Fleming declared after a few moments thought. 'A public place like that, open to every Tom, Dick or Harry.'

'Just as in *The Purloined Letter*.'

He'd obviously never read Edgar Allan Poe, but he followed me along the path. 'We're just wasting our time.'

'At least it's something we can follow up,' I replied as the first houses of the village appeared out of the darkness. 'If you've got a better idea…'

The Cromarty Arms closed early on Mondays; there was no noise, no light to disturb Church Street from its torpor. As usual, the iron gate of the Courthouse was open, as usual the clock on the tower stood at half past four. Nor was there anything unusual at the main entrance with its stone cross. By the light of Fleming's torch we checked the surroundings. There were footmarks on the rain-soaked lawn; they led towards the west and soon we could feel the crunch of glass under our feet. The lower half of a sash window had been raised.

'Give me some light,' Fleming said.

The windowsill wasn't very high but he had some difficulty climbing up onto it because of his bad leg. I heard him swear as he squeezed through the narrow opening. Then there was a dull thud and his body tumbled down inside. I called out twice but there was no response. I was going to climb in myself when the astounded face of the warden appeared in the beam of the torch.

'Oh, my God,' she said as she opened the door for me, 'I thought it was him coming back.'

'Him who?'

'The automaton. The walking automaton.'

She switched on the light in the west room. The remains of Thomas Urquhart were scattered over the floor: cogwheels, springs, bits of metal and wicker framework, scraps of cloth, porcelain. Scott Fleming, lying below the window, was scarcely in a better state. Only semi-conscious, he was groaning, his bald head sporting an enormous bruise.

'It looks impressive, but it's not much,' the warden said. 'I held back on the blow.'

Her drab hair, done up in curlers, reminded me of Aunt Catriona. Her man's pyjamas, two or three sizes too small, revealed her muscular forearms.

'I went to bed early because of the match tomorrow, but I couldn't get to sleep so I thought that a little nightcap... I switched on the light on the stairs, but not here, there's a full moon and I don't like people spying on me from the street. Then, as I went into the cubby-hole I heard steps outside and immediately after the window was smashed to smithereens. I'm not a scaredy-cat, but all the same... I squatted down behind the door, with my head just high enough to see through the glass panel, and I saw him cross in front of the window.'

'What did he look like?'

'I told you, like the automaton. A curved moustache, a blue suit with braided epaulettes and lace cuffs. He had an old dark lantern, like in the pirate films. I couldn't see his feet, but he must have been wearing boots or heavy shoes. He made quite a noise when he went to have a look at the stairs. He must have been worried about the light. He waited a moment, then he came back in the room and stood in front of Sir Thomas' desk. My eyes had adapted to the darkness, I could see him better and better but he was concentrating too hard to notice me. He didn't take his eyes off the automaton, it was as if he was expecting it to speak to him. And that's what happened: he put a coin in the slot, the little tune was played and Sir Thomas said his piece. He listened attentively, making the same gestures at the same time as if... as if he was a reflection in a mirror.'

The warden seemed pleased with her metaphor. As for me, I was silently berating myself for being an imbecile: I'd just realised what wasn't right about Sir Thomas' tomb. Fleming's groans grew a bit louder.

'Perhaps we should call the doctor all the same.'

'Yes, we'll call him. What did he do then?'

'He… he took out his knife. Oh, look, he forgot it. There it is.'

It was a big hunting knife with a finely carved horn handle. And a long, sharp blade. Impressive.

'Obviously the automaton's not a living being, the knife couldn't hurt it, but all the same when he stabbed it in the chest I had to put my hands over my mouth to stop myself crying out… It's been there for so long, hasn't it? It's stupid, but my first thought was: could it be repaired?'

Wrapped in thought, she picked up a porcelain knee.

'The next moment I had an answer to that. Not content with stabbing it, he demolished it. Broke it up piece by piece. Its clothes, its head, its body. He was searching for something, but couldn't find it. He started looking all round the room and that's where I recognised him: the laird from Cromarty House. But I'm not entirely sure, there was something odd about him, he was feverish perhaps… I remember the day he came to open our new cricket pitch, he shook my hand… but his eyes didn't have that glint then. He looked very old, very frail, whilst this evening… He stood there for a while, not doing anything, then he had an idea. He took out the panel under the desk, tapped the sides of the compartment. With his knife he unscrewed something and the disc appeared. A rubber disc, like the one that does the music and the voice of the automaton.'

Fleming had sat up. He was rubbing his head and fluttering his eyelids. I gestured to the warden to go on.

'He put it on the machine and set it going. It was the same voice, but not the same words. He listened to it once, and then again and a third time. At the beginning he was furious, I could see him quivering with rage, he even tore off his moustache. But then, after the voice had finished the third time, he took a deep breath and smiled. Then he left the way he'd come, by the window.'

'What did the voice say?'

'I couldn't understand it all. Too much crackling. But you can listen to it if you like, the disc's still there, all you have to do is to put the needle on it. While you're doing that I'll go and get some ice.'

I've often wondered if our great-grandchildren will feel as uneasy hearing our recorded voices as we do with those of our ancestors. Doubtless they will. It's not simply a question of the advances in technology, voices — I mean the voices of the dead — are *intrinsically* different. Something comparable to the corruption of the flesh happens to them. Or did our forebears perhaps realise, at the moment they spoke into the microphone, that these ridiculous scraps of sound, engraved in wax or some other material by a no less ridiculous mechanical process and infinitely reproducible, were going to live on after the incredibly sophisticated and fundamentally unique piece of apparatus that was their own person? Then their voices take on a tragic or grandiloquent tone: they are addressing the future, knowing full well that the future is not interested in them, and that gives their voices inflections worthy of Hamlet.

Ah, my Thousandth! There you are at last. Why didn't that damn German invent a machine in which our voices could meet. Copulate together, instead of this vocal masturbation that releases its sperm to no purpose whatsoever in the great silence of death.

What can I tell you? Deep down inside you know everything already. The story began in the mouth of Thomas Urquhart and that is where it ends. Rounded off, finished, perfect, like all good stories.

I met her in Florence, in the Boboli Gardens. On that terrace that looks out over the countryside to the south and from where you can see San Miniato. She had pretty big tits, which didn't particularly interest me, but also a mouth large enough to swallow the campanile of Santa Maria del Fiore. Separated from an Irishman who was a seed merchant (there are some things you can't make up!) she had kept the ridiculous name of O'Flaherty, but was a direct descendant *of the celebrated man of letters, James Braco of Merchiston. After that very first evening in the Cavour her labial rotundity and her palatal cavity held no secrets for me, but I saw it as my duty, on my return to Scotland, to enjoy them one more time in that foul little cottage, reeking of geraniums, outside Stirling, where she spent her time producing daubs of hydrocephalic dogs. In return for a good dose of my seed (which, it appears, was of much better quality than that of her ex-husband), she allowed me to consult her family archives, where I found Learmonth's letter. If you are here, then it's because you have read it as well. I slipped it into my pocket after I'd done up my flies.* Exit Mrs O'Flaherty.*

One night I went down into the crypt. It was magnificent, my thousandth, magnificent. The sneering skull of Sir Thomas, clean and smooth as ivory, and those gems inside whose fires were ignited by my lantern: six eternal stones scattered on the road to death...

And then... And then the diamonds literally ran through my fingers. Like water. Like life, spunk and Veuve Cliquot. There were six of them, and a few months later, just enough time for me to fill a few cunts and empty a few bottles, there was just one left. I'd be hard pressed to tell you where the others went, apart from the one I gave to Catherine Grant. But the sixth — ah, the sixth... it's thanks to that one that I constructed my masterpiece. I wrote the novel you have just read — what am I saying? — that you have just lived through! A French engineer designed the desk and the automaton for me. He doubtless overcharged me a bit, but who cares? The desk is infinite, perfect, like a book inside the author's head before a single line has been written down. Its shape shifts as, one by one, the drawers reveal their intermediate secrets which are to the ultimate secret what the minister is to God. Each combination is one sentence among the infinite number of possible sentences, it shines for a few seconds with the incomparable brightness of that which is, *then sinks slowly into the melancholy murmur of* that which was *or floats for ever in the limbo of* that which could have been.

Without you, my thousandth, none of this would have been possible, for it takes two to make a book: the one writes, the other reads. The one pulls, the other pushes; one tangles the threads, the other unravels them. At the end the bobbin is empty, there's nothing left.

Are you disappointed, my thousandth? You mustn't be. We've lived through a marvellous adventure together. And there is no other.

Eternally yours

Alexander

'What was all that gobbledygook?'

I looked at her without replying. I thought I had heard, among the final crackles of the disc, the sound of a kiss. Images from my stay in the House were going round and round in my head, like the scraps of film assembled by Bruce and Wallace. Fleming groaned again when the cloth filled with ice cubes was applied to his head; as I slipped my hand into his pocket to get the revolver, he muttered something inaudible.

'Call the doctor,' I said. 'I'll be back in half an hour.'

'By the way, what were you two doing here?' the warden asked with a frown and a meaningful glance at the gun.

∞∞∞∞

'I didn't expect you to come alone, Miss Guthrie. Would you like a cup of tea?'

The hayloft of the old barn was dimly lit by a candle that cast his gigantic shadow onto the laths and beams of the ceiling. I approached cautiously through the rubble and piles of planks from the dismantled stalls. Shapes emerged from the gloom around me: a rack, a drinking trough, horse-shoeing equipment hanging from the walls.

'Personally I don't like tea, it's Barbara who's got me into the habit. It has the advantage of not having much taste so you can drink it frequently. It gives a rhythm to the day, if you follow me.'

'No thanks.'

'Do come up. And put that barbarous instrument away. I'm not dangerous, I've never killed anyone.'

'Move away from the ladder, please.'

There was a sigh, then the shadow receded. I climbed the rungs without letting go of the gun. A gust of wind made the rafters above my head creak.

Urquhart was sitting on a heap of hay, in his short sleeves, Sir Thomas' wig and suit at his feet. He flourished his teacup and gave me a melancholy smile. On the floor, close to the fork, were a kettle, a gas stove, a large envelope and a dictionary. I remained standing, at a respectful distance.

'Par isn't very bright, but he's stubborn. How did you manage to get rid of him?'

'He won't be long coming.'

'What a pity. I do so like our little chats. Don't you?'

'I'm sorry, but I'm the one who's going to be asking the questions. How did your brother die?'

'Foolishly. Excuse me but these boots really hurt.'

He took them off, giving little squeals, then felt round in the hay for an old pair of slippers that he put on with a sigh of pleasure.

'Stupidly, even. It was strange, such a clever man, so sure of himself. When he came back he hadn't changed in the least. It was in forty-nine. No one saw him arrive that night, he came round the back; I was reading in my office when he tapped on the window. His clothes were a bit moth-eaten, true, and you could see that he hadn't been to the barber's for ages, but apart from that he was his old self, the same as ever with his swagger, his "my friend" and his golf clubs. "Come, my friend, don't look at me like that, I'm not a ghost." He immediately made himself at home, sat down opposite me and lit a cigar. "Zounds! There's nothing like home sweet home! I'm going to lock myself away here for a while. James, you really do look like death warmed up... and you're letting this house fall into rack and ruin. But I'll soon put things to rights... With what money? Don't you worry about that. From now on — and until I set off on further adventures — I'm the master in this house." I felt what I had always felt when faced with him: jealousy, a kind of disgust, a raging desire to get my hands round his throat and, stronger than all that: fear. I had come out in a cold sweat. Once again I was going to give way to him, obey him. And I visualised the hell he would make my life if I once more ended up under his thumb. Taking my courage in both hands, I told him it wasn't possible. That when he left he had abandoned the house, his children and all his rights along with his duties. I well remember his reaction: he looked me up and down, as if he was deciding which piece of my body to cut off first, then he threw himself back in his chair and burst out laughing. "James, my dear friend, it looks as if, despite all appearances, you have acquired a little self-confidence. I like that, brother, I like that very much. We'll settle this between men, as in the good old days. Like the Duries of Durrisdeer! A good old duel by candlelight, in the barn." I'm not going to fight you, Thomas. "Who's talking about fighting? Do you imagine I want to skewer my dear twin brother? It's just a little contest, old chap, come on, be a sport." '

Urquhart emptied his cup, hesitated for a moment, then threw it over his shoulder.

'I don't know why I accepted. I don't know how I got here with that blasted gold club in my hand and that blasted dark lantern that hardly lit up anything. It was quickly over: I was on my back with Thomas' club across my neck. "Ah, my friend, that's what's always been wrong with you: your footwork or, rather, lack of it." He was really enjoying himself, he was in seventh heaven. "What a pity I haven't got my camera." He took a step back to get a better view of my discomfiture, pretending to take pictures of me. "You really are grotesque, flat on your back, straw in your hair." He took another step back. I could see what was going to happen... the fork behind him... the edge of the loft coming closer. Some emotion stirred within me but I couldn't say if it was sorrow or pleasure. He tripped over the fork and fell backwards, thrashing his arms like someone swimming on their back. Even before I went down, I knew he was dead. The noise, you see. The cracking of the vertebra…'

Sir James remained silent for a good minute. Hands on his knees, he was rocking back and forward; he suddenly seemed to feel cold.

'I picked him up and I said to myself, "Is that all?" I mean, he wasn't very heavy. I carried him to the crypt and all the way I kept asking myself what he would have done if the opposite had happened, how would he have dealt with my body. Would he have put it on his back? Would he have dragged it by the shoulders. Yes, that would be it, I'm fatter than he was. I could almost feel his hands under my armpits, almost hear him grunt with the exertion. Sir Thomas's coffin was the easiest to get at, on the floor, close to the entrance. 'Good,' I said out loud. I put the writer's remains in another coffin then laid my brother in that one, but as I was bending over him, about to close the lid, I suddenly felt dizzy. My heart stopped beating, I wasn't breathing. I was cold, stiff, motionless, and yet I continued to see, to think. I was still alive. I felt as if I were both of us at the same time, he and I, the dead body and the living man. And my head was full of those questions that had plagued me ever since I'd been able to use words: "Why am I me? Why is he him?" So I went to get my knife and chopped off his finger so that no one would ever know *who* was in the crypt. No one. Not even me.'

'But you made a mistake. You cut off the middle finger of his *right* hand. As if it was your reflection in a mirror.'

'Is that so?' Sir James said with a frown. 'Pooh! It doesn't matter any more'

For a few seconds he disappeared in the hay, looking for his cup. Once he'd found it he stood up, jaunty again, to pour himself another cup.

'For the first few weeks I tried to go on as if nothing had happened. As if Sir Thomas were still in Germany or some other country… But then I started getting ideas — projects, dreams I'd been unaware of before. The treasure, for example. I'd never been interested in it. "You've no imagination," he used to say. But now, little by little, I started to look for clues. To have a go at the desk. I'd already opened a few drawers when Barbara arrived. And I realised — until then I'd never looked at a woman — I realised that I'd changed, was no longer the same man, but not entirely a different man either. I was *us*. The first time I disguised myself and went to her room, I could read it in her eyes: she admired *us*.'

'Where is she now?'

'In the Royal Highland Hotel in Inverness. But I won't go to join her. It's over. We fought against the desk together, opened all the drawers apart from the last. By day I was James, with my slippers and my dictionaries. At night… at night I was… I don't know who I was! Then you arrived, my dear…'

Then he gave me a look that I won't forget that soon. Nothing had changed in his features: his inexpressive mouth, his slightly receding chin, his flabby cheeks. But I had the impression that someone had slipped in *behind* that face, that a pair of unknown eyes had occupied Sir James' sockets and were subjecting me to intense scrutiny.

'My *dear* Miss Guthrie I've often watched you while you were asleep, you know? In your little bed, with your little candy-pink nightie. You didn't look particularly formidable and yet… and yet I immediately realised that the desk had found its master, that Alexander had found his "thousandth". It was only a question of time. And now it is finished. Sir Thomas can rest in peace, the secret of the treasure has been found. As for me, I will soon depart — I've found the door.'

'The door?'

He tapped his head. 'The one in there, inside my head.'

He picked up the large envelope: *Diagnosis: strong indications of the existence of a venous aneurism in the left temporal lobe; pathological risk of a cerebral haemorrhage; surgical solutions: nil; proposed treatment: nil.* What a magnificent invention these ultrasound scans are! Just look at that. Isn't it splendid? It's there, d'you see, under that big dark patch. And what a way of putting it: "nil nil", like the result of a rugby match. I know it off by heart. *Prophylaxis — x-i-s, not c-s-i-s — Prophylaxis: the risk of a vascular cerebral accident is increased by strong emotions, physical exertion, sexual intercourse, excessive hilarity...* Emotions and sexual intercourse produced no effect. All that's left is laughter. I'm not sure I can manage it, but I'm going to try. It's intimidating, like everything you do for the first time. Would you stay with me, Mary?'

He went to the end of the loft, then came back into the light, took a couple of steps towards me and a couple of steps back, like an actor looking for the right place to start his monologue.

'Just a minute...'

'No. I've been waiting for years already. Thomas was right. What a fine way to go. To go and join him. *We* will be *us*. Now let's see...'

He cleared his throat. He closed his eyes, opened them again. He was concentrating so hard he looked funny. The first sound he produced was a stomach rumble; he was clenching his jaws and fists. He panicked for a moment, but he fixed his eyes on mine and suddenly seemed more relaxed. He made two further efforts, more convincing this time. I was fascinated by the performance.

'Yes,' he said, 'I think I see how it works now.'

Once more he closed his eyes and this time the laugh came. An awkward laugh, hesitant. A novice's laugh. His face lit up. 'That's it! That's it exactly. This laughing's very amusing, you know. Off we go then.'

He gave me a little wave, a bit like my father when he set off to work.

∞∞∞∞

Sir James didn't die, but when the aneurism ruptured, it destroyed most of his brain functions. In a vegetative state he was admitted to the neurological ward of an Inverness hospital, the one where his grandfather Stephen had ended his days.

The day after his attack I went to the Royal Highland Hotel, but Barbara Foyle had already packed her bags and left. I never saw her again.

The police, after a routine investigation, concluded that Sir

Thomas' death was accidental so that he could now rest in the comfort of his own grave in Cromarty graveyard. There were only four mourners at the burial: Fleming, the twins and myself. Scott Fleming doubtless wanted to make sure his enemy was well and truly dead. Throughout the ceremony, with a bandage on his head, he kept giving me venomous looks: I had deprived him of his revenge. He hadn't spoken a word to me since the night at the Courthouse Museum and didn't even say goodbye as he left the graveyard. I never saw him again either.

Since that night I had taken up residence in the Cromarty Arms, waiting for... what? I spent the days wondering what I was doing there. Putting down scraps of sentences on paper, ideas that led nowhere. One week after the events I received a letter from the twins and, for the last time, set off for Cromarty House.

After the wretched winter we had been through, the roof was in an even worse state. At the top the walls were oozing moisture, one of the first-floor shutters was swinging on its hinges. The whole building looked sick and sad in the driving rain, rather like a book that has been frequently leafed through without care and left askew on the corner of a shelf.

The hall was icy cold. It still stank of cat and old floorcloth in equal proportions. A quick glance at the door to the south wing; another at the portraits pockmarked with damp and whose subjects were more and more coming to resemble John Merrick, the elephant man. The 'laughter closet' scowling in its corner; the staircase, strips of the red carpet with its bizarrely twisted brass fitments and rods. And the twins emerging from the north wing and coming to meet me.

'It's very simple,' said "Wallace" as he ushered me into the projection room. 'Legally we don't exist.'

'Our father never recognised us,' "Bruce" went on, 'and our uncle didn't adopt us so we have no right to the estate which, anyway, will soon be seized by the creditors; after everything that's happened ten new ones appear every day. And if we're still allowed to use the name of Urquhart, it's because "people have to have a name" as the coroner said.'

'We were subjected to a psychiatric examination. According to the shrink, the individual going by the name of Wallace Urquhart is suffering from a serious paranoid psychosis with a tendency to schizophrenia…'

'While Bruce suffers from "a simple manic-depressive state with no adverse effect on the personality." What that idiot psychiatrist doesn't know is that he examined the same person twice. We swapped jackets — and symptoms — in the waiting-room.'

'What, in practical terms, is going to happen to you?'

"Bruce" gave his brother a quick glance. 'In practical terms, as you put it, Wallace Urquhart will be admitted to a charitable institution for the mentally ill in Fortrose…'

'…while Bruce can stay in Cromarty, with Eagle. He will even undergo therapy that will consist of being entrusted with certain simple tasks of benefit to the community.'

'But that's unfair!' I exclaimed.

'Exactly! With what right should one of us spend his time taking his ease in the lap of luxury and the company of the most diverting specimens of humanity…'

'…while the other has to file minutes of meetings or sweep up dead leaves and, what is more, swallow the awful grub produced by poor Eagle every day!'

'So we decided to swap roles as often as possible. Every Saturday Bruce will go to visit Wallace in Fortrose. We will arrange things so that we get a few minutes alone together. That will be enough to fool them. Thank you for your expression of sympathy, Miss Guthrie, but, as you can see, everything is turning out for the best…'

'…except that once a week I'll have to put on your dirty clothes…'

'…and I'll have to wear your old shoes that stink like a midden.'

They continued to exchange caustic remarks for a while. Not knowing what to do with myself, I wandered round the room; someone had taken almost all the reels of film off the shelves and swept the hundreds of yards of celluloid into a corner.

'Come on, let's stop this stupid game, Bruce. Miss Guthrie hasn't come to watch our ten thousandth argument.'

'You're right, Wallace. The fact is we have asked you to come...'

Again they exchanged glances. The privilege of concluding this sentence seemed to depend on some incredibly complex order of precedence.

'We have asked you to come,' "Wallace" eventually went on, 'because, to our great regret, we find ourselves in a situation in which we are compelled to withdraw our offer.'

'As you can see, we no longer own anything. The bailiffs have already confiscated our reels and most of the furniture. They're going to come tomorrow to collect the more cumbersome pieces: the wardrobes, the pictures in the great hall, our Cinemeccanica IVE projector...'

'...and the desk.'

My heart missed a beat. I imagined with horror Sir Alexander's masterpiece in the middle of an awful middle-class drawing-room: some old biddy would keep her visiting cards in it and her holiday snaps. A retired deputy chief fire officer would write his memoirs on it...

'In a nutshell: we're broke. On top of that we'll be occupied with demanding tasks day and night. One of us will have to behave as if he's insane...'

'...the other as if he's of sound mind. That, as I'm sure you will agree, hardly leaves time for matrimonial projects.'

"Bruce" nodded sagaciously, before adding in melancholy tones, 'As for our life's work, I very much fear it will remain unfinished.'

'And it's best like that!' "Wallace" exclaimed. 'The world has hardly digested the Copernican revolution. It's not ready for our *Cinema*.'

"Bruce" avoided my eye and adopted his contrite look: 'I hope you will forgive us, Miss Guthrie... and that you will not take us to court for breach of promise of marriage, like Mrs Bardell in *The Pickwick...*'

'Don't be a cretin! Mary's far above all that.'

'Of course, Wallace, you're right... In fact,' he cleared his throat and his fingers twiddled an imaginary thread, 'it's in order to beg your forgiveness that we have invited you to the ceremony.'

I gave them both a questioning look.

'Do make things clear, Bruce. People can never understand what you're getting at.'

'We're going to... give Laura Hunt her freedom back.'

'And all the others.'

'To... cast them out... into the infinite space... of the cosmos. Do you follow?'

'Let's get on with it, Bruce, let's get on with it. I'm sure Miss Guthrie has other things to do.'

Keeping his eyes fixed on me, "Bruce" went over to the screen and tore it down. The window behind it appeared, with a heavy curtain over it. Behind me I could hear "Wallace's" footsteps, then the hum of the projector, accompanied by the smell of dust scorching on the bulb. "Wallace" came over to join me as scraps of film followed one after the other on the curtain, strangely distorted by the folds of the material: people dressed in black gathered round a grave; a dead crow nailed to a door; a big ship sinking in the ocean. At the exact moment when Laura Hunt appeared, "Wallace" gripped the back of my chair convulsively.

'Now, Bruce!' he said.

His brother hesitated. Then, reluctantly, he opened the curtain. Light poured into the room. The picture of the actress, with her pretty little face and her white rain-hat, was imprinted on my retina for a moment; then, quivering, she merged with the foliage of the tall trees in the park.

271

CHAPTER XII

The razor in my hand, my cheeks covered in shaving soap, I contemplated my reflection in the mirror. A little iceberg of foam detached itself from the ice-field and slowly slid down my neck to the little cavity between the tendons. It was too long since I had really looked at myself. Almost three months. Since Scotland-France and the night I spent with Mary Guthrie. After that Scotland had lost every match, taking the wooden spoon in the Five Nations, and I had regularly got drunk, only opening the bookshop for a few hours a day, sometimes not at all. My reflection frowned and made me look at the rings under its eyes, its sallow complexion: *All this is your fault!* Someone knocked on the door. It must be a neighbour come to borrow something, or a door-to-door salesman.

I looked down at my skinny thighs, the slight bulge of my stomach, my penis.

Ecce homo.

They knocked again.

The existence of the person outside my door seemed to depend entirely on my ability to imagine him or her. I wiped off the foam with the towel. A very, very faint hope tried to spread its wings in my breast, but I wrung its neck. I put on a dressing gown and went to open the door. Lewis marched straight in, folded his arms and looked disapprovingly at the unmade bed and the sink crammed with dirty dishes. He removed the glasses and empty bottles from the table and replaced them with a bulky envelope. For a moment I thought he might be about to roll up his sleeves and clear everything up, but he just shook his head and said, 'I've just been to the hospital. He wants

272

to see you.'

'Is he very bad?'

'No worse than yesterday. He just needs to talk to you. It's important. And he'd like you to take him *that*,' he added, pointing at what was left in one of the whisky bottles.

'I didn't know he was allowed to drink.'

Lewis laughed. 'Pooh. Allowed? And you, are you allowed? Do you ask permission to ruin your health day after day? He at least can argue that in his case there are attenuating circumstances.'

Feeling uncomfortable, I poured the contents of the bottle into a little flask I could hide in my pocket. Lewis kept a close eye on me, waiting for me to make a slip, to spill a drop.

I was astounded to see that it was half past three. The time Mr Mitchell was in the habit of coming to the shop; he must be stamping impatiently outside the closed door. I flushed with shame.

'Err… I have to get dressed.'

Briefly putting his reserve to one side, he gave me an impish glance. 'Yes, that would be a good idea.'

When I came back from the bathroom in my crumpled blazer and dirty flannels, Lewis was looking out of the window. 'I've brought you a manuscript, Mr Krook. The last one I'm going to publish. It concerns you. And Scott Fleming. If you should want to learn more about your father.'

'Thank you.'

'I also wanted to say… Don't disappoint Arthur. Please.'

His words were going round and round in my head as I made my way to the Royal Infirmary. During his first days in hospital Walpole had made me talk about the bookshop a lot; I had had to invent odd details about certain clients, imaginary sales. As I told him all this, I was trying to guess how far he was being taken in. In vain. His eyes sparkled but I couldn't say whether it was with pleasure at hearing of the place and the people he loved or from amusement at my lies. Then, like a coward, I'd taken to going less frequently. The previous week I'd just telephoned to see how he was doing.

It couldn't go on like that. On the way to the hospital I went to Greyfriars Kirkyard and did what Walpole had expressly asked me to do: I cleaned his wife's gravestone. Not having thought of bringing an implement with me, I scraped away the dirt with my fingernails.

'He's having an X-ray,' said a tall, powerful nurse I hadn't seen before. 'Wait by his bed.'

Then she added in admonitory tones, 'I hope at least you've been vaccinated,' as if not only my own well-being depended on it but the smooth running of her section, perhaps even the whole operation of the National Health Service. Walpole had doubtless finally worn out the patience of Peggy, the pretty brunette with the bronzed knees, unless it was just her day off. The other bed was also empty — *exit* the old man who used to listen to Jeannie Robertson on his phonograph, beating time with his hand covered in freckles. In his place were a pillowcase and blanket neatly folded on a clean sheet. The curtain between the two beds was mauve, like that in the confessional in Campbeltown.

The pile of books on Walpole's bedside table reminded me of his last appearance in the shop, the Monday after the match. Robin and Lewis were there. 'I've come to caress them.' And he did, he caressed his books. 'So little time. So little time to read you all... We have, what, fifty, sixty years? Almost nothing. All these books we've not read... All those marriages we missed out on — for they are marriages! Books and their readers get married, they even have children! Little homunculi that never leave our brain but have lives of their own, that grow up and die with us... They even have names, names in italics: *Humphrey Clinker, Moby Dick*... Ebenezer, would you be so good as to get a cigar for me?' Gingerly he took a first puff at it, but his cough didn't come. And his eyes started to shine again, just as they used to. "I've still got a little time left, haven't I? The time for... a few books. But which ones, oh God, which ones? Help me, my friends, help me please.'

After a few moment's hesitation we all set about the task. We elbowed each other out of the way at the shelves, tore the stool out of each other's hands; never had there been so much activity in

Walpole's Bookshop. Eventually we had made our choices and lined up clutching our finds. Sitting behind his cash desk, Walpole looked like the judge in some laborious treasure hunt.

'*Uncle Silas* by Sheridan Le Fanu. But of course, Lewis, why not? It's what they call a minor work, isn't it? I like minor works, they're like minor chords, they often move you to tears... Oh, look, *Othello*.' He smiled as he held the little Arden Classic in his hands. 'You're quite right, Robin, we've never really finished with Big Bill, have we.' Suddenly he froze. '*Our Mutual Friend*, Mr Krook! That's the only Dickens novel I've never... Every year I think about it, but then... How ever did you guess? Once I quoted Mr Podsnap and his odd gesture and you thought I was talking about a customer! Marvellous, Eby, marvellous. Just imagine, a Dickens novel I've never read, it's like... an extra life.'

Crash! The sound of the trolley hitting the swing-door. The nurse lifted Walpole up as if he weighed nothing at all and put him back in his bed.

'No more than fifteen minutes,' she decreed, 'he's tired.'

He stuck out his tongue when his new warder had turned her back and shook my hand warmly, keeping hold of it for some time. 'I can see that you've been to visit Mildred. What have you done with your ring?'

'There's something I have to tell you, Arthur...'

'It's not necessary. Mitchell was here just now. Do you think he asked how I was doing? No. He didn't even wish me good afternoon. "I want to have a word with you, Mr Walpole. Your bookshop isn't opening during the advertised hours." He kept looking round from time to time as if he wasn't quite sure what kind of place this was. I said, nice and quietly, "If you remember, Mr Mitchell, there has never been a notice with opening times on the door."—"*Here!*" he replied tapping his forehead, "they're in here." '

Walpole imitated his shrill, peevish voice perfectly. When he was pretending to be Mitchell, the smile vanished from his lips and his nostrils quivered with repressed fury.

' "I hold you... I hold you personally..." He didn't finish the sentence. Perhaps he'd finally noticed all this apparatus. There are no drips in Meredith's novels, you know. It calmed him down, at least a little bit. "Mr Walpole, I wish to express my most strong disapproval." '

Mouth open but without making a sound, Walpole shook his head and his right hand at the same time: it was the gesture that had replaced laughter for him since his cough had become too painful. It looked like some secret code or a piece of stage business from an extraterrestrial drama.

'But I managed to bring him round: "I'm terribly sorry, but he's ill."—"Ill? who's ill?" The poor bugger had no idea what the situation was. He stared at the drip with a look of alarm. "Mr Krook, my partner. He's got the flu. But he's on the mend. The bookshop will be open tomorrow, at the *advertised hours*."—"Ah, good. The flu. That changes everything, of course. Tell him…"—"Tell him what, Mr Mitchell?"—"Tell him that I thought his interpretation of *Beauchamp's Career* was brilliant, though entirely fanciful. Please pass on my wishes for a swift recovery. Goodbye, Mr Walpole." And he left, just like that, without a backward glance. You would be well advised to reread *Beauchamp,* otherwise he'll shoot your thesis full of holes.'

A further Martian laugh. I didn't know where to look. And the word 'partner' had just exploded in my confused mind, like a time bomb.

'Moreover you do look a bit peaky, Ebenezer. Come now, don't take on like that. The life of a good bookshop isn't measured in hours, not even in days. When Mildred… went, I closed for two months. When I opened again they were all waiting on the doorstep. Famished. And in that regard I've made certain arrangements. Did you bring the you-know-what? Thank you. It would, of course, be better with a good cigar, but still…'

Walpole put the flask to his lips, took a mouthful and immediately started to cough violently. He went bright red; he was choking. I hardly had time to hide the flask in my pocket before the nurse burst in.

'What's going on in here?'

She gave me a nasty look as she picked up the oxygen mask. 'Breathe in this.'

Mouth open, eyes bulging, Walpole shook his head.

'You will put this mask on, you stubborn old mule, or I'll fetch Doctor Cameron.'

The name seemed to make an impression on Walpole. He surrendered, not without giving me a look, just as he put the mask on, full of terror and despair. His cough subsided; he could breathe more easily through the impersonal hum of the machine.

Satisfied, the nurse busied herself about the room for a while then came and stood, hands on hips, in front of us. 'That's enough for today. Visiting time is over.'

Walpole held up his hand with the fingers spread, an imploring look on his face.

'All right,' she said after some hesitation, 'Five minutes. Not a second more.'

Hardly had she turned away than Walpole took off the mask.

'The old battleaxe. I hate her. But she's nothing beside young Cameron. He wants to fix this wretched contraption to my nose. He wants to take away my last utterances. This mask is death… the face of death. We must hurry, Eby, she'll be back soon. Quick, sign this.'

He'd opened the drawer of his bedside table and was holding out a document to me that had the letterhead of a Princes Street lawyer. At first the information in it hardly penetrated my consciousness, but then a few sentences emerged form the legal mumbo-jumbo: *It is hereby agreed that Messrs Arthur Walpole and Ebenezer Krook shall henceforth be partners in the commercial enterprise that will hereafter operate under the name and style of "Walpole and Krook Booksellers" as hereinafter provided… On the death of one of the partners the survivor shall enjoy full possession of the above named enterprise subject to the condition that the survivor shall continue the commercial activity of booksellers which is the stated object of the said enterprise… In witness whereof the parties hereto at Edinburgh have set their hands this twenty-seventh day of March One Thousand*

Nine Hundred and Fifty-four.

'I can't accept this, Arthur. It's too much.'

'Don't be ridiculous. I'm not giving you a present, I'm attaching you to a ball and chain. I'm providing you with a miserable income, an unhealthy workplace, miles and miles of bumf, a herd of emotionally disturbed customers — old men who are going to die on you one by one — leading, in all probability, to bankruptcy. The age of publishers and booksellers is coming to an end, Eby; soon it will be that of the "suppliers": people who work in the shade to exploit all human activities, dealing indiscriminately in whatever turns a profit, be it books, jars of mustard, socks, information, fridges, caster sugar or love stories. What does content matter? The only thing that matters is delivery. The conveyor belt of the Suppliers is already up and running, delivering superfluous useful articles and useless superfluous articles. Carefully gauged and priced emptiness. The day will come when goods will only serve as a pretext for delivery; when books will appear in the shops and disappear a few months later without having been bought or read or even opened. They will pass like waves to be swallowed up in the great ocean of silence. All that will be left will be the foam. The dregs.'

'There's still time to think it over, Arthur.'

'On the contrary, time is short. The founding principle of Krook & Walpole must be set aside! We can no longer afford to wait fifty years, we must act quickly before the dictatorship of the Suppliers is firmly established. Save what can be saved. Gather all the endangered species in your ark, those of 1905, of 1925, even those born last year. It is the supreme task I am offering you: be the last bookseller.'

It was impossible to back out. I picked up the pen. As I appended my signature to the pages of the contract, a strange calm came over me; I had the feeling I was giving birth to a new Krook — a Krook who was in chains, true, but viable. The only viable one.

'Perfect! Now let's drink to it.'

Eyes closed, he moistened his lips, then held out the flask to me. At the last moment, however, he frowned. 'Just a moment. I may be wrong but have the feeling you've had enough to drink during these last few days. Do you think the ark wants a drunken Noah at the tiller. What a pity you haven't got your ring.'

Without knowing what he was getting at, I took out the cord round my neck.

'Jolly good. It's going to save your life and this is how it'll do it.' Taking the diamond, he made a little scratch on the glass flask, just below the level of the whisky.

'There: thus far and no farther. I'm not interested in the history of the ring. What matters is that from now on it is the guardian of your soul. Keep it on your finger. Let it shine, Eby, let it shine! You know...'

The words died on his lips, as if carried off on a trolley gliding along the corridor.

'I had a dream, Eby,' he went on after a moment. 'I don't believe in the transmigration of souls but I do believe in that of books. I believe that Joseph K. is an avatar of Dickens' George Silverman; that Tristram Shandy is reincarnated in Dr Faustroll. All books are made from the same material that circulates unendingly down the centuries. I know this because I saw it in my dream. It was in a great gothic hall; the books were floating in the ether, linked to each other by long crystal tubes through which a marvellous... a marvellous diaphanous fluid poured with letters, words and sometimes even faces, trees, houses floating in it. Right at the top, beneath the vault illuminated by unreal light, were the founding fathers: *The Odyssey, The Aeneid,* and a little below them the first crystal arteries were dividing and forming a network... *Gargantua, Don Quixote, Gulliver.* The fluid never stopped flowing, it passed through the books, irrigating them, then continued on its slow descent. And, Eby, guess what — I saw *Martin Eden*!'

As slow as a hearse, the trolley was approaching, door by door. 'Right, then. The dragon will be back soon. Go and open up the shop for Mr Mitchell.'

Snuggling down in the pillows, he added, 'Thank you, my son. I really feel much better, you know. It's the little bookseller, he's moved on. Now it's your guts he'll be gnawing at. I think I'm going to be able to finish Dickens with complete peace of mind.'

Night was falling as I left the hospital. I got to MacAvoy's just before it closed, bought what I wanted and went back to Anchor Close, disdaining the prodigious pub. All the way along Holyrood Park a vague odour of spring tickled my nostrils. It followed me as far as the Royal Mile, mingled with exhaust fumes. There was also a briny smell. In Edinburgh you often forget that the sea is quite close and when the cries of the seagulls sound over the Old Town, you have a strange feeling that they must have flown across an immense stretch of dry land to reach us.

The letter box was crammed full of orders, catalogues and bills — bills above all. Mr Mitchell had pinned a sheet of paper to the door on which there was a single huge question mark. I removed it with a smile. One of the bulbs burnt out when I switched on the light, the other had been dead for several days and there was no replacement. I unearthed a candle in the cubby-hole. Holding the candlestick, I walked up and down along the shelves, looking for the ideal place. I chose a low shelf, in a corner, which our customers hardly ever looked at. To make room, I put some books on the shelf above. *Martin Eden* and *Homage to Catalonia* stood out proudly in their brand new binding — a little too new, perhaps. I couldn't say whether the austere Henry James, the fiery Stevenson and the delicate Edith Wharton appreciated their new neighbours, but the two promoted tomes, aware of the privilege they were enjoying, modestly huddled up together against the upright of the bookshelves. After a moment's reflection I added *Bartleby, The Diary of a Superfluous Man* and *Notes from the Underground.* On the shelf I stuck a label on which I'd written:

A book + a book + a book + a book + a book = a man.

Francis Krook's equation.

I blew out the candle. Silence. No one out on the Royal Mile. Standing under the fanlight, I observed new feelings inside myself. *My* bookshop? No! The place no more belonged to me than it had the previous day: the little bookseller in my stomach had already taken things in hand. Little by little the presence of the books calmed my wildly beating heart, just as a wall can absorb the vibrations of door that's been slammed.

It was the moment. The moment of what, I couldn't say. The moment, that's all.

Epilogue

They were there, by the roadside, on a little strip of grass overlooking the valley: Ebenezer Krook, Robin Dennison and Lewis Rosewall. An unfrocked priest, an alcoholic Communist journalist and a homosexual publisher close to bankruptcy — a fine trio for a funeral! But old Walpole would have approved, of course.

We'd had problems finding the place. Shortly after Melrose there was a fellow sitting by the road doing nothing. 'Scott's View? You can't miss it. Keep straight on until the crossroads with the big oak and then turn left.'

'The big oak,' I said after we'd set off again, mimicking his Borders' accent. 'And how does he think we're going to recognise it? That's all there is here, trees.'

Mary didn't seem to be in a hurry to get there. There was a vague smile playing about her lips. 'Don't tell me you can't recognise an oak tree, André Borel. I presume they have a few in France, don't they?'

'I don't like this lack of precision. If we were in the town I could find Big Oak Street on the map and locate the place for certain. Which clearly demonstrates the superiority of language over object.'

She'd guffawed. It had been happening quite a lot since we'd got married. Lacking relevant experience, I wondered if that was in the nature of things, if it was one of a certain number of more or less codified details which are part of building a life together. For example the odd way she had of using my whole name, André Borel; why not just André? It seemed to me that these irritating little gibes had come a bit too quickly, that they would have been more appropriate for an old couple who had become blasé rather than for two young lovebirds.

I parked beside Rosewall's picturesque bone-shaker. While we were getting out of the car, Krook was wrestling with the lid of the urn. He turned to look at us and Mary immediately stiffened. It was a simple urn, pewter, I think, with a bulge that looked like a fat belly. Poor Walpole, who had ended up so thin.

We kept at a respectful distance, after all we weren't the real mourners. The lid finally gave way, with an unfortunate sound, given the circumstances. A *phut,* like a tin of food being opened, reminding us that the urn was just an ordinary object, doubtless mass produced, which slightly spoilt the symbolic nature of the moment. Rosewall put his hand on Krook's shoulder, Dennison patted him on the back. Then, with an abrupt movement, Krook emptied the urn at their feet. At least that was what he thought he was doing. No one had felt the gust of wind coming, a simple *epiphenomenon* of the complex interplay of masses of air circulating among the hills of the Southern Uplands. It blew the ashes all over the three men: their clothes were dusted with it. The journalist had even swallowed some.

'Good God!' he said, spitting on the ground. He rinsed out his throat with whisky and passed the flask round. The three men had a drink then silently spent a minute dusting themselves down. Finally Rosewall put the lid back on the urn.

'I'm sure Arthur would have loved that.' They all burst out laughing, almost simultaneously. Their faces were still smudged with ashes. They looked like miners or classical actors slumming it in a horror film.

'I'm going to talk to him,' Mary simply said.

Seeing her approach, Dennison demonstratively headed for the only available bush nearby while Rosewall walked back across the road. That suited me, I needed to talk to him about the book.

The previous day Mary had finished correcting the page proofs. From the apartment we had rented on Princes Street you could see the Castle, pale in the sharp June light, and also the windows of her aunt's flat. The vacation was approaching. The vacuum. I was both relieved no longer to have to hear the *rat-a-tat-tat* and the *cling* of the Remington and terrified of the silence that would have to be filled. She had tidied up the proofs by tapping the sheaf of papers on the desk.

Sir Alexander's desk. I was still unhappy about that wedding present. Not because of the price, outrageous though it was (it so happened that my mother had just sold an apartment in Châteauroux the one where my great-uncle Évariste, the family eccentric, or paranoiac according to some, had devoted thirty years to his worship of Charles Dickens). But it was much too big for the sitting-room. That was our first open disagreement. Mary turned out to have more fighting spirit than expected, showing fiendish cunning at alternating seductiveness and threats. I'd thrown in the towel. Now that baroque piece of furniture came between us both as the repository of memories from which I was excluded and bearing a future the main part of which escaped me.

'I feel like Breacan's dog,' she'd murmured. 'I've dragged the body up onto the shore. What should I do now?'

I had no answer to give. Although I made a living from analysing other people's books, I've always regarded writing as a vaguely reprehensible activity requiring unmitigated brazenness, much naivety and a good dose of vanity. An unpublished manuscript, one that has not yet been validated by exegesis, seems to me as different from a real book as an egg is from a chicken. It's something formless, spongy, sad. However, even *Old Goriot*, even *Madame Bovary* have been through that embryonic stage. Split between derision and envy, I had watched Mary's manuscript grow.

A cloud passed over the Tweed. I caught hold of Rosewall as he was heading for his car. 'Are you really going to publish it?'

He removed his arm from my grip. 'Yes. It will be my last book. The printer is a friend of mine. He has a stock of old paper that he doesn't know what to do with. I'm going to publish it, then I'll call it a day.'

'But it brings in real people. The Urquharts, for example.'

'The dead don't sue.'

'Krook?'

'He couldn't care less. Anyway, it's not really important since I haven't sufficient funds to get copies on bookshop shelves. It will be a stillborn book, a phantom book. Ebenezer will be the only one to sell it — if he wants to.'

Rosewall put the urn in the boot. I was watching Krook and Mary out of the corner of my eye. She had her head down and was speaking quickly, like someone at confession, and in a slightly whiny voice I'd never heard her use. He was looking away.

'I still can't understand why she didn't change the names,' I went on. 'Skimpole instead of Walpole, for example. Duval instead of Borel... Duval, it sounds good. A name for a Frenchman in an operetta — a Frenchman for a Hollywood scriptwriter keeping going on bourbon and Marlboros.'

'One can never tell what goes on in writers' minds, Mr Borel.' He screwed up his eyes before adding, with a hint of mockery, 'Are you concerned for your reputation?'

'No. For hers. She's about to start a thesis. All it needs is for one of her future students to chance upon the book. You can imagine what it would be like to address a lecture theatre full of sniggering students when you've written that kind of stuff.'

'Let's say she'll bring a whiff of the maverick to the university staff room. That's not necessarily bad for her career.'

The confabulation on the other side of the road had finished, with no other noticeable effect than a slightly more pronounced frown on Krook's face and the suspicion of a tear perhaps in the corner of Mary's eye. Dennison reappeared from behind his bush, buttoning up his flies and whistling cheerfully.

'At least do something about those slippers. I don't know how often they crop up in the manuscript. They're a veritable obsession.'

'There I might be able to negotiate two or three cuts.'

'And that ending? Don't you think it's a bit... abrupt?'

'All endings are the same,' Dennison said as he walked past.

'He's right,' Rosewall agreed, with a nod of the head. 'Things have to end one way or the other, is that not so, Mr Borel?'

A little later, in the car, I watched Mary out of the corner of my eye.

'Just now he laughed with the others,' she said as she wound up the window.

'Who did? Krook?'

'There's something different about him but I can't say what it is.'

She seemed both pleased and saddened by that. I waited for a minute, then remarked casually, 'Talking of Scott, it seems that on the day of his funeral his horse, that was pulling the hearse…'

'…stopped at Scott's View. Everyone knows that… My God, do you realise? He laughed…'

'You told him, about the baby?'

'Why? Isn't it obvious enough?'

We had decided to drive on to Berwick to see the sea. The Tweed had widened. Now it flowed on majestically, pulling us along with it. Towards what? Feeling uncomfortable, I wriggled in my seat and crashed the gears.

'Precisely. He may want to recognise it.'

'Recognise it?' She laughed again. No one will recognise the child. It will be an unknown. A blank book. A babbling story with infinite possibilities. Like the desk. In fact, only one thing is certain…'

She left the sentence unfinished. Despite the closed windows, the sea air filled the car. There was a gleam in the distance, then something white, immense and lazy: a wave.

'What is certain?'

'That it will have the blood of the Urquharts.'